For anyone who ever feels it's impossible to believe in themselves.

I believe in you.

And for Kaia, always.

THE BOOK OF THE WATCHERS

VOLUME II

Angel of Earth & Bone

TORY GUYON

THE BOOK OF THE WATCHERS

VOLUME II

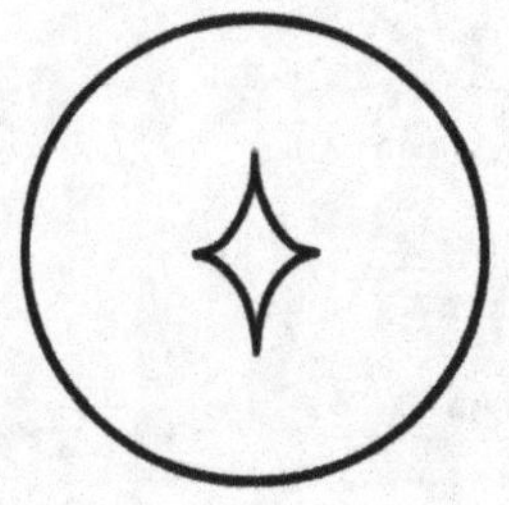

ANGEL OF EARTH & BONE

HILDUR

QUEEN OF THE ELVES

120 YEARS AGO

It was never a good sign when an angel came to Earth.

As the Queen of the Elves laid yet another soldier's helmet atop the smoldering pile of skulls and mangled metal, she could only imagine what kind of terrible omen awaited her when two shot down from the sky.

She inhaled sharply. A rotten stench coated the air—death, blood.

They'd already brought war; what else could the archangels possibly want from her?

Placing her palm on what remained of the fallen soldier, she resumed her prayer with a curt sigh. *"Leyfðu mér að reika um skóga þína, leyfðu mér að renna meðfram ám þínum—"*

"Hildur." A voice interrupted her.

She hadn't sensed their footsteps, but the Angel of Earth's essence, her words, pulsed in the scorched dirt, in the deep canyons of her fjords, in the icy slopes of her mountains. The earth spoke to the angel—fields rustling and canyons yawning and trees curling in worship—but now, it cried for help.

The pointed tips of Hildur's ears twitched. The scent of morning dew cut through the filth and the frenzied roar of a sea drifted on the breeze—the Angel of Water was here, too.

"Gaia," Hildur addressed the Angel of Earth. Her hand remained on the lifeless body. She didn't want to let go; didn't want to face what she had lost. Her eyes too dry, her soul too empty to cry anymore.

"We need to discuss our next move," Gaia pressed.

Once a powerful queen, now a widowed, desperate woman struggling to hold the seams of her kingdom together, Hildur barely had a shred of dignity left to face the archangels.

But this, this was too much.

"You turned my realm into an elven burial ground." Slowly, Hildur looked over her shoulder. Her lavender irises flared—sharper than twin daggers. "And now you want to talk strategy?"

The angels glanced at each other. How curious. They were nervous. Hildur could only wonder what kind of scheme they were concocting telepathically.

"We need to." The Angel of Water stepped forward, her robes fluttering in the endless wind, her piercing blue eyes hopeful. Little did she know that all hope had been buried with the dead. "Chthonia may be retreating, but we can't let up—"

"So send your kind to the slaughter," Hildur snarled, turning to face them fully. "It's a never-ending battle between your realms. Go fight it somewhere else. You've done enough to the Huldufólk."

The sky cracked open. Lightning parted the dark clouds, striking one of her mountains. Rock and ice fell swiftly down its face, slamming into the ground far below. A plume of mist rose from the pile.

Mira, Hildur thought her name was, flinched as if she'd been pinned under the debris.

Then the world fell silent, as if it were holding its breath. Even the whines of the dying cavalry had quieted. A ripple of hurt shot through the elf queen, but she kept her jaw tight and her brows folded, her heart stronger than stone— it was the only way to rule, even if the deaths of her people ate her up inside.

"We've summoned every Nephilim within the Arctic Circle." Gaia's pearly white wings quivered. Hildur wasn't used to seeing them untucked, so out and free, but she supposed it made a powerful statement on the battlefield. "No one is answering the call. We cannot uproot people from their homes."

Hildur's eyes narrowed. "What exactly do you think you've done to mine?"

The elf queen stepped over a dismembered hand. Blades of grass sprouted under the thuds of her boots. Ancient magic rushed her veins and gathered beneath her footsteps, leafy tendrils coiling over the dirt, over the open grave of a once-flourishing fishing village.

The angels stilled. They didn't swallow, they didn't inhale. Two ivory statues as stark as delicate snowflakes against this muddy, wretched world. The only thing that moved was their stares tracking, *scrutinizing*, the elf.

"Because this war is on *my* soil, because the Huldufólk are not Empyrean blessed, does our ruin mean nothing to you?" Hildur spat through clenched teeth. "Are we nothing but weeds for you to stomp on?"

Mira's shoulders fell. "Of course not. You are our partners." She reached out, but Hildur shook off the touch, the metal of her armor clanking, the dried blood staining the silver brown.

These angels, with their pristine feathers and their freshly pressed velvet robes. What did they know about partnership, about sacrifice? They'd been holed up in their towers half this war. She'd been fighting alongside her people the entire time.

"I will not have history repeat itself," Hildur said, drawing air into her lungs, curling her rich tawny fingers into a fist so tight the joints cracked.

More rocks slipped down the mountain face, the heavy stones grating against the ice and echoing across the fjords.

Mira dropped her chin. The heavens followed her cue, storm clouds swirling and swollen, threatening rain. Another bolt splintered the sky; the light flickered off her soft features. Thunder growled like a ravenous cave troll in the distance.

"A legion of archangels is on their way," Gaia pressed. "We can't give up now."

"Dear Gaia"—the elf queen's voice cracked, raspy from the battle calls she'd made to her elven army over the clash of blades and violent rips of flesh—"I have nothing left to give."

An icy wind blew across the grounds, biting the cheeks of the angels so they were red and raw, whipping loose strands of Hildur's strawberry blonde hair out of her braid.

She returned to the pile of bodies, quelling a sob that was dying to be let out.

Bringing her middle and pointer finger to her lips, she sealed each visible dead elf with a kiss before shakily grabbing a nearby torch and igniting the makeshift pyre. Heat pressed against her armor as she finished her prayer. This time the angels stayed quiet. She deserved as much—to mourn her people, her land, in peace.

For ten short minutes, nothing but the crackle of the fire made it to Hildur's ears. Then she moved, her legs leaden, thighs screaming. The bones littering the ground snapped like sticks beneath the defeated drags of her feet.

A single tear slipped down her cheek as the flames grew behind her, and she went to leave the battlefield for the final time.

"Hildur!" Gaia shouted.

"We are done," the queen seethed. She didn't bother to turn around; her eyes remained fixed on the glacier in the distance, on her castle wavering like a mirage, and the snowcapped mountain behind it.

It wasn't the first war the elves had been dragged into, but as Hildur walked away, she vowed it would be their last.

PART I
ANGEL OF RUIN

CHAPTER I

ALRIGHT RIVER, NOW CLIMB ONTO HIS BACK."

I stared at Shanley, then back at the werewolf—the one I supposedly needed to climb. "Ex-excuse me?"

"Haul yourself up his side and situate yourself between his shoulder blades. Here…" Shanley tilted her head towards the beast's jowls—which I wouldn't be caught anywhere near—and pitched her very human voice to the low whine of a canine, giving what I assumed to be a command.

With a chuff from his snout, the wolf crouched a little lower.

Wide blue eyes, freckled honey-beige cheeks, and golden-brown hair reflected in his midnight stare, the only pieces of me that might have remained the same after discovering I was half-angel—Nephilim—and the heiress of the Angel of Water.

"There, should be easier now." Rolling up her sleeves, my friend dropped to a knee and interlaced her fingers, the cup of her palms ready to hoist me up. Her skin was dry from long days at the coffee shop, and calloused by the repeated transition from hands to paws.

Little grooves indented her forearm—bite marks. The ones near her wrist were definitely new. I'd worked countless shifts with her at Kona Koffee before I got fired, and she had a story for every scar: boozy late-night wrestling, unlucky run-ins with vampires, and simply Turning at the wrong place, wrong time.

But these marks… these ones she tried to cover with her flannel sleeves. These ones she wasn't proud of, didn't joke about.

These were from tending to a beast far worse than a grumpy customer.

These were from Chet Jennings.

Forget the claws and fangs and godlike strength he'd been granted after being bitten at the full moon party earlier that summer—just his name sent a chill down my spine. The thought of facing him tonight…as not only a witness to his carnage, but a victim of it long before…was enough to make my pulse thrum off beat.

A wail erupted from the thick of the forest, curdling the mist. It couldn't be Chet: he'd already be at Crescent Rock under the watchful eyes of the Council of the Moon—the Elders who made up the governing body of all the local werewolf packs—impatiently waiting for his trial to begin.

But Chet wasn't the only thing that lurked in the night, wasn't the only monster who'd made it their sole mission to destroy me.

Shadows coiled in the darkness as if they were living, breathing things. Without the light of the moon, it was damn near impossible to see.

Breath a wisp in the air, I glanced behind me. Nothing but fur and trees. The steel gazes of Shanley's pack tracked my movement.

Most of the wolves were bare, but some of the larger ones had packs strapped to their backs. Clothes. Around the others, a couple shreds of fabric shone bright against the damp forest floor. Sometimes, Shanley had once told me while we were mopping up spilled milk, the urge to Turn came on too quick, too strong, and even the nimblest, most experienced wolves couldn't get undressed fast enough.

I placed a shoe in Shanley's hands, my fingers knotting in the beast's mane. "This won't hurt him?"

She shook her head, ashy blonde strands flopping over her temples.

Of course it wouldn't hurt him. Kenny was all muscle and brute strength in every form. Pressing my heel into Shanley's palm, I hiked myself up onto his massive shoulders with such effortless grace I would have never, *ever* believed I'd be capable of. But…

I was stronger now. Faster. Keener senses. Still couldn't outrun a werewolf, no matter how much Empyrean magic—Source—I'd inherited from my mom.

Shanley wiped her palms together, brushing off the dirt. "River, you good?"

I nodded, tucking my fingers under Kenny's long outer chestnut coat to hide how badly I'd started trembling.

He huffed out through his nostrils, paw scuffing the earth, ready to run. I willed myself not to focus on the way his claws indented the soil, how when he rose on his hind legs, standing tall and proud, my head grazed the lower branches.

How, once he took off, there would be no going back.

In less than an hour, I'd be facing Chet on the stand.

I could still feel the heat of his nasty breath, his saliva smearing over my skin… A chill rattled my shoulders. How was I going to relive his public attack at the bonfire, and the private one in his bedroom, in front of Elders, witnesses, *strangers?*

"Stay low while we're running," Shanley said.

My head snapped in her direction, sticky thoughts of Chet dissipating for now. I'd get through this for her. Because no matter who bit whom that smoky night at the beach, it was her pack, her territory, her problem to solve—and from the little I knew about werewolf politics, punishments were vicious.

I inhaled, the air sharp and minty. I wanted to bring Chet down. But, more importantly, I wanted to be there for Shanley like she'd been there for me all summer, wiping my tears, dragging me out of bed past noon, forcing me to do the unthinkable—*socialize.*

"Keep your grip tight on the ruff of fur around Kenny's neck. I'll be right alongside you."

In a flicker of movement her hands had tripled their size. Fingers curling, palms swelling, tufts of fur sprouting along her knuckles…

She had started to Turn.

"When I howl, it means we have ten seconds till take-off," she added, but those final words were torn apart by a shrill whimper as her flesh and muscle tore and transformed.

A familiar sense of unease hollowed out my stomach. It didn't matter how many demonstrations Shanley had given me—hearing bones crack and reset, watching facial features morph and sharpen never got easier.

Fixing my gaze on the starlight trickling down through the canopy, on the dark outlines of the redwoods, I waited for her to finish shifting, wincing at every godawful snap of her limbs.

Prickly dry leaves crunched beneath the heavy thud of her feet, now paws, as she stalked to her position at the front of the pack. Velvety ears perked, and she drew her nose towards the sky. A melodic *oooooowwww* poured out of her throat.

The others slowly pitched in, each wolf's cry different, distinct. Some low and lively, others guttural and longing, all blending into something—a presence that rang in my ears, my jaw, through my whole body, and blanketed the woods long after they'd stopped.

Kenny rocketed us forward, the howl of the wind replacing the song of the wolves.

I settled into position, focused on keeping my spine arched, my knees locked around his ribs. The powerful shift of his shoulders dug into my legs, my quick gasp lost to the stinging air, my ponytail waving like a flag in the wind as we raced through the night.

The wolves darted through the trees, infiltrating the forest like wraiths. Little by little, the group splintered off, disappearing into the darkness.

I remained hunched, peering over the wild ruff of Kenny's neck, poised to avoid getting a branch to the face. Still, it was definitely possible with my luck, in a wilderness this dense and at the speed we were going. My wide eyes darted around, teary from the wind—bark, shrubs, bushes all whizzing by in a deep green blur.

A silhouette sprang up on our left, twisting towards us. I flinched, nearly slipping off before I grabbed a fistful of fur.

Obviously, it was just a werewolf—probably Shanley. I waited for the flash of a tail, the streak of a pewter coat. My ears perked for the gallop of heavy paws.

Goosebumps prickled my skin, and an ancient pulse of power rushed up my arms.

My fingers brushed my collarbone, reaching for the lapis necklace as if my mom's heirloom might miraculously appear. It didn't, of course.

It'd been stolen off my neck by trusted hands—the very same ones that had cupped my chin and tangled in my hair and grabbed my face for the perfect kiss—and placed into the claw-tipped clutches of the Greater Demon, Finis, leaving me weak. Powerless.

Dry wind stung my cheeks, and for a second, I wasn't racing through the fresh mountain air, but fleeing the burning darkness, the ruined Boardwalk behind me, Ryder's vengeful screams echoing in the night, my best friend, Javi, limp in my arms.

The silhouette skittered between the trunks, working to keep its stride.

My pulse galloped in my chest. After I banished Finis to the vile realm she crawled out of, I never actually found out where her hit men went. For all I knew, it could have been one of them stumbling through the thick mess of brambles.

Whatever it was, it didn't belong with this pack.

It was following us.

The temperature dropped, each inhale an icy stab to the throat.

Ryder. These were his woods. He was out there. Somewhere.

Like Javi, he'd nearly been killed during the attack at the Beach Boardwalk. Not at the demon's hands—at *mine*. And not before admitting he and his brother were part of the Night Stalkers, willing pawns in Chthonia's game to overthrow the angelic realm of Empyrea, abduct me, and siphon my powers.

And I'd fallen right into his trap.

Bet he never guessed I'd get away.

I could still hear the lilt of his accent, his haunting last words sharper than the arrow he'd been aiming at my heart. *Make this easy on yourself, River. We have already fallen.*

Here, it was louder than ever.

River.

Here, it was like his essence was woven into the canopy, into the soft crush of leaves.

River.

My heart leapt in my chest. Traitor.

"River," I heard him call.

Impossible. There was no way that was anything more than the whistle of the wind.

No way I was hearing voices again, especially his, after months of straight silence from the ones who used to haunt me daily—the other three elemental archangels—the Watchers.

I squinted into the dark, peering between the flashes of tangled trunks and ivy.

There was nothing but sporadic shafts of light barely piercing the thickest shadows. Nothing but the rustling of the branches in the summer breeze. It must have been that.

Kenny followed the pack with another sharp turn. Around us, the forest thinned, pale boulders and hard plots of soil puncturing the pine-riddled ground. More moss, more stars, less overgrowth. Nowhere to hide.

I whipped my head around, scanning the edge of the wood.

A flash of color. A howl. A wolf darted out. Then another and another, as the pack drew back together. Familiar brownish-blonde speckled fur darted to the front. Shanley. I blew out a sigh of relief.

A grove of redwoods rose up in an otherwise empty field. A temple of sorts, made of stone and bark. A white glow emanated from the heart of it, spearing back into the grass like fronds of the missing moonlight.

Crescent Rock—it must be. My shoulders slumped as we reached the hidden meeting place, but the aching fear curled around me.

I was now minutes from facing Chet on the stand.

From facing his fake tan, fake smile, fake charm.

"You ready?" Shanley took a hit of her vape, quickly stashing it in her pocket. She'd already changed: black jumper cinched at the waist; jacket draped over her shoulders; jowls replaced by high ivory cheekbones.

Booties hitting the ground, I smoothed out my navy slacks—a gift from her girlfriend, Mau. My whole outfit was, actually: the ribbed shirt, the bold lip, the bow in my hair, all of it styled by her. All of it too fashionable. Too itchy. But for tonight, I needed the armor.

Wolves trotted past me, speedy and silent. Several had shifted back to two legs. No one spared me a second glance.

Well, at least I blended in.

A lithe arm linked around Shanley's. Mau effortlessly slid in beside her, looking radiant as ever in her human form. Red lips set in a thin line, she fidgeted with her tight knit dress. A slight tremor rocked her hands as she worked the fabric, then dragged a fingernail to sharpen the corner of her winged liner.

She was nervous. Shit.

Heat flared on the back of my neck.

Shanley ran her hand through her windswept hair. "Let's go in. Opening remarks start in a few."

The lump that'd formed in my throat kept me from answering.

"You got this, girlie," Mau whispered, before she and Shanley disappeared.

I wished I had someone to link arms with. Someone to wholly lean on. Someone to fill the empty void in my heart.

I wished I had Javi. But he was still in a coma, recovering from the demon attack, and it was *my* secrets, *my* lies, *my* schemes that put him there.

If only I'd let him in on my life, as best friends do, he wouldn't have snuck out after me.

If only I'd told him the honest truth, he wouldn't have ended up atop the splintered wood and mangled metal as a pile of barely breathing, bloodied rags.

If only.

Willing my feet forward, I sucked in a breath and walked towards the open-air sanctum, alone. That feeling that someone was there, that someone was watching, never seeming to go away.

CHAPTER 2

I PASSED THROUGH THE REDWOOD TREES, FINGERS skimming the bark. Colorful flashes of fur sprinted past me, furry tops of ears and the occasional wet snout brushing against my legs.

Shallow breaths clouding on the night, I waited for the last few werewolves to pass, Mau and Shanley becoming mirage-like slivers as they drew deeper into the heart of Crescent Rock.

It fell quiet, like the world was holding its breath. The swish of tails, the hushed pads of paws all lost beneath a sudden veil of silence.

Darkness pressed in. Sticks snapped behind me. Warm air brushed the back of my neck.

I turned, supernaturally fast, biting back a scream as my shoulder clipped a tree trunk. A lone wolf sprinted past.

That's it. I panted, heart beating in my chest like a war drum. It was only my angel senses fine-tuning to pick up the smallest details, the softest sounds, the subtlest shifts in energy.

I inhaled on a ten count, trapping the breath until my pulse slowed.

Without the Voices, my brain and my body bounced back quicker now, or maybe I was just getting used to the sensation of magic. About damn time, after eighteen years.

Still, I could have used the Voices' interjections to tell me whether or not I was dealing with a straggler or a monster. With them gone…every minor scuff of a heel, every shift of a branch had the very real possibility of being something more.

I was always on edge, always looking over my shoulder. And even though the Angel of Fire, Akosua, had severed our connection in support of Chthonia, an even more twisted version of *hell*…

I was always waiting for her and the others to return.

I rubbed my upper arm, the spot sore and tender from knocking into the tree. For sure another bruise. It'd go right above the one I got yesterday, when I stumbled over my swifter, stealthier feet racing down the stairs to the beach.

And the one next to *that* matching the fading welt on my temple, when I'd given a small tug on my surf leash just to have the board come flying at my face.

This time, I simply shook it off and walked on until I reached the back of an outdoor amphitheater.

Hundreds of piercing, eager eyes landed on me.

Was every wolf from every district within their territory invited to this? One pack member's problem was everyone's, I guessed.

So much for a low-key entrance.

Even though the energy tore through me like a set of sharp claws and I wanted to run and hide… I raised my chin high, picked a staircase, planted one foot in front of the other, and wove through the terraced seating. Paying less attention to the humans sitting on the low cobblestone walls and the werewolves sprawled on the grass behind them, and focused on the more pivotal things—like breathing.

My eyes darted around. For Shanley, for Mau, for any familiar face. I found one, glaring up from a seat near the front of the amphitheater.

Chet.

The breath I'd been taking lodged in my throat.

He'd lost his fake tan. His gaze was wild, darkened by the shadow of the crescent-shaped rock I could only assume this clearing was named for. Even dressed as he was in a full suit and tie, it was clear he'd been off the roids and out of the gym, likely kicked off the water polo team, far from the overinflated jock I'd last seen.

I could see what I'd taken from him. But no one—my hands curled into fists—no one knew what he'd taken from me. Tonight, I'd expose him for what he truly was.

Chet's lip curled. He was out for blood too; I didn't need to hear a single word to know that.

My gaze drifted behind him to the stage, where five people waited on thrones that had been carved out of the massive rock face.

The Council of the Moon. They almost looked bored.

While their faces wore the marks of battle—faint pocks, and fine lines—I was shocked at how young they actually were despite being considered *Elders*. My dad had grayer hair and more weathered skin than they did, and he was in his late forties.

Werewolves didn't live long—something about the stress of Turning and what it does to the body: organs growing and shrinking, limbs bending and snapping. Every time they shifted it shaved another few months off their lives.

The beings in front of me… there was no way they were older than thirty, thirty-five tops. The one in the middle tilted his head, a silver scar slitting across his warm beige jaw catching in the low light. With a raised brow, he cleared his throat.

Shit. I was staring.

Trying to coach my face into something in the ballpark of neutral, I scurried down the few remaining steps, attention drifting to the other side of the aisle—finally locking eyes with Shanley, her gaze even more translucent in the starlight. I beelined to the open seat next to her, heel skidding on a patch of moss.

Moisture dotted my upper lip, and it damn near killed me to have Chet see me sweating. I didn't have to face him to feel how his dangerous smirk drilled into me, how every part of him had been honed into a threat.

I knew what he was thinking: *keep her quiet, submissive.* No chance, Chet.

The same Elder who'd given me the odd look rose from his throne.

Not a single breath, not a whisper of the wind floated on the night—just the heavy fabric of his emerald mantel sliding over the stone, as he prowled towards the front of the stage.

"Rise." His voice echoed off the rock, bellowing across the clearing, into the marrow of my bones. In one swift movement, the entire audience rose to their feet. I staggered up, a breath too late, my cheeks hot. "Let us honor our ancestors and receive the blessing of this new moon."

Tilting his head back, the ends of his jet-black hair skimming his broad shoulders, he let out a howl.

Those in human form raised their chins while the beasts angled their snouts.

Staring up at the stars, I swallowed a breath, and the song of the wolves erupted around me. Their howls wove together as if this was their form of worship, the chorus building, strengthening until their lungs couldn't take it, and they fell back into silence.

"Tonight, we will hear from Shanley Galloway, Pack Leader of Santa Cruz City, District Three, and Chet Jennings, fledgling, pack to be assigned, to gather more information around the night he was Turned. Any other grievances will be discussed after, if time permits."

Murmurs spilled and spread like water seeping through a crack in a dam. I couldn't make out what they were saying, but I could feel it. The franticness, the fidgets. I tugged at my cuffs, stretching out my sleeves.

The man raised his arms, quieting the crowd. "In June, the evening of the Strawberry Full Moon, there was an altercation at Davenport Beach, resulting in a member of the Santa Cruz City Pack biting mortal Chet Jennings, which led to him Turning." His gaze swept the assembly. "A direct violation of both clause fifteen of the No Hunt Order, and article nine of the Werewolf Accords."

I turned towards Shanley, trying to get a read. But she was stone-faced, her eyes fixed on the stage. Leaning back, I managed to snag Mau's attention.

We're fucked, she mouthed.

My stomach dropped.

"We already know who's responsible for this." The Elder's dark brown stare roved the front row, landing on a Santa Cruz City Pack member a few people away from me.

Antonio ducked his head, a fierce shade of red spreading over his suntanned cheeks.

To me, Chet had always been a predator. In fact, I'd almost forgotten he was just a mortal dude before the bonfire. And while it royally sucked that he had literal fangs and claws and some form of supernatural power now… it was hard to hate the one who bit him. Antonio hadn't meant to Turn him. And Chet threw the first words, landed the first punch.

I'd fought back too that night—a couple nights, actually—I just didn't happen to possess the gene that turned someone into a werewolf.

"As leader, Shanley will take ownership of her pack's actions and walk us through what happened before we call witnesses and determine a resolution." Quirking his fingers, the Elder beckoned her forward. "As the bylaws require."

Shanley stirred beside me, her throat bobbing as she let go of Mau's hand and trudged up the small set of stairs that led to the stage. She slid behind a podium that blended in so well with the rock, I hadn't even noticed it at first.

"With gratitude, Elder Ivan." Resting her forearms on the stand's surface, she took a deep breath. "The night of the Strawberry Moon, Chet Jennings found his way to our monthly bonfire. Still unclear who invited him or how he found out about it, but at this point, I doubt anyone is brave or stupid enough to admit it."

It had gone so eerily still, even the air felt tighter—as if everyone had sucked in a breath and was holding it in.

"Not only was Chet a bother to my pack—he was a dick to my guests, crossing lines from the moment he arrived."

"Why were mortals invited to this gathering in the first place?" the woman on Ivan's left demanded. She jutted out her hand, chunky emeralds and sapphires glinting from the rings on her fingers, her skin as dark as the midnight sky. "This situation could have easily been avoided."

The others nodded.

"You're right, Elder Jesalynn." Shanley dipped her chin. "As a result, we've postponed any future large gatherings."

"It's a step," Jesalynn said, glancing at the Elders, "but these events need to be outlawed completely."

Aside from Ivan, who narrowed his eyes at something in the distance, the remaining three mumbled their agreement. I resisted the urge to turn around to see what he was so interested in—I owed my friend my full focus.

Shanley's throat bobbed. "With all due respect, that's not why I'm up here." The Elders snapped their attention back to her. "I'm up here to defend my pack member. He shouldn't be held accountable for someone else's bad behavior. Did things go too far? Yeah. But that's what happens when you're pushed to the brink. If Chet wasn't already so bloodthirsty, I doubt anyone under my rule would have responded that way."

"Provoked or not," Jesalynn said, her eyes flashing, "you know the punishment for breaking article nine."

"I know." Shanley's voice twisted with the hint of a sob that felt like a jab to my gut. "And as his leader, I take responsibility. I'm here to take his sentence for him."

"You're willing to die for your pack member?" Jesalynn raised an arched brow, her face curious.

My blood froze.

Shanley gripped the sides of the podium. "I am."

Mau shot up from her seat, fangs sharpening, hair lengthening, clothes already in ribbons on the floor, her furrowed stare fixed on the Elders, deadly. Around me, the pop of dislocating joints rang in my ears and snarls echoed across the stone. Towards the back of the amphitheater, someone shrieked, either in threat or in fear.

I gripped at my knees, holding myself still in the chaos, trying not to be sucked down by the crushing guilt. Death. Hot tears pricked my eyes. She hadn't told me death was on the table.

It wasn't *fair*. If I had known…

Chet's toothy smile, the way his grip had stamped my wrist, the words that had spewed from his loose lips, flashed in my mind. And that gnawing fear, it still tore through me, like a set of sharp claws.

Ugh. I should have just ignored him at the bonfire—should have walked away from him at Grad Night, and even before then, when he'd locked eyes with me at that house party. Then it all would have played out so differently.

No one deserved to die for this. But mostly… Chet didn't deserve to *live*.

I couldn't help but glance over to where he sat. He hadn't budged, seeming to relish the anarchy. He craned his neck towards me, raising his lip to show off his new pair of sharp, pointy teeth.

Put those damn things away. I glared at him.

He was ready for this.

Ready for blood.

"ENOUGH!" It wasn't so much the command, but the underlying snarl that had me whipping my head towards the stage.

Shouts quieted. Bodies stilled. Tension swelled.

Mau froze in front of me in wolf form, poised to charge, silky black hair along her spine standing on end.

Ivan stood tall and feral, anger flashing like lightning in his dark eyes. I could still feel Chet's hungry stare, practically salivating… I dug my fingertips into the slab of rock I sat on.

"Let's not get ahead of ourselves and talk of death." Ivan left his perch, making his way across the platform one strong and purposeful step at a time. Instead of stopping in the center, he headed towards the very lip—towards me. Frowning, he glanced at the wolf in between us, her claws still indenting the concrete. "Back down, Maureen. No matter how mad you are, you cannot evade the law."

Déjà vu hit me harder than a sack of bricks. Those words: *back down*. They sounded too familiar, stirring a dark, anxious part of me. Ryder had given me that warning the last time I saw him, the night he betrayed me and handed me over to a demon—*you can't outrun them.*

A growl trickled out of Mau's throat. She eased off the stage, coming to sit at my feet.

Ivan's lips twitched. "We need to give Chet and others a chance to speak." He gestured across the aisle, and I fought to stop from looking at him again, my enemy sitting there grinning back at me. Giddy. "Then we'll discuss as a council and determine what happens from there. No one is being sentenced to death"—his mouth quirked, like he was fighting some kind of grin as he slipped a final word under his breath—"yet."

I shifted in my seat. How the hell was this funny?

Somebody's *life* was up for grabs.

"Galloway, you're dismissed," Ivan said, returning to his throne. "Jennings, you're up."

Out of the corner of my eye I could see Chet stirring, his thick frame tromping up one end of the stage, while Shanley dashed down the other and took the seat next to me.

He took his place behind the stand, an eerie sparkle in his eyes. "Thanks, Elder Ivan."

My shoulders stiffened at his deep drawl. Full of authority. Full of confidence.

"And thank you, my great Elders." It was no more than a purr as he turned to acknowledge the Council of the Moon. "For hosting this assembly and giving me a fair shot at joining the Pack."

"Make your statement," Jesalynn ordered, her tone making it clear she was not interested in the façade. Good. Maybe she'd be on my side.

"I can assure you the bonfire was nothing more than a…" He paused, throwing the final word at me. "Simple misunderstanding."

My shoulders flinched as if he'd actually struck me.

Really? That's what he wanted to call this?

There was no misunderstanding when he'd slipped off my clothes when I was blacked out drunk and he put his hands on me. No misunderstanding when he'd attacked me—and the others—at the bonfire because he couldn't handle rejection.

Something cracked in my chest: a sob—my heart. Shanley squeezed my hand, which at some point had curled into a fist.

"I was having a little lovers' quarrel." He licked his lips as if the lie were sweet nectar. "It would've been resolved if Galloway had just stayed in her lane. But as you know, she likes to put her nose in other people's problems."

Unease washed over me in a cold sweat.

"We were close to hashing things out when this so-called *Pack leader* grabbed me by the shirt collar and chucked me into the crowd. Naturally, I bumped into a few people. Antonio was too belligerent to realize it was an accident."

Shanley's lips curled back, her pupils shrinking to pinpricks.

"He threw the first punch. What's a guy to do?" He shrugged. "I defended myself."

"That's not how I remember it," Shanley spat, a touch too loud in this quiet, dense space.

"Galloway!" Ivan bellowed from his throne.

"What?" Shanley hunched forward, resting her elbows on her bouncing knees. Hair had started to sprout from her ears. Oh, God. She was unraveling. This wasn't good. "Respectfully—this is bullshit. Wolves are bound by honor and truth. How can you even entertain these lies?"

"Silence!" Ivan's voice cracked off the massive rock formation like thunder. "You've had your time to speak."

"Hardly," Shanley grumbled. The Elder met her with a vicious stare.

Jesalynn cut in. "Regardless of who started it, we still have a very dangerous situation on our hands. A mortal has Turned, and the stories do not match up."

"You're right, Elder Jesalynn." Chet smiled. It was disarming. "I'm the victim here. I was bitten. What reason would I have to lie?"

All the hair on the back of my neck prickled. Of course I knew Chet was lying but I didn't get his motive. He'd absorbed all the strength and power he could ask for—he'd been granted a brand-new life. Shanley was trying to take the fall anyway. What was his play?

"Shanley has been part of this pack since she was a pup. Lying is not in her nature." The Elder interlocked her fingers. "That said, I also know her loyalty is boundless and fierce."

"I think it's time we call up witnesses," another Elder chimed in, his chin sharp and jutting, brows wiry and thick.

"Yes." Jesalynn nodded in agreement. "The fledgling has made his statement."

"Very well," Ivan said.

Pangs of fear zapped my stomach.

"Who are we calling to the stand first?" Jesalynn asked.

Shanley stood, the breeze of her swift movement brushing my arm. "I'd like to invite my guest, River Harlow."

The single other woman on the council took me in in one swift, speculative glance. "An outsider?"

"Ah." Ivan clicked his tongue. "The *Nephilim.*"

Interesting tone there, but it wasn't the first time someone spat the term at me like it was something to be ashamed of. I shrugged it off, choosing to focus on my breaths instead, keeping them even and deep.

Jesalynn pursed her lips. "Nephilim do not hold court here."

"With all due respect, River's more of a pack member than that mongrel is. She was there at the bonfire." Shanley's gaze turned glassy. "And on the receiving end of his antics."

"These are Pack politics, not Empyrean." Jesalynn tilted her chin, a tiny display of empathy. "Given the size of this gathering, I'm sure many others witnessed the altercation. Surely one of them is willing to take the stand?"

I gulped, a ball of fear lodging itself in my throat. Leaning back in my seat, I glanced down my row at Antonio, his head bowed.

"None of us had even heard of Chet before that night," Shanley continued. "River has known him for years. If anyone can provide a true testament to his character, it's her."

"Regardless of their history, she does not hold the lycanthrope gene, therefore her words are inadmissible in this c—"

"I'll allow it." Ivan waved his hand before resting it back under his chin.

Jesalynn swiveled in her seat. "On what grounds?"

"Amendment to article fifteen of the Werewolf Accords—added after the turf war with the vampires in the eighties."

A silver-haired Elder whistled, muttering, "Bloody time for those involved."

Jesalynn's face froze, incredulous.

Ivan shrugged, almost nonchalant. His eyes darted to Chet, who was still standing at the podium, something relayed in that narrowed stare.

Turning to face forward, Jesalynn asked Chet directly, "And what is your relationship to this witness?"

He brushed a wavy strand out of his face. "River and I have a complicated history."

I bit down, pressure building in my temples.

It was simple, really. I said *no,* so he decided to set my world on fire.

"Explain," she said carefully.

The corner of his lips teased at a smirk. No doubt he was gearing up to humiliate me. "She has a little crush."

Hot rage flashed my face, my neck, my chest.

Rolling up his sleeves, he exposed his muscles, or at least, where they once were. "I was supposed to go to college for water polo. She was going to stay here and finish high school."

"Minors cannot testify without parental consent," Jesalynn cut in.

"Oh." He fisted his mouth, holding back a laugh. "River's not a minor. She was a senior last year. She just didn't graduate in June like the rest of us."

Pins and needles struck my skin at what was sure to be hundreds of eyes falling on me. I wrapped my arms around my stomach, sinking lower, attempting to blend with the silhouettes of the humans and wolves.

"And with me being in the kennels these past few weeks, adjusting to…" Chet gestured up and down his body, breezing over the subtle changes I'd missed from trying not to look too hard—the scruff on his chin, his broader shoulders, his thicker neck—now glaring. "So, forgive her for some of the things she might say. She's dealing with major separation anxiety."

The dreaded whispers came, like I knew they would. Unable to look at him—at *anyone*—I glanced at my hands, wringing them tight in my lap.

A growl rumbled against my leg. Mau.

"It's okay," I whispered, running my fingers through the raised fur on the back of her neck. "I won't let him get away with this."

"Jennings, take a seat." *Finally.* "Nephilim, come forth." Ivan gestured me forward with an open palm.

Desperate to keep my legs steady, I slid off the low wall, the pavers slick under the soles of my feet.

Anxiety pummeled through me, a restless drumbeat, as I made my way onto the stage.

Up here, the breeze deflected off the rock, nipping at my clothes, my hair. I cleared my throat, the acoustics of the clearing catching the sound, projecting it like a natural megaphone.

"H-hello. My name is River," I said—I think. All I could hear was the pounding of my heart and the howling of the wind and the emotion in my voice, but not the words.

My knees buckled. Gripping the sides of the podium's top, I held myself up as much as I hid behind it. I needed air. I needed to *breathe.*

Drawing in a deep inhale, I slowly counted to ten.

Hundreds of beady eyes glittered in the dark. Waiting. Watching. This was going to suck, but I'd gone through worse—I'd *actually* had Chet breathing down my neck before.

My slow intake of oxygen helped quiet the overwhelm—a trick from my therapist.

The thought of Dr. Fairmore sent a pang of guilt through me. I hadn't visited her grave in weeks. And to this day, this hour, this heart-rattling second, it was her words that got me through the overwhelm.

Take a deep inhale, she used to tell me. *Hold it in.* She'd wait a beat. *Good, now release.*

So, I did. And with that exhale, the panic, the fear, the urge to run away, all escaped.

It felt like it took forever to find my voice again. But I did.

"I'm here on behalf of Shanley, leader of the Santa Cruz City Pack, as witness to Chet's behavior at the bonfire—and before then," I said, just as I'd rehearsed.

"Yes, we're well aware of that." Ivan's voice boomed behind me. "Get on with it, girl."

I flinched at the sharpness of his tone. Had I been standing behind one of those standard wood lecterns they used at the community college, it would have toppled over.

"Yes, your honor, I mean your Elder, uh—" Muffled laughter swept over the crowd. My temperature must have jumped a thousand degrees.

"Silence!" I knew it was Jesalynn from the multiple times she'd spoken. "Let her speak."

The werewolves obeyed.

With some difficulty, I swallowed and continued. "Chet and I do have history. Months before the bonfire, at a party not too different, he assaulted me. That was the first time."

"*Liar!*" Bug-eyed and spitting, Chet sprang out of his seat.

"Sit down, boy," Jesalynn ordered.

He bared his teeth, straining against two poor souls ordered to grasp him by the arms and bring his ass to the bench, the only things holding him back from rushing the stage. From me.

I picked at the skin around my nails, the cuticles red and screaming. "And the last time he touched me without my consent was at the full moon party."

"Objection!" Chet stood.

"It's true. Before Shanley pulled him off me, he was threatening to—" Saliva rushed my mouth, that bitter taste of pure, unequivocal fear burning all the way down. "To do it again. After I got away, I wasn't close enough to see what happened with Antonio. But if there's anything I know about Chet, it's that he throws a tantrum when he doesn't get what he wants—"

"This is clearly speculation," Chet snarled. "Why is she still up there? Someone get this bitch off the stage!"

My raised voice bounced off the stone. "Chet, will you let me fucking speak?!"

Branches rustled at the far side of the clearing, drawing my gaze to where a silhouette darted between the redwood pillars. I blinked, and there was nothing but stars, fur, and trees.

Leashing the anger, I tried to refocus, my sweaty palms gripping at the stand.

"Nephilim," Elder Ivan called, his voice sharp in warning, "we aren't here to traffic in speculation. You are a witness, here to share what you witnessed."

I nodded jerkily. "After he Turned," I forged onwards, the details growing more vivid with every word, "he sought me out. He pinned me to the ground, waved his claws in my face, and brought his fangs closer and closer… And then Shanley came to my rescue—again."

When I dared a glance over to Chet, he stilled in the grip of his companions, his nostrils wide and breath steaming out. A slow grin spread across his sharp features. Knowing. Deadly.

I should have chosen my next words more carefully, but I was so fucking tired of making myself smaller for him, and that smile ignited me with rage. "He wreaked havoc as a privileged, upper-class kid with all the time and money in the world. I can't even imagine the destruction he will cause as a werewolf—"

A glint of silver whirred past me, barely missing my cheek. My hand shot up instinctively.

I assumed it was Chet breaking free from the pack, his claws cutting the air, coming for me. But he… he was still there with that smug look on his face.

"Elder Blaise!" someone screamed, pointing at the wall of rock looming behind me.

I turned, my palm slamming over my mouth. Blaise, the silver-haired Elder, lay at the foot of their throne in a crumpled, facedown heap, dark liquid pooling beneath their emerald robes in a creeping puddle.

Jesalynn and another leader crouched beside them, exchanging frantic looks of disbelief. The tips of bloodied, battered feathers stuck out from Blaise's side. An arrow.

Dread turned my insides leaden.

More screams, pure terror, infiltrated the amphitheater. I whipped back around.

I hadn't been imagining it. Hundreds of beings snaked through the redwoods, all in dark hoods and leather jackets. A uniform fit for a thief or assassin. For a supernatural syndicate. For a Night Stalker.

My heart clenched as if a fist had taken hold of it.

Gaze roving the tree line, I squinted, trying to differentiate the night from the wraiths in the all-black outfits—trying to see through the flares of fur and flailing limbs, as the assembled burst from their seats, a rush of bodies all seeking the safety of the woods.

For once, I didn't shrink. I didn't hide. Even if every bone in my body was telling me to.

One intruder stood at the top of the steps, the others cascading around them like billowing wisps of shadow. They flicked off their hood.

The earth dipped under me.

It was Ryder's older brother, Leif.

CHAPTER 3

Leif tilted his head, a snarl chiseled onto his face. He was draped in shadow and leather, his blonde bun shiny and slicked, no strand out of place, and his bright eyes were dark with bad intentions—like a twisted mirror of his dark-haired, smirking brother.

He stared directly at me with bloodthirsty purpose, the way a predator stakes out its prey.

I drew in a tight inhale, the air heavy, harsh on my lungs.

Maybe he'd signed a deal with the devil again, maybe this was revenge for escaping the first time, or maybe this was hatred for tempting his brother away from their ruthless syndicate—although, it's not like I'd really succeeded at that. But from the way his gaze stayed fixed on my face when he dipped his starlit jaw, reached over that muscular shoulder, and pulled an arrow out of his quiver…

I knew he was here for me.

Did that mean…? I gulped, my throat burning with terror. Did that mean Ryder was here, too? My chest ached as if it'd already been punctured.

In one breath, I might see him. In one breath, he might shoot me.

It was that night at the Boardwalk all over again, Ryder's betrayal familiar and stabbing.

My eyes darted around the clearing—around the beasts and humans fleeing, the clash of teeth and steel from those fighting.

The wolves were outnumbered. The shadows consumed everything. I ground my jaw, my head snapping away from a crumpled body. Clearly, the Night Stalkers were here for more than a fight.

They came here to kill.

"River!" A familiar voice rang out amongst the others—desperate, screaming. Shanley. I met her stare. She violently patted at the air. "GET DOWN!"

I ducked just in time, the sharp tip of an arrow whistling over my head. It landed behind me, skittering across the stone. My heart flittered wildly, crashing against my ribs.

Adrenaline gathered in my chest, then expanded outward like a balloon, pain and pressure building and shooting to the scars on my shoulder blades, my fingers, the rest of my limbs—in between it all, a feeling I couldn't mistake for anything else: a faint pulse of magic.

Maybe if I just wished, if I focused hard enough, I could unleash it like I had that night at the Boardwalk, even without my mom's necklace—the conduit for my powers.

I narrowed my eyes, tracing over the little view I had of the forest behind the crescent-shaped rock, desperate to find a source of water in the darkness.

I was usually good at this, parsing through the environment, everything made clearer by my angel senses.

But the chaos, the blood, the tears, the screams… It was like a fuzzy, red filter had been smeared over the world, and I couldn't see through it.

Back flush against the podium, I craned my neck, managing to catch a glimpse of Chet—the people who'd been restraining him were now cold lumps on the floor. Everyone around him had fled. Teeth bared, he glared up at the stage.

Something was off. He hadn't run away.

I followed his line of sight. Despite the carnage, Elder Ivan hadn't moved from his throne.

Seeing him there provided no relief, no matter how badly I wanted to believe that the leader of the werewolves was about to go claws-out and fight off the attackers.

But he was too still, too calm. The more I studied him, the more unease prickled my skin.

He wasn't snarling, he was… smiling. Like he was *proud.*

An icy chill washed down my spine, seeping into my bones.

He was in on this. They both were.

Chet was no surprise. I didn't know Ivan. The stings of betrayal I was feeling were more about the secrets that'd been whispered, kept from their own kin. This was supposed to be a safe space for wolves.

Finis had spewed the bogus idea of bridging the realms before I banished her to hers: angels and demons and every species all "coexisting" together by whatever means necessary—violence—and with Chthonia, the devil's realm, in charge, of course… I guess I didn't realize how far, how deep the message had spread.

How so many people willingly chose to side with evil.

Shadows infiltrated the stage—Night Stalkers in their all-black uniforms—grabbing the other Elders and throwing them to the ground.

With a violent roar and a flash of dark hair, Jesalynn shifted into her massive wolf form. The Stalker before her was nothing but shredded skin and leather by the time I could blink.

I jolted back, hitting my head on the thick stone podium. Ears ringing, I gritted my teeth against the swell of sharp pain.

A pair of combat boots appeared before me, splattered in dirt and blood. I didn't let my eyes trail any farther up. Ignoring the pounding in my skull, I whirled out of my hiding space and ran. I hopped off the stage, landing on the slick stone between two werewolves.

I'd recognize the shape of their snouts, the color of their fur, the loyal gleam in their eyes anywhere: Shanley and Mau.

A figure landed before Mau, their approach lethally silent except for the whir of their red-tipped blade. Yellow-slitted eyes glowed beneath their hood.

My friends swept into formation, becoming a shield of snapping jaws and fierce growls.

Another being dropped into our space. Hissing, they swayed their head from side to side. I stepped back, staggering into the eroded edge of the stage. They slithered closer, a forked pink tongue darting out of the darkness under their cowl.

More growls filled the air, but at that point, I didn't know who they were coming from.

With a chuff, Shanley pointed her nose towards the wilderness. *Go,* she seemed to say. She lowered into a crouch, mirroring Mau. With a final throaty warning, they lunged.

I darted towards the trees, jumping over bodies, skidding on moss, splashing through shallow pools of fluid.

My stomach turned.

There were too many shadows, too many people bleeding out. I could help. And yet… I kept running, kept my face straight ahead, kept my gaze locked on the thick foliage.

Shanley had told me to flee, but who was I kidding? I would have done that anyway.

Bands of pressure tightened around my heart. *Coward,* it thumped.

Wavering at the threshold of the forest, I watched the streams of light shining down from the clearing get swallowed by the dense wall of trees and undergrowth.

Selfish. Thump. *No better than a demon.* Thump.

A devilish scream curdled the night.

Not allowing myself to turn around, I dove into the darkness. Thin branches whipped my face as I sprinted through the trees. Pine leaves tugged at my hair. Even bolder shadows dotted the night—I knew better than to assume they were redwoods.

The brush rustled a few feet over. Someone carving a path beside me.

Shanley? Mau? Relief eased the ache of my muscles. Lungs stabbing, I slowed.

Fumbling for my phone that'd been stashed in my pocket, I tapped the screen—no bars, that was a given—and shone it in front of me. The trees were colossal. The leaves were still.

The air was heavy with silence.

"Sh-Shanley? Mau?" Despite the effort to be quiet, it felt like every hushed syllable, every labored gasp, echoed in the night—like the wild pounding of my heart was covering the sound of someone else's footsteps.

The hair rose on the back of my neck.

If it was a friend, they would have shown themselves by now. A twig snapped.

I held up my light, shining it over a wall of ferns. "Who's there?"

And if it was an enemy, they surely would have pounced by now.

Another snap. A crunch. Behind me this time. My breath caught in my throat.

I whirled around. "Show yourself!"

Swearing the branch ahead was an arm and the gnarled trunk a torso, I peered into the woods.

"I'm armed!" I added, even if it was untrue, even if my voice was quaking.

A deep chuckle came from the shadows, and it was like a bullseye shot right to my heart. I'd heard that laugh—many times—but not once in over a month. Not since he'd completed his blood oath and handed me over to the demon at the Boardwalk.

"Ryder?" I forced a harsh tone, and it still came out breathless.

No answer, but I could feel the heat of his gaze burning through the dark.

And if I lifted my phone, I was sure a pair of gold-green eyes would reflect the light. "Is that you?"

A silhouette shifted within the grove.

"Run." The command wove through the trees, the wind, my bones. It was him, but his tone was gritty, strangled, like someone—or something—else was trapped inside him and he had to fight to get a word out.

Part of me ached, a much bigger part than I'd like to admit.

He was tortured, and I wanted to heal him. I wanted to see him, talk to him. Touch him. I stepped forward.

The forest fell silent.

"Silly girl." A whisper, a snarl. Him, but not.

It stopped me in my tracks, that flare of wanting warring against the broken pieces of my heart. Ryder had once helped me find my power, but just as quickly he'd taken it away.

What would happen if I took another step towards him?

Dead leaves crinkled beneath the soles of my feet.

And another?

"Go," he spat. "Now."

My heart rammed against my rib cage. "Are you saving me?"

"Maybe." The word was dipped in venom. "Or maybe I just like the chase."

Low, solemn howls echoed off the tree trunks. The wolves. Shanley, Mau. I bounced on my heels, leaning in their direction. Debating.

Out of the corner of my eye, there was a blur of movement, muscles lunging, leather.

Slipping on the wet soil, I ran away from Crescent Rock, away from my friends, away from it all. Faster and faster, not looking back, not letting myself sink into the guilt of leaving them—even though they'd told me to.

When the woods thinned, I didn't stop, not even when the golden fields surrounded me.

Finally, I turned my head, and I could have sworn there was a shadow in the distance behind me.

I cut through the eucalyptus, weaving in and out of a thicket.

Pins and needles danced along my tendons. Every inhale burned. But I'd keep going until I was sure Ryder wasn't following, and even then I'd plow on, only stopping once my legs gave out—because that was better than an arrow through my heart.

I glanced at my phone. A single bar. That wouldn't do shit out here.

Phone service would be better down by the road, which is where I thought I was heading. Not only would I be safer down there—it was paved.

My foot slipped into a gopher hole, and I staggered forward, slamming into an outcrop of pale rocks. Ugh. Chest heavy, I pressed off the stone. Hobbling down the rolling hillside, now more rock than grass, I crouched beneath the sharp juts of conifers, climbed over boulders with such chalky residue it turned my pants and my palms white.

I slid down a near-vertical rock face, my legs shaking under my weight when I stood up at the bottom, and the steep edge I'd landed near crumbled like sand. Calves aching, I leapt back.

Suspicion was already humming through me, a whisper of intuition tickling the hairs on the back of my neck. And then I saw them: aliens, peace signs, names, a compass rose, doodles carved into every spare inch of this fragile rock.

I bent down, running my fingertips over a pair of letters. *NS.*

Like a pitiful, nervous prey animal, I froze.

This wasn't a random cluster of steep sandhills. These were the moonrocks.

Which meant the Night Stalker compound was hiding in plain sight, somewhere in the vale below. Ryder hadn't been hunting me—he'd been herding me.

CHAPTER 4

RYDER, THAT BASTARD. I GLARED UP THE HILLSIDE AS if he'd be standing there, looking down at me with that devilish smirk.

Scanning the dark horizon, I crept along the rock face, hiding within its shadows, trying to gauge a better path to escape. As I moved closer to the bottom, the sandhills towered over me, eroded and menacing.

I leaned over the edge. Pine needles and fractured rock littered the ground, and probably bones—*mine* if I wasn't careful. If I didn't stay calm.

Of course I'd wind up here. If I craned my neck, I could make out the looping letters of the rooftop's sign just over the thick fence of trees.

The glaring reflection of a floodlight bounced off the curve of the *W,* the swirl of the *A,* the *O* hanging on for dear life. *Wizard of Auto.*

My fingers curled in on themselves. I knew better now— that the auto body shop was merely a front for the Night Stalkers, for their black market, blood oaths, and nefarious deals.

And of course, the crumbling pale rocks curved around the buildings, providing only one way in or out: through the compound.

Biting the inside of my cheek, I eased myself down the rest of the delicate slope. Fully aware that one misplaced hand, one slip of my shoe, could end in a gnarly fall. Worse, it could attract attention.

I hopped off the last outcrop, sinking into the dirt that lined the dense wall of pine. Light flickered through the trees—a flash of metal, the glitter of sand-crusted glass.

It was quiet. Probably a ruse.

Even if most of the Night Stalkers were still attacking the werewolves, there had to be a guard or two patrolling somewhere, waiting for me to stumble through, ready to enact the next phase of Ryder and Leif's plan, whatever that was—finally hand me over to Chthonia? Torture me? Siphon my Source in one of these salt-worn buildings?

Because killing my therapist, putting my best friend in the hospital, stealing my mom's necklace, and outright betraying me wasn't enough. No—tonight's ambush and that murderous gleam on Leif's face made it clear I was still being hunted.

Easing through the row of trees, I darted to the closest building, throwing myself against its peeling emerald wall. My back scraped against its bumpy surface.

Rusty pipes, sheds due to collapse at any moment, old motorcycles, and lots of junk twinkled beneath the stars… but no peddlers, thieves, or assassins. No misfits. No Night Stalkers.

Maybe I was stealthier than I thought.

"Stop right ter."

Two pairs of hands clamped down on my arms.

Dread washed over me, breaths quick and panicky, heart beating out of my chest. My eyes darted around. No Ryder, no Leif, just the dwarf in front of me, and the two at my sides.

Dropping my shoulders, I faked an air of indifference, even if I was shaking inside.

"You got me." I glared down at the dwarf, his red beard bright against his pale pink skin.

I tried to elbow the other two off, but their grip was as unbreakable as iron.

The head dwarf matched my furrowed stare. "Yer goin' to need to come wit us."

I'd figured that was coming, but still… my mouth went dry. I only hoped the tremble in my bones didn't make it to my voice when I asked, "Where?"

His unruly brows dipped inward. "To see te Wizard, of course."

The words struck me like darts.

"The Wizard?" I repeated, slowly, adding time. "Doesn't he have more important things to do?"

"Probably. So, ye can imagine what his reaction will be when he has to stop what he's doin' for…" Even in the dark, his inquisitive gaze bored into me. "This."

This—cataloguing me not as a threat, but more a thorn they needed to pluck out of their side. He tilted a brow, his eyes sweeping over my clothes. Maybe for weapons.

If they were expecting me, they would've known I was defenseless—powerless. But clearly, they hadn't been briefed. They had no idea who I was.

I played into that. "What, an inquiring customer?"

"Yer still a trespasser." He gnashed his teeth together, metal caps glistening. The sound cut into my skull, and I bit back a scream for help that I knew he would only silence.

Turning his back, he walked towards the moonrocks, where the stones caged me in.

The leaden weight of fear nearly shoved me to my knees.

I didn't move until fingers dug into my bicep. "C'mon," one of the remaining dwarves growled, "we don't 'ave all day."

"Can you lighten your grip a little?" I bit out, feet skidding in the dirt.

In reply, he tugged on my arm as if it were a leash. I was flung forward, my shoulder almost popping out of its socket.

A flash of recognition crossed his features. "I know who ye are."

"No, you don't," I said quickly. Much too quickly. "I'm just a customer. Here with a business proposition. First-time visitor. You don't know me."

"Yes, I *do.*" He threaded his fingers through his moustache in contemplation, until his eyes lit. "Yer Ryder's girl."

I flinched at the name. Shit, the dwarves *did* know me. I'd be delusional to think otherwise—to think I'd actually outsmarted a bunch of veteran criminals.

Stomach roiling, I swallowed thickly against the sting of bile. "And who are *you?*"

"Te name's Nemuik." Gravel crackled beneath his boots as he watched me for a reaction. I didn't give him one, keeping my expression neutral. "That ter's Declan and up ahead is Grum."

I glanced at the dwarf on my other side. His grip was

firm but noticeably gentler. Most of his mouth—his entire face, really—was buried in his russet beard.

With a sharp twist of my arm, we followed Grum around the building, broken windows and their bare interiors flashing by. My heart skipped. Was that the room where Ryder signed his blood oath? Where he'd vowed to hunt me down?

"So, Ryder and Leif made it back already, then?" I asked, trying not to stumble over their names. They still tasted bitter, but I'd say anything to fill the silence, which was sharper than the blade gleaming at Nemuik's hip.

"What now?"

"From the Council of the Moon?" No answer. "Crescent Rock?" Disbelief had my voice pitching up. I knew I was dealing with criminals here, but surely slaughtering dozens of innocent werewolves wasn't a typical checkbox on their to-do list. "With the rest of the Night Stalkers?"

"What are ye goin' on about?" Nemuik snapped.

Suspicion pricked at my skin. "There were hundreds of you there. It was an ambush."

"Exactly what are ye tryin' to insinuate, girl?" His beady eyes narrowed in impatience, but his gaze bounced across my face, like he was looking for something.

I glared right back. "Nothing, I'm telling you *facts*. Leif led the whole attack."

"Our crew done no such thing."

"Who was it then?" I side-eyed Declan. He seemed equally confused. Or maybe that was disinterest? Hard to tell with all the hair. Either way—this was weird. "They were dressed in all black."

"That's yer evidence?" Nemuik snorted. *"They were dressed*

in all black," he repeated in a shrill tone he must have thought sounded girly. An attempt to mock me. It made my blood boil. "What good do we 'ave attackin' a bunch of mangy mutts?"

"Watch it," I snapped. "Those *mangy mutts* are my friends."

"Pets, friends, whatever they are," he harumphed, "I stand by what I said. It wasn't us."

I kept my chin high and my face forward, careful to keep the nerves twisting my stomach from reaching my face. "Don't you dare make me feel like I'm crazy."

They were there. I saw them—*ran* from them. The Stalkers were obviously trying to disorient me, and I hated to admit… it was working. My shoulders caved in.

With another yank, Nemuik steered us down a dirt strip that could hardly be called a trail.

Panic and Source roared to life in my veins. I staggered at the rush of blood, the sudden awareness of just how hard my heart pounded, just how much I wished I could escape.

"Yer better off not runnin'," Nemuik advised, as if I was stupid enough to try. "Or askin' questions or makin' silly assumptions. Ye say ye got business to do? Get to it and go."

Like Ryder and Leif would let you release me, anyways. The thought was so loud, I could have sworn it left my lips in a frantic breath.

Tingles surged down my arm, collecting beneath the dwarves' firm grips. My magic was desperate for a way out, every dig of their fingers only feeding its power like oxygen to a flame. But there was no escaping for either of us here. There was nothing but darkness and rock.

Through a break in the trees, something stubborn and firm ground against the packed earth. I couldn't see it; I could hardly hear it over the drum of my racing heart. But I felt it, a dragging in my teeth, my bones. A body? A rope?

Light flickered ahead. Fire burned back the night. Under the orange glow of torchlight, I could make out the pale slabs of rock, dead leaves, and a rusty old door the first dwarf— Grum—had just finished opening.

Nothing but darkness waited inside. I scanned a dilapidated sign that'd been staked into the ground next to it: *Moonrock Mine.*

"In we go, little Nephilim." Grum took the torch out of its bracket, the flames dancing in his golden eyes. "Don't be shy. Te Wizard is waitin'."

CHAPTER 5

WITH THREE ARMED DWARVES AT MY BACK, THERE was nothing to do but step inside.

That grating sound, something heavy raking through the dirt, came and went again. The door, I now knew. We were locked in.

Grum elbowed his way to the front of our group, the light from his torch bouncing off the narrow mining shaft. I'd tasted the musty, damp air just standing at the threshold—in here, it was suffocating.

Clearly, this wasn't the front door. The dust and lack of footprints, along with the debris crunching beneath our feet, gave off the vibe it hadn't been used—let alone swept—in years.

I kicked the dirt to clear my path, nudging aside a few random sticks. Dozens upon dozens littered the floor, so bleached it must have been ages since they'd seen the light of day. Under my heels, they cracked and split with the lightest touch, crunching…

My stomach dropped. Those were not twigs.

Those were… bones. Femurs. Spines. *Skulls.*

Oh my God. I was going to be sick.

"A message if yer lookin' to loot our realm." The whisper shattered the silence like it was a pane of glass.

Irritation slipped past my clenched teeth. "Was that meant to be reassuring, Nemuik?"

"'Twas meant to be a warnin'."

"I've been sufficiently warned, thanks." I didn't care that it echoed through the tunnel, that the snap of it made the pointy tops of his ears twitch.

Who in their right mind would loot this place?

A draft blew through the corridor, batting at the torch's flame. Its fiery tendrils flickered, softened. I clutched tight onto my captors, fear lancing through me.

Declan raised a wiry brow at the touch. I didn't let go. If that light went out, no way was I letting myself end up on the floor with those bones.

Although that might be better than what waited for me up ahead.

The air grew heavier, the silence thicker. The floor a death trap of skeletons, the tunnel feeling even tighter. And the ceiling seemed to get lower and lower, eerie shapes gathering in clusters overhead.

Throat dry, I rasped, "What is that?"

If they said bats, I might die.

"Crystals." Grum raised his torch.

The translucent blue rocks glimmered in the fire's reflection. They were everywhere now, growing out of the damp earth, dotting the ceiling like stars.

"In its heyday, 'twas an excavation site." Nemuik grabbed a fallen shard. "All te greatest warriors, all te finest hunters, all te realms was fightin' for a piece of Moonrock Mine."

"Why?" My eardrums popped, and the sound of my voice, the tread of our footsteps, rushed at me as if I'd been underwater.

"Mined wit dwarven magic." He held up the sleek fragment of crystal, twisting it in the firelight. "Then forged into weapons that'll memorize yer enemies, gainin' power wit every drop of blood. After two or three brawls they'll start singin' when yer foes are nearby."

He stashed the shard in his pocket.

"So, is the operation on hiatus, or…?"

"Nah, 'tis over. Too much fightin'. Too much lootin'. Too many deaths. Most te mines collapsed in te Loma Prieta eart'quake. This is one of te only shafts that survived. Now we jus' use it for te ghosts and te prisoners." He wriggled his bushy brows.

Wonderful. I wondered if I should ask aloud which I was to be.

I bit down on my lip. We treaded on. Around us, light rippled off the crystals and the path finally grew wider.

Voices carried into our corridor, which emptied us into a much larger, much busier chamber—and much, much brighter. Crystals glistened from every spare inch of space, mimicking a clear, cloudless, sky.

My heart leapt: there were a dozen or so offshoots splitting from this main room. One had to lead outside. My arms were now free of the dwarves, I could make a run for it.

That hope immediately died when I noticed they were all patrolled by guards of various species and sizes, all strapped with weapons, decked in spiky leather, and supernaturally still—aside from their heads, which slowly tracked us through the cavern, over the dinged mosaic in the center and to the foot of a black dais.

As we passed a dimly lit tunnel, I met the icy glare of some kind of cave troll. I jerked my eyes away.

Staring is quite rude, Ryder once told me. I hushed that inner voice real quick, but the reality was… I couldn't help it if I tried. Everywhere I looked there was something terrifying, something magical.

"What is it we 'ave 'ere?" a very displeased being bellowed through the circular room.

It drew my attention forward, to the dwarf sitting on the glossy, onyx throne.

The Wizard. King of the Night Stalkers.

My fingers curled, digging into my palms like claws. After what I'd witnessed at Crescent Rock tonight, I could wring his meaty neck right here.

"Well?" Tapping his knuckles on an elaborate wooden snake head that'd been carved on the stiles, he sized me up with his visible eye. A patch fixed over a tight skull cap covered where his other one might lie. "Ye got somethin' to say, Nephilim?"

Plenty, but he had more.

My tired gaze roved the dais to the grisly beings fanned around him—at least a dozen dwarves and trolls, creatures with scales and horns—Ryder and Leif missing from the crowd. They must not have made it back yet.

Drawing in a breath, I went to form words, but the bloody scene from the tribunal flashed before my mind. I cringed at the thought of all the battered crimson fur, at what might have happened to my friends, at their solemn howls that'd been echoing through the forest as I ran—like a coward.

The Wizard leaned towards an associate, blue eye narrowing. "Somethin' wrong wit her?"

"With *me?*" I didn't even mean to say it. It just flew out of my mouth between one choppy breath and the next. "The Night Stalkers massacred dozens of innocent people tonight. I know you have no morals, but do you have no laws? No rules?"

Every pair of eyeballs whipped to me. Nothing except the slow drip of the stalactites broke the tense silence. I bit the inside of my cheek, trying not to flinch at each splash against stone.

The Wizard's lips broke into a sinister smile, teeth sharp and glistening. "Got a sense of humor, this one, don't she."

Hands as strong as iron locked around my biceps again. Declan and Nemuik.

Huffing air out my nose, I gritted out, "Nothing about this is funny."

"Then why ye crackin' jokes?" Darkness swirled beneath his wispy lashes as he pinned me with a knowing look.

My stomach flipped. He knew something was wrong. He just wanted me to cooperate in front of all his loyal subjects.

I wasn't going to let this go.

"You're a smart man." I wrestled against the grip of the dwarves at my sides, not missing that every hand and claw in the chamber slid to their sheathed weapons. "And as leader of such a well-oiled syndicate, I'd be shocked if you didn't keep tabs on every member, on every contract that gets signed here."

A hiss slithered in the air, raking over my skin. I could have sworn it trickled from one of the mouths of the serpents on the arms of his chair, but that was impossible. They were ornamental, like gargoyles sculpted onto a steeple.

"Especially ones that call for blood." My jaw was so tight I barely managed to get the rest out. "Especially if it meant sending hundreds of your Stalkers on an ambush. Or maybe you just turn a cheek when the hush money is right."

The Wizard sat back in his throne, loosely draping his elbow over the armrest, the snakes unmoving but poised to strike. With the blood rushing in my ears, I'd probably just been hearing things. He sucked his teeth, as if something was stuck between his molars.

"Throw 'er in the pit."

The dwarves dragged me across the room, towards one of the more secluded tunnels.

"Wait! Let go of me!" I bucked against their grasp. "WAIT!"

The chamber shook with the force of my shout. Nemuik and Declan lay in a heap, bug-eyed, mouths gaping. Source charged my blood, the air, my breaths. Condensation beaded the smooth face of the stone, vibrating with power. *My* power.

I drew in a ragged breath. I couldn't let them see what this was—an accident. That would be deadlier; it'd reveal the crack in my armor.

So, I did nothing to soften the snarl on my face or the glare in my eyes, even if the hushed creak of bows and the whisk of spears whispered through the room.

Even if they were all aimed at my chest.

Water flowed in thin rivulets from the walls to the floor, pooling beneath the soles of my feet.

"That's right." The Wizard's eye stayed glued to my hands, as if they were a pair of rare, fatal weapons that might rip him apart if he tore his gaze away. "Yer that Angel of Water."

A wave of subdued realization fell over the room. I kept my expression bored.

"Tough contract, that one." A chunky ring glistened in the light as he twirled the braided end of his beard. "Almost didn't 'ave te Stalkers take it when that Grater Demon approached me wit it."

"How considerate of you." I pursed my lips.

"I heard ye escaped her clutches, ye stealthy little ting." He released a wiry gray strand of hair from around his finger. "Ryder and Leif wanted to pursue ye after." My heart stumbled, the words hitting an aching part of me. "I declined their request. By syndicate standards, their work was done. Not our business what 'appens to ye after. How's that for yer morals?"

Tears stung my eyes. I clenched my jaw, holding them back. Foolish. I was so foolish to think Ryder only betrayed me because he'd been bound by blood and honor. But the Wizard said it himself: Ryder had delivered me to his client, Finis—he'd completed that job *thoroughly*—and yet he was still hunting me.

I just couldn't figure out why.

"But now that yer standin' right 'ere…" Veins popped out of his weathered skin, that quiet hiss from earlier slithering in the space between us again. "It'd be easy to pop ye in a sack and deliver ye to Chthonia meself. I'm sure tere'd be a very large reward. A very large reward indeed…"

My breaths rattled in my lungs as Nemuik and Declan shifted closer.

"Whatever it is," I quickly lied, "I can offer more."

"Te devil pays well."

I stiffened. I don't think it really hit me who was haunting me, hunting me, until he said that. The Night Stalkers were just a tool, loyal only to each other and the ones that hired them—it was hell itself that put the bounty on my head.

"Was it money or morals stopping you from coming after me further?" I questioned.

He shrugged. "We all got to feed our families, little Nephy. No offense to ye."

"Oh, that makes it better." Cold sweat swept over my neck.

Bearing my weight on my hip, I glanced at my rippling reflection in the shallow puddles at my feet. A spark of magic shot through my veins, giving me a small burst of confidence. And an idea…

They couldn't hand me over if I was one of them.

"I offer you my service." I twirled my wrists, the Wizard's associates taking a step back at the fluid spin of my joints. A deathly smirk curled my lip—they didn't need to know I had no idea what I was doing, that I'd spent the entire summer trying to summon my Source only to fail every time.

The Wizard's forehead crinkled. He was considering.

"Nah." With a casual wave of his tattooed hand, he summoned his cronies.

"Wait!" I said again. The dwarves froze midstride, wincing at the power in my voice.

The Wizard raised a salt-and-peppered brow in assessment.

"Give me any job you want," I said smoothly, pushing back the thoughts about what they might have me doing.

Survival, wasn't that their big thing? Well, now I was in survival mode, and I'd do just about anything to get out alive—including swearing allegiance to a supernatural syndicate that may or may not have ambushed my friends.

"We don't offer jobs," he said. "We offer contracts."

"Fine." I spit out the word before I changed my mind. "Give me a contract."

"Ye'll be bound by magic."

"Figured."

Resting his chin on his knuckles, he tilted his head. "Ye know what kind of tings we do around 'ere? Or do ye need remindin'?"

A shiver wisped up my spine, my gaze lifting from the throne to the skulls strung like a garland across the back wall. He wouldn't have me kill someone right off the bat… would he? I was too in my head. My confidence was slipping.

"No," I said simply, even though my voice faltered.

Mischief twinkled in his eye. "Then we 'ave ourselves a deal."

"Great. What are the terms?"

"Been lookin' for somethin'. Need ye to find it and steal it."

Thievery. Better than cold-blooded murder—but still. I crossed my arms.

As if he read the movement, he added, "'Tis this or te pit."

A casual ultimatum.

I bit the inside of my cheek until the metallic tang of blood coated my mouth. The pain was easier than fear—it kept me from squirming, from revealing everything with one silly flinch.

"Alright," I ground out. "When do we draft this up?"

"Now."

"Ok." My heart fluttered. "You got a pen?"

The Wizard's mouth drew into a toothy grin. "Oh no, little Nephy. Our contracts aren't signed wit pens." He whipped out a metal tool with a pointed tip. My face paled. It was a tattoo gun. "Tey're signed wit needles."

CHAPTER 6

THE TATTOO GUN BUZZED TO LIFE, THE END DIGGING into the air, warming up to drill into my flesh.

"I thought tattoos were reserved for the blood contracts…" I started, trailing off as my gaze roved over the dwarves and other supernatural beings hanging around the outskirts of the room—intricate markings curling out of their cuffs, their collars, sweeping up their necks.

They were practically covered from head to toe in tattoos.

"Seriously?" Irritation made my voice sharp. "You want me to brand myself? Can't we just sign a piece of paper and call it a day? I won't back out, I swear."

"'Tis our custom." The Wizard flexed his fingers, the wispy ink on his knuckles bending with the movement. "What's te matter? Ye afraid of te ink gun, little Nephy?"

"No," I said, before the insinuation took root and everyone found out how scared I was. My hands balled into fists. "Fine, then. Are you going to do it right here?"

Pushing off the serpentine armrests, he rose from his sleek onyx throne. "We'll head to te parlor."

With a flick of his chin, he gestured to the dark, mildewed passage in the corner, guarded by the massive troll. Great.

This time I didn't flinch when the dwarves grabbed my arms, didn't shout when they led me to the near-pitch-black tunnel and the troll waved me off with a sinister, stumpy smile. Didn't fight when we trudged up a snaking, steady incline and reached the ground level.

The light from the parlor cut through the musty air, falling in shafts across the rocky path. My captors released their grip, the skin tender from being pulled and pinched and tossed around.

A single leather chair, bolted to the floor, awaited me in the middle of the room. Thin lines were scratched all over the material—I tried not to think of how they might have gotten there.

The artist prepared her workstation, needles of different lengths glistening in the soft orange light. Dyes, guns, herbs, body parts in jars, all sat atop the metal tray. I did not want, or need, to know what part of the ritual those were for.

"You giving me a tattoo or performing surgery?" I joked, attempting to shake some of the anxiety.

Shoulders tensing, the artist slowly craned her neck, snarling lips protruding between the thick strands of her braided, white beard. I withered at the look, effectively shut up, and tucked a loose strand of hair behind my ear.

An iron door tempted me from the far side of the room. Through its porthole I could make out the flowered emerald wallpaper of what seemed to be some kind of hall—maybe making a run for it and finding Shanley was an option I *really* should have considered more.

A metal hand situated below the porthole rapped its silver claws against the door.

I blinked. Obviously, I was just seeing things.

That logic was quickly lost when it then scurried to the handle and with a crude gesture, turned the lock. My jaw dropped. *Rude.*

"Any thought as to what yer goin' to get?" a voice asked. It was hardly a whisper, but nonetheless, my palm flattened against my chest.

A dwarf, much younger than the others, one I hadn't seemed to have noticed, stood at my side. With a vinyl apron and an armload of supplies, he had to be the apprentice.

I cleared my throat, squeaking a bit. "Didn't think I had a choice."

"Ye won't if ye don't decide before ye get in that chair." He kept his tone a touch lower as the others in the room only seemed to grow louder. "Otherwise Yudfren chooses for ye."

I spared a glance at the artist, who was tinkering with the settings on her tattoo gun.

"And she doesn't have the, uh—" the apprentice continued as his boss began to rattle the tool, "patience to find one ye like."

"Thanks for the heads-up…"

"We're ready for ye," Yudfren bellowed, severing the chitchat.

My heart thundered in my ears, each beat slamming against my rib cage in rhythm with my shaky steps.

The eyes of the previous customers tracked me from their photos on the wall as I crossed the room. Hundreds of missions, memories, forever captured within the gallery of frames.

Most of the beings in the photos were smiling—an expression the outright opposite of whatever was happening on my face.

Hard to tell from where I was standing, but I could have bet money the guy in the picture in the top left corner—his ivory skin, his dark hair contrasting with his bright eyes, beaming with a sort of happiness I had hardly ever seen him wear—was…

"Get in, sister."

My stomach lurched, but I did as I was told. Sliding onto the worn leather, I squinted at the overhead lamp shining straight into my face. Black spots danced before my eyes, fluttering like tiny, winged insects hypnotized by the warmth. Like moths, or—

"So, what's it goin' to be?" The artist put on her gloves, the latex snapping against her tattooed wrist, leaving a red ring on her pink-tinted skin. "Or shall I select for ye?"

"A butterfly," I stated, the imprints from the bright bulb fading from my vision. "A monarch butterfly."

Yudfren shuffled through the ink, the bottles clinking together. "Where de ye want it?"

"Um…" I pointed to the inside of my left wrist. "There."

Someone dragged over a stool, the metal bottoms of the legs scraping across the hardwood floor. The Wizard plopped onto the seat, gray eyes burning with excitement.

"Care to tell me the terms of this contract? It's not like I'm going anywhere," I said wryly. The tattoo gun clicked on; I flinched at the shrill buzz filling the room. "And I could use a distraction."

He threaded his fingers, resting his elbows on the edge of my seat. So laid-back for a king of the underground.

"Been lookin' for an artifact. Resembles a large pearl—can be shaken like one of those Magic Eight Ball tings. Operates like one too."

"Why don't you just go to Target and get the knockoff?" I teased; my saccharine smile met a gruff, blank stare. "Alright, where is it?"

"Natural Bridges."

The location unlocked a core memory, one I'd buried deep within: my mom and I climbing rock walls and scaling ledges, poking through tide pools and seagrass. "I'm familiar."

"Tere's a cave about a half mile in. Te Stalkers have marked it in te rock."

I didn't remember any sea caves—and the currents never allowed us to leave the natural bridge of stone and shallow pools against the bluffs.

"Already lost a few men on this mission."

"Lost?"

"Te others went mad."

"And what makes you think I can do it?" I couldn't even get inside the damn Santa Cruz Lighthouse, the watchtower literally *dedicated* to the Angel of Water. My odds were not looking great here.

"We've tried dwarves, goblins, trolls, but none speaks to te water like ye do," he said. "Ye were made for this—and I've run outta Nephilim."

Yudfren adjusted my arm with a rough twist. I winced and turned my attention back to the Wizard. "I can think of two very capable Night Stalkers off the top of my head who are also part-angel. Why don't you just ask them?"

He lowered his head, tight-lipped.

"Let's stop pretending here." The cool sting of an alcohol pad met my wrist. I waited for Yudfren to finish and dropped my voice. "When are you finally going to tell me what's going on with your syndicate?"

The hairs on the tops of his ears twitched. Yudfren barked an order at her apprentice. I took the opportunity to slip a few more words in.

"You can try to silence me all you want, but I'm not an idiot," I whispered harshly. "You knew of the attack. You didn't order it—but you also didn't stop it."

The Wizard tapped the leather cushion.

"You're taking the fall for them, aren't you?" I said carefully, his shiftiness, the knowing gleam in his eye, the other dwarves' confusion, everything falling into place. "Why?"

"S'what family does."

Family. From the little I knew about Ryder's, he'd lost his parents when he was five. Leif had naturally morphed from older brother into that father figure role.

And the Night Stalkers… they were more than a band of unruly misfits—they were all they had. Ryder and Leif must be like sons to the Wizard.

Sweat beaded his temples, one of the few parts of his face not covered in ink or hair. "Afraid my boys 'ave fallen into somethin' much darker than organized crime."

My nose squinched. "What's worse than that?"

"Organized warfare."

I broke out in goosebumps as if the temperature had suddenly dropped. "So, if it wasn't your Stalkers that invaded Crescent Rock… whose were they?"

"Tere's a fringe group. Didn't tink much of it, to be honest. We get a lot of those 'ere. Serve a lot of 'em too." He met my gaze. "But this one, it's gainin' steam. Usin' my resources, recruitin' my men, causin' chaos where we 'ave no business causin' chaos."

My stomach sank. "Like tonight."

Emotion brewed in his visible eye—disappointment? "What kind of leader are ye if yer own syndicate is actin' behind yer back?"

Yudfren swiveled around.

The Wizard cleared his throat and straightened his spine, slipping back into that gruff, ruthless mask. "So anyway, tere are markings in te stone. Ancient ones in a tongue we cannot read. 'Tis a boundary, spelled to repel certain beings."

"Or the ones with sticky hands," I muttered.

The artist hovered over my veins, giving them a tap.

With my wrist clean, she wasn't going anywhere, which meant I wouldn't get any more information out of the Wizard.

I sighed.

Aside from the unpredictable magic I was working with, state parks closed at sunset. To get to this remote a location within Natural Bridges, not only would I have to hop the gate and sneak past the rangers, I'd have to scale quite a bit of eroded rock.

Come to think of it, the circumstances around this mission had to be *perfect* for me to succeed. "Say I meet the requirements and am allowed into the cave… What if it's just full of water?"

He wiggled his fingers. "Weren't ye just threatenin' me wit those special powers of yers? I'm sure ye can figure somethin' out."

Well, shit. I'd really dug myself into a hole with that one. "All this for a magical eight ball?"

"Te Pearl of Truth is for a very special client."

"What happens if I f—" Words tangled on my tongue as a sharp tip dug into my skin.

"Keep talkin'. It'll help wit te pain." He gestured to my wrist. "Interestin' choice, by te way. Natural Bridges bein' a monarch sanctuary. Looks like it was meant to be."

Surprise flared through me, numbing the discomfort for a beat. I *hadn't* put that together.

Out of the corner of my eye, Yudfren grabbed a sheet of gauze.

"What happens if I fail?" I managed to squeak out between the relentless stings.

But when the needle arced over my vein… every ounce of awareness, every last bit of confidence left me, and I almost passed out. Then I felt it—a small second pulse, beating in my wrist. And an urge, a tug on my intuition, drawing me away from the room…

It was all too much. My eyes fluttered shut. Instead of the steady tick of the tattoo gun, I heard a whooshing, like ocean waves crashing on jagged, hollowed-out rocks.

And then I saw it under my eyelids, clear as day: a pearl, shining like a beacon in the night, lodged within a crevice. It was bigger than I'd imagined—about the size of a softball.

The thick outer layer protected a shimmering, iridescent interior that swirled with the steady rhythms of the tide.

"The Pearl of Truth. I see it," I whispered when my voice finally found me. The vision vanished, as if I'd spooked it.

When I opened my eyes, the unbearable sting was gone. The space around me had grown far less stuffy—the dwarves had actually given me some breathing room, spreading out along the walls.

Filling my lungs with air, I glanced down at my arm. A small butterfly spread its near-translucent orange wings across the upper left corner of my wrist, permanently perched on the tendon. No wonder it hurt like hell.

"It starts wit a pull, a gut feelin' ye simply can't ignore." The Wizard stepped forward, his eyes glowing wild with magic. "'Tis te enchantment of te ink. It'll lead ye like a compass—no matter what ye do, where ye go, that naggin' sensation will be tere till ye complete yer mission."

My insides flopped, as if the butterfly had taken flight in my stomach.

"If ye fail or if ye decide to abandon te task, te pain will start growin', spreadin', till it hijacks every one of yer senses." His words landed like the chanting of a hex. "Nephilim, ye are bound till this is fulfilled. And I want it done tonight."

I blinked. "You can't be serious."

The Wizard shook his head. The sound of my voice seemed to help him snap out of it—from whatever that just was—his eyes fading, the magic dimming. "Yer lucky it's dawn. Ye got te whole day to plan."

It's not like I had sleep to catch up on or friends to check in with or a life to get to…

"Lots of shiny tings in that cave," he warned. "Don't be tempted. They say it's haunted by te souls of those who are lost at sea."

Disbelief shuttered the funny tingle in my veins. "Great. Are we done here?" I swung my legs over the side of the chair. The Wizard shot back to dodge my knees.

"One more ting. Nemuik!" he barked. "Ye go wit her."

"What?!" Nemuik stepped forward in protest. "Why me?!"

"Don't ye ask questions! 'Tis protocol to have a scout for rookies. She's one of us now."

Skin flushing a vibrant red, Nemuik went back to his position, toothy glower fixed on me.

Well, at least my plan worked: I was the newest member of the Night Stalkers.

CHAPTER 7

Where are you? The dreaded dad text hit my phone the moment I left the junkyard and crossed the Wizard of Auto's boundary. A flurry of other notifications popped onto my screen, the messages all blending together:

We're ok!! Are you ok?

Come home this instant.

Your dad's looking for you.

River, you need to answer. It's Javi.

My heartbeat stuttered in my chest. Time itself seemed to stop.

He's awake.

It was daybreak. My dad was livid I had been out all night, but at least Shanley, Mau, and the City Pack were alive—not good, but not dead. And my best friend, Javi, had finally opened his eyes after weeks in a medically induced coma.

Drop me a pin, we'll take you to the hospital.

When a glimmer of red cut through the swells of dust and Shanley's Honda rolled up the road that led to the compound—to the literal middle of fucking nowhere, where I'd bluntly been ordered by the dwarves to *walk*—I almost sank to my knees.

I slumped into the passenger's seat, Mau filling me in on the aftermath of Crescent Rock from the back. Ivan fled, Chet fled, dozens of werewolves missing.

The world shot by in a blur of gold streaks and yellow fields. But my mind was racing faster.

The constant pulse of pain shooting up my arm, the vision of the Pearl smushed between my thoughts… I felt myself drawing inwards.

Was this how Ryder felt about me? I'd been his mark, his mission to hunt me inked onto his arm. Had I lined his every blink, his every breath, every beat of his heart—like the Pearl did mine?

A hand cupped my shoulder. "Riv, you okay?"

Mau's hushed voice snapped me out of it. "Yeah."

At least for now.

I gave them the lowdown of what I'd seen and heard at the compound—leaving the tattoo out. The werewolves had also heard rumblings about this so-called fringe group, but they weren't so quick to believe the Wizard's innocence in all of it.

"Bloodthirsty criminals," Shanley growled.

"Sociopaths," Mau spat.

"Cruel," they both said. "Lawless. Vile."

And those were the kinder words they used to describe the syndicate.

I slunk farther into my seat, hiding my wrist in my sleeve. What would they think if they knew I was one of them? Even if it was the last resort I had?

Shanley zipped into the hospital's driveway, tires screeching as she pulled up to the curb.

"Want us to wait for you?" she asked.

I shook my head. "I'll text my dad."

Getting out of the car, my steps were so unsteady I thought I might faceplant, the blood rushing to my head. I went to close the door, meeting my reflection for a second—the haggard mess of my hair, the dirt and faint scratches streaking my cheeks, the flash of magic behind my blue stare.

I darted inside, that wild, lawless girl in the reflection haunting my thoughts.

She was me—but not.

Wiping my face, running my hands through my tangles, I rushed through visitor check-in, slightly surprised they didn't turn me away.

I'd been here almost every day since the accident—since Javi had been infected with the Greater Demon's hellish Source—the process so ingrained in my head I could probably find my way to him blindfolded.

I leapt up the stairs to the second floor, sprinted down the far-left corridor, and halted at the fourth room on the right. My hand stilled on the handle. On a ten count, I inhaled, holding it in—just like Dr. Fairmore would tell me to do—then released it and pushed open the door.

"Get the fuck out."

His words hit me so hard, I staggered halfway out of his room. I didn't expect the anger. I absolutely deserved it, but... I just didn't expect it.

"Javi, I—"

"Don't!" He held up his hand, and it killed me to see the pain from the movement flash across his face, as he accidentally tugged the IV taped in his elbow. "Don't take a step closer."

Still stuck in the doorway, I leaned against the frame. I hardly even recognized him. The dark circles under his eyes, the wan skin, the slur to his speech, the machines surrounding him…

"Javi, please. Let me explain."

"I don't want to hear it." Instead of their usual softness, his brown eyes were hard as he scoped me up and down. He paused on my bloodied collar, on the layer of dirt dusting my shirt, scrutinizing. "You look like shit."

Probably should have done more with the baby wipe Mau handed me in the car, but it had lain limp in my hands because, even now, I could hardly concentrate on anything but the Pearl.

"Have you been up all night?"

I nodded, biting down on my lip, the burst of pain dulling the sharper pull of the tattoo's magic.

"It's so funny," Javi continued harshly, with a cold laugh. "You're standing in front of me but you're like a ghost. I don't recognize you. I don't know you."

"You do." I took a cautious step inside. "I'm River. Your best friend—"

"A best friend wouldn't lie. Wouldn't pretend. Wouldn't live a double life." His words were like a dagger twisting between my ribs. "You're no friend of mine."

I shrunk in on myself, shoulders curling. My eyes burned.

What had I done? Who had I turned him into? The last time we spoke—before he ended up here—he was mad, confused, but he still… *cared.*

When I sent him my location the night of the demon attack, I hadn't anticipated he would show up. Maybe that's where I went wrong. Maybe I didn't believe he would come because if it were reversed, I'd have an excuse—too tired, too sad, too anxious—heart the text and go to bed.

But he was the better friend. The better person.

A single, silent tear slipped down my cheek. I blew out a shaky breath, fighting to keep the rest of them in.

"You're upset?" He leaned forward, patterned gown slipping off his shoulder, a blistered, irritated scar poking out. "How do you think I feel?"

Chin dipping towards the floor, I bit back a sob, my lungs spasming.

"I had to defer my admission to UCSB. I have to learn how to walk again. I'm going to be stuck in this miserable place for months. Months." His face twisted with pain. "Meanwhile, you get to go off and frolic and do whatever you want."

Looking up from the scuffed tile, I took in the cold room around us. There was no color in this space. No vibrancy, no life. Not even a sliver of natural light made it past the closed curtains.

Guilt devoured me like a hungry, flesh-eating virus. "I'm… I'm sorry."

"It's not fair." Javi threw himself back into the starchy pillows, the words hoarse—like he'd repeated them a hundred times before. "Are you even going to summer school, or did you give up on that, too?"

Too. Like I'd given up on life—given up on us. Given up on him. I just wanted to keep him safe, and I failed. Worse, I'd snuck around and kept secrets about my angel lineage, lied to his face about Ryder, and gotten him to hate me in the process.

"There's a few weeks left," I choked out.

His hardened stare turned glassy. "And what are you going to do after? You can't work at Kona Coffee forever."

"No." Heat crept up my neck, scorching my face. "I can't." What remained unspoken hung between us.

"Oh my God." He shook his head, and it wasn't disbelief that laced his tone—it was palpable disgust. "You got fired."

"Right after the incident," I said, almost too ashamed to admit it out loud.

"Figures," he murmured.

"Do you want to know what happened?" I scooted closer, testing out the shorter distance. Maybe if I told him everything, from the beginning… It might not repair the damage, but at least he'd understand—I hadn't even given him that chance. "That night at the Boardwalk?"

Another shaky step, then another, and another, until my legs hit the edge of his bed.

His upper body tensed. "It's all my family's been able to talk about this morning. The storm, River, her psychotic break, the fact that I never really mattered to her. I think I've heard enough."

"They weren't there." A zing of relief softened the nerves. He didn't remember Finis, the Source, the portal to Chthonia. "Don't you want to hear what happened, from me?"

Air blew out from his lips with a sharp *tsk*. "You know, I could deal with a broken heart. I was going to shoot my shot regardless, and if it didn't work out…" he shrugged, jaw tightening at the discomfort. "I can't fault you for not loving me back."

"But I did love you." My words twisted into a cry. "I *do* love you."

He held out his arm, blocking me from treading closer. "You're entitled to your feelings, even if they're messy. You know what I find unforgivable about all this?"

My fingers shot to my mouth, and I feverishly bit the nails as if I were a scavenger that'd gone weeks without food.

"Instead of being up-front, you led me on. Instead of being honest with me, you lied. And after thirteen years of friendship, of me being the only person you could rely on… you didn't trust I would show up in your darkest hours."

"I didn't think you would…" I trailed off, stopping myself from proving his point.

"OF COURSE I WOULD COME!" The monitor next to his bed started beeping shrilly, the sound piercing my eardrums. "Because that's what friends do, but I wasn't a friend to you. I was just a placeholder until something better came along."

I cupped my chin with my hands, placing my middle fingers on my earlobes to drown out the noise of the chirping machine. "That's not true."

He shook his head.

His mind had been made up.

And even if I knew in my heart his accusations weren't true, my actions said otherwise. I was selfish. So selfish.

Unredeemable.

I whispered, "What do you want from me, Jav?"

One side of his mouth quirked up in an easy, dimpled, smile, and for a second, I thought I might be hallucinating.

"Honestly, nothing. Now go," he ordered. "And please… just… don't come back."

The pain struck me like a gut punch, sucking all the wind from my lungs, hollowing me out.

Palm cupping my mouth and tears slipping down my face, I backed into the hall, stumbling past a smear of white coats and blue scrubs and automatic doors that didn't open fast enough—

I burst onto the sidewalk, the day too bright, too warm, too promising. I gulped down air as if I was starved of oxygen, each inhale burning.

Javi's words, Chet's stare, Ryder's betrayal, the gravity of the night before crashed into me with a flash of a pearly white object and a flare of tainted magic.

I didn't know where I was going, I just had to run, had to get as far away as possible.

As I stumbled around like some kind of idiot, my shoulder clipped the person walking past me.

"Ow! Seriously?"

"Sorry," I mumbled, hand shooting to my arm, rubbing at the soreness.

"River?"

It took effort to draw my gaze up from the ground. When I did, surprise shot through me—the person I'd run into was Javi's older sister.

I swayed to the side, still unsteady on my feet. "Jade."

"What is wrong with you?" Narrowing her violet-sparkle-dusted stare, she said, "Are you high or something?"

"Of course not." I wiped the salt from my face with my sleeve. "Just tired."

At one point, Jade and I had been friends, but all I got from her now was a frigid glare.

There were bags under her eyes, and her warm copper cheeks were sunken like she was equal parts sad and haunted.

"Shouldn't you be at Berkeley?" I blurted. Anything to fill the awkward silence, although I'm pretty positive we *both* heard the frantic pounding of my heart.

"I should," she said, "but I'm not."

"Javi's up."

Pursing her lips, she raised a brow. "Why do you think I'm here?"

Of course, duh. She must have driven down from school at like four in the morning, right when she got the news. "I'm s—"

"Save it." Her jaw worked back and forth. "I need to get inside. I know my mom went to grab him some clothes and his comics, and I don't want him to be alone. But I want you to know one thing." With a slow, controlled step, she closed the distance between us, her stare boring into me with a special kind of fury. "You leave my baby brother alone."

I didn't move, didn't so much as breathe.

"I don't know exactly what happened that night, but I know Javi, and I know you." She jabbed a hot-pink nail into my collarbone. "The recklessness isn't what gets me. It's the audacity to think my brother wouldn't come running after you."

Gulping against a dryness that'd withered my vocal cords, I nodded.

"If you took your head out of your ass for one second, you would have seen how much he loved you. Always there for you, always going out of his way for you, and what does he have to show for it? Four metal plates in his head and six screws in his knee." A gust of wind tousled her shoulder-length hair, the shiny black strands glistening in the sun. "Just admit it. You didn't love him back. You just used him to fill the hole in your heart."

I inhaled wetly, sniffing against another spate of tears.

"Was it worth it?" Her tone was ice.

"No," I squeaked out.

Crossing her arms, she gripped herself tightly, as if it took everything in her to hold herself back. "What were you even doing out there in the middle of the night—*in a full-on tsunami?*"

"I didn't know..." That the demon would be waiting. That Javi would take the shortcut through the Boardwalk instead of going straight to the actual destination I sent him—the Santa Cruz Lighthouse. "I didn't know it was going to be that bad."

"We're in a climate crisis, River. Every natural disaster is bad."

There was nothing natural about this, about Finis's serpentine face and the way it twisted in the moonlight, about the dark, demonic magic that'd turned our amusement park to rubble and infected Javi's mortal body like a poison...

But I couldn't tell her that.

So, I not only carried the guilt of that night—I also carried the full truth of it.

Jade whisked past me, her flip-flops slapping against the concrete. "I wish you were in there instead of him."

Me too, Jade. I wished it every day.

As I stepped off the curb, the blaring *honk* of a horn had my heart jumping, instinct pushing me back. A shuttle accelerated past me, the driver's curses muffled by the wind.

I wished it had flattened me, honestly.

Another honk. This time more subtle, coming from the parking lot. I whipped my chin in that direction, towards a hand waving out the window of a small SUV. My dad.

Turning on my heels, I headed for his car. I only hoped with Javi waking up and the tearstains on my face he'd just leave me alone.

I opened the door, the AC a cool kiss over my face and hair.

"Hey, Riv."

"Hey." I slid onto the seat.

"How was it?"

"Horrible."

The car reversed.

Muscles rigid, I waited for the questions, the judgement, as I picked at the dirt beneath my nails—but they never came. The faint tune of the radio, the hum of the tires, the hiss of the air were the only things that made it to my ears.

"I'm sorry," he offered.

"Thanks." Sliding down the leather, I let my shoulders fall.

Sleep should have come easy after being awake for so long, after hours of running and adrenaline and fighting to survive and having my heart shattered over and over again—but my brain wouldn't turn off. I couldn't stop *thinking*.

I rubbed my forehead, trying to ease the throb that had gathered behind my skull.

Home, I just needed to get home, take a shower, and flop into bed. Nothing could reach me there.

Stabbing pain shot up and down my arm. Gripping my sleeve, I pulled the cuff well past my knuckles to hide the butterfly. This cursed tattoo.

Another secret to keep. Another thing eating me up inside.

It pulsed, a biting reminder of its power—as if the visions weren't enough. Attempting to shield myself from my dad's curious gray eyes darting over every minute, I nuzzled into the seat, the Pearl of Truth shining bright in my mind.

I glanced at the sky. Pearl.

Closed my eyes. Pearl.

Took a breath. Pearl.

When Ryder took his blood oath, was it my face that haunted his thoughts?

"Damnit." I shot up, the seatbelt tightening over my chest.

An awkward jumble of sounds came from the driver's seat. "Everything alright?"

No. I took a mission bound by blood and magic, and now I was losing it. "Yeah," I lied.

We turned down a main road. The dizzying push and pull lessened, the swell of impulse fading, the pain dulling into more like a bruise versus a constant prick.

Strange.

My dad veered left, and the feeling came back suddenly, achingly. I sucked in air too quickly and gripped the seat.

We went down another road—right—and with every turn of the engine, it faded. I eyed the street signs, caught a glimpse of the hazy blue horizon ahead. We were headed in the direction of Natural Bridges.

"Wow." My fingers drifted to my lips. Didn't mean to say that out loud.

My dad cleared his throat, shifting in his seat.

"It's a…" I gave him a tight smile. "Beautiful day?"

"Yeah." His grip tightened on the steering wheel, sun-tanned knuckles turning bone white, as he unknowingly took me closer and closer to my target. "It is."

I glanced at where my shirt covered the orange and black of my tattoo.

The Wizard had given me less than twenty-four hours to complete the contract. A favor, I realized. Any longer and the enchantment in the ink might turn my brain to mush.

Adrenaline bloomed in my chest, equal parts maddening and addicting.

Indeed, it was a beautiful day to steal a magical pearl.

CHAPTER 8

"YOU MADE IT." THE WORDS LEFT MY LIPS IN A CLOUD, dispersing into the chill coastal air.

In his all-black ensemble, he could have just been another shadow.

"I'd rather be sleepin'," Nemuik growled from within the hood of his cloak, "but I had no choice."

I pulled up my sleeve, the faint lines of my fresh ink glistening in the starlight. "Me, either. Should we get friendship tattoos to match?"

"I been waitin' 'ere since sundown, I hope ye know. Ye better 'ave come armed wit more than just jokes!"

My brows dipped together. "Armed? As in weapons?"

"Why, why me?" he huffed. Tarnished silver glittered from his pocket, quickly followed by a fractal of crystal. A dagger.

He withdrew it, and I leapt back, scrambling to put some distance between us, nearly tripping over a root. The dwarf flicked the blade forward in quick, stabbing motions, no doubt aiming for my guts.

"What are ye doin'?!" he snapped. "Are ye tryin' to get us caught?!"

"You're the one trying to stab me!" The words were muffled behind the shield of my fingers.

"*What?!*" he whisper-screamed, eyes darting to the park's entry gate and the small hut that housed the rangers. His hands fisted at his sides, hood rustling with the movement. A sliver of moon danced over his fuming red cheeks. "Why would I be tryin' to *kill ye?!*"

"I don't know. Easy target?" I was too shocked to come up with a reasonable answer, too on edge from the night before.

"Ye may be te one wit te contract, but it's my arse on te line here," he snarled, slicing the dagger through the air. "If ye fail, I fail. Listen 'ere, girl… if ye go into that cave without any sort of weapon, yer bones will be just another decoration on te floor. Capiche?"

Nodding in understanding, I gulped down the rising fear.

He spun the blade between his fingers before offering me the pommel. "Now get yer shit together. Failure is not an option t'night."

"Right. Great pep talk." I grasped the hilt, the cool metal biting against my skin. The intricate grooves of the steel handle were dotted with specks of clear blue—shards of crystals, the same kind that I had seen covering the dwarfdom, were welded onto the blade. "I've got it now."

It slipped from my grip, landing tip down, nearly impaling my toe.

"For te love of te saints," he cursed under his breath.

"Sorry, this was probably expensive," I murmured, stumbling to grab it, a flash of heat searing my temples and neck. "Um, where exactly do I put it?"

The whites of his eyes reflected in the dim light. "Take this." He passed me a scabbard with runes stitched into the leather.

"Thanks." My fingers were clammy, even if the coastal air was crisp and chilling, as I attached it to my waistband. It looked ridiculous on me. Like I was playing dress-up.

The last time I'd held a weapon, it was the smooth shaft of an arrow, the curved wood of a bow. Ryder's.

"Nemuik…" I tried not to let the hesitation seep into my voice, but I had to know, in case I didn't make it out alive, in case I didn't get another chance. "This odd obsession I have with the Pearl, does it just… go away once everything's done?"

Air steamed out of his wiry-haired nostrils, and he waited a beat, as if taking extra time to decipher my words. "Once yer mission is complete, ye don't 'ave a target, so yer huntin' instinct naturally fades."

And there I had it. Ryder and I meant nothing, then.

"Got it." Even though I didn't say his name, the way my voice quavered must have made it apparent.

"Te tattoo is what may have brought him to ye, but those feelins', they belonged to him," he added, unprompted.

I shook it off, the reality of it already sinking into me like claws. Did he not know Ryder had only pretended to like me to complete his own contract, or did the dwarf just not realize how good the guy was at his job?

"Anyways." His boot scuffed the dirt. "Ready?"

Pulling on the strings of my hoodie, I gave Nemuik a tense nod, feeling anything but.

"I can only lead ye to te half-mile marker," he warned. "Too dangerous for me after that."

"Too dangerous for *you?*" I raised a brow. "Aren't you a ruthless killer?"

"Not a great swimmer. And, ye know, te area is spelled."

"Ok," I blew out the word, my confidence leaking out with it.

Knees bent, shoulders hunched, he crept down the small hill into the sand dunes below.

I didn't think, I just went, trailing his silent footsteps, hoping the midnight mist blanketed our silhouettes from any rangers still lingering about.

Once we reached the damp band of water-soaked sand at the foot of the bluffs, he held up a hand in signal, and I froze. Something skittered across the shelf of tide pools above—too big to be a crab.

Back flush against the salt-crusted edge, I leaned just far enough to see onto the ledge.

Round black critters scurried over the small pools, oblivious to the rising tide—and, so far, to us. As often as the ocean swept them out, they crawled back in, no stone or hole or shell left untouched.

More confused than anything, I asked, "What are those?"

"Scuttlers. Scavengers."

"Should I..." I inched forward, poking my head back out—barely ducking in time as a long-forgotten piece of fishing equipment flew off the cliff and landed in the damp sand. "Be concerned? They look like giant, tailless tadpoles. Angry ones."

"Nah, jus' don't get close." He didn't even flinch when a group of them jumped off the rocky shelf and sailed over his head, fighting and spitting like a savage pack of hairless chihuahuas. "Extremely territorial."

Digging into his pocket, he pulled out a bag.

I eyed the speckled balls within the plastic. "Are those…?"

"Jawbreakers." After pouring out a palmful and popping a few in his mouth, he stashed the rest. "If one of 'em gets out of line, pop 'em." He demonstrated with a quick, jabbing motion.

"Is violence the solution to all your problems?" I asked.

He shrugged. "Most of 'em."

"Wouldn't a golf ball do more damage?"

"I can't eat golf balls."

Rolling my eyes, I fell back into position.

Using my knowledge of the ocean, I listened to the waves as if I was getting ready for a rough paddle out to the surf lineup: memorizing the pattern of the tide, timing the heavy crashes, weighing the icy silence.

Fourteen seconds.

I breathed deep, the Pearl of Truth parting my thoughts like a beacon in the night. A plan laid out before me, a puzzle unfolding. I closed my eyes: I'd have fourteen seconds once we got to the half-mile mark to descend the jagged shelf of rock, make it past the rip current, and get inside the cave before the next wave came and swallowed me up.

Water slammed into the rocks. My eyes thrust themselves open. I could do this.

Using the barnacle-studded cavities dimpling the side of the bluff for handholds, we climbed up onto the ledge of tide pools positioned above the raging sea—a natural bridge, of sorts.

A blast of salt water sprayed our clothes. I was already drenched, and we were nowhere near the cave. This was going to be a long, cold night. I should have worn my wetsuit.

Scuttlers scurried towards the end of the reef, growling, snapping at our footsteps.

Nemuik waved them off with an irritable huff. "Oh, quiet, ye good-for-nothin'…" A wave breached the natural bridge, snatching a group of them perched on the edge.

With one arm out for balance, the other skimming the wall of dirt that made up the bluff, I trailed behind the dwarf.

The mist grew thicker the farther we crept, curling around our limbs as if it could drag us out to sea. My pulse sped up, thundering in my ears. I didn't see Nemuik—I could barely see the brittle rock in front of me.

My next step landed on nothing. I caught air, a sharp scream slipping past my lips.

Without thinking, I threw my arms up until my fingers found purchase on the stone, waist and knees slamming into the jagged edge. The sharp rocks bit into my skin, but at least I was able to drag myself up. I peered over the near-invisible recess into the foamy waters below.

"Tere's te marker."

I followed Nemuik's voice until the outline of his braided black beard and leather jacket broke through the fog.

He stood next to a serpent's head spray-painted onto the crumbling bluff.

"Te sea cave is tere, down below."

We turned towards the ocean, the coastal haze dispersing long enough for us to make out the arch of the ancient cavern.

Its gaping opening seemed to swallow the waves and even the tiny bit of moonlight, trapping them both in its depths.

I twirled my wrists, flexing the joints. The thin scabs on my knuckles caught a hint of the moonlight, my hands still raw from many painful, failed attempts at trying to break and enter the Santa Cruz Lighthouse—a place that supposedly *belonged* to the Angel of Water and bridged Empyrea with Mortal Earth. If I couldn't even get in there, how the hell was I supposed to get in here?

A chill raked over my spine. "What are you going to do?"

He plopped a candy in his mouth. "Stand guard and eat jawbreakers."

A draft tunneled through, nipping at our clothes, its low howl echoing off the walls of the cave.

Words unsteady as my legs, I whispered, "Is it true? What the Wizard said? That it's"—my jaw clamped down—"haunted?"

"I've only made it this far." Nemuik gripped the sides of his hood, flopping it back over his head. "And 'tis not in yer best interest to hear what happened to te souls who were ordered to come 'ere and fetch te Pearl."

Fear twisted my stomach. I reached inward for a thread of elemental power—my Source. It skittered deeper, a quiet passenger, watching, waiting, lurking in the silence.

"Ye got a plan?" His gaze remained fixed on the entrance.

I fidgeted with the cuff of my hoodie, pulling it up my arm. The orange hues of the butterfly brightened against my skin as I brushed my thumb over the thin, raised lines. Pain rippled in its wake; I was hit with a vision so hard, my hand shot out and gripped the closest sturdy thing in front of me—which happened to be Nemuik's shoulder.

There: in a pool, a grotto, near the outer chamber, lay the Pearl of Truth. Wedged in a crevice, partially submerged beneath the silt and sand, shimmering like a tiny moon. Shadows crept in, calling from darker corners, until they whisked away the image of my target.

From what I gleaned, the cave was empty.

Nemuik cleared his throat. "Ye good?"

"Yes," I said, springing my hand back, those fingers going straight to my mouth. "Any other last-minute advice?"

"Don't die."

Rolling my eyes, I spat out a sliver of fingernail. "I'll try to remember that one."

I couldn't make any promises, though.

Carefully, I lowered myself down the craggy ledge to yet another level of tide pools, my shoes skidding on the algae, slipping into puddles deep enough to wade in.

"Ok, Nephilim?" Nemuik's voice was muffled by the salty gusts of wind, and when I glanced back, he was bracing himself against it, hands in his pockets, shoulders high. "Good luck."

Water sprayed my sides, the bitter cold of it stinging my cheeks. The swell crashed onto the limpet-covered surface I was standing on, dousing my ankles.

The wind picked up as I treaded farther from the bluffs—closer to the cave. The tug of my tattoo a siren song, pulling me onwards, until I reached a jutting point in the natural bridge.

A cord of intuition banded around my chest. From here, I could make out the notches carved into the stone above the gaping hole of the sea cave's entrance: the runes that made up the spelled boundary.

Most of the swirling, intricate marks, I couldn't place. But there was one in the middle I'd recognize anywhere: the teardrop with the two four-pointed stars lining the upper lefthand corner. The Empyrean symbol for water.

My heart leapt and my tattoo pulsed, adrenaline prickling my veins. Instinctively, my hand crept to my collarbone, grasping air instead of my necklace that bore the same symbol.

None speaks to te water like ye do, the Wizard had said. He knew about this. And because it was a symbol that represented the Watchers—the angels—perhaps that was why all those other poor creatures had met their end trying to retrieve the Pearl.

Another breaker smashed into the point, almost knocking me off my feet.

I centered myself, brushing off the stir of hope and focusing on how the hell I was going to get in. The surf was tricky here. It made the entire cave inaccessible, really. But I guessed that was why it was the perfect hiding spot for a magical artifact.

The ocean pummeled every surface, water sloshing against the reef, the current stealing any unanchored object in its path. It wasn't worth the risk of closing my eyes and trying to channel my Source again when one rogue wave had the strength to sweep me out to sea.

I'd known I was going to get a little wet, but this…

I was going to have to jump. Jump, and bodysurf in.

There literally was no other option.

Searching for any signs of a sneaky rip, I started the count to fourteen. I'd coast along the bridge of rock, avoid the messy backwash in the middle, then ride the waves into the shallows. Daring one more glance at a very confused Nemuik, I leapt.

The soles of my feet sliced through the water first, the icy shock freezing me to my core as my legs, chest, head, and the rest of my body joined the frigid world beneath the surface.

Unrelenting pressure suddenly pushed me down, as if a wave had broken over me. But that was impossible. The next set wasn't for another twelve seconds.

I had timed it *perfectly.*

Another blast from above yanked at me. The force was so strong it thrust my mouth open, water rushing down my throat. Clamping my jaw shut, I wiggled my toes, dipping for the sandy bottom, scraping against… nothing. A twinge of panic seized my muscles. I was way too close to the shore for it to already be this deep.

Something brushed my arm—something slimy, something quick. Maybe a harbor seal, or a tangled bulb of kelp, or a more chilling thought: a soul.

The Wizard's words echoed loud and clear in this weird abyss: *They say it's haunted by te souls of those who are lost at sea.*

Seaweed tickled my wrist—or was it a limb? Flinching, I waved it off, bubbles whirling around me. A thicker object brushed my ankle. Another curled around my hand.

Air slipped through my teeth in a steady stream. My lungs were *aching.* But something was definitely there. Its touches felt purposeful—like prodding fingers.

I opened my eyes. They burned at the salt.

Impenetrable black surrounded me. I'd been thrashing at nothing, wasting my oxygen on nothing. But the longer I stared into the murk… the more it seemed to stare back.

Screaming faces morphed out of the shadows, curious hands seemed to reach from the whirling grit, a haunting presence dragging me *down, down, down* to where there should have been sand, but there was nothing except darkness.

Light flickered in the corner of my eye. I swung my head in its direction, my slitted gaze snagged on the leather hooked to my waist, the clasp undone, waving like seagrass in the current. The crystal of the dagger.

Feeling had started to leave my limbs. My pulse had started to slow. But I reached for the sheath, the movement sluggish, out-of-body, as if I were watching myself.

My fingers fumbled with the flap, barely bending to grip the steel. The longer I struggled, the more if felt like I was becoming a phantom, and the phantoms were becoming… real.

They grabbed at my arms, my legs, their hollowed eyes hungry, pleading, their murmurs mixing with the turbulent whooshes of the tide.

We cannot bear the sound of your beating heart, they seemed to say. Come, live with us in ruin, and whisper the songs of the sailors. Don't be scared…

But I was. I was so, so scared. And maybe that's what drove me to swath the weapon through the water, through ghostly muscle and incorporeal limbs. Fear made me fight against whatever supernatural force was pushing me into the depths.

A spark of warmth stuttered in my chest. A flare of magic—a flame going out.

Shoulders twitching, lungs collapsing, I squinched my lids shut and looked in, reaching for that spark.

I wrapped my entire sense of being around that flicker of hope—my Source. Using it as an anchor, to pull me *up, up, up,* until I burst through the surface.

Crisp, salty air stung my lungs in a burning gasp. Whitecaps rushed towards me. Before I could catch my breath and dive under, the current hooked me in its grasp.

Flailing and spinning, I fought against it, even though my strength was totally, utterly spent.

Then a voice. Two. Ones I thought I'd never hear again, wove themselves onto the breeze, into the stormy sea, into my pounding heart, screaming, "STOP."

Two of the Watchers had reached me. How, I didn't know. Our connection had been severed. But I listened. I stopped. I let my body drift, riding the waves until the bottoms of my feet finally found sand and the ocean carried me in.

Stumbling, I dragged myself to shore, sopping and shaking. At the edge of the surf zone, I dropped to my knees, palms sinking into the damp, waterlogged ground, dagger sparkling in the moonlight beside me.

Salt water, hot and acidic, poured out of my mouth.

After a good retch, I rose to standing, glancing at the arched stone ceiling overhead.

I made it.

CHAPTER 9

THE BREAK CRACKED LIKE THUNDER AGAINST THE beach, bellowing off the smooth stone walls.

I turned to face the opening. From here, the coast was invisible, and all I could make out were the midnight waves and the star-dotted sky.

Foamy water trickled over my toes. The tide was rising—it had already filled most of the grottos, and would fill this entire chamber, soon.

I lightly swept my fingertips over my tattoo. The vision was clear: the Pearl of Truth was in a crevice, but there were a million of those. And they all looked the same.

Legs still adjusting to the soft ground, I took an unsteady step forward, tiny pebbles and fragments of shells sticking to the soles of my bare feet. Wait a minute. Where the hell were my shoes? Turning back towards the waterline, I eyed my drenched pair of high-top sneakers that'd somehow slipped off me, flopping against the small beach with the swash.

I snagged them, thrust them onto my sandy feet, and trudged deeper into the cave, dipping my arm into the small pools, peering into the many nooks and holes.

Droplets of condensation plinked in a steady rhythm, keeping time with my heart.

A shale outcrop jutted into my path. Light flickered behind it, pulsing like a fire. I swallowed hard. I thought no one else had access?

Dwarves, goblins, and trolls hadn't been able to cross the boundary... but I had. Was that who this cave was for—people like me? People descended from angels?

Outside of Ryder and Leif, I'd never met another Nephilim. And after dealing with them, I wasn't sure I wanted to.

Creeping closer, I eased my dagger back out of its scabbard. I was probably holding it wrong, but whatever—it was better than nothing.

Air locked in my lungs; I stilled, waiting for a sign of who or what I might be facing.

Brandishing my weapon in front of me, I rounded the corner.

No one was there.

Blinking, my hand dropped to my side. But there was...

An altar?

The warm light from burning, half-melted candles danced across my face. Wilted orange and white petals littered the floor and an oval tabletop.

What was this place?

Lowering to a crouch, I ran my fingers along the curved stone, my skin scraping over the blue gems studding its surface. Lapis. Just like my missing necklace.

Realization barreled through me, tightening my lungs until my breath hitched.

This wasn't just a cave. This was a shrine dedicated to the Angel of Water. My mom.

The starfish statuettes, the dried sand dollars, the winged figurines placed in the center of the slab… offerings, to a guardian who would never come.

A draft swept through the chamber, but it came from the wrong direction. From the back, where there should have been… nothing.

Slowly, I stood. Grabbing a votive, I followed the rustle into the dimming light, into the heart of the cavern.

"Hello?" I said, my voice disappearing into the shadows.

I wasn't ready for what might answer back. A ghost? A Nephilim? My mom? She'd died ten years ago, condemned for leaving Empyrea and choosing to live and love amongst mortals, but something was in this chamber. I could feel it, a curious, cautious essence, hovering in the unlit corners.

Soft light glowed from within the darkness. Hues of red, green, and yellow radiated from a wall, reflecting in a small, stagnant pool. I peered across, but the shapes were fuzzy this far out.

I slipped into the pool, my leggings, hoodie, *everything*, already sopping, and held my candle aloft. The silt was velvety against my skin, the water cool but not as frigid as the ocean.

It was the depth and the darkness that had my heart racing.

Halfway across, I was up to my waist. Then quickly after, to my chest. And even faster, to my neck.

The candle flickered, and I tried not to shiver as I gazed at what'd been carved into the wall: the Empyrean symbols for the Watchers.

All burned with color, as if they'd been painted on with bioluminescence. All except one.

I went to move closer, but the bottom dropped off. With zero energy or desire to tread the murky water, I stayed where I was.

A green circle with a four-pointed star in the center. That was Gaia, Angel of Earth.

Two yellow spirals with three four-pointed stars. Fei, the Angel of Air.

Four stars curling around a red flame. Akosua, the Angel of Fire.

And a teardrop with two four-pointed stars, but it was unlit.

Because the Angel of Water was gone.

A heavy boom echoed through the chamber, a wave against rock.

Shit. The tide. The *Pearl.*

Scanning the symbols one last time, I waded back to the edge of the pool, vowing to come back with a wetsuit and a surfboard soon.

When I stepped out of the water, the night air hit me in one frigid punch. I wrapped my arm around my stomach, trying to lock in the heat. It was useless.

Shivering, I headed back to the cave's entrance, my feet shuffling over gravel and sand. I placed the candle on the altar and whisked past the jutting shale and continued on towards the front.

The dips and hollows that held nothing more than puddles when I first came in were now full to the brim, seawater trickling over the edges. I stood in the outer chamber, the tide lapping at my ankles.

Think, think, think, River. My mom must have known this artifact was here. Where would she hide it? Would she be okay with me giving it to the Night Stalkers? I shook that worry away—it wasn't like I had much choice. And she wasn't coming back to claim it.

Water trickled in, faster and farther, sloshing in my high-tops.

In my last vision, the Pearl lay half-submerged in a grotto. Between then and now, the water level had risen by, I don't know, a few feet? And there'd been hints of darkness, but not enough to swallow the little bits of candle and moonlight.

Which put it somewhere close to…

Spinning on my heels, I trekked towards an outcrop halfway between the entrance and the altar. It had to be in one of these pools, flanking the sides of the cave.

I hurried to the one on the right, nothing intuitive guiding my decision. But the liquid looked slightly less foamy, which was a plus. Wincing, I stepped in, the freezing ocean water numbing my skin. I dipped down to my waist, my arm skimming the rock, blindly reaching in crevices.

The next set hammered the beach, whitecaps rushing towards me, knocking me back.

This wasn't going to work. It was too aimless. I closed my eyes, inhaling a steady stream of air. I opened my palms and held them at my sides, my fingers bobbing on the water's surface.

"Come on. Help me!" A whisper, a plea, an unfinished prayer, spoken not only with words, but with my heart, with every fiber of my being. Was anyone listening? The universe, the angels, the essence in this cave. My mom. I felt a vein in my temple pop.

PLEASE. HELP. ME.

Wind rustled through the cavern, whipping at my sodden hair, swishing the tide. Shadows whirled before my lids, crackling candlelight. My hands met cool air.

I stumbled back a step as my eyes shot open, my spine digging into the pool's rocky edge.

Water, there should have been water, I should have been up to my waist in water. But the element was gone, as if… as if it had been sucked back out to sea.

Jaw tight, I turned around.

Every grotto had emptied. Someone, something had answered my call. I flexed my fingers, Source tingling from the tendons up and over my body in one shimmering wave.

Wobbling out of the hole that was once a full pool, I strode to the other side of the chamber. The pull on my instincts turned heady and visceral—magnetic.

Hermit crabs clicked their claws angrily, skittering into the nearest divot as I slid into the hollowed-out space. It was identical in size and shape to the other across the cave, but something about this one felt… different.

Reaching into a damp crevice, I brushed away the loose pebbles, my hand grazing the slime and the grit and the chipped shells of sea snails, until it landed on something round and smooth.

Muscles shaking—from the cold, from excitement, from the dwindling magic—I pulled out the Pearl of Truth, cringing when I scraped its side on the narrow cavity. Removing the bits of algae stuck to its glossy outer layer, I weighed it in my palm.

It was like I held the entire world in my hands. Nothing felt more right. More true. I was meant to find this, to hold it. How was I supposed to give it up? I wouldn't, I couldn't—

A burning sensation tore through my scabbed wrist. The flash of pain cut off my train of thought. This wasn't me. It was the tattoo. The true challenge wasn't finding the target.

It was turning it in.

I considered the consequences of not giving it back as I flipped it between my hands, the extra touches fueling the rush, the Pearl glistening with every twist.

Beneath the surface, its shimmering white substance parted at my movements—as if this wasn't a pearl at all, but a glass object made to mimic one.

Huh. So it really *was* like a Magic Eight Ball.

Maybe I could just give it a little shake.

A flare of green, a hint of blue broke through, growing brighter, more *alive*.

As soon as I stopped, the misty interior thickened, shrouding the secrets within its core.

"No!" I surprised myself with the cry that echoed off the cave walls.

Without thinking, I shook the Pearl harder, throttling the damn thing until my arms felt like they might fall off—until my teeth ground together so tight it gave me a pressure headache and, finally, the inside diluted with color.

This time when I stilled, fragments of a scene floated to the surface.

Full, flowered meadows. Deep valleys, winding rivers.

Black, volcanic sand. Miles of untouched beach. Moss-covered cliffs, roosting birds. Rainbow streets, cozy taverns. Glaciers, ice—*so much ice*.

What was I looking at? A glimpse of the future? Another world?

A pale building on a bluff with a red-roofed tower. A lighthouse. Someone knocking—no, banging on the door. A young woman in a blue sweater, hair in a messy braid, *desperately* trying to get in.

The angle shifted, and I could almost taste the earth in the air, almost feel her frustration, as if it were… I swallowed against a knot of fear that had lodged itself in my throat.

The girl in the Pearl of Truth was me.

And then, between one furious blink and the next, the vision changed. Day became night. It was still me, but this River was fuming—this River was hopeless.

Stomping and kicking and screaming on the tower's doorstep while everything, everyone around her burned. The vast, rugged coastline scorched to dirt. The fields not lush and full of life but holding the ruins of a fallen city, a dying fire to indicate every razed home and building.

The moon shone. There might have been stars, but the sky was covered in red and green brushstrokes that glimmered and twirled. And in the soft light, horned beasts stalked the horizon while women were dragged by their hair, children were stolen from loving hands, and desperate beings were left to cry over their dead.

Ash billowed beneath my other self's footsteps, settling on the ground beside the bodies. A half-burnt corpse looked up at me, its face twisted in horror.

Death covered everything. Ribbons of flesh, severed limbs, torn wings—remnants of what seemed to have been a war.

Rain began to fall, dousing everything in scarlet. Horror seized both mes—within the Pearl and standing here in this empty cavern—because those weren't raindrops at all.

It was blood.

I tore myself from the scene, and the momentum carried me as I slipped backwards, splashing into a pool of dark liquid.

Had I landed in blood or water? Wind carried the sounds of whips cracking, of people screaming. Fear rushed through me as the candles sputtered. Reality wobbled; for a moment I couldn't tell which me I was, if I was the River clutching the Pearl, or the one inside it.

Muscles tight and locked, I planted my feet firmly in the sand, the wake lapping at my clothes.

With every rattling breath the night, the cave, the cold, the tide came whooshing back to me. My chest rose and fell sharply. It had just been a vision, and during it, at some point, the power holding the sea back had folded, and now the water was rushing in.

The grottos overflowed. The waves crashed overhead. I had to leave now.

I crawled out of the pool like a dripping swamp monster, pausing on the bank. Angry surf rammed the cavern's entrance, the current stealthy and sweeping, sucking up every little thing in its path. And with the—acid singed my throat—*ghosts* lurking in the murky shallows, I couldn't imagine even attempting to go that way.

I turned the other direction, where the path meandered into a pit of black, the Pearl of Truth lighting my way. The symbols on the wall were little more than fuzzy wisps of color as I passed them, faintly glimmering like a mirage.

Back here, the darkness was palpable, a sentient thing. It was the essence that filled this cave, watchful, illusory. I swore the chill running up my spine was actually a claw.

No way I'd turn around to confirm it.

Out of sight, out of mind. My useless mantra did nothing to tame the fear, but at least it kept my legs chugging forward.

Ahead, the path split in two. Footsteps slowing, I held up the Pearl, bathing the chamber in light. Someone else had been here and lit the candles, and no one in their right mind would choose to dive through those waters. One of these forks must lead out.

Nothing major stood out in either tunnel; they were both old and musty, both carved into the rock. I shifted towards the one on the left.

The ever-burning light in the artifact sputtered, shadows flickering over the walls. Heart thrashing against my ribs, I backed away, its luminance growing steady once more as I turned to the right.

Well, that settled that.

Turning away from one hungry maw of darkness to the other, my quick feet padded over the dirt. That sensation, someone—something—was watching, listening, *breathing* on me never left. I couldn't shake it, not until I crawled through a narrow shaft, squeezed through a smaller hole, and stumbled into the starlight.

Head swiveling, I was able to gather the gist of where I'd ended up: on the sloped top of the cave, where it met the bluffs. I was out, but I couldn't call myself safe, not yet.

Grasping onto roots and rocks, I snaked along the crumbling wall. Goosebumps flooded my skin. The other tunnel must go deep inside the earth. I definitely wouldn't be exploring that one anytime soon.

The fog had dissipated, thank God. If I didn't have a clear view of the bridges, there was no doubt in my mind I'd slip and fall into the raging sea below.

I rounded a corner, my stomach tumbling at a precarious drop-off. A white circle whizzed over the tide pools like a shooting star—a snarling, spitting thing clambered after it. What the—?

The dwarf's cackle drifted in the air, his shoulders bouncing up and down with mirth.

He was throwing his jawbreakers across the rock as if they were tennis balls.

The pathetic flock of scuttlers jumped away from his candy projectiles, chomping at each other, stains of sugary dye dripping down their damp, onyx skin.

Even with his back to me, I could *just* feel Nemuik's diabolical, toothy smile.

"I thought those were for emergency measures," I deadpanned.

Spine stiffening, he stole a glance back at me, and the color drained from his face.

Once he seemed to determine I wasn't a ghost, he cleared his throat. "Jus' tryin' to pass te time. Ye took bloody hours in tere."

"Here." I thrust the artifact into his grasp. The second it met his hands, my tattoo flared one final time. A farewell. "It's done."

"I'll be damned." Awe softened his hard expression. "Te Pearl of Truth."

A twinge of sourness curdled my insides as I watched him fawn over it like that. Mine—it was mine. The urge to steal it out of his hands was almost paralyzing. My gaze zeroed in on him, as if he were a target I needed to dispatch.

I staggered back.

It was just the pull of the tattoo, I told myself, just its magic diluting my emotions in a heady aftershock.

I breathed deep. With every crash of the waves, every inhale of salt, the painful wanting faded from my body. *It wasn't mine.* I exhaled. *I had no claim to it.*

"Shall we?" The dwarf tossed the artifact into a rucksack. As it plopped inside, I swore a sword glinted beneath the swirling matter. Blood flowed like wine. Red-slitted eyes fumed.

"Why do they call it that?" I wiped my brow on my dirt-crusted sleeve. "Pearl of Truth?"

"Reveals te truth," he stated flatly, the tip of his beard twirling around him, flapping in the wind like the sail of a ship.

"Obviously," I said with a saccharine smile. "In what sense? Past? Present? Future?"

"Te outcome of whatever path yer on." He thumbed his sheath. "Any more questions?"

I got the feeling no more were allowed, but I asked anyway. "Who's the client?"

"That's confidential. Stalker business only."

"In case you hadn't noticed," I gritted out, showing off the butterfly on my wrist, "I'm one of you now."

Red bloomed on his light fawn cheeks, the tip of his

nose, the tops of his ears. "Fine," he spat, before turning on his heels. "Te Wizard."

Suspicion lit like kindling.

"What would he want with it?" I needled, trailing his footsteps over the rocky shelf.

"Knowin' te future is power. Maybe he doesn't want it fallin' into te wrong hands."

"The king of an organized crime group is the right hands?"

"Tere not te worst ones."

"Whose would those be?"

In a flash of silky hair and midnight shadow, he spun and shoved a dagger into the small space beneath my chin.

"Lots of questions." He drew upward, pushing the sharp tip into my skin. "Did someone mess wit somethin' they weren't s'posed to?"

"No." My lips hardly parted, afraid the movement might force the blade further into my flesh. Nemuik pressed in. "Ok—yes," I choked out.

Cold night air filled the space between us as he withdrew his blade and stepped back.

I wiped my neck. A tiny bit of blood smeared my hands. "Are you joking?"

"What did ye see?" he pressed.

My jaw fell open. "You cut me!"

"'Twas jus' a pinprick." He waved it off like it was no big deal.

"Ugh." Hands balling into fists, I let out a huff, too amped up to hold it in, too angry to stop and think about what I was saying. "I saw death. War. Beings being wrangled and rounded up. And then there was me, at the center of it all."

The tide roared, slamming into the cliffs. My heart pounded just as loud.

Elbow resting on his knee, Nemuik stared out at the horizon. "Tere's a storm brewin'."

Despite the unruly surf dancing in his dark eyes, I had a feeling he wasn't talking about the weather.

My knees buckled, fighting to sit and rest. "It truly was hell on earth." Just like Finis promised. "I wish I hadn't seen that."

Nemuik sighed. "That's te downside of soothsayin'. S'possible te know too much."

"I mean, how do I just go on with my life knowing all this?" Acid burned in my chest. I'd never felt so helpless. "And that there's nothing I can do to stop it?"

"One ting I know about destiny," he said, running his fingers through his long moustache. "S'not linear. It can be changed."

"How? I'm just one person, and I'll shoot it straight, Nemuik: I'm a fuck up." I held out my hand, counting my faults with my fingers. "I haven't technically graduated high school, and I'm about to fail my final course that would get me my diploma, *again*. I lost my job and most of my friends. I have no idea how to use my Source…" I tucked in my lips, swallowing the rest of the words, already overwhelmed by it all.

The dwarf's wiry brows dipped. "Ye got to believe in yerself first, Nephilim."

As if it were that easy. I kicked a stray rock, and it tumbled into the sea.

"C'mon," he said, sheathing his weapon. "Let's head out. Maybe te Wizard can help us decipher yer vision. What it means, where ye were, all that."

"I was near a lighthouse—" I said it out loud, and my stomach dropped, as if I were free-falling from one of the surrounding bluffs.

My eyes went wide and for a moment, I was inputting the coordinates I'd found scribbled on the back of my dad's lighthouse article into my phone's search bar all over again.

I stopped breathing; my heart was beating too fast…

Then I was pitching the idea to Ryder at a magical pub, that there were structures housing portals for the Watchers to access Earth, convinced of it even if he'd shut me down.

I glanced at my knuckles, at the raw, raised scabs…

And then I was pounding on the stubborn door at the Santa Cruz Lighthouse, the Pacific Ocean wild and unruly at my back, my Source buzzing in my veins as if to say *this is home, this is home.* But I was unable to get in, no matter how many times I tried…

The memories rose and fell like the tide.

The structure I'd seen in the Pearl of Truth wasn't a lighthouse. It was a façade, retrofitted over time to look like an average coastal landmark, but it was really a bridge between worlds.

Just like the simple brick structure at the end of the grassy bluff, casting its beacon over the city of Santa Cruz. Unbreakable stone, unhackable locks… No amount of sweat or Source or will could get that thing open. It was impenetrable, really.

But it was only one of four.

Imagine our shock when the western watchtower did not fall, Finis had told me when she and her Night Stalkers had intercepted me while I was on my way to that very spot. *That a child took the place of the Angel of Water.*

"To your watchtowers," I muttered Akosua's infamous words under my breath.

"What ye say?" Nemuik's pointy ears twitched. "Ye were near a what?"

"A—" Source fluttered next to my heart. "You know what? You head to the compound without me. I have something to do."

He narrowed his eyes. "Ye need to close this out. Tere's paperwork."

"Forge my signature," I said, before whisking past him.

"Ye can't jus'—"

"Oh!" I tossed over my shoulder. "Can you give the Wizard a message for me? I quit."

CHAPTER 10

"Iceland?" Mau blinked, her long lashes fluttering. "Really?"

"Yep." I held up my phone. The pale lighthouse on the screen was an exact replica of the one that had been revealed in the swirling mist of the Pearl. "This is where I was in the vision—where the war took place. Where I need to go."

The wrinkled scrap of paper I'd found in my dad's files earlier that summer, covered with the scribbled coordinates for the other watchtowers—well, fragments of the numbers, at least—slipped out of my grasp, drifting to the floor. Mau bent from the edge of my bed to pick it up.

Shanley ran a hand through her ashy blonde hair, pinning the strands. "I don't know, Riv. Why not try the lighthouse on West Cliff? We can head there right now."

"Because we've already tried that one." Literally all summer. Snatching my duffel from the closet, I groaned at the thought of attempting—and failing—to unlock the tower on the point again. "It won't open."

"And what makes you think this one will?" Mau handed me the torn paper. "River, I love you, but this feels—"

"Impulsive," Shanley cut in, tapping her fingers on the plush arms of my corner chair.

"It's not, I promise." Smiling, I unzipped my bag, but I wasn't fooling anyone. "I've thought a lot about it."

"Oh yeah?" Shanley crossed her tattooed arms, her pale skin flushed against her t-shirt's crisp, white sleeves. "You got home from your little adventure at five this morning. It's ten AM. You're telling me you've had time to sleep and think on it before jumping to this decision?"

I pulled open a drawer, catching a glimpse of my reflection in the vanity's mirror. No amount of concealer could hide the bags under my eyes. No amount of sleep could clear my mind of the death I'd seen in the Pearl.

Tossing the duffel onto the bed and filling it with a thick stack of leggings, I continued, "When I was in that sea cave, I found symbols for the other three Watchers carved onto the wall. Earth, air, and fire. They were all glowing, except for water."

Mau shifted her shoulders. Shanley spun the silver ring on her pointer finger. I didn't miss the way their eyes quickly met.

"And of course it wasn't lit. *Of course* the lighthouse won't open. It's the watchtower for the Angel of Water, who's *dead*, and I—" I still didn't know what I was. Something between angel and human; heiress and cursed; powerful and powerless. I shook my head, not wanting to dive into all that, so I settled on: "I'm like a cheap knockoff of the real thing. When I was in that cave though, and I had that vision, I *felt* something. Fate, a purpose, a presence, a higher power—I don't know. *Something.*"

Shanley leaned forward. "Remind me how you discovered that cave again?"

"I was…" Exploring? Surfing? Playing roulette with my life? Ugh. I'd left that part out for a reason. If they found out I'd worked with the supernatural mob they blamed the werewolf attack on—even if it was a last resort, even if I'd already quit—they might never forgive me.

But this was exactly what I'd done with Javi. Underestimated our friendship, assumed he wouldn't understand. Kept secrets. And look where that got him—got us.

I chewed the inside of my cheek. This was going to blow. But I couldn't keep any more secrets. I took a seat next to Mau, the mattress dipping beneath me.

"I haven't been completely honest with you." My hands twisted in my lap. "When I was at the Night Stalker compound I… took a contract with them."

"*What?!*" they said, the word half a mortal shout, half a wolf's snarl.

"I wanted to tell you on the way to the hospital, but I couldn't bring myself to. Not after what happened at Crescent Rock, not when you hadn't had time to process everything."

Mau stayed silent, her mouth gaping.

"So, did you mean to go there?" Shanley leapt up, her footfalls thudding across the floor. "Did you think they would help you more than us?" Hands digging into her hips, she nodded at Mau. "Your friends?"

"No!" I shot back, my palm hovering over my heart. "I promise you, there was no other way. It was a last resort."

"Five people died. Dozens of others were injured." Shanley's eyes lingered on my wrist. Her lip curled with the start of a growl. "And now you've bound yourself to our sworn enemy?"

"They were going to hand deliver me to Chthonia if I didn't do something drastic. Please. I've lost—" My voice cracked, and I took a quick gasp of air, my chest caving. "Everything. I can't lose you, too."

"We're not going anywhere." A firm grip wrapped around my trembling hand. Mau. She shot a look at Shanley, who had started unpacking the clothes I'd put in my duffel. Which, fine, it wasn't even a big enough bag anyway. "It's all just very fresh," she continued. "The packs haven't even been able to mourn. And now that we know who sent you to that cave…"

I pulled a stray string on my comforter.

"How do we know the Wizard didn't set this up?" Mau leaned back on her palms. "It'd be convenient to get you to a remote place, in a foreign country, all alone."

"He's not powerful enough to influence an object like the Pearl." I gnawed my lip.

"But he is resourceful enough." Shanley's low growl rumbled the ice in our drinks. "It could've been someone in his arsenal of crooks."

"They wouldn't set up another Night Stalker. That's why I took the contract in the first place: for protection. I know it's hard to believe, but they actually have a code of ethics."

"'Thou shall not kill each other, just everyone else'?" Shanley muttered under her breath.

Despite the heaviness in the air, the corners of my mouth quirked. "Something like that."

"I just can't believe Elder Ivan, dude." Blowing air past

her lips, Shanley fell back into the chair. "What would possess him to betray his own kin?"

As if Finis were right behind me, hissing her mission to bridge the realms and rule the Earth and unleash demons in my ear, I dug my cheek into my shoulder. "I think I know."

Both my friends fell lethally silent. If their claws were out, I was sure they could cut the tension with an audible tear.

"This… fringe group." Slowly, I stood. "The one the Wizard told me about, the one you mentioned had made it onto the Pack's radar but wasn't considered a real threat. It is." I eased the ruffled clothes into a neat pile. "They want you blaming the Night Stalkers. They want us all fighting."

Shanley's forehead crinkled. "Why?"

"Because it's easier to cast their influence," Mau said, her tone distant.

"Exactly." I opened my closest, dug through a tight row of jackets, and pulled out my thickest wool sweater. "Their ideals are extreme."

"Fanatical," Shanley chirped.

"But radical," Mau added. "Realm-changing. And in a world that's been abandoned and left to govern itself—when the angels created it by rebelling against their own laws and mating with humans to create the Nephilim in the first place…"

"It could attract the right person." Even with the heat from the summer day stuffing up my room, a chill crawled up my spine. "A person tired of being second to mortals, of being the so-called *lesser* species.'"

"A person tired of being collateral," Mau finished.

"Ivan." Shanley winced, and it pained me to see the hurt flash over her face. "I guess there were signs."

"A superiority complex is not a sign of treason." Mau flipped her jet-black bob, the tiny amethysts on her nails sparkling in the light. "He was the patriarch of the wolves. An alpha we could trust. And he played us for fools."

"Even the strongest leaders can be led astray," Shanley muttered.

"Even archangels." I dipped my chin.

They looked at me expectantly.

"Akosua." I placed the sweater next to my duffel.

"River…" Shanley started. "How do you know the others aren't in on it, too?"

"Gaia and Fei?" My throat tightened on their names. "I know this sounds weird… but I could hear them when I was struggling outside of the cave, and I could almost feel them when I was inside."

Mau's dark stare softened. "Even though Akosua cut off your connection?"

"Yeah." I nodded, pulling out the paper with the coordinates once more. "I hadn't heard their voices for over six weeks—not since Grad Night, or around then." The paper shook in my hand. "Telepathy aside, there were plenty of other ways to reach me."

Shanley pursed her lips. "Do they have cell service in Empyrea?"

"We don't even get service in the redwoods!" Mau threw up her hands.

"I was thinking more along the lines of a portal disguised

as a lighthouse?" I shook my head, a ghost of a smile on my lips.

"Oh, yeah, that would work, too." Shanley grinned. Mau rolled her eyes playfully.

"These structures connect Mortal Earth with Empyrea. I assumed it was a me thing, but with the growing threat of Chthonia, what if the western watchtower is inaccessible to all of us?"

"Locked as a safety precaution?" Mau said.

I nodded. "The Watchers' Source is strongest when there are four. Four elements, four angels, four watchtowers, four cardinal points."

The carpeted floor creaked beneath my pacing feet. A drying wetsuit hung on the back of my open bathroom door. I snatched it off the hanger and rolled it up.

"There's no Angel of Water," I continued, "The Angel of Fire has dipped and joined the enemy, and so the wards are hardly stable as it is. It's not safe for Earth or Air, which is why I need to go to them. The tower in the vision, the one still pulled up on my maps"—I gestured to my phone, sitting unlocked on top of the bed—"is the northernmost one. Gaia's."

Mau steepled her fingers. "First of all, I think we need to work on this negative self-talk. You *are* the Angel of Water." A flush heated my cheeks, but she didn't bat an eye, pressing on. "Secondly, it can't be safe for you, either. After what we've seen, nowhere is."

"Then it looks like I'm a target anywhere I am. Here." I rolled my neck. "Iceland. Might as well go somewhere I can find help."

Reaching under my bed, I pulled out an old backpack I'd used on camping trips with my dad. Dust particles danced in the light.

Mau asked, "What about summer school?"

"I'm going to fail anyways."

"Again?" The tiniest hint of pity shone in her face. I tried not to let it faze me.

"Okay, just admit it." I held the crushed pack to my chest. "You don't think I'm cut out for this."

"Of course we do, Riv." Mau gave me a sympathetic pat on my arm and glanced at her girlfriend. "You have our support. But it doesn't mean we fully agree. How do you know Gaia will help? If your watchtower is locked, wouldn't hers be, too?"

"Look. I couldn't stop the attack at Crescent Rock; I can't bring those werewolves back to life." My voice cracked. "I can't fix what I've ruined. I can't alter the past. But what if I can change what happens next?"

"Alright." Shanley spoke softly. "How can we help while you're gone?"

I exhaled shakily. "Who's in charge in place of Ivan?"

"Elder Jesalynn."

"And no one's seen Chet?" I asked as I dumped the pile of clothes into my backpack.

They both shook their heads.

Damn. I'd been seriously hoping he'd be part of the body count. "For now, I'd station some extra lookouts. Especially in your district, Shanley. Anyone who's friends with me, is an enemy to Chthonia. They'll do whatever they can to get to me—to get to my Source—as we've seen…"

Shanley stood from her chair and cracked a window. A rush of air circulated through the room. "Got it."

"Other than that," I swallowed against the dryness in my throat, "tend to your pack. I know they're hurting. I know you're hurting."

Mau gave me a tight smile. "We will."

"What about your dad?" Shanley raised a brow. "He cannot possibly know that you're doing this."

With gritted teeth, I flashed her a smile. "Can you help with that? He likes you."

She buried her face in her hands. "Yeeeaaahhh, he's going to hate me after this." Peeking through her fingers, she asked, "when do you leave?"

"Tomorrow. There's a flight at noon." Snatching a corduroy hat off my dresser, I popped it on my head. "Then I'll find a hostel, go to the lighthouse, track down Gaia… and stop a war?"

"You make it sound so easy," Mau teased.

"I think the closest pack to Iceland is in Finland, right, babe?" Shanley paused—waiting for Mau's silent confirmation, I assumed. "Maybe they can give us a report on any weird activity or beings you should stay away from—like elves. I've heard a thing or two…"

"Perfect," I said, hardly hearing her as I smushed another wetsuit into the bag. "Alright. I think I'm done packing. Now I just need to spend my life savings on this plane ticket."

Mau delicately sorted through the top layers of fabric. "Girlie, have you even looked at the weather?"

Shanley leaned over. "Two wetsuits? What is this, an excuse for a surf trip?!"

"I can't help it, I'm a *water angel.*" I laughed, playfully tossing the words right at Mau. "Surfing is in my blood. Iceland has swell! Now get!" I swatted them away with a smile.

As I buckled my backpack, my stomach twisted in a chaotic tumble of butterflies and nerves.

I was going to Iceland. I was going to find Gaia.

And nothing, no one, could stop me.

PART II
ANGEL OF DARKNESS

CHAPTER 11

CRISP EARLY MORNING AIR WOVE AROUND ME, NIP-ping at my loose hair, biting into my bare hands.

I'd been in Iceland for less than two hours and it already felt like the island was trying to blow me away. My numb fingers tapped on my notes app, pulling up the directions to the hostel Shanley had given me—a recommendation from the Finland pack.

So, I was already on Rainbow Street, clearly: bright red, orange, yellow, green, blue, and purple stripes ran along the entire length of the road, gleaming against the dark of the asphalt.

Now I just needed to find the right alley…

Tucking my phone into my pocket, I breathed into the cups of my palms to heat my hands and scoured the cobblestone lanes tucked between the colorful buildings.

Nothing screamed hostel. My stomach, on the other hand, was fiercely grumbling at the earthy aroma of coffee and something oily—*burnt cheese*—wafting from the line of cafés.

Tourists clinked their mugs, picked over souvenirs, and stuffed their faces with pastries that had to be the culprits behind the smell in the cozy warmth of the buildings.

A prickle raised the hairs on my arms. It wasn't a choice to freeze my ass off out here, but I had to find my hostel.

I turned away from the windows, hoisting my backpack up to give my shoulders some relief, walking until I reached the courtyard of a curved, white granite cathedral—the end of the block.

Still no hostel.

I was beginning to think I'd been punked or I was just really bad at directions.

A water droplet splashed my cheek. Rain, again.

Flipping the hood of my windbreaker over my hair, I hustled beneath an awning.

A flutter of movement across the colorful road caught my attention. Two people, the only other brave souls who seemed able to bear these frigid morning temperatures, disappeared into a narrow street—an *alley* I hadn't noticed despite checking nearly every building—with a swish of their long, tweed jackets.

Backpack flopping against my tailbone, I scrambled after them, but between one blink and the next they just… vanished. I stopped mid-stride, the thin air stinging my lungs.

What the—? How did they just disappear?

The alley didn't seem special; it was merely a path between two thick, stone walls. No doors, no gutters—no wonder my eyes had breezed over it. And it was long, far too long for them to have run down in one second. It stretched out in front of me, glaringly empty. There wasn't even a dumpster to hide behind, or in.

An iron arch marked the entrance, which felt a bit gothic for such a modern and vibrant area. The curves and swirls came together in the center to make a design that put it somewhere between nautical and floral. My eyes went wide. It was a compass rose, a symbol I'd seen at the moonrocks and at that magical pub Ryder had taken me to so long ago.

My heart thumped loudly in my chest. This was supernatural-marked passage. Annað Ríki Hostel had to be down there.

The moment my foot stepped under the arch, another world unfurled around me, as if the bare cobblestone alley was nothing but a canvas that the magic painted over in one, shimmering sweep.

I spotted the figures I'd originally seen and trailed behind them, nearly jumping out of my skin when a pair of shutters opened and a buzzing creature I could only describe as a fairy started watering the flowers in their window boxes.

I was so caught up, I didn't see or hear the scooter until it swerved around a pothole and almost flattened me. I had to practically fling myself into a wall as the driver whizzed past in a blur of green spikes.

Shanley had mentioned these kinds of beings lived more out in the open in the Nordic countries, but damn, there was hardly any effort put into concealing themselves. They lived so… authentically. Freely.

Meanwhile, the strangers I'd been following leapt up the steps of a busy parklet and tossed their jackets onto the last empty bench seats. I caught a glimpse of their faces as they turned their heads—one with horns, the other with silver pools for eyes—totally unbothered.

I was not the strangest thing here, not by a mile.

Keeping my steps light, I walked up the small set of stairs, gripping the banister tight.

Sunlight poked through the clouds, reflecting off a pair of brass-plated double doors. The name I'd been looking for, Annað Ríki Hostel, hung in mismatched letters over the frame.

I'd made it. With a sigh, I pushed open a door and entered a lively common space.

The air was thick with espresso and magic.

Careful not to hit anyone with my outrageously big and overfull backpack, I shimmied between the long communal tables, still managing to graze the backs of heads.

Every hunger pang tempted me to drop my stuff on the floor, right then and there, and head to the spread of cheeses, meats, and scones.

A more informal seating area lined with warped bookcases and antique lamps that gave off the coziest vibe led me to the check-in area. I wove through the aged chairs and clunky side tables. My foot hooked on a leg—not a furniture leg, a human leg, I realized—but it was too late, I was already falling into their lap.

"Oh my God." I shot up, but my backpack pulled me down, and I scrambled like an overturned turtle. "I'm so, so sorry."

Beneath a long set of lashes, he glanced down at his stained linen shirt, the material damp against his dark brown skin.

"It's… fine." His voice was warm but cautious. Slowly, he stood, holding an empty paper cup and a sticky baked good. "But can you get me a napkin?"

"Of course." I scurried to a table, my gigantic bag almost knocking out someone else, and grabbed an entire stack. "Here."

Placing his breakfast on the armrest, he lightly dabbed at his shirt. A smirk spread over his lips. "Be careful where you fling that thing." He nodded to my backpack. "You could really take somebody out."

My face burned. "Sorry. I might have packed an extra wetsuit. Or two."

"Diver?" He raised a thick brow.

I shook my head. "Surfer."

Curiosity lit his face. "Have you been in Iceland for long, or are you just getting in?"

"I got here this morning. From California." My jaw clicked as I held back a yawn. "I'm beat. I'm also uncoordinated. Doesn't make the best combination."

He chuckled lightly, the twists of his hair sweeping out from his beanie to skim the tops of his shoulders. "Me too. I mean, I'm tired—I have a little more swag." The corners of his eyes crinkled with the trace of a smile. "I just got off the night shift." He held out his free hand. "I'm Gunnar."

"River." I met his firm grip, his skin soft and delightfully warm, thawing me from far too long out in the uninviting chill I'd been wandering around in all morning. "Nice to meet you— although…" I bit my lip as I sought the words, pushing a stray lock of hair behind my ear. His eyes twinkled down at me as I quickly added, "I wish it were under better circumstances."

Laughter shook his chest—his sopping-wet chest. I cringed, embarrassed all over again.

"So, what do you do for work?" I asked, changing the subject before the flush returned to my cheeks.

"Security... of sorts." Eyes narrowing, he tilted his head,

as if realizing something I didn't. "I'll save you the trouble of going to reception. Check-in isn't until four." He strode to the bar, leaning against the counter. "You can place your bag behind here if you don't want to lug it around until then."

"Are you… sure?" I asked, already slipping off the thick straps.

"Yep. My friend works here—she won't care." He curled his fingers to gesture for me to hand it over. "Bring it here."

"Oh, thank God," I breathed, as the weight left my shoulders for good. I stretched my arms overhead, relishing the lightness. "That feels so much better."

"Ekkert að þakka."

My brows dipped inward. *Huh?*

"It means 'no problem'." A breeziness draped his tone. "You don't need to thank me."

He turned to leave.

"Well, at least let me buy you a coffee." It came off a little desperate but, honestly, the last thing I wanted to do was be alone. And Gunnar was nice. And a local. Maybe he could fill me in on the lighthouse. "I owe you one," I added, forcing a coolness I didn't possess. "Literally, since I'm the reason you're wearing yours."

Not a single part of him moved. Not a blink, not a breath. It was supernatural, really. He was thinking. The gears were turning, intrigue and suspicion flashing across his umber eyes like lightning on a dark, stormy night.

Maybe he was just being nice, and I had overstepped. Maybe I did just need to go my own way. Or maybe that fringe group had in fact reached Iceland and he was realizing who I was…

Sweat dotted my upper lip.

"Alright." He returned a full smile, brighter than the anemic sun outside. It melted some of the anxiety away. "But in order to function like an actual person right now I'm going to need something stronger than drip coffee. Cappuccino?"

The words puttered out of me. "Yes, of course! I need like a quad."

He pulled out a stool.

"Thanks," I said, plopping onto the seat.

"Hey, G!" a waitress called from the other end of the bar, flashing a big, toothy grin. She poured a round of coffee, wiping up stray stains with a rag.

"What's up, Frey?" He removed his beanie, placing it on the counter. The pointy tips of his ears poked through his hair.

Surprise inched its way up my throat, but I wouldn't let it out. I shook my leg, the tip of my shoe tapping against the subway-tiled wall.

Clearing dirty plates along the way, the waitress made her way over, her steps so fluid and graceful she might as well have been performing ballet. "I was wondering when you were going to make it in. Long night?"

Gunnar pressed the heels of his palms into his eyes. "You have no idea."

She grabbed a scrunchie off her wrist, pulling her long, strawberry locks into a pony. A line of silver hoops stamped her cartilage, all the way up to where the top of her ears came to a sharp point.

I tried—I really did—but I could just *feel* my eyes tripling in size and the air escaping my lungs. I'd seen enough movies, read enough books, even heard Shanley speak about them briefly to know…

Elves. These were elves.

She tilted her head at me, cheeks flushed from exertion as she hefted the stack of dirty plates to her hip. "Who's this?"

"This is River. She's staying at the hostel." He swiveled in my direction. "River, this is Freyja."

"Nice to meet you," she said, her voice guarded.

A fold appeared between her brows. Shit. I was staring.

"Nice to meet you too," I said quickly.

Gunnar propped up his elbows, resting his weight on the counter. "Can we please get two *quadruple* cappuccinos, Frey?"

"You got it." With a wink, she drifted gracefully over to the espresso machine, wiping her hands on her apron.

"So, River," Gunnar drawled, "what brings you to Reykjavík?"

"It's…" Of course he'd ask that. Anyone would. It was an obvious, normal, question—but one I stupidly hadn't planned an answer to. "I have a relative here. Uh, extended family. Well, more like a family friend…"

"Your drinks." Freyja dropped two steaming mugs in front of us.

That was quick. Supernaturally quick.

Eager to have an excuse to dodge the question, I grabbed mine and took a sip. The rich, earthy notes settled on my tongue. "This is the best thing I have ever tasted."

"Traveling will do that," she laughed, heading to a customer flagging her from the other side of the bar.

Gunnar looked at me expectantly.

"Yeah, so that friend, she's kind of like a great aunt? I just graduated"—*lie. You're a liar, River*—"so I thought I'd come out here… to visit and explore. I've never been out of the country before."

"Does she live in the city center?"

"No, she's…" My fingers twisted in my lap, the edges of my nails scraping together.

Ugh, why was I so jittery? I was oceans away from home, the Finland wolves hadn't reported any suspicious behavior, nobody here knew who or what I was…

Unlocking my phone, I pulled up the browser, the tab still open on the map. A marker hovered near the watchtower coordinates. "She lives out here, somewhere."

Gunnar leaned over the screen, his forehead furrowing. "Not much out there. A geothermal swimming pool and a couple of guesthouses. There's also an old village, but that was abandoned decades ago."

And a lighthouse, I waited for him to say. I mean, it was there—on the map. But oddly, he didn't mention it.

Suspicion picked at my insides like a crow gnawing on carrion. "Are there any buses that go out there?"

Gunnar blinked. A few times. I swore he was studying me closer.

"If you think that's where you'll find your aunt… let me tell you, there are no people out there. Just a lot of wind. And ice. And puffins." He said it so casually—too casually— as if it were the least important place in the world.

It only made me more skeptical. But before I was able bring up the watchtower, Freyja reappeared.

She untied her apron, plopping it in front of us. "What are we up to today?"

"Sleeping," Gunnar replied with no hesitation. "And it sounds like River might be trying to catch a ride to *Dyrhólaey. Vitavellir.*"

Didn't know where that was, but assuming it was the location on the map, I went along with it.

"Ah," she said, her voice pitching up. "What for?"

"Family," he responded smoothly. "A great aunt."

"Interesting." A look passed between the two of them. It was subtle, but I didn't miss it. They were scrutinizing me just as much as I was them. What for, I didn't know, yet. "Not many people out there," Freyja said, like she and Gunnar were reading from the same script.

When I didn't acknowledge that, his fingers tapped an uneven rhythm across the bar top. "Not many at all."

My eyes narrowed. Were they speaking in code or something? How many times did they need to say that?

"Well..." Cheeks raising in a close-lipped smile, she twisted out from behind the counter. "I'm off. There's a south swell coming in."

My breath caught in my throat, my heart fluttering. If there was one thing that could get me to ignore their questionable comments, ignore all my responsibilities, it was the opportunity to catch a wave.

"You surf?" The excitement in my voice was tangible; I cringed.

"I do," she said with a laugh. "You?"

I nodded. God, I was practically salivating.

"Want to join me?" Her gray eyes burned brighter, as if they were crafted from the arctic sea themselves. "We can try to find your cousin's house after."

"Aunt—"

"Right, right." She swatted the air, silver rings glinting on her golden-brown fingers.

Trapping the air in my chest, I took a beat to decide, while Gunnar texted someone and Freyja grabbed her bag. Part of me was still a little weirded out. I was probably just jet-lagged. It was just my sleep-deprived brain tricking me into thinking the world was against me—that they were against me—and I had nothing to worry about. Gunnar and Freyja had been nothing but kind and welcoming.

"Let's do it." The rest of my words tumbled out in one, quick, excited string. "I hoped to fit in a surf sesh, but I wasn't sure I'd get the chance. I packed my thickest wetsuits just in case!"

"One can never have too many," Gunnar quipped, stashing his phone in his jacket pocket. "Fair warning: I'm sleeping on the way. Night shift."

"You get your beauty rest. It'll take us a little over an hour." Freyja playfully cupped his cheek before turning to me. "Grab your stuff, River. We're going surfing."

CHAPTER 12

HEAVY WAVES PUMMELED THE SHORELINE—NOT EXactly what I'd call inviting. The frothy edge of the tide rushed up the beach, drenching my surf booties, the pair I'd been *this close* to leaving at home. I wriggled my suddenly damp toes back and forth, the arctic chill radiating down to my bones.

A blur of black streaked through my peripheral as Freyja slipped into the water. Sliding onto her board, not a hint of fear in her determined strokes—even as the break crashed around her, on top of her—she seamlessly glided under, popping out on the other side of the whitewater.

Strands of her sopping pink hair stuck out from her neoprene hood. Soon, she was so far out it was like the ocean had swallowed her whole.

My turn.

Heart pounding, I waded to my knees. Saltwater flushed my wetsuit; a shudder lapped up my spine. Before the cold had me second-guessing this decision, I hopped onto the wooden board Freyja had let me borrow and started paddling.

Swallowing a lungful of air, I dipped beneath a wave as it began to topple.

It slammed into the ocean's surface above me, the power radiating to my back, pushing my board out in front of me.

I flinched, bubbles swirling all around. In these waters, hesitation was deadly, and I knew better than to work against the current.

So, I let it spin me around, let it hold me under for a second longer than was comfortable—it was part of the process, being pushed to the very limit. Just part of the thrill, not knowing if the rush was from excitement or fear.

I thrust my board against my chest and propelled myself upwards, breaking through the choppy surface in one fluid stroke.

"*Whoo!*" An excited shout ripped out of me.

I barely had enough time for an inhale before I had to dive under again, and another wave crashed directly above.

This was, by far, the most brutal paddle-out I'd ever endured. It must have been twenty-five minutes later when I reached the lineup, my breaths shallow and visible in the cold air. If my hands were any indication, the color must have drained from my face—every limb had gone numb. I couldn't actually feel the smile on my face, but I knew it was there.

"You made it!" I recognized that voice, but it still surprised me—I hadn't even heard her swim up next to me over the hollow roar of the ocean.

"And it was nothing short of a miracle." I opened and closed my mouth like a fish, trying to clear the pressure from my ears. "That was gnarly."

Freyja laughed, her nose and cheeks tinged red from the cold. "Now comes the fun part." Eyeing the next set rolling in, she lowered herself onto her board. "I'm taking this one. See you soon!"

She paddled fiercely, then popped up to standing and disappeared under the curl of the wave—along with my view of the shore, the sparkling strip of black sand beach barely visible over the crest.

"*Whoo!*" I cheered, clapping when she resurfaced and rode the momentum all the way in. Leaning back on my hands, I bobbed on the midnight blue ocean.

Emotion stirred in my chest, mingling with the adrenaline surging through me. The wind rippled off the coast, biting my cheeks, stealing tears as soon as it whipped them up.

Water swirled around me, lapping at the top of my board and pulling at my booties, as if the current were a pair of hands waiting to drag me in.

I felt her here—my mom. In the rugged beauty, in the tumble of the sea.

But most of all, I felt myself. I felt the part of myself I had lost after that night at the Boardwalk, the part that had gone dark. Stirring, waking.

So much shit had happened, it was weird to call myself happy, especially because I was here to stop a war—but that's what I was, finally back in the waves.

Tilting my head, I gazed at the clouds. No raindrops, but if there was anything I'd learned in my short time here, it was that the weather was not to be trusted.

Small shadows blotted out the moody sky, bolder than a passing cloud—smaller, too, and headed for the pillars of lava stacked along the coastline, the lichen cliffs dotted with flares of bright orange. *Puffins,* I realized, as another one flew in from the sea.

My stone-cold heart melted right then and there.

Folding my chest onto the deck, I started to paddle, cupping the water in quick, purposeful strokes.

I swerved into position, hands scooping, legs kicking, feeling the ocean's force building beneath me, until the nose of my board teetered over the top of the wave.

Only at the very last second did I shoot up to my feet and lower into a crouch.

I carved my way into the barrel, a bubbling channel of water trailing my fins. Ducking beneath the curl of the wave, I stuck out my arm, fingers skimming the fluid wall.

Gaze fixed ahead, mind focused on the glide, I could have sworn something hovered in my periphery, that something was watching me—but that was ridiculous, I was in *the middle of the ocean.*

Still, the hairs rose on the back of my neck.

Maybe my leash had come undone and was flapping around in the froth. Careful not to tilt the board, I stole a quick glance at my feet—and the Velcro still strapped around my ankle—then at the dark blue tube spiraling around me.

There was definitely a presence in here. Something powerful and alive that my angel senses picked up amongst the salt spray, kelp beads, speckles of sunlight, and shadows.

Realization struck me like a bolt of electricity. It was the essence in that cave at Natural Bridges; it was what emerged within me as I floated on the water, watching the birds.

It was me—my Source.

Whipping my face forward, I righted myself, digging my toes into the wooden surface of my borrowed board.

The circular opening ahead grew smaller and smaller, closing in as the wave curled in on itself. I didn't want this moment to end. And I couldn't believe it took me this long to understand that it didn't have to. I was an angel of water. I grinned, knowing Mau would chide me for that, because she was right—I was *the* Angel of Water.

Hands at my sides, I thrust them forward, pushing against air and calling on that thrum in my veins. The barrel stretched with the motion. I felt it move and shimmer, tremble and twirl, as if it were an extension of my soul.

I wanted to keep going forever. But there was a bluff up ahead, my arms were tired, and my brain was starting to sputter. Every thought, every muscle not keeping me functioning at the most basic level was dedicated to channeling my power.

Just as happy exhaustion tugged on my knees and filled my head with lightness, I shut that part of me down, like a light switching off, and the barrel slowly tapered out.

Riding what was left of the wave all the way in, I hopped off in the shallows.

The ocean lapped at the shoreline, as if it'd been nothing other than lazy and calm, no sign of the angry, spitting break or the undertow.

Cheeks sore from the chafe of the wind, the rub of the salt, and the cheesy smile that was vying for a permanent spot on my face, I trudged up the steep bank to a sprawled-out woven blanket the two elves were lying on.

Hearing my footsteps, Freyja sat up. "Have fun?"

Pretty sure that was obvious. Tingles flooded my body as I laid my board on the hot black sand. I set my hands on my hips and a satisfied exhale left my lips.

"I cannot wait to do that again," I confessed.

She squinted. "Those were some interesting moves out there."

Gunnar crossed his hands above his head to block the sun. "Where'd you learn those?"

"My dad." A twinge of panic crept into my voice, but I gulped it down.

With the clouds, the rocks, the distance to the shore, there's no way they saw what I just did—no way. Again, they were just being nice, and I was just being paranoid.

Freyja tilted her head. "Pretty impressive."

I bit my bottom lip, trying to hold back the dopey grin.

Gunnar reached into a tote bag. "Need a towel?"

Nodding, I scooped the fabric from his hands and wrapped it around my shoulders.

"Should we go?" Freyja suggested.

"Yeah." Gunnar's eyes darted to hers.

So many things passed between them in that tick of silence. That wasn't weird. Wasn't weird at all.

"Perfect," Freyja said, her tone gravelly and low. "I'm sure your *great aunt* is going to be so excited to see you, River."

NOTHING. THERE WAS absolutely nothing out here.

Just bumpy highways, green hills, rocks covered in lichen. Every so often, we'd pass a red-steepled church, and the occasional guesthouse. Wild horses sprang up every few miles in shaggy clusters.

Gunnar leaned over the center console. "Assuming she doesn't run a B and B?"

"Not that I know of," I muttered, cursing myself for such a ridiculous excuse.

Freyja glanced at me, turning down a narrow road to reveal another stretch of nothing.

"Should I keep going?" she asked, but a different question colored her tone.

I nodded, gritting my teeth—wishing for a town or people or any sign of civilization to magically spring up out of the lowlands.

All I got was more empty countryside, more horses. More awkward silence.

"I think she lives near a lighthouse." It was a bold move given the verbal gymnastics they'd done to suggest everywhere *but* that structure. I had to say something to keep us from driving in circles, though.

"Interesting," Freyja said.

"Interesting," Gunnar echoed.

Heat flashed along my upper lip.

A single bluff rose out of the flat coastal fields, like a gnarled hand reaching into the sky. If I peered hard enough, a small speck of white popped against the horizon.

Breaths turning shallow, I sank into my seat. The watchtower… we were already driving towards it. Interesting indeed.

Stacks of stone flashed past my window, littering the otherwise bare plain. Pockets of them seemed to be arranged in a somewhat orderly fashion. Demolished houses. Crumbling buildings. Grass jabbed through the rubble, telling a tale of life and loss.

Gunnar's voice came from over my shoulder. "What's left of an old elven village."

"What happened to it?"

"It was destroyed," Freyja gritted out. A gust of wind shook the windows. "Here—"she shoved a sweater at me. "You need another layer. It's going to be cold out there. Wear this."

Her tone could cut glass, but that wasn't what made the goosebumps raid my arms.

I glanced at the long sleeves, rubbing the fabric between my fingers—blue, wool—exactly what I'd been wearing in the Pearl of Truth. I gulped, and it burned all the way down.

These weren't just the ruins of some ancient settlement. These were the remains of war.

Rain and time had washed away the blood, but I swore I saw the stains between blinks. Swore I tasted the ash on the air between breaths.

The Pearl was right, something terrible had happened here. And now I couldn't figure out if it was a history lesson or a warning of what might come. Or an even more disturbing idea: what if I wasn't here to stop a war—what if I was here to start it?

Oh God.

"Does everyone know about this place?" It was one of those thoughts that happened to get spoken aloud, but I was curious about their way of life. About what got shown, what stayed hidden, who I might have seen in the Pearl.

"Yes," Freyja said shortly as we reached the base of the bluff and started our crawl up the steep incline.

I stared out the back window, the wreckage growing smaller in the distance. "You aren't afraid of mortals stumbling across it? Of finding out about you?"

She shrugged. "Half the population here already believes in the hidden folk. In elves. It's not considered weird; it's just part of life. Part of the culture."

"Unless we're using Galdur in the open," Gunnar chirped.

"What's Galdur?"

"Elven magic—" he started to say, until Freyja cut in.

"Which would be against elven law." She gripped the steering wheel tighter, glaring into the rearview mirror to lock eyes with me. "Back to the point though. Most our quirks go unnoticed."

Had to agree with her there. Regardless of the mental filter humans had that caused them to overlook most supernatural things, most were too distracted to put together the pointy ears, the grace and the stillness, the immortal glow to their skin, anyways.

Obviously, I was no elf.

But I imagined—whether from heightened elven senses or the fact we'd met in a magical hostel—they knew I wasn't human either.

Freyja tucked a stray strand of hair into her braid. "The mortals here respect us, and we live alongside them peacefully."

Ryder had once told me a similar story, about the different species preferring to disperse into society, to blend, if it was a viable option for them.

My fists tightened at the thought of him. Every muscle in me did.

"Here we are." Freyja pulled into a spot in the empty, unpaved lot and cut the engine.

Aside from the fierce wind jostling the car, it was quiet.

The elves stared at me with tilted chins and knowing gazes.

"Well…" Head swiveling, I took in the blustery, desolate cliffside, noting the lack of buildings—and people. I tugged on my collar, the space getting tighter, hotter. "This is a bust."

"Perhaps we should head back," Freyja suggested flatly.

I twisted in my seat. The lighthouse was *right there,* identical to my vision—down to the salt-stained ivory sides and the red circular tower. I had to at least try to open it. Who knew when I'd have the chance to come back? Sure, I could book a tour, but…

"I need some fresh air." My heart thudded so savagely against my ribs that I was positive they could hear it. "Do you mind if I step out for a sec?"

I didn't wait for a reply.

Fingers grasping the handle, I flung the door open and practically jumped out before a forceful gust slammed it shut. No clue what they said, if they even answered. But I felt their watchful eyes piercing me in the back like daggers my entire walk up the loose gravel path.

A slitted square column of smooth, pale stone stood in front of me. No door, which meant it must be on the other side. The ocean side.

The moment I disappeared from the elves' view behind a corner, I felt my jaw release, tension melting from my body.

Safe from prying eyes, I hurried to the entrance. I reached for the handle, pressing as hard as I could.

It didn't budge.

I doubled down. Now, with both hands, I tried to force it open, frantically shaking the handle, ramming my hip and shoulders into the wood. Mau knew it'd be locked. Deep down inside, I knew it too, but I still tried with all my might. "C'mon, you stupid thing…"

"It won't open."

All the air left my lungs in a gasp. "I"—hand shooting to my chest, I stepped away from the door—"I didn't realize you were there."

Arms crossed, Freyja and Gunnar stood on the terrace, where the concrete path met the grass. Unmoving, unblinking, like two majestic, elven statues. They were a decent amount of space away if I needed to slip past them and run. But considering how fast and silent they had proven themselves to be, eh, maybe running wasn't the right call.

I pulled at my frayed cuticles. "Ready to head back?"

A low howl whipped across the cliffs, rustling my damp hair.

Freyja took the first step closer. "That aunt of yours, what's her name?"

"Um." Heat gathered in my cheeks. "Gaia?"

"That's an old name." She crept closer. "One that has roots. History. You know what it reminds me of, G?"

Gunnar bit back a coy smile.

"A very important Empyrean figure." Chest inches from mine, she halted, her tall frame drenching me in shadow. "What kind of soul-searching are you doing here, exactly?"

"I—" I choked on the words, my throat closing off.

The jig was up. They knew. Of course they fucking knew.

"I was waiting for you to come clean on the way here." Freyja's suspicion raked over me in one long, judgmental sweep of her eyes. "I humored you by driving in circles. Humor me and tell me why you're here, angel."

The air seemed to tighten around us, turning heavy and charged, almost unbreathable. I sucked down a burning inhale with some effort. "What's it to you?"

Her hand moved to her waist—to the blade sheathed there. Gunnar followed suit.

My body went rigid, and I pushed out the truth. "I saw myself here in a vision."

That wasn't enough. Apparently, the elves needed more to release their grips from their pommels.

"I need to talk to Gaia. We used to… communicate." Wasn't sure that was the right word, given that her voice used to infiltrate the sounds of my everyday life and I'd just had to listen and deal, but I went with it.

"Then you should know it's locked," Gunnar said. A warning lined his tongue.

"Kind of hard when she just up and disappeared. Did you know *that?*" I probably should have stood down, but the lack of sleep and my rising frustration did me no favors. "If I don't find her, this entire realm is at risk of war. And if what I saw on the way here was the result of the last one, you don't even want to know what this next one will bring."

I moved to go around them. Before I could, Freyja held up a palm. Damp earth erupted out of the concrete, a wall of lawn and stone spewing up like a geyser.

My arms flew to cover my head, and I squinched my lids shut until the clods of dirt no longer rained down. When I opened my eyes, her expression had hardened, narrowed. It was all wrong.

"Was that a threat?" Freyja barked.

"What?"

"Who sent you?"

"No one."

"Don't lie to me." In one smooth flick of her wrist, the dagger came between us.

Flinching as if she'd actually struck me, I said, "This feels a lot like an interrogation."

Her teeth bared in a humorless smile. "It is."

"Are you serious?" I curled my fingers into my palms, willing my body to stop trembling with unspent adrenaline. "If anything, I should be asking *you two* why you're so protective of an Empyrean landmark. Who sent *you?* Who are you looking for? Who do you serve?"

The knife glinted, sharp as Freyja's eyes. "Watch your tongue, Water Angel." So they hadn't missed my little stunt in the ocean. "You know nothing of us. We serve no one but our queen."

"You're on our land." Gunnar's lips stretched into what should have been a smile, but it held not even an ounce of his original charm. "And we protect it at all costs."

Sun broke through the clouds, dancing off the sharp tip of her blade, still pointed at me.

A pang of hurt cleaved my chest. I hadn't done anything to them. I didn't deserve this.

Limbs tingling with rage and power, I stepped over the hole she'd blown in the concrete. In defiance. In opposition.

She rolled her neck. "Oh? Does someone have a statement to make?"

My body buzzed with nerves and something that felt a lot like magic. As I tightened my fists, a thick haze gathered overhead, eclipsing the sun.

The tide beat onto the crags below like a steady drum. Here, we were never far from the water, and the element seemed to surge through my body, a rush of strength that harmonized with my fear and anger. The ground trembled beneath our feet.

"That's enough!" Gunnar shot between us, arms out as if they were shields. "It's time for a field trip."

"What?" I spat. "No."

"Yes." He sighed, a kiss of a breeze twining through his thick twists of hair, the clouds scattering. "An angel is sneaking around, trying to breach the realms? You need to pay the Elven Queen a visit."

"Breach the realms?" I scoffed. "You've got the wrong girl."

Judging by Gunnar's and Freyja's darkening stares, they didn't care.

"Fine," I huffed, out of options, anyway. I'd meet their queen. Unfortunately for her, I was all out of smiles and charm. Those things didn't suit me, anyway.

CHAPTER 13

Neither of the elves acknowledged me. They hardly even glanced at each other as they stomped to the car, pushed me into the back seat, locked the doors, and drove away.

We raced down a wet, slick road towards their queen. My hands twisted in my lap as I picked at the frayed skin. I'd been full of adrenaline on the bluffs, but now it was waning.

Now I was scared.

Their accusations echoed in my mind. Their words thrown and weapons pointed as if I were the threat, as if I were the enemy.

Mountains rose to the left, the sharp, snowy peaks cutting into the sky. The vibrant grass that carpeted the foothills gave way to glistening ice fields. Snow no longer merely capped the summits but cascaded down the cliffside. The hum of the tires and the off-and-on patters of rain were the only sounds to break the silence for hours.

Freyja pulled into a near-empty parking lot just as a few remaining tour operators were packing their shuttles full. Arctic water surrounded us—trickling down the mountains, running off the massive glacier, flowing into a vibrant lagoon and then into the stormy sea.

The chill of it crept into the car, frosting the windows, turning my breaths into little puffs of clouds.

"Get out," Freyja barked. Gunnar gave me a small smile and opened my door.

I stepped out of the car and put my hand to my brow, squinting against the sun. The waning light coated everything in a warm, orange glow, igniting the fragments of ice into fiery diamonds.

"Where are we?" I dared to ask.

"Jökulsárlón Glacier Lagoon," Freyja replied, popping up beside me. "The entry point to the Kingdom of the Huldufólk."

My blood ran colder than the glacier sheeting the horizon.

Gunnar headed for the narrow waterway that divided the fresh waters of the lagoon from the salty ocean, motioning for us to follow. "Come."

Freyja angled herself into my line of sight, arm outstretched, beckoning—or maybe she was just trying to block me from running. I took in a tight inhale, the icy air sharp on my lungs. And I walked, head low, legs heavy, as they brought me to…

A boat.

Freyja jerked her chin at it. "Get in."

It didn't look like anything more than a quintessential rowboat as it rocked against the dark shore. Expecting Gunnar to bust out an oar—and maybe hand it to me—I was surprised when he tugged a small motor on instead.

"You coming?" he asked, although it was clear it wasn't a question.

"I'd listen to him," Freyja whispered in my ear. She backed towards the vessel, wiggling her fingers. Taunting.

I frowned so hard I could feel my face wrinkling.

She just laughed, one foot already in the boat.

Anger flickered through me. Source gathered in my chest, like I was sucking up all the energy from the elements, as if I were my own conduit. And maybe I could be. I'd have to be.

With a hard glare, I did as I was told.

Gunnar gave me a nod of approval when I stepped gingerly onto the wood beside him. "Remove your earrings and any other jewelry."

I might have expected such an outlandish request from Freyja, but Gunnar? It sent my Source skittering. "What?"

"You heard him." She tabled her palm. "Your jewelry."

My hands shot to my earlobes. "Why?"

Her slate gaze pinned me as if I were an unruly child, but she only smirked in reply.

"The mermaids," Gunnar finally supplied.

Mermaids?!

"They're attracted to shiny things." Freyja unclasped her own white-gold chain from around her wrist, then unclipped the many hoops from her ears. "Wouldn't want to get pulled under. Now hand it over."

Hesitantly, I pulled off my rings and plucked out my studs.

Curling her hand around the goods, she reached for a tackle box nestled under an overstuffed duffel beneath the first row of seats.

The boat rocked as I sat down, the wood creaking. "What are you doing with them?"

"Keeping them out of sight." She shut the lid. "And keeping us safe."

My muscles trembled, anxious, unspent energy zinging through me.

Gunnar took his position by the motor. "You ready?"

Whether I was ready or not, he reversed us away from the shore. We headed into the lagoon, away from the ocean, towards the glacier.

The air thinned, chilled. My cheeks turned numb, my lashes froze, and my nose felt pretty much nonexistent. Resting my elbow on the edge, I peered into the turquoise water, my reflection broken up by pieces of floating ice.

"I wouldn't do that," Freyja murmured.

The mirror image of myself pursed her lips. "And why's that?"

"So we don't have a catastrophe, I'll repeat myself: they love shiny things, and your eyes are as bright as a royal jewel."

My shoulders stiffened, but I refused to let the concern slip into my voice. "Oh please, as if they'd actually rip my eyes out of their sockets."

I shook my head, but instinct stirred within me. I so badly wanted to prove her words didn't bother me, that violent mermaids were just a creative story meant to scare me…

A shadow flickered just beneath the surface.

Then a splash on the starboard side.

I whipped around, heart hammering. Rippled rings disturbed the water, but that was probably from a piece of ice or our boat or a fish.

Probably.

Freyja leaned back on her hands at the bow. Her long neck arced, braid trailing to her waist. A thin scar ran along her jaw, so faint I would've never noticed if her golden-brown face wasn't kindled by the hues of dusk.

"See something you like?" she taunted, eyes closed.

"No!" It came out a touch too loud, drawing a smirk out of her. Cheeks searing, I turned to the water, just in time to catch the spotted head of a seal dip under. "So, are we going to talk about what happened back there?"

"Hmm?"

"At the lighthouse?"

"What about it?"

I twisted to face her. "You cornered me, accused me of trespassing, and pulled a knife on me?!"

"Mm-hmm, right." Why did it sound like she was half-asleep?

"I'm sorry, am I boring you or something?"

She shrugged, not a care in the world in those loose shoulders. "Just doing my job."

"Isn't your job at the hostel?"

She sighed. "That's more of a side hustle."

"Fine. What are you doing now?"

"Getting you to the Queen of the Huldufólk." Another dodgy answer out of her. A yawn.

Sharp pain radiated from my thumb, and a drop of blood smeared my pointer. I hadn't even realized I'd been picking at the dry skin around my nails. "What exactly is she going to do with me?"

"Who knows?" Freyja finally opened her eyes, a fiendish grin parting her cheeks. "Feed you to Helgustaðir's spar dragon? Or deliver you to the trolls? Perhaps lock you in the dungeons beneath the castle—"

"That's…" Panic scraped my insides, clawing up my throat. "That's enough."

"Sometimes at night I can still hear the screams of the last prisoner she took." Elbows resting on her knees, she leaned forward. "Such a terrible fate…"

"*Stop!*" The force of my shout reverberated across the water, splitting off a chunk of an iceberg, violently rocking the boat.

The motion underfoot flung me to the side. I grasped the railing before I could fly overboard, my knuckles white.

"Impressive." Freyja's words were steady, but her arms were out, palms flat against the bench.

Behind me, Gunnar's mouth hung open in similar shock.

"Sorry, I—" I started to say, but the words died on my lips.

Two of the most unusual beings I'd ever seen shot out of the water onto a floating sheet of ice. At first, I thought they were seals. But their movements were so deliberate, so artful—winking giant black eyes, webbed hands combing their stringy hair, the most godawful voices cooing a tuneless song. I lifted my hands to cover my ears.

A slight shake of the head, so minor it could have been passed off as a tic, was all that Freyja did to signal for me to keep my hands where they were.

Gunnar stood, sweeping into a bow. "Beautiful day it is, ladies."

Screechy giggles tore into my eardrums, and it took every little muscle not to flinch. Freyja shot them a brilliant smile, waving and covering her heart as if she was addressing the queen and not—*mermaids,* I realized.

"Indeeed," one sang, slapping her fish tail against the frozen surface.

The other fanned herself, as if she were moments away from fainting, delicate but deadly claws whizzing through the air. The edges of her tail were still submerged. Under the water, it glistened like a vibrant coral, the dusty pink scales shimmering with her titters.

Adjusting her spotted body, she slid off the ice with hardly a splash. I held in my breath as a line of bubbles drifted closer to the boat. To us. The elves were still fawning, still smiling, unbaffled. Guess I was alone in that.

My forced grin slipped when fingers—human fingers— clasped the rail. But they quickly changed, turning green and slimy. Turning webbed.

Long, ruby locks swayed like strands of algae in the current, the mermaid's head splashing through the surface with one graceful bob, water dripping over her porcelain skin.

It wasn't long before the delicate freckles, the rust-colored gaze, the sweet pearly smile, turned rigid and splotchy and amphibian. Her ears disappeared completely, nose flattening to a couple of mere slits.

Whiskers lengthening, she fixed her gaze on Gunnar, her enlarged pupils rimmed with a faint trace of her human irises, but soon those were lost to her seal form, too.

Oddly, she held up a fork. The bent metal reflected in

the light as she waved it in the air like it were as dainty as a silk handkerchief.

Gunnar plucked it from her hand, then took her webbed fingers in his, the clear mucous coating of her skin glistening like dew as he brought them up to his lips.

A giggle scraped her throat. I fought to hold in a gag.

My eyes watered, the corners of my mouth dragging down at the strong scent of fish that coated the air. Freyja kicked my ankle, her smile so sharp it could cut throats. A warning to not break the façade. I sat up a little higher, willing the bile to stay in my stomach.

"We must be off now," Gunnar bowed. "Do you grant us safe passage?"

"Yesss," the mermaid croaked.

My stomach lurched. Oh no. I covered my mouth with my palm, holding everything in. But the smell, the boat ride, the wave of nausea: it was all too much.

Her head snapped towards me, her patchy strands of hair—no trace of the vibrant red except in the tips floating in the water—whipping around her rubbery shoulders.

"Everything alright with this one heeere?" She swam closer.

A heave pushed its way through me. I nodded, trying to play the game. God, though, her breath was more rancid than rotten meat, the scent seeping through the cracks of my fingers no matter how tight I clutched my face.

"She's fine, fair one. Just a little seasick," Freyja purred. But I knew there was a command under all that flattery, a silent one directed at me.

Curiosity flickered in the mermaid's dark stare before something else—rage, hurt—engulfed it.

She bared her teeth, that brilliant flash of white now yellow and jagged like a piranha's. "Do you not admire my beautyyy?"

"No—I mean yes," I started, choking on my words. "You're stunning, I'm just..." Acid burned my throat. The mermaid that'd been perched on the floating slab was gone. A groove in the ice indicated where she'd slithered off, a small wake rippling against the side.

"You'll have to forgive my friend." Freyja effortlessly moved to sit next to me, draping herself across the seat. An artless pose, but a strategic one that blocked me from the mermaid's glare. "She freezes in the presence of such sovereignty."

A quiet splash sounded next to the rowboat, this time behind me.

"You knowww, we haven't collected a tithe from the elves in quite some tiiime," the creature sang.

"I think one is duuue," a second voice grated.

Oh God, please don't say my eyeballs. Sweat lined my brow.

"Very well." Gunnar's casual curtness bellowed behind me. "We'll address it with Her Majesty promptly."

"Once we arrive at the kingdom." Freyja waved as if the issue was a bothersome thing she could simply toss away.

"No." The wood groaned and rocked in the second mermaid's strong grip.

Freyja stumbled forward, and suddenly there was nothing between me and the first mermaid.

My arms swung out for balance, but my heart dropped to my stomach. Her wide, dilated pupils were unmoving, unblinking. Already fixed on me—as if I were a bullseye, a prize.

Or worse, food.

"You cross our waters as you please. You disrespect our presence. You pay it now." Her words held no semblance of the flirty singsong. It was deep and longing and full of… hunger.

Freyja's shoulders stiffened as she straightened herself. Gunnar shifted his weight.

"Alright." Freyja reached beneath the seat for the tackle box. "How's a silver dollar? Or a vintage broach? That'd look lovely around your neck. Or maybe a pearl comb? So beautiful with your hair." Her words were full of compliments but clipped with anger.

The mermaid's cackle scraped against the wind, as if it didn't belong in this world. "No. We are not interested in your trinkets. We will take our payment in flesh."

I blinked. A few times. Flesh? That couldn't be right.

Gunnar shifted his weight. "We didn't bring any meat."

"Sure, you diiid," the first mermaid gargled.

Oh God. I could see where this was going… I wrapped my arms around my waist, as if that could protect me from the bone-crushing jaws of a cannibalistic mermaid.

"And we haven't dined on elf in a long, long tiiime."

Freyja swiftly stood. "That's because it's outlawed."

I glanced at the fists tight at her sides. She flexed her hand, the veins popping back into place—and I stilled. She was missing half her pinky.

"And," Freyja retorted icily, "we protect you from being slaughtered by the whalers in return. I'd say that's a very fine deal. No elf, but at least you get to live."

"Ah!" The first mermaid put her hand over her heart. A mockery of sympathy. "Are we upsetting the queen's most treasured Eye?"

I tilted my head. The term didn't ring any bells, but I stashed it away to question them on it later—provided there would be a later.

"Oh pleeease," the second mermaid crooned. "You know she was a daddy's girlll."

Was?

Freyja's corduroy jacket flew off, her hands now making quick work of her shoes. My breath sputtered. She'd used those manicured fingers, the ones tugging off her wool socks, to threaten me with her magic earlier.

Why wasn't she using it now?

A cluster of scar tissue gleamed along her bicep where the skin drew back, hollowed out like a bite mark. Goosebumps tickled my arms, my pulse ringing in my ears as she continued to strip, down to nothing but a camisole and leggings.

She was about to jump in. When she was teetering on what could have been no more than two inches of railing, Gunnar grabbed her by the waist.

The mermaids pointed and laughed.

Freyja thrashed against him.

I glanced at my backpack, still tucked beneath the first row of seats. If I could reach that, I could snag the dwarven dagger I'd packed. But the boat swung wildly, like a wooden pendulum. I was stuck. It was going to tip.

Water whirlpooled around us, slamming against the rudder, crashing over the bow, each hit to the hull moving in time with the mermaids as they circled the boat like frenzied sharks.

Warmth splintered off my chest, tingling down my arms. My Source. The elves weren't calling on their powers, but maybe I could call on mine. I unfurled my fingers. The boat pitched sideways, the edge skimming the water. I swallowed a sharp gasp of air as my hands shot out to the sides, my elbows locking to keep me from going overboard.

A small, rectangular object slid across the wet planks. The tacklebox.

I lunged for it, not really sure what I'd find, or even really what I was looking for.

The top compartment snapped open, salt-crusted treasures spilling out. A ballerina figurine with a moldy tulle skirt. A rusty spoon, a silver brush, a locket with a broken hinge, dozens of bobby pins. Nothing but worn-out trinkets and trash.

Honey-beige skin and darting eyes danced in a reflection at the bottom of the box, so panicked I almost didn't recognize them as my own. A tiny handheld mirror. I grasped the thin handle, my face pinched in the splotchy glass. Intricate swirls threaded the metal, pressing into my clammy palm. A shadow stirred behind me—a flash of smoky green.

I spun to catch what'd sped by in the reflection, but it was too late. The mermaid was clambering over the side, the wood splintering beneath her claws in preview of what she wanted to do to my flesh.

The mirror slipped from my grip, shattering on the floor.

A wave of hot, fishy stench clogged my throat.

She was singing, screaming. Whatever noise she was making, her breath was just as vicious as before; I was choking on the odor, writhing at the sound. It curdled my senses, drowning everything else out, the uncanny version of a siren's call.

Fingers digging into my ears, I gritted my teeth, twisting to find the elves.

Slick, membranous hands wrapped around my ankle, knocking me down onto the deck. With my free foot, I kicked until my dirty sole stamped her nose and she withdrew with a hiss.

I thrust my foot out harder. A growl rent the air.

Nostrils flared, and the seal-bodied huntress hurled her upper body forward with no other motive than to crush and kill.

"River!" Gunnar, pinned beneath the blubber of the other bloodthirsty merfolk, slid the mirror my way. My fingers wrapped around the gilded handle. "Hold it up!"

Wielding the frame like a knife, I thrust it forward.

The mermaid stopped midair, coiling in on herself— her wail so unbearably loud it could have broken the glass if it hadn't already been in shards. I covered my ears, nearly dropping the mirror, the earsplitting shriek carving its way into my bones.

Springing to his feet, Gunnar darted over to me, his hand wrapping around mine.

Together, we shoved the antique forward until the

mermaid slunk over the edge and disappeared into the lagoon. Unclasping our fingers, Gunnar tossed it to Freyja.

She caught it in one hand and thrust it in front of her, forcing the convulsing, wailing being back into the water—hanging over the side until the cries faded to gargles.

Then there was nothing… nothing but our heavy, haunted breaths in the silence.

"You know what they say," Freyja deadpanned, considering her perfect reflection in the remnants of the mirror. "Flattery gets you everywhere."

CHAPTER 14

MAGIC GETS YOUR FARTHER." RISING FROM THE SODden wooden planks, I slumped onto a bench seat. "But yeah, sure, flattery is nice and all."

Freyja threw on her jacket, sparing me an unamused glance.

Gunnar wasted no time and slipped past me to the engine, revving it to full speed. The loud hiss cleaved the silence; its vibration rattled my head and my teeth, swishing the layer of water and glass spread over the bottom of the boat.

My fingers curled around the wood. They stayed that way, for at least an hour or two, as the glacial landscape passed us by until, finally, I said, "seriously?"

"What?" Freyja sat, resting her back against the bow, cheeks red and chafed.

"Why didn't you use your magic back there?" I fought to keep my voice loud over the howl of the wind.

"Why didn't you use yours?"

I gripped the edge tighter, the skin stretching over my knuckles. "I'm the captive here."

The temperature dropped, coaxing tears out of the corners of my eyes. Freyja wove her hands through her hair, redividing it into three thick strands.

"And regardless, I shouldn't be saving *you.*" The merfolk's tuneless croon ripped through my mind. "After all, aren't you 'the queen's most treasured Eye'?"

Her fingers froze. "What did you say?"

My body swayed as we drove faster between the icebergs, turns growing tight and desperate.

"You're right, angel." Pulling the elastic from her wrist, she tied off her fresh braid, slinking forward to rest her elbows on her thighs. "I am. And it's in your best interest to shut up and do as we say."

A frown tugged at my lips. Twilight settled in around us. Gunnar lit a small lantern on the bow; it swung wildly in the wind, casting Freyja's face in warm light and wicked shadows.

"So, you're like royal guards?" I asked.

Freyja's laugh was far from lighthearted. "That is far too simple a term."

It was Gunnar, back at the helm, who provided an actual answer: "Eyes are all-seeing, all-knowing—and quick to dispatch any threats to their Kingdom."

When I first met him at the hostel, he was talking about his shift, how tired he was. I had thought he was a local employee, maybe even someone working at the hostel like Freyja. But no doubt he'd been out all-night sleuthing for the elf queen. "Fine, royal spies."

The motor slowed. Silence settled over us, heavy and jarring, as we drifted towards a small dock.

Without the buzz of the throttle, my voice came out deafening. "And what, surfing and waitressing is part of the job?"

She glowered. "It can be."

"A queen's best soldiers aren't always the most useful at her side," Gunnar added, as he maneuvered us against the bottom of the sparkling glacier, lining up the boat's frame to the dock at its foot.

He cut the engine and anchored us to a metal bar, knotting the rope so tightly his hands shook, and tossed the duffel and my backpack—which were miraculously still stashed beneath the first row of seats—onto the planks.

One foot on the deck and the other on the dock, he held his palm out, expectantly.

Freyja took it, stepping onto the platform with a toss of her hair.

With her safely deposited, he repeated the gesture, his hand extended back towards the boat. Waiting. "You going to stay there all night, angel?"

Maybe.

Something splashed in the distance. My chin swiveled towards the darkness.

Maybe not.

Springing onto unsteady feet, I let him guide me off the vessel, legs wiggly at that first step on somewhat-solid ground.

He swung the duffel over his shoulder and headed for the glacier. "We leave at dawn."

Freyja marched behind him, the dock groaning with the thud of their boots. Dawn?

"You know, some would consider this kidnapping?" I grabbed my backpack and scurried after them, a relentless chill in my bones. At their silence, and clear lack of concern, I added, "So what are we supposed to do now?"

The frigid night air stung my raw skin, a slash with every stride of my legs.

Gunnar slowed at the threshold between wood and snow. A fresh coating of powder dusted the ground.

He again held out his palm. Hushed words left his lips—whispers of a spell, of a dialect long lost. A ball of light ignited in his hand. With a gentle toss, it floated up into the air, hovering a few paces before him. My insides fluttered.

"Sleep." He peered over his shoulder at me.

"You expect me to sleep after *that?*" I sputtered.

Using his magic to light our way, he headed inland, his pace slower, less urgent. "At this point, expectations aren't something I have for you."

"I could say the same," I grumbled, my sneakers sinking into the snow.

Yes, it was pitch-black and freezing, but these were severely less dangerous circumstances than the open water filled with flesh-eating mermaids…and he was going to call forth his power now?! Freyja ripped apart the earth at the lighthouse—Galdur, they'd called it. I'd witnessed firsthand that there was more to it than party tricks like this.

Clearly, I was missing something here—but I couldn't imagine they'd willingly share their secrets with a so-called prisoner. So, for now, I just waddled behind, trying not to faceplant on the slick ground, and came up with my own theories.

Maybe the elven magic behaved similarly to my Source and needed a conduit to act as an anchor? Or… maybe the type and intensity was different, depending on the elf, kind of like how Nephilim abilities worked?

Ryder would know. The thought rose, unbidden, with a ring of truth to it. Ugh. *Stop it.* I swatted it away as if it were nothing more than drifting snow.

The sky unfolded above us, wisps of color swirling between the stars, painting the deep blue canvas in vibrant glows of pink and purple and green.

Even if I wanted to escape—even if every fiber of me was fighting against this excruciating walk up the glacier—the auroras were a reminder: I'd seen them in the Pearl of Truth.

I was supposed to be here.

In this godforsaken, deadly, polar place.

Gunnar's light grew brighter. It cast the cold world in a warm, yellow glow, sparkling up the slope to a near-vertical wall of ice. Holes punctured the face—footholds, handholds.

My knuckles went white. Oh no, were we supposed to climb that?!

Tripping over clumps of ash and wood scraps, some of the few signs of life littering the worn path, I jogged to catch up with the elves. They were peering inside the many cavities dotting the sheet of translucent blue.

"This one's good!" Freyja called, her voice echoing off the hollow inside.

With a tilt of his chin, Gunnar led us into the heart of the ice, his Galdur glistening off the opaque walls. The duffel slid off his arm, thumping to the hard ground.

I followed it warily with my eyes. "What's in the bag?"

"Body parts," Freyja chirped with no hesitation.

I stilled at the edge of the cave, wind nipping at the wet, frozen strands of my hair.

"Sleeping bags, water, food, axes, crampons." Gunnar rolled his shoulders, a chuckle shaking his voice. "Get in here before you freeze to death. And take that backpack off. You'll need all the rest you can get before we hike the glacier."

Hike. Ugh. I knew it. My backpack dropped to the floor with a thud.

Kneeling next to a ring of stones that held the remnants of a campfire, Gunnar took his magic into his hand and, as if it were melted wax, poured it onto the pile of charred logs.

Flames crackled to life, pulsing warmth over my cheeks while a bitter chill danced at my back. Rubbing my palms together, I reluctantly inched closer.

Freyja rolled out three mats, topping them each with fresh socks and a sleeping bag.

My brows furrowed. "Coincidence that there's the perfect amount of stuff for all of us, or was this kidnapping planned all along?"

"Well, we have to pack enough gear for ourselves, and we always carry extra in case…" She looked me up and down with those arctic eyes. "…the situation permits."

I blew out a sigh. I guessed it could be worse. At least they gave their captives beds.

After taking her heavy outer garments off, Freyja draped them over a boulder and plopped herself on top of her makeshift mattress.

Gunnar kicked off his boots, curling into his bedding.

The middle one remained open, inviting.

My body ached for rest.

Blowing warmth into my hands, I took another step inside, then another, and another, and the next thing I knew, I was fully in the ice cave, nuzzling down into the fleece.

Shadows from the fire flickered overhead, twisting with each loud snap.

Freyja rolled onto her other side, facing the embers. "Interesting day."

"Yep," I said to the ceiling. "Very interesting."

A soft whistle floated up from Gunnar's bed. I held in a laugh. He was already snoring.

Goosebumps broke out over my arms as a blast of cold hit me. The sweater Freyja had let me borrow was much better than what I was originally wearing, but it was damp and did little to retain any heat in these glacial temperatures. I burrowed deeper into the blankets.

"What were they saying about your dad?" It was hardly a whisper; I wondered if I had even said it out loud. And I sure as hell didn't expect an answer.

"The truth."

At first, I thought I was imagining it, until she flipped onto her back and her gaze briefly locked with mine before stalwartly fixing on some point far above our heads.

"My father was Commander of the Eyes, the queen's right hand. The most intimidating warrior you ever laid eyes on—who wore honors from hundreds of battles, someone they wrote *rímurs* about"—a smile leached the strength from her voice—"but he always had time for me."

A tentacle of guilt snuck around my chest as I thought about all the time my own dad had carved out for me.

"What about your mom?" I asked hesitantly.

A darkness crept over her face. "Too busy for me. It was my dad who actually spoke to me during the Jól festivities, my dad who snuck me an extra slice of cake after dinner and read me bedtime stories and took me to see the royal huskies."

"Did you grow up in the castle, then?" Interlacing my fingers, I rested my palms on my stomach. "Since he held such an important position?"

"Yes." She held her hand in the air, twisting it in the soft light. "Devoting myself to the kingdom, becoming an Eye, working my way up the ranks, felt like the best way to honor him."

And here I was, cutting school, surfing every day, griping about the legacy my mom had left me. Unlike Freyja, who had literally joined an army, I had spent the ten years since the loss of my parent hiding instead of being the person she wanted me to become.

Turning onto my side, I tucked my hands beneath my cheek in a makeshift pillow. "What happened to him?"

Her arm dropped to the mat. "He died."

"I'm sorry." I'd heard the phrase so many times—after my mom passed away, after my therapist was slain, after Javi fell into a coma. They were useless words that wouldn't change a thing; but they were the only ones I knew I could actually get out against the wave of sympathy roaring through me.

"Many people died in the Cross-Realm War." Her face crinkled in the sort of smile meant to hide strong emotion and brush it off, but I'd seen a flicker of her grief. It was the same kind that haunted me: the kind that never went away. "In that way, he wasn't special at all."

My throat twisted into a knot, but I swallowed the feeling down.

"The mermaids found him on the rocks beneath the lighthouse cliffs. Apparently, he was the perfect lunch specimen for them."

Oh God, she wasn't implying they…I leveraged myself up onto my elbows, desperate for fresher air.

"We never got his body back." At whatever my face held, she bit out a cold laugh. "But then again, most were unrecognizable anyway."

I inhaled sharply, but the oxygen didn't reach my lungs.

The vision from the Pearl of Truth played before my eyes: the blood, the ash, the loss, me screaming at the watchtower door. A cough ripped its way out of me. I gasped for breath, but the air was too cold, burning my throat, like swallowing fire and ice at once.

Freyja thrust a water bottle into my hands. It could have been poison for all I knew, but I chugged the entire thing. "You good?" she asked haughtily.

"The Cross-Realm War." I gritted my teeth, fighting against the spasm of my lungs to force a normal breath. "It was there. It happened there."

Freyja pulled a stray stitch on the zipper of her sleeping bag. "Mortals visit Dyrhólaey for the view. We visit to remember. Why do you?"

I glanced over my shoulder, my eyes sweeping the shadows in case something else was listening. But it was just us.

"To stop it from happening again." I forced the words out, holding my voice steady even as my breath hitched. "I had a vision before I came to Iceland. It wasn't a lie or a threat when I told you that earlier. I saw the remnants of war. And what's weirder? I was there. At this point, I'm not sure what that means, if it was a scene from the past or…" I gulped. "A premonition of what's to come."

Freyja turned her gaze to the fire.

My nerves twisted in my chest. "I didn't come to infiltrate your kingdom or spy on your court. I came here to find the Angel of Earth." I had to tread carefully here. Allegiances ran deep, and even if she'd made hers to the elven queen, that didn't mark her as trustworthy. "I obviously wasn't going to outright tell you that after knowing you for two seconds. Demons have a bounty on my head—if I'm wanted at home, how do I know I'm not wanted abroad?"

I paused, and in that shallow breath I waited for a twitch of the ears, a stretch of the spine, any quiet signs of loyalty to Chthonia—but there was nothing but stillness from her.

So, I continued. "Do you know what I find interesting, though? Those same demons are just as territorial over the watchtowers as you are. And they don't belong to either of you."

Freyja's shoulders slightly flinched. There it was: a sign. I didn't know of what yet, but one of my points had finally struck her.

"Coming here… It felt like I was finally doing something right." My words were no longer aimed at her but at the ceiling, as I dipped my head back and stared at the cracks in the ice as if they were stars. "I've lost so much. I've put so many people in harm's way." I blinked against the burn of tears: the werewolves, Javi, my therapist, all staring back at me when I closed my eyes. "But who was I kidding? My mistakes are like scars. I have to live with them forever. And I'm the biggest of them all."

Freyja shifted in her bedroll. I could feel her stare, but I couldn't sense what was behind it.

I pulled my legs to my chest, resting my cheek on my kneecap. "Anyways, the lighthouse is locked, you've taken me captive, and now I'm back at square one: no idea how to find Gaia."

She pursed her lips as if she were debating. "The queen might know." My head perked up. "But before you get too hopeful, her priority is protecting her kingdom, not entertaining the whims of her prisoners."

Desperation chipped at my confidence. "Any tips for getting on her good side?"

"Address her properly. Don't ask questions. Listen between the lines. Speak only when spoken to, and never, ever forget: you are not our guest." Uncertainty filled the space between us, turning the air heavy. "You are our enemy until proven otherwise."

"Thanks," I said, more out of courtesy than anything.

"I don't know who's worse." Rustling in her sleeping bag, she flipped onto her other side. "The demons who start the war, or the angels who drag us into it."

CHAPTER 15

Three days.

We hiked that damn glacier for *three days* before reaching the elven border. Each day was the same, and the view never changed. Ice, ice, and more ice. My eyes burned from the unending white.

Other than the pulse-rattling climb up the vertical ice face in the wee hours after leaving the cave, it'd been a relatively flat journey. Boring, but flat.

I kept waiting for a kingdom to grow on the horizon— for the barren plateau to give way to some sort of path or city or even just a tree in the distance. So I was justifiably confused when the two elves stopped in the middle of what, to me, looked like the exact same stretch of crystalline white we'd been walking through for three days.

"What are we waiting for?" I asked, kicking at the snow. A puff of it rose up, caught in the wind, and blew back in my face. Freyja smirked, but didn't move her gaze from whatever it was in the distance.

"For the sun to reach the highest point in the sky," Gunnar replied patiently. "Then the kingdom will be revealed."

It sounded made-up.

My eyes found the sun: blanched and weak, barely yellow, in this colorless wasteland.

"Here." He knelt in a fresh layer of powder from the storm that'd been raging the night before—that had kept me up until the crack of dawn, turning my hair into icicles.

With gloved hands, he shoveled the snow aside until he reached the bottom: a layer of glistening, grayish-green stone. He ran his fingers along a deep groove.

I tipped my head. "So that's what's underneath."

Still squatting, he kicked his chin in the other direction. "There's the citadel, over there."

Heart leaping in my chest, I peered into the horizon.

Nothing.

"Wow, I can't believe it," I deadpanned. "More ice and snow." I wanted to cry, my legs ached so badly. I'm pretty sure I had frostbite in unspeakable places. And I vowed to never eat another peanut butter-flavored protein bar again. "Am I missing something here?"

More eye rolls. More smirks.

Spindrifts danced over the frozen tundra, shrouding the world in whorls of bluish white.

Unlike the frigid air of the blizzards we'd endured, this settled over my skin and clothes in a soft layer, bringing with it the smell of damp soil after a storm. After a numbing few days in the cold, I'd forgotten that sensation even existed.

I breathed it in, iciness stinging my nostrils.

Wind gusted around me as I stepped over the parted snow, whispers threading through my hair, tossing the few unbound strands across my face. The second my boots hit the ground, all I could see was light. I blinked against it—the sun bouncing off the glacier, I figured.

I shielded my brows and squinted up towards…mountains.

My jaw dropped.

Not just mountains—sleek, spiraled roofs. Sparkling blue towers. Curtain walls. Battlements. Arrow slits.

In the blink of an eye, an entire structure seemed to have magically carved itself out of the ice in front of the snowy peaks. The castle.

I rubbed my eyes with my palms, just to be sure I wasn't seeing things.

Nope, the fortress was still there, even with the spots now dotting my vision.

"You coming, angel?" Freyja tossed over her shoulder, already paces away. Gunnar was a speck in the distance.

Borrowed crampons crunching in the snow, I raced to catch up, still not used to the footwear.

Beneath all the layers, heat broke out across my skin.

After multiple days of nonstop wind and rain, it felt weird to be sweating. Even weirder to feel something other than mind-numbing boredom and pangs of hunger: stirs of excitement. I slipped off my backpack and tugged off my sweater, tying it around my waist.

The walk must have taken the better half of the day. My legs were *screaming;* my stomach, *grumbling,* my eyes and any visible skin, *stinging*.

Finally, we approached the castle grounds.

Two enormous columns of ice flanked the opening of an outer wall—as if keeping watch. Just beyond it, the pathway ended abruptly. The castle glistened on the other side of a moat.

A crack thundered on the air. The left column had started shaking then lifted the lower block of its build, which happened to be in the shape of a *foot*. It crashed onto the ground, snow flurrying beneath its frozen toes.

My gaze flew up the chiseled ice that made up its ankle, its knee, its leg, my eyes widening at the jagged pieces making up its torso, chest, shoulders, neck, and finally, its diamond-shaped head. Pupils blinked to life, little sapphires beaming beneath frosted brows.

Shriveling in the shadow of this glacial behemoth, I almost forgot about the other one—almost. But then it too withdrew from the wall, the ice cracking and grumbling as it stretched its joints after who knew how long.

Both lumbered forward and, in a powerful movement much swifter than I expected, clinked their spears together and thrust them to the ground, forming an X across the path.

"Who goes there?" the giant directly in front of me bellowed.

I shrank into myself.

Gunnar held his fist against his heart. "Gunnar Stelpths, third son of Rohan and Romedyr, Eye of the Queen."

"And I," Freyja said, stepping forward and mirroring Gunnar's gestures. "Freyja Argon, first daughter of Odin and Hildur, Eye of the Queen."

"There are three," the guardian on the left rasped, as if his vocal cords had been frozen and were finally thawing. "Name yourself."

I would have, but the syllables caught in my throat.

Freyja's gray eyes narrowed on me. I could practically hear her thoughts commanding me to speak.

"Now would be a good time," she muttered. "Their preferred method of punishment is stomping."

"R-River," I squeaked. "First, um, first daughter of Corbin and Mira Harlow."

See? I was no one interesting.

Freyja raised an eyebrow at me. "Your title?"

Was hoping no one would catch that.

I tapped my foot in time with my racing heart. Keeping it generic, like angel, felt like the best option—at least, until I knew the elves could be fully trusted.

But then I made the mortal mistake of dropping my gaze, which went straight to the ice monster's foot—the same foot that would rather stomp me to smithereens, that had dark brown, almost red flecks along its sole—and it just came tumbling out of me. "Angel of Water."

Gunnar and Freyja went lethally still.

Bringing my hands behind my back, I feverishly picked at my cuticles, raising my chin in false hubris. Hopefully they didn't see through it.

Hopefully they didn't hear each twist of my gut, each frantic pound of my pulse.

Hopefully they hadn't sworn allegiance to Chthonia.

Guess I'd find out soon enough.

The weapons clanged and I flinched, but the guardians only lumbered to the side, their spears pointed to the sky, not my heart.

Behind them, the drawbridge lowered with a groan. They were allowing us to pass. My breath caught in my chest.

"Welcome to Lokahryggur, also known as Hamarinn, Kingdom of the Huldufólk."

With their massive, sculptured bodies no longer blocking the way, it was a straight shot across the bridge to the pristine inner courtyard, sweeping birch trees peeking through the portcullis.

The elves bowed their heads in reply and marched across the frozen wood. With an ungraceful dip that probably looked more like half a squat, I skittered after them.

Gunnar shot me a knowing smile.

He didn't seem like my mortal enemy. But then again, for all I knew, he could be walking me to the guillotine right now.

A shudder worked its way up my spine.

I paused on the threshold, the air dense in my lungs, energy thick and piercing. There, a rustle in the frost-tipped grass; a trickle in the frozen river; a crumble of the rockface.

My gaze swept the area. There wasn't a soul in sight.

Hairs rising on the back of my neck, I continued on.

Just because I didn't see them didn't mean vigilant eyes weren't watching.

CHAPTER 16

On the outside, the grounds were a vision of ice and glass.

I tried to take it all in, my eyes darting wildly as I clattered across the frozen moat, using every muscle to make sure I didn't slip and tumble off into the frigid waters below.

Vines broke through the snowpack, creeping up the fortress's glistening walls. White-and-blue banners topped the battlements, flapping in a piercing wind. A clear chute rose out of the turrets towards the back, cutting through the mountain's highest peaks.

Ice led to tile as we passed through the gatehouse into a courtyard of ivory stone. The castle's many buildings and curtain walls curved around it. A large willow tree loomed in the center; from here, I couldn't tell if it was carved from ice or if the glassy leaves were natural.

A servant carrying one too many baskets of laundry dashed in front of me, stepping on my toes. I quickly moved, just to knock into a group of elves who, judging by all the pearls and silks and upturned noses, had to be part of the royal court.

"Sorry!" I squeaked, scurrying away.

A sudden and very welcome blast of heat thawed me to my bones, the air inviting and electric despite the frost-laden rose bushes and the silver sky above.

Pulling off my borrowed gloves, I flexed my fingers in the warmth, the feeling returning slowly.

The castle was enormous, glassy towers sparkling in the afternoon light, the tallest of its spires lost to a blanket of mist. My head kicked back. I couldn't even begin to count the floors, the royal banners draped over every white marble railing that wasn't in the clouds.

My gaze dragged to a shadowy corner, as if a magnet were pulling it, to an unassuming set of stairs leading down. Tendrils of darkness seeped out from its depths, the stones around the entrance slick with ice. Shivers broke out across my body, despite being across the courtyard.

What was that place?

Just as I took a step towards it, a guard appeared, slamming the cellar doors shut. Only then, at the clang of the metal, did I realize I had made it halfway to that corner in some sort of daze. I turned to find myself alone.

Hustling to catch up with Freyja and Gunnar, I fought my curiosity each time a hall splintered off from the courtyard, wrestling against the impulse to stop and examine the giant willow as we walked beneath its sweeping white branches.

A trio of elves inconveniently stopped to gawk in the middle of our path. Funny enough, their stares weren't pointed at me—the completely out-of-place stranger—but the two I'd arrived with.

One of them rushed forward. I jolted away, and my elbow grazed a branch hanging over the path. Ice crystals cut into perfectly shaped leaves dangled off the peppered bark, clinking together. I reached out to steady it.

The glistening foliage was cool against my skin as I wove my fingers along the stems.

"Uh-uh." Gunnar's deep timbre echoed through the court. "No touching. Either of you."

Face flushing immediately hot, I retracted my hand, and the rogue elf faltered back. They watched me with wide, jealous eyes as I rejoined Gunnar and Freyja.

"You need to be restrained." Freyja's tone was flat, unamused.

I couldn't tell if she was joking.

Gunner didn't acknowledge either of us. Not until we reached the far end of the courtyard and halted at the bottom of a stone ramp.

"Crampons off." He unzipped the bag he'd been lugging around for three days straight. I unclicked my extra footwear and tossed them in.

The clink of metal on metal echoed in the hollow space.

"River, your backpack," he ordered.

I happily dropped that.

Two other elves, in chain mail and slitted helms with sigils on their chest plates, appeared at the top of the ramp, coming straight towards us, moving in perfect synchrony. Even the sheaths at their hips swung in tune: one knife, one long sword. The tip of a battle ax peeked out from behind a shoulder.

We were being greeted by knights armed to the teeth.

Great.

On an abrupt halt mere inches from us, they raised their gloved hands in salute.

I shifted my arm to return the gesture, only to reconsider midway, tucking a nonexistent hair behind my ear with a cringe.

Freyja and Gunnar didn't hesitate to greet them back, immediately launching into fervent conversation after—in Icelandic, of course. Through their layers of steel and the heavy accents, I didn't glean much. But it didn't take an understanding of their language to know what they were talking about: me.

Especially when Freyja pointed right at me, switching to English for my benefit. "This is her."

At her cold smile, I blanched.

One of the guards grunted. The other's head swiveled towards me. Neither spoke a word. They returned to formation, one clanking iron foot in front of the other, marching back the way they came. Wiggling his eyebrows, Gunnar followed, lips raised in that classic smirk I'd come to know and expect.

Freyja nudged her head in their direction. "Go on, you."

Not having any other choice, I fell in line.

Soon, red carpet replaced the pale stone beneath my dragging feet. A corridor arched around me, the walls lined with marble and gold and oil paintings, all the classic signs of royalty. It could only mean one thing: we were nearing the queen.

Nearing my judgement.

Shoulders hunched, I tore apart my cuticles, the familiar sting comforting.

Silver-plated doors carved with creatures out of fairy tales rose from the end of the hall, stretching from the floor all the way to the ceiling. They opened without any command on our approach, the gilded throne room peeking out above the knights' feathered helms.

My pulse raged in my throat.

What was Freyja's advice for the queen? Curtsy, listen, ask no questions, expect nothing, accept that I'm an enemy until proven otherwise…

We neared the threshold. My footsteps slowed, stopped. It felt like the werewolf tribunal all over again, except this time I had no friends here for support. I had no one to save me.

The blood rushed in my ears.

A grunt came from behind me, followed by a shove. I stumbled into the hall. Every eye fell on me. And there were plenty in here, all outright staring. Seriously, the entire royal elven line must have been gathered in this gold-kissed room.

I skipped over them completely, my gaze darting to the tall, muraled walls arching over the windows, the vivid colors, lines and brushstrokes spilling onto the ceiling.

We halted beneath a chandelier. It was carved out of ice, every tassel frozen solid despite the ceaseless warmth.

Breaking formation, the two guards strode to the foot of the dais, Gunnar taking a position next to them.

Freyja went straight for the throne, shoulders back, spine straight. Her boots hit every carpeted step with a firm thud. I could only imagine the intensity in her stare, and I was thrilled to not be on the receiving end of it, for once.

Pausing at the top of the platform, Freyja bent to the woman in the wooden seat—the wood similar to the peppered white bark of the tree with the icicled leaves—and kissed her, once on each cheek. Bold, even for someone labeled the queen's most treasured soldier, given the others stayed on the main level and fanned around her.

"Good to see you back in one piece." The monarch's voice was light in the air, lyrical like a songbird, honey incarnate, every word enchanting. With a toss of her hair, Freyja flittered to the side, situating herself into the only other seat—the one next to the queen.

That didn't seem right for a guard.

With a narrowed gaze, I looked away from Freyja, readying myself to address the queen.

Every thought evaporated when I met her pale violet eyes. They flared brighter, rooting me to the spot, sucking all the oxygen out of me. A voice inside me screamed to look away, but it was so small, so faint, it was easily swallowed by the magic, by her beauty—a natural beauty as rare and moving as if she had been sculpted from the mountains.

My legs shook, knees giving in to an overwhelming pull to a kneel. I didn't necessarily care to fight the urge. I had already forgotten where I was, what I wanted. I was ready to swear fealty. I was ready to give her everything.

And then the elf queen turned away, her strawberry-blonde strands whispering over her lap. It broke the spell, her glamour ceasing, my lungs and muscles spasming, my knees locking rigidly to standing. My next inhale was a wheezing gasp.

Mantle trailing behind her, the queen descended from the dais. Her beaded silk dress hugged her tall, lithe frame, swishing with every silent step. Her eyes pierced me, but they'd changed, darkened, more of a deep indigo now. I couldn't tell if it was scrutiny or curiosity that flickered in her gaze.

The guards looked tense as she approached me—muscles ticking in jaws, eyes locked on every movement.

I tapped the sides of my thighs. Should I smile? Wave?

One of the soldiers behind her shifted their weight, grasping their pommel.

I gulped. Nope, I wasn't going to do a damn thing. I brought my hands together, and even that might get me tackled at this point.

A brilliant smile pushed the queen's strong cheekbones higher. "Thank you, my gracious Eyes, for escorting our guest to the realm of the Huldufólk."

Guest. That's the last thing I considered myself—I'd been warned against it, actually.

Was this a test?

Gunnar and Freyja swept into bows so low their noses might've touched the floor. "It is our honor, Queen Hildur."

Hildur. That name rang a bell. Freyja had said it when we announced ourselves to the giants.

And then she'd kissed the elf queen upon arrival.

Then she'd taken a seat next to her on the dais.

Our conversation in the ice cave played out in my head: father passed away, mother too busy, raised in the castle. My stomach dropped. Freyja wasn't just *the most treasured Eye of the Queen*, she was her daughter.

She was the princess.

I dug my nails into my palms. Whatever. She had her secrets, and I had mine. And now they were all out in the open.

"So," Hildur said, peering down her nose at me, her tawny skin radiant and flawless—like her daughter's. There were no other sounds, except the drag of fabric, as she slowly circled me; it felt like my heart had ceased to even beat. "What is your name?"

"River," I managed to say without my voice cracking.

"River." She stressed each syllable, testing it out. "What are you doing in my kingdom?"

My gaze slipped from her face, wandering over the crowd.

Heat seared the back of my neck. Was I really supposed to explain it all now? There must have been two hundred people in this room, half of them armed guards.

Drawing in a sharp inhale, I held it and counted to ten. Afraid to move—afraid to speak.

"Go on," the queen urged, now on her second lap around me. "Explain yourself."

"I'm looking for the Angel of Earth. I tried her watchtower, but as you know, it's locked." I started out strong, until murmurs from the assembled elves had anxiety clawing at me from the inside out all over again.

Hildur's long fingers came to rest beneath her chin. I took it as a silent command to go on.

"I'm told you might be able to, uh, assist with that," I continued, fighting to keep the fear brewing within me from playing across my face.

She held her elbow with her other hand. "I'm afraid you have been misinformed."

I didn't move—didn't even dare breathe—biting my own tongue.

"That watchtower is locked for good reason." She tilted her head, her diadem sparkling. "What is yours for trying to break in?"

Face pinched, I shot Freyja a glare. We'd talked about this in the ice cave, and this was not the note we'd left on. What kind of story had been spun to her mother?

Hildur smiled, and in that coldness, I saw her daughter. "You know Gunnar and Freyja weren't the only spies on the Dyrhólaey cliffs. The birds, the wind, even the hills have eyes for their queen."

"It's not what it looks like." Freyja might hate me for this next part, but I needed some ground to stand on. "Just ask the princess. I'm not your enemy, Hildur."

The queen snapped her spine straight, her eyes flashing with ice. "I am not your friend; I am not even your acquaintance. To this kingdom, you are nothing but a prisoner—an enemy, at that. Mind your tongue. You are lucky to even address me as *Your Highness.*"

"Please, *Your Highness.*" I gritted my teeth, Source swirling in my veins, mingling with the adrenaline pushing me to run and settling in my thighs until they started to quake beneath me. "I had no idea this was going to cause so much trouble."

"Any—*all*—who try to breach the realms go straight to the ice dungeons." A chill blew over me with her threats. "This is elven law. We do not make exceptions, no matter if you're a pixie or the highest-ranking seraphim. There's room for everyone down there."

I shifted on my feet. "I'm not here to start a war with you." In one fluid *clink*, the guards unsheathed their weapons. "I'm here to stop it."

Hildur raised her hand, the only thing stopping a blade from slitting my throat. But I had to act quickly—I could sense that she wouldn't keep her loyal knights off me for long.

"A bold statement, I know, and I'm aware I don't look like much, but I had a glimpse of that war in a vision. The death, the blood, the screams…" The scene played out in my mind, and I hadn't realized it until now, but the people who were left scrambling and hopeless were mostly… elves. "It's been haunting me every day since. And it took place on those very bluffs, just outside the lighthouse."

A muscle in her eyelid twitched.

"Regardless of what I saw in the vision, I know more pain and suffering is next." I drew in a slow breath, measuring my words. Across the dais, Freyja threw me a look that said, *Careful.* "It's all part of Chthonia's plan to bridge the realms so they can re-create hell on earth. No one is safe from that. Not even you."

It was probably a trick of the light, but I could have sworn the queen's face paled.

That look was just the glimmer I needed to go on. "Whatever is coming to your land is coming for us all. Finding Gaia and the rest of the Watchers might be the only thing that can stop what very well could be the apocalypse."

"The Watchers," the queen tsked. "What do the archangels care about the elves? Empyrea deserted our kind long ago when they left us with their broken mortals and their fallen gods."

I tried not to sink into myself, to not let my confidence shutter. This line of thinking was exactly what Chthonia preyed on. Clearly, I wasn't going to change the queen's heart permanently, but maybe I could change it for a moment.

"Think about the last war you were dragged into," I said, projecting my voice so she would not mistake my words. And maybe so the other elves in the room would hear it, too. "I know it decimated an entire village. Probably more. I know you lost family, people you love." Behind the queen, a light flush crept over Freyja's cheeks. "And I know you'll do whatever it takes to stop it from happening again."

The bloody scene from Chet's tribunal floated to the top of my mind. My heart twisted. All those innocent lives lost. All the panic and chaos. Because of me.

"This is your chance to save your kingdom." My eyes widened, pleading. "Release me. Let me into the watchtower. And we can figure this out with Gaia. Together."

The queen's eyes narrowed to slits. "I have to say, this is the most creative story I've heard in at least two hundred years of prisoners groveling for mercy at my feet."

"W-what?" I was too shocked by the accusation to notice the thud of boots, the clank of steel prowling forward.

"Take her away." She swatted the air before turning back to the dais, as if I were nothing but an annoying fly buzzing around her throne room. *"Isdýflissur."*

A firm grip locked around my bicep. "No," I begged. My other arm was captured. "No! Get off me!" I turned wild eyes on Freyja and Gunnar, but they met my panic with a coldness that turned my heart to stone.

With a rough tug that nearly pulled my arms out of their sockets, the guards dragged me across the room. The chamber doors were flung open, a loud crack reverberating off the walls—wood slamming against stone.

I knew where they were taking me. Dread pressed against my chest. I'd seen the entrance to the dungeons— that icy cellar door in the courtyard.

There'd be no miracles there.

Eyes darting to the chandelier, I funneled every drop of power rushing through my veins into each of those dangling ice crystals. As the guards bore me off, I caught a flicker of movement above.

Or maybe that was just my body, trembling with fear, panic shaking the whole room.

My waist cleared the doorway.

No. I wouldn't let them take me to that abyssal pit of hopelessness. Wouldn't let the look of knowing pity twist the faces of the elves I'd stupidly considered friends.

Digging my heels into the ground, I silently called to the water.

With a chime, the ice fixture jolted.

My ankles passed the doorway. In moments, they'd lock me out forever.

I clenched my hands into fists, ground my teeth, and focused every thought, every beat of my heart on the fear, the magic, the rage.

The ceiling rumbled. Hairline cracks erupted around the chandelier's mount.

Judging by the widened stares, the sharp gasps, the rustle of silk shoes—people fleeing—I wasn't the only one who noticed.

And just in time. Another breath, another pulse of Source, and the chandelier broke off from the ceiling. In a glittering shatter, it crashed dead center, where the queen and I had been only moments before.

Screams erupted. People ran, ducking for cover. Splintered shards of ice ricocheted off the columns, the floor, sticking to hair and velvet robes.

Hildur did not move from the middle step of the dais. Her lips parted just barely, lavender gaze electric and accusatory, piercing over her shoulder at me.

Palms raised, the guards backed off, their faces feral with fear.

Minutes passed like hours; the queen scrutinized me with each ticking second. Finally, she cleared her throat, and fully turned to face me.

"You have my attention, Angel of Water."

CHAPTER 17

ELL, NOW IT WASN'T JUST A SECRET BETWEEN FREY-ja, Gunnar, and me: everyone knew I was the Angel of Water.

Within the span of Hildur calling forth a handmaid and that handmaid, Helga, escorting me to my rooms, word had traveled throughout the entire castle. As we trotted down the halls, servants gasped and hid, courtiers parted and whispered. Even the fake knights in the metal armor displays seemed to turn their heads as we passed.

The hall Helga escorted me down wasn't any different than the rest: ivory stone ceilings and walls illuminated by floating balls of warm, white light.

Given I'd just been upgraded from prisoner to guest of honor, I probably should've been a little more on guard, paying attention a tiny bit more—I probably should've been walking a little more briskly, like Helga, but after three days of hiking, on top of twelve hours of air travel, my legs would not go any faster.

So, when the pitter-patter of her feet disappeared around a corner, I simply didn't have it in me to scurry after her. In fact, without her frantic, darting eyes, I slowed my pace, taking in the tapestries, the art, the statues of elves and beasts carved out of ice.

One canvas in particular drew me in: a pale blue sky with a marble pantheon parting the wispy clouds. Winged creatures and a mix of beings that could have been Nephilim or elves or another human-like species fought between the sun and the untouched landscape below—a forested bluff overlooking an unruly sea.

A water droplet splashed my cheek. I shot back, glancing at the ceiling.

There were no water stains, no signs of a leak. My gaze fell back to the picture, eyes widening. It'd been days since I'd hit a real bed, so sleep deprivation was definitely kicking in. At least… that's what I told myself as I backed away and hurried after Helga.

"Your Grace." She was waiting dutifully in front of a set of mirrored doors at the end of the long, vaulted passage. "The elevator."

Really? My brows dipped together. We must've walked up dozens of staircases, and now she wanted to take the lift? Equally shocking was the fact that such a modern piece of equipment existed in a fortress like this.

But I didn't question it as the doors slid open, and a pleasant bell greeted us, like metal chimes clinking in the wind. I stepped inside, leaving streaks on the pristine surface with my dirty shoes—marring the smooth sheet of glass.

Glass. As the doors closed, I realized they weren't mirrored at all; they were see-through. Same with the walls, the floor. We were standing in no more than a glass box.

My stomach dropped, and there was no doubt in my mind that my entire body would be next, shattering the surface and tumbling down the glistening chute.

Helga came up next to me, her should brushing mine. "For your first time, it's best not to look down."

Right. Swinging my head up, I focused on the ceiling instead—it was also made of glass, to my dismay. Tightly compacted snow glinted behind it.

"Himinn Tower," Helga said, unprompted.

It took me a moment to realize she wasn't speaking to me but to the elevator itself, because at her voice, the cart lurched. My heart leapt into my throat, and we shot upwards.

The walls were free of railings, of anything I could latch onto, and I *needed* to latch onto something. Without thinking, I took Helga's palm in mine. Her skin was cold and fair, like she'd been sculpted out of the snow. She gripped back and, despite the temperature, there was a warmth in the gesture, as she gently patted the back of my hand.

Still, saliva flooded my mouth, my gut churning nervously.

It was dark. Cramped. And we were zooming upwards in a box made out of the most breakable material in the world.

I pulled on my collar.

Shadows roamed over the transparent walls when suddenly, the entire world went white, and I squinted against the flare of daylight.

Slowly, I unclenched my fingers, breaking off from Helga. A crystal-clear view unveiled itself before and below us—the valleys, canyons, smoking chimneys, and snow-laden hillsides stretching out for miles in all directions.

We were traveling up the side of the mountain.

The landscape was stunning, endless, a new pocket of the panorama exposed every second we climbed. I blew out a frosty breath, the anxiety slowly giving way to excitement.

Another windchime signaled our stop. The doors crept open. Helga stepped out promptly into a foyer. "Welcome to Himinn Tower, also known as Sky Tower."

I strode to the center of the cylindrical space and did a slow spin.

It was immediately obvious how this part of the castle earned that name: instead of walls, there were windows filled with expansive views across the elves' wintry realm.

Thankfully, the floor was the same natural tile that filled the castle below. And from what I could see, so was the single corridor branching off this entry room.

My insides fluttered and, for the first time in days, it wasn't due to being threatened or scared or chased. It was beautiful.

"There are four suites on this floor." Helga whisked past the seating area on silent feet, leading me down the hall. Stone soon replaced the windows, the warmly lit passage mimicking the ones on ground level. "Your rooms are here. You will go to the queen's private quarters for breakfast. I will fetch you in the morning."

Meeting the monarch was daunting enough, but the locked doors drew my gaze. "Who's staying in those?" I nodded to the ones farther down the hallway.

Helga's lips pressed together into a line. "They are occupied by other visitors." There was no room for questions in that tone.

Dropping the subject, I approached the circular handle to the room she'd indicated was to be mine.

My pulse ticked in my neck. I wasn't sure what I was afraid of; I'd been granted amnesty, and even if the queen were to change her mind, I was the furthest I could possibly get from the dungeons, probably hundreds of floors above them.

Still, I remembered that eerie draw, that pull. A sense that wasn't entirely my own, like I was feeling someone else's dread, someone else's hopelessness and terror.

My hand was shaky as I gave the handle a twist and pressed the door inward, and the uneasiness floated away.

When the elf said *rooms,* she wasn't kidding. This wasn't a room; it wasn't even a suite. It was pretty much a small apartment—I was hardly one foot in, and I could already tell it was bigger than the one my dad and I shared in Santa Cruz. Epic didn't even begin to cover it.

"Sorry!" Helga squeaked from behind me, her voice timid and rushed.

Sorry for what? The chic, tufted seating area? The tray of pickled veggies, cheese, meat, fish, and bread on the coffee table? The wall of books, the crackling fire, the panoramic view overlooking the mountains?

I turned just in time to catch the thick fabric of her green dress slipping out of the room.

The lock clicked.

"Wait!" I sprinted towards the door and jiggled the handle, banged on the surface with my angry fists. But it wouldn't give. "Rude!" I shouted through the thick wood. No clue if she heard me.

So, I was still a prisoner, then, just in a pretty, gilded cell. Pressing my ear to the door, I waited for the faintest sound of skittering feet, of soft breathing, but Helga had disappeared. The hall had fallen silent.

I was alone.

Sulking in the entryway wouldn't get me anywhere. With a sigh, I pushed off the frame and explored my temporary home—my cage. Crossing a hand-loomed rug, I walked over to the coffee table and picked up a grape. The sweet flavor burst in my mouth.

Next, the chewy, salt-crusted bread.

Guess it could have been worse.

"Enjoying your meal?"

I gasped, a piece of food lodging in my throat. Was someone in here with me? Hitting my chest, I coughed the bite down before I could choke to death while my head errantly spun to find the source of the feminine voice.

Other than my red-faced reflection in the mirrored cabinets, hutches, and drawers, not another being was in sight.

Movement pulled my gaze downwards, to where the fire flickered in the hearth.

Just above the coals, a face winked back at me.

I jumped back at the sight of a floating head crafted out of the flames, tripping over the velvet couch seat, landing in a mountain of frilly, beaded pillows.

A head. A face. *In* the fire.

"Oh, poor Helga just arranged those."

"You—you talk." Dryness crept into my mouth. "But what… what are you?"

"Someone they needed to keep quiet."

My jaw dropped.

"Kidding!" The flames sputtered from an invisible draft. "I'm a fire nymph."

I scooted to the edge of the cushion, peering into the blaze—at the distinct pointy nose, the dancing eyebrows, the lips parted in a smile. "What are you doing in my fireplace?"

The kindling crackled, as if the spirit stuck inside was… laughing. "I live here. What are you doing in my room?"

Fair point. "I was brought here against my will."

"That explains it."

"Explains what?"

"Why the servants came in so hot and bothered today. Sweeping up all my piles of ash, replacing my logs—I'd been collecting those for *years*. And the spiders, they didn't even stand a chance. No warning, no nothing. Although I think I enjoy people more than arachnids. For the most part."

My attention darted to the ceiling, the crown molding chipped and worn; to the walls, the floral paper peeling at the corners; and the bookcases, thick layers of dust gathered between the spines.

At first glance, the place had seemed fit for a queen. But as I looked closer… things were out of place, poorly hidden, quickly breezed over, as if the staff had been in a rush to clean up.

"It's been so long since anyone's been up here. I'm positive the court forgot I existed. I haven't had a chance to talk to anyone in a long time. Am I doing it right?" The fire shuddered. "Am I talking too much?"

I shook my head, dropping my gaze to a runner at the foot of the white brick that made up the fireplace, a large stain fading the intricate pattern. It'd also been way too long since I had had a conversation like this—with someone who had no ulterior motive.

Even if that someone was a talking inferno.

Leaning forward, I brought my elbows to my knees. The element warmed my cheeks. "What's your name?"

"The last visitor called me Eldi. It means fire in Icelandic. What's yours?"

"River."

"River." She paused. "You remind me of her."

"Who?" My heart stilled.

"The last visitor. Her name was…" The flames spit. "I can't remember."

"Helpful." I eased back into the cushions, nostrils twitching at the hint of mildew.

Smoke plumed. "What? It was over a decade ago!"

"Are you getting fiery with me?" Biting back a smile, I laid my head back and closed my eyes.

"You know, there's a bed through those double doors."

"I figured." My lids shot open. "Are there any other entrances I should know about? Or exits, for that matter. Secret ones, perhaps?"

"There's the window. I've heard it opens. Can you fly?"

"No." Shoulders caving, I settled into the cushions, letting my breaths slow.

"Not much use to you, then. Although, I've seen the skyline in the mirror. When the sun hits the mountains at certain times of day, like right now, it looks like they're on fire. Alpenglow, they call it. There's really nothing quite like it. Maybe you could check it out, you know, on your way to the bedroom?"

"I'm too tired to move." I was too tired to open my eyes again. Almost too tired to talk.

"Are you at least going to close the curtains?"

"No."

"Okay, well… good night."

"Good night, Eldi."

CHAPTER 18

Thunder cracked. The tide bellowed back, the force of it shaking my bones. Back flush against the weatherworn wall, I hid beneath the lighthouse's tower, blending with the shadows.

A cry rang out, so close it could have been next to me, but it somehow felt lifetimes away. The sky rippled, the air splitting apart like a piece of torn fabric, as things not of this world—things with horns and fangs and murder in their eyes—poured out.

The temperature plummeted, the cold snaking up my spine. A dark cloud of those beasts swarmed the countryside, devouring everything, everyone in its path, leaving a trail of skeletons behind.

A snarl tickled my ear. I turned. A demon, lurking in the darkness with dripping, open, jowls…

My eyes thrust themselves open. I clutched at the air, sitting up in one sharp gasp.

Insistent knocking echoed from the entry, jolting me from the nightmare into reality. The elves. The castle.

"Your Grace?" Helga's words were muffled behind the heavy door. "Are you decent?"

"Uh, yes." The door creaked open. "No!" I stumbled to my feet. "Give me five minutes!"

I glanced at the hearth, the fire nothing but glowing embers. Shit! Was Eldi okay?

Grabbing an iron pole, I poked at the burnt logs and piled another one on. My heart sank. Did I kill her?!

"Ow!" A raspy voice ignited with the flames.

The tool slipped from my grip. "Sorry, Eldi! I thought you were a goner."

"You can't put me out that easily," she mumbled. "Where are you running off to?"

"I'm late!" Tripping over my feet, I darted to the bedroom, clipping a small table with my hip. An entire plate of macarons and a jug of what looked and smelled like wine crashed onto the hardwood floor. "Damnit."

"Everything alright in there?" Eldi called.

"Yes," I lied, ignoring the urge to bury myself under the covers of the four-poster bed. Instead, I beelined for the bathroom, catching a glimpse of my backpack on an accent chair. I was surprised to see it sitting there. I'd assumed it had been confiscated upon arrival.

Gold arches, silver accents, and fluffy pink towels failed to mask the reality of the room: a leaky faucet, a massive chunk missing from the tile, splintered mirrors—a kingdom in disrepair. No shower, but the clawfoot tub was full. That was convenient, at least.

I dipped my finger in the water. Disappointment washed over me.

Cold, freezing cold. It must have been pulled last night. I sighed. Obviously, Galdur was better used on more important things than a bath, but a small shred of me had hoped the warmth had been preserved with elven magic. Nope.

There was no time to drain it and refill it, so, I stripped off my crusty clothes, my phone falling out of my pocket and clattering to the floor, and in I went.

ONCE DRESSED IN a striped long-sleeved shirt and black jeans, I snagged the dwarven knife Nemuik had given me from the folds of clothes in my bag.

Still shivering from what was pretty much a cold plunge, I scurried to the couch, booties dangling from my fingers, and sat down.

"You're in a hurry," Eldi commented.

"I'm meeting with the queen." Unrolling a pair of socks, I slipped one over my numb toes. "Yesterday, I somehow convinced her not to toss me into the ice dungeon, but today's a different day. I assume she'll want to discuss the vision that brought me here, Chthonia's plans, stipulations for unlocking the watchtower." Wiggling my other foot into the cotton, I said, "But who knows if she'll be as forgiving. Got any advice?"

"I once heard a visitor say it's best to just smile and nod."

"Well…" Moving on to my shoes, I slipped the leather over my ankle. "I'm not good at either of those things."

"You don't have to be good; you just have to play. With the elves, it's all a game."

I nodded, clipping the dagger's sheath to my waistband.

The flames crackled. "And I know it's not much coming from a burning pile of sticks, but I like your smile."

My cheeks lifted with the corners of my mouth. "Thank you, Eldi."

Quickly weaving the strands of my damp hair into a French braid, I rose.

The glass in the mirrored furniture shook against the thud of my boots as I strode to the entryway, my shadow billowing over the floor, parting like wings in the shafts of natural light.

"Oh!" Eldi called after me. "Under no circumstances should you enact elven law."

Halfway across the room, I stilled. "What?"

Another set of knocking, *pounding,* on the door, pulled my focus.

"Even if it's your last resort," the fire nymph continued. "Don't do it."

"Your Grace, are you ready?" Helga's voice, meek as ever, was barely audible over the pounding of my heart.

Blood rushing in my ears, the only thing I could think to ask Eldi was, "Why?"

"You'll get what you want, but like everything in life…" She trailed off, a lick of blue twisting with the flames, sadness coating her voice. "It comes at a cost. The elves are cunning. Creative. They'll use your words against you, even the ones you do not say."

Realization hit me like a solid punch to the gut: the dry jokes, the tips, somehow knowing where everything was despite being caged in an iron grate.

"Eldi," I said, my voice shaking. "Did they put you in there?"

Another knock rang out from the door. "My lady, the queen has stated she is going to come up here herself should you not open the door. She has also stated you will not like it if she does."

"Eldi?" I whispered.

"Go!" With a flare of sparks and smoke, the nymph's face disappeared within the flames.

Even with the fire burning in the hearth, a chill ran up my spine.

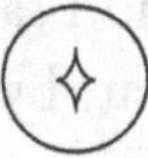

A CLOCK CHIMED. Silverware clinked. Throats cleared and bobbed.

I said nothing. Looked at no one—even if they stared at me—just slurped my lukewarm porridge.

The goosebumps hadn't left my arms. I did not want to end up in a fireplace.

"So." Hildur batted at the corners of her mouth with a frayed cloth napkin. "When did you take her place?"

My spoon froze in front of my mouth. "Whose?"

"Your mother's." The queen leaned back in her chair, a servant answering the cue and grabbing her empty plate. "Unless you're Mira in disguise?"

Shaking my head, I took a bite of my breakfast, pushing the bowl aside. "Um, recently."

"Interesting. I thought archangels weren't allowed to birth children. How ever did that get approved?" Reaching for the teapot, she poured herself a cup, tendrils of steam wafting in the air, condensation lining the cracked spout. "Or did it… not?"

My grip tightened on the unpolished utensil. Eldi's

words echoed in my mind. *The elves are cunning. Creative. They'll use your words against you, even the ones you do not say.*

This could very well be a trick, but one thing was for sure: Hildur was testing me, reading me; she was playing chess and going for checkmate.

I sat a little higher, pushed my shoulders back, got in the game. "What does it matter? I'm the one who broke your chandelier. Clearly, I am who I say I am."

"You do owe me for that, by the way." Such a strange remark for a kingdom that wore gilded threads and ate with silver spoons.

"Add it to my bill." I tossed my floral napkin on the table.

Taking a cautious sip of her tea, Hildur set down her cup, the chipped porcelain clinking against the saucer. "Alright. You want to know the truth?"

I schooled my expression into one of practiced boredom, the same one I wore in summer school. The only hint of my fear was my fingers picking themselves to shreds in my lap.

When the queen didn't immediately continue, my gaze skimmed the rest of the room. Freyja's eyes glimmered with curiosity in the adjacent seat. Even the servants seemed to creep closer, linger longer.

Hildur frowned infinitesimally, either at the idea of telling the truth or at the added attention. "I haven't seen Gaia in over a decade." Her gaze cut past me, as if she were seeing through the solid silver doors, down the long stretch of corridor, past the arctic tundra, to the tower on the bluffs.

A decade. I fought to stay still, but the timing made my shoulders jerk. Ever since my mom's passing.

"But even so, it was pretty sporadic to run into any of the Watchers after the Cross-Realm War." My heart stuttered. Did that mean Hildur knew the others? Fei, Akosua—my mom. Her irises flared electric as she continued. "Dragging entire kingdoms to battle over a centuries-old conflict that isn't ours, and will truly never end, isn't the politest thing to do, but if it were me, I'd at least have the decency to face the aftermath."

She leaned forward, and I kept my spine straight, fighting the urge to look away.

"Is that why you're here?" Her voice made the place settings rumble. "Did they send *you* to finally clean up the mess?"

"I—I…" A tremor worked its way into my teeth, my bones. "No. Look, I can't change the past. But I want to help shape the future, so the Cross-Realm War doesn't happen again."

As if I were about to fill her in on the latest neighborhood gossip, Hildur whispered, "And how are you going to do that?"

That look made me dig my nails deeper into my skin.

Glancing at my fingers, my attention snagged on the faded yellow marks staining the white tablecloth. Huh. Maybe they missed laundry day. Or maybe her beloved, thriving kingdom was falling apart behind a façade of splendor.

My chair scuffed the torn rug as I scooted back. "By finding Gaia."

"What do you need her for? This is elven territory, and you have an audience with the queen." She narrowed her gaze. "Are you powerless?"

So much disgust in that word: *powerless*. To her, it meant useless, and that was one thing I couldn't afford to be.

"No!" Yes. Kind of. Ugh. I could just feel the bitter pride radiating across the table from Freyja.

"Gaia—the *Watchers,*" Hildur said, a hint of a snarl lining her tone. "They locked themselves up in their pretty little towers over ten years ago, never to be seen or heard from again." Her cool hand slipped over mine. "Leaving the rest of us to rot."

I stiffened, my body temperature plunging beneath her cold palm. "What if they did that to protect us?"

Lips tight, she raised a brow. One slip of the tongue—that's all the reason it would take for her to kill me or throw me out.

"My mom's death opened up a weak spot in the archangel's wards. Believe it or not, that magical barrier protects everyone, no matter if you call yourself mortal or supernatural. Closing their doors could have been a last resort."

Especially with Akosua joining Chthonia. But it was impossible to tell how much the queen knew, how much she was gleaning from me.

And what she might do with it.

Inspecting the jewels sparkling on the gold bands on her fingers, Hildur said, "I have tired of this talk of war."

I slipped my hand out from her grip and pushed my chair back.

Her palm lay flat on the table, frost spreading out beneath it as she glared up at me.

With eerie calm, I rose. "I thought you would care more about your people."

"Watch your tongue, angel. You know nothing of war." Her face, a rich tawny beige that glowed against the icy realm like a tiger's eye, blanched with ire. "I care about my people now. I cared about them a century ago. The battle cries still came to my door."

"Did you have a chance to stop it?" I managed to keep my voice steady, despite every bone in me shaking with rage and unchecked magic. "Or were you too *tired* of all the war talk then, too?"

A plate shattered against the herringbone floor, hurried footsteps rushing to clean it. Freyja's arctic eyes were on me, a hand secured on her waist.

It was clear nobody talked to the queen like that, but I didn't care.

"Dear girl." A hint of a smile played at the corners of Hildur's mouth. "I've had this very conversation in this exact room more times than the history books can date. For me, it's simply a case of déjà vu."

My hands clenched at my sides.

She stood, shooing the servants darting to her aid. "So long as Chthonia and Empyrea exist, there will always be a side. This time the elves will not choose. We will not help."

Source swelled from my fists; the ceiling began to rumble, crown molding breaking off the corners, cracks slithering up the walls. Frozen water jutted out of the fissures, leaving a line of glistening icicles.

Our breaths clouded in the air as the room grew colder. "Forget my vision, forget the Watchers, forget the growing threat of Chthonia's supporters. This is... different. It's not war. It's Armageddon."

Hildur's gaze swept over the icy seams in the walls, a flash of power circulating in the lavender of her eyes.

"If you'd rather hide out in your frozen palace, be my

guest." My fingers curled around the lip of the table, knuckles going white. "I will find a way inside Gaia's watchtower. To hell with your elven laws."

Plucking a frostbitten lupine out of the vase closest to her, she regarded me over the sea of flowers that had been fresh literal moments ago.

Color flushed her face, the look of twisted anger gone. But something even more peculiar brightened her stare, as if I were a rare object she might choose to acquire. "Very well."

"Very well what?" Confusion shot through me, snapping the tether I had with my magic. In an invisible wave, it ricocheted towards me, knocking me back a step, and the room stilled.

"Kristjan." The queen barely had to raise her voice. The door creaked open and an older man flurried in.

Hildur drifted towards the threshold, the long, belled sleeves of her dress draping behind her and sliding against the floor with her skirts. Pulling off his wool cap, Kristjan greeted the monarch with a bow, pushing his spectacles up his freckled nose.

Servants flocked to the table, clearing the dirty dishes, most covered in a sheet of frost. Their conversations were fluid and hushed.

"What do you think you're doing?" Freyja's gravelly voice was shielded by the bustle of quick-working hands.

"Me?" Jabbing my finger in Hildur's direction, I whispered back, "Does she enjoy being this difficult, or does she really just not care about the fate of her kingdom?!"

The clanging of China masked Freyja's venom, so no one but me was stung when she bit back, "Mind your place.

Most wouldn't dare challenge the Queen of the Fair Folk like that."

"There's nothing fair *about* you guys." I gripped the top of my chair, droplets of water flecking the wood. "And exactly when were you going to tell me you were the crown princess?!"

"Did I need to?" Freyja crossed her legs; she was the only one who hadn't bothered to get up, and from her perch she somehow still managed to hold the high ground. "Didn't think you'd be staying long."

I rolled my eyes.

"Besides," she continued, "making it known to outsiders that I'm the heir to the throne is a threat to my security."

"Target on your back? Filling a powerful woman's shoes? I can relate." My teeth pressed down. "But it's not like you'd want to try to."

I'm not sure why it surprised—or even bothered—me that she was as cagy as her queen. I'd kept my title a secret, too. Still, I couldn't ignore the sting of hurt in my chest.

Freyja opened her mouth to fire off another witty retort, but it was her mother who spoke first.

"River." Hildur clapped her hands twice, a perkiness to her brisk steps. "I will help you find the Angel of Earth."

My attention snapped to the queen, every part of me homed in on what she was saying.

"As I have said before, the watchtower is locked. It cannot be opened. However…" She paused, pursing her lips, as if debating whether she should stop. "There's a hallowed cave deep in the fjords. The Nephilim call it Jarðarbæli, earth's lair. I cannot guarantee she will be there or that you won't die in the process, but it's a starting point for your search."

A tickle of adrenaline crept up my spine.

"But," she added, her purple eyes somber, "there's something you must do for me first."

CHAPTER 19

THE WIND WHIPPED ALONG THE BALCONY, HOWLING off the sides of the castle, a light layer of snow skittering over the frozen river below.

"This moat." Hildur waved her hand over the top of the rail. "What use is it if it's frozen solid?"

Fingers numb, I gripped the thick stone, the raw air burning my face, stinging the tops of my ears. "Not much…"

"You say an Armageddon's coming." Her cheeks flushed at the icy chill. "Anyone could pass this river as it stands now."

"And you want me to do…" I dared a glance at Freyja, who was hiding a laugh poorly disguised as a cough. "…what, exactly?"

Flabbergasted, the queen turned to me. "Fix it."

Face pinching, I met her violet stare. "You want me to fix it right this second?"

"You want me to ask twice?" That look, like she'd never in her life had to ask for something a first time.

Gulping, I turned my attention back to the moat. "How?"

"How did you rip my chandelier out of its socket? How did you decorate my walls with ice crystals? Kristjan." Releasing me from her bitter gaze, she called her courtier over. *"Gakktu úr skugga um að stíflurnar virki."*

His pale eyes darted between us. Honestly, I wasn't sure who scared him more.

"So, are you ready?" the queen continued.

"What?" I balked. "No."

"What's the issue?"

I gestured to the open doors, to the elves gathering at the threshold, eyes wide, lips swift. "The issue is you're forcing me to perform like a show pony."

"Do you blame them? They're curious. Not every day you get to see the Angel of Water perform feats for the kingdom."

I crossed my arms. "Yeah, well, my powers aren't magic tricks."

"We'll all have frostbite if you take any longer," Freyja bit out from the other side of her mom.

I leaned over the railing, just so I could glower at her.

"Oh, River," Hildur said with a tight smile aimed at the small crowd, "with that attitude you'll never make it far. Humor me. You're confident in your skills, are you not?"

Hot air blew out of my nose. Maybe if we stood here long enough, the ice would just melt, and we'd all be on our way. Popping up on my toes, I craned my neck to try and see beyond the turret, which was blocking the view of the mountain.

A stroke of lustrous blue glimmered beyond the icy tower. I pressed myself farther, until the dramatic cascades of a waterfall came into view. It was frozen solid: the water caught in the action of falling, the mist scattered like ice pellets, the spray stuck in midair.

Setting my heels back on the ground, I asked, "How long has it been like that?"

"Long." That was it. That was all she gave me.

"Have you tried anything else to thaw it?"

With a tilt of her head, she pursed her mouth and raised a brow.

Okay, so that answered that.

Dropping my gaze to the moat, a permanent frost dusting the fronds of grass that lined the banks, I followed the grooves in the ice. Thin, black veins shimmered between the sheets of vibrant turquoise—threads of dark magic. Unease hollowed my heart.

Assuming they'd tried to use their own source of power—Galdur—with no success, why was she so convinced mine would work? And if it didn't, then what? No Jarðarbæli? Tossed out onto the glacier? The guillotine?

I turned back to the queen. Expectation emanated off her in almost tangible waves; the pressure felt heavy on the air.

What was I supposed to do? Questions were clearly forbidden, and I couldn't tell who she was keeping the answers from: me or the hundreds of clueless elves huddled along the perimeter.

Perhaps both.

"Okay." Shivering at a particularly frigid gust, I gripped my arms tight across my chest. "I clear this and get the river flowing, and you'll take me to Gaia."

"Yes."

I glanced over my shoulder, and spotted Gunnar, a statue of uniformed muscle, his navy-blue coat and stamped beret popping against the sea of beaded dresses and metallic threads.

Attention back on the task, I released a controlled exhale, then slowly filled my lungs with the crisp morning air. Opening my mind to every sound, every scent, every quiver of light and shadow—striving to reach that space in my chest between body and soul, between bones and blood.

Nothing.

The same nothing I felt when my fingers reached for the space under my collarbone and met only air. I couldn't do this, not without my mom's necklace—my conduit.

Despite the chill, nervous sweat beaded my temple. My nails dug into my palms.

Defeat slithered its way into my thoughts. These weren't the right circumstances. Every time I'd called on my Source, I'd done it in a moment of panic without really thinking about it. Now that I wanted it, needed it, it wouldn't come. I was in way over my head. This was a horrible idea; I'd never be good enough—

A voice, one I'd never physically hear again, filtered through my thoughts. *Allow yourself to feel,* my therapist used to say.

I didn't deserve her words, not even in memory.

If Dr. Fairmore had been assigned any other patient, she'd still be alive. But they killed her—Chthonia's fringe group, maybe even Ryder himself—to get to me. I wished I could ask her: was there something else I was supposed to feel besides the utter desperation, the rage, the longing, the pain of her loss?

Powerful.

The word flashed across my mind like the crack of a whip, shattering the wall I'd built around my heart.

There. A faint tremor began beneath the ice. A whisper rose across the slick surface. A bead of water slipped down the icicles. A shadow flittered over the bright turquoise hue.

My Source. It was here.

While I felt a rush of elation, I hadn't earned anything from my audience—not a flinch, not a single bat of an eye from the elven queen, her daughter, her court.

Flexing my hands, I pushed out in the air, as if I were pulling the ice apart, hoping the motion would direct my Source to follow the movement, just like it'd done when I was surfing in the Atlantic Ocean. This time it didn't work, of course. Stubborn-ass magic.

Or maybe... maybe the dark power woven into the block was stronger than I thought.

Prickles of doubt speared my concentration, but I wouldn't give up. I'd made it all the way here. Water magic was in my blood.

I could do this without my necklace.

I'd just have to try really fucking hard.

Mentally swatting away the intrusive thoughts, I poured all my focus into the element I was named for. My entire being—every ballooning of my lungs, every beat of my heart, every clench of my muscle—dedicated to releasing the water from whatever evil spell had come upon it.

My hands went white as the blood rushed away from my fingertips.

A loud crack shook the castle's foundation.

Gasps came from inside, a chorus of panic and awe. Even the queen betrayed her fear when her hands shot to the railing, holding tight. I grimaced, redoubling my focus.

Darkness crept into the corners of my vision with each pulse of pain shooting to my head.

A fracture split the frozen river in two. It skittered up the waterway to the bottom of the falls, slabs of ice descending into the electric-blue depths.

The air quaked. A deafening roar filled my ears.

A cool breeze rushed past my face. The sharp whine of swords sliding out of their sheaths followed, as the royal court took a giant step back.

Hundreds of glacial shards blew out from the falls, pulverizing the frozen sheet that the river had become as the natural flow returned. I ducked under my arms, chips of ice bouncing off the railing, the banks, the stone.

Water plunged into the pool, shattering the silence, pushing the remaining ice blocks downstream.

A rumble echoed beneath my feet. Was the balcony shaking, or was that just me? I turned towards the castle. Everything—the sounds, the light, the world—seemed to move in slow motion.

My brows crumpled. People were applauding? Shouting, clapping, stomping their feet...

That—that couldn't be right.

Beside me, Hildur straightened, looking annoyed as she brushed errant snowdrift from the skirt of her gown. "Well," she snarked, voice low in my ear, "don't keep them waiting."

Clutching my stomach, I followed the directive of the waving, smiling queen—giving the elves a painful, pathetic bow. It was all I could muster; my muscles were so sore. The burnout hit suddenly, as if I had just run a marathon, leaving my body quivering and achy.

Their answering cheers echoed off the snowcapped mountains at a level my ears simply could not handle. I blinked rapidly. I was seeing double, triple. I needed to sit down.

I caught Gunnar's eye. He was watching me closely, as if he knew something was wrong.

Oh God.

I took a deep breath. I would absolutely die if I passed out in the center of this balcony, in front of everyone, in front of *him*—the cool, elven guard.

"Alright," I clipped out, swaying against a world that felt like it was spinning underfoot. "I did it. Can we go?"

"Oh," the queen simpered. "It's far too late. Another time. Tomorrow."

"Are you serious?" My jaw dropped.

"Does it sound like I'm joking?" She walked briskly towards the open doors, her royal subjects in tow, dress flowing behind her in a wave of velvet and silk.

Pain radiated through my temple. "What am I supposed to do now?!"

"Explore the castle," she said, waving me off. The court dispersed, going back to their duties, as if this were some kind of halftime performance.

"You can't do that!" I called after her, but she had already disappeared into the belly of the castle.

"She's the Queen of the Huldufólk," Freyja purred, swinging in front of me so she could walk backwards and talk. "She can do whatever she wants."

"Where are you going?" I huffed.

"I'm going to spar."

Uh, I most definitely wouldn't be doing that. Not that she invited me, anyways. "Where did Gunnar go?"

"Huh." With a sly grin, she tilted her head. "Wouldn't you like to know."

"What? No, that's not—" I hadn't meant it like that. I slid my pointer and thumb across my brows, the pressure building behind my eyes.

And just like that, between one heartbeat and the next, I was alone.

Well, at least I wasn't sentenced to my rooms as if they were a jail cell. Might be worth checking on Eldi, though.

"Got yourself in a pickle, there?"

I glanced up.

His eyes struck me first: a glacial blue, almost translucent. The rest of him was just as shockingly beautiful it hurt to look at him—and that wasn't just from the overstimulation of using my Source.

"Who are you?" I didn't mean to come off so exasperated, but I really was not in the mood for small talk. I needed peace, quiet—not some dude leaning against the archway, arms crossed, chiseling out lean lines in his forearms.

"Flóki." He slowly spun a dagger between his fingers, the sharp tip indenting his skin. "That was quite a show."

"Show?" I scoffed. "That wasn't for entertainment purposes."

With a twitch of his lips, he ran his thumb along his blade. "Whatever it was, we needed it around here."

"What?"

"Magic."

I peered at him closer then: pointy ears, towering frame. He was elven. Wisps of dark ink marked his lotus-white skin, a vivid contrast of dark and light. A chill ran down my spine, either from the temperature or the intense way he tracked my movements.

"Don't you have Galdur?" Pushing off the railing, I did my best to trot across the balcony and into the vaulted hall on my rubbery legs.

"Wait! Do you know where you're going?" He propelled himself after me, matching my strides. "Let me be your tour guide. It's River, right?"

Well, he had two things correct: I had absolutely no idea where I was going, and I could only assume he knew my name because every servant, soldier, and subject was spreading it like wildfire.

Shooting him a quick glance, I kept my pace, too proud to slow down. "So, are you an Eye, too?"

He nodded, the silver hoops puncturing his cartilage glistening in the light. "Stationed in the highlands. They brought me here for Haustgildi."

He gently steered me around a corner, clearly knowing where we were going.

I stared down at where his hand met my shoulder, the rings digging into my flesh, my brows coming together until he lifted it. "Haustgildi," I repeated, doing my best not to butcher the term. "What's that?"

"The annual harvest festival." Now with a deathly cold palm grazing my lower back, he guided me down a spiral staircase. I didn't bother to shrug him off—exhaustion was seeping into my bones, turning the whole world fuzzy. "Well, technically it's meant to be a yearly thing, but we haven't had one in decades. Maybe Hildur is showing off for you."

It surprised me to hear him drop her name so casually. Addressing a royal by their title was a sign of respect—all the elves did it, even ones super chummy with her, like Gunnar. Who was this guy?

"Yeah, maybe." I slid closer to the wall, away from his wandering hands, even if it left me more exposed to his wandering eyes. The unsettling blue flickered over me, drinking me up.

"If you're not here for Haustgildi, what brings you to Hamarinn?"

"I'm shocked you don't know." Even I hadn't missed the whisperings from the servants bustling through the halls this morning—that the Angel of Water had arrived, that there had been talk of war. "Were you not in the throne room for my very public debate with the queen? Or are you too good for the goss?"

"There's little that I think I'm too good for." His smile turned asymmetrical, jerking up at one corner. "Maybe I just wanted to hear it from the girl herself."

Windows were sparse in this stairwell, the darkness thickening, crowding, almost like it was a living, breathing thing. I quickened my pace, nearly missing a step.

"Are you nervous?"

"For what?" My heart raged in my chest.

"Jarðarbæli."

"So, you do know why I'm here."

He shrugged, eyes seeming to drill into my own.

"Should I be nervous?" I made every attempt not to sound like it, but a tremble shook my words, especially as

I remembered Eldi's. *They'll use your words against you, even the ones you do not say. Creative. Cunning.*

"Most people would be." Cupping his chin, all sharp lines and harsh angles, Flóki added, "But then again, most people wouldn't dare enter the lair of the Angel of Earth."

"Most people don't need to confront the Angel of Earth."

"You'd be surprised."

It was almost enough to stop me in my tracks. "Do you know something I don't?"

"I know lots of things." He wiggled his thick black brows. "Hey, that's an interesting scabbard, where did you get it?"

"Huh?" I glanced at my waist, completely forgetting what I'd fixed to the belt loop that morning: the runed leather holster holding my crystal blade.

Déjà vu swept over me in a flash of nervous heat. That question… it held the same faux innocence, the same prodding tone, as when Leif once asked me about my necklace—and he had used that information to unleash a demon and steal the one thing helping me channel my power.

Chances were that Flóki had no motive and was just a natural creep. But I wouldn't let myself fall victim again, in case I was wrong. So, I shrugged, fighting off the swell of unease.

"A friend," I lied. "Are you actually going to tell me these super important things, or just keep talking sideways?"

"You've got an attitude on you, haven't you?" He chuckled. It raised the follicles on my skin like the hiss of a venomous snake.

Shafts of warm light danced off the walls. We were getting closer to the landing. Relief flooded me when we rounded a corner and entered the open-air courtyard.

Spotting the passage that led to the elevator, I darted to its portrait-lined hallway. "I think I can find my way from here."

"Are you sure?" His boots thudded behind me. "I haven't even gotten to show you any of the best parts. Ískastali has the best library in the realm, and don't even get me started on the pantry."

"I'm good, thanks!" I forced my knees up, breaking into the closest thing to a jog that my exhausted body would allow.

"C'mon, I know you're hungry!" His words echoed behind me.

"Not right—*oof!*" Shoulder colliding with another's, I rebounded, cupping the sore muscle. "Sorry!"

Looking up from my hand, recognition quickly replaced the pain.

Umber skin. Raven ringlets. Equally surprised brown eyes.

The air whooshed out of me in one invisible punch. "Dr. Fairmore?"

CHAPTER 20

"RIVER." MY NAME SOUNDED UNCERTAIN ON DR. FAIR-
more's tongue, like she too was rationalizing that I was
there. But I wasn't the one back from the dead.

She was.

Crushing and melting the ice had taken a lot out of
me, but I didn't think I was on the verge of hallucinating. I
blinked. Once, twice, and a few more times, just to make sure.

"What—what are you doing here?" I could hardly form
the sentence.

"I… After I escaped Chthonia's henchmen, I had no
choice but to flee." Her deep brown eyes sparkled with
something—shock. Hope. Incredulity. "I have to admit,
when there were whispers that the Angel of Water was here
in Hamarinn, I didn't believe it."

Tears dotted my lashes. How was she here? I'd visited
her grave; her face haunted my dreams; I'd blamed myself
over and over for her death. I bit the inside of my cheek. If
I could hold it together in front of hundreds of people, I
would not break down in this hallway.

"But it's true." A hint of a smile quirked her gaping
mouth. "My God, it's true."

Shooting right past the formalities, we drew each other into a tight embrace. The threads of emotion I'd been able to keep tightly wound snapped, and I was crying into her shoulder, the hot tears burning my cheeks, slipping over my jaw.

I didn't deserve this hug. I didn't deserve her.

Tight black curls brushed the side of my cheek, lavender and honey and a spritz of salt infused in each strand. It was such a familiar blend of smells—reminding me of home, of those therapy sessions that changed my life, of all the reasons I had to live.

Finally letting go, I took a step back, wiping my nose on my sleeve. I glanced over my shoulder, checking for Flóki—to find the hall silent, empty, as if he'd never been there in the first place—before turning back to Dr. Fairmore.

Looking at her face… I still saw the shredded office, the dark magic, the cemetery.

She'd died. And I didn't know by whose hand—the Night Stalker offshoot or the demon posing as my therapist—but at this point, it was all the same. I'd mourned her. I'd—

"I don't understand," I said with a sniffle. "You had a headstone and everything… Is this magic? Are you really here, or is this my exhaustion and my Source playing tricks?"

Her lips curved up, but sadness haunted that knowing smile. "Come."

She walked into the courtyard, the long hem of her dress dangling in a drip of sage fabric across the stone.

I matched her idle strides, noting the shadows billowing and fluttering around her as if they were… wings.

The towering mountains loomed above the open ceiling, their jagged silhouettes cutting into the sky—no clouds, just sunlight, and the sparkling branches of the icy willow draping over our path.

She led us to the heart of the tree, the limbs forming a perfect shield from listening ears and prying eyes. "After our last therapy session, they attacked me in the parking garage."

They. My nails dug into my palms, Ryder's name a dry lump in my throat—but I had to ask. I had to know. "Who were they?"

"I don't know exactly." As she parted the foliage, her sleeve slipped down her arm. A scar marred her skin from the top of her wrist to her elbow—that was new. "They were wearing masks; and from the moment they captured me to the moment I escaped, they didn't take them off. But they bore the marks of Chthonia fanatics—inverted pentagrams, goat-headed figures—on their skin and their clothes."

Acid churned in my stomach. They'd taken her—tortured her, by the look of that scar and the other one I caught, a good slice along the side of her neck.

She ducked her head. "I wanted to be there for you—"

"No." I placed my palm on the tree trunk, and the cool bark dug into my skin. "This is all my fault, Dr. Fairmore. You don't need to explain yourself." *I don't deserve it.*

"Call me Olivia," she said. "And I owe it you. Owe it to her."

My pulse drummed in my ears. "Who?"

She finally glanced up, her eyes shiny with unshed tears. "Your mom."

"Why?" I fought to steady myself, the ground feeling like it might slip out from under me at any second.

"Because I told her I would look out for you."

The air turned heavy. "You… you knew my mom?"

Nodding, she continued weaving through the leaves, the ice clinking around her with the soft echoes of a windchime. "It's not often an archangel befriends a Nephilim—but Mira always preferred the company of those of us stuck on Mortal Earth. I more than knew her. She was a dear friend."

Shock blew through me. There had always been a spark of familiarity to her rose-tinged face, because I'd seen her—met her—before she showed up as my new therapist that fated day.

Pushing off the tree, I staggered after her. "I met you that one summer. At the beach."

Most of the memories before my mom's death were fuzzy, as if they'd been plucked from my head, but that sunny afternoon in the cold sea and the hot sand came rushing back to me.

"I was walking my dog." Tossing her chin over her shoulder, she gave me a glassy smile. "You just adored him. Do you remember?"

"Yes! The fluffy white one. What was his name?"

"Henry," we said at the same time.

The dog had kept me occupied while my mom and Olivia spoke, their words hushed and quick.

Now that I thought about it… "That happened a few times—us running into each other. It wasn't a coincidence, was it?"

Stepping out of the branches, she waited for me on the other side, her silhouette wavering like a mirage behind the dense curtain of ice. "No, it definitely was not."

"Why—ow." I pulled a twig out of my hair. The limbs

twisted around my own, snagging on my braid, until I stumbled out the other side. "Why the secrecy?"

"To protect you." Turning on her heels, she headed for a vaulted corridor. "The laws for the angels are not like the ones you know. There's no such thing as forgiveness—no room for mistakes. Mistakes are sin. Sin is treason. You commit treason, you are sentenced."

"I mean, my mom must have known that when she decided to date my dad in the first place, right?" I asked as we approached a crumbling stone stairwell blanched with what looked like salt. "She was an archangel. That's millennia of life and laws."

With soft steps, Olivia descended. "Yes, but what you have to understand is most angels who serve the Court of the Creator *do not feel*. They exist in a realm of order, and anything that threatens to disrupt that order is chaos. Chaos cannot exist in Empyrea."

I followed her without hesitation, light playing off the walls. "Even more reason to just walk away from him…" I grumbled. My heart cinched in my chest, as if to remind me, *Easier said than done.*

"That'd be the easy answer, wouldn't it? Especially for beings that experience no human emotion. But the Watchers were created in the image of *mortals*. Mortals are equal part order and chaos. They're moody and messy, beautiful and cruel. They're complex. They're not perfect."

We rounded a corner, the passage abruptly pitching into shadow.

Torches guided our way downward, illuminating my former therapist's silhouette in a warm glow.

"Despite this very big difference," she continued, "the Watchers are still bound to the same rigid laws as the others."

"That seems unfair."

She tsked. "Truly."

A faint trickling of water rippled in the distance—pipes, or maybe runoff from the glacier pooling beneath the castle floors.

"But…" My brows furrowed. "Didn't a bunch of angels come here and, you know, fall in love? Make babies? Get corporate jobs?"

"You're funny," she said, a tinge of laughter coloring her words. "Being sent to a world after a lifetime of order, witnessing the intricacies of human interaction…" She shrugged. "I'd be tempted. Wouldn't you?"

"Even if it were a death sentence?"

"Oh, it's much worse than that. Death would be a courtesy." A tremor worked its way into her shoulders, and I imagined we were, in our mind's eyes, seeing the same gruesome images of the Fall. I'd never forget those cries of despair, the air full of decay and hopelessness in that glimpse of the past Madame Myrian had shown me in her crystal ball earlier that summer. "But for some, experiencing the emotions that make us human, even if only for a brief moment in time, is better than an eternity of feeling nothing at all."

She slowed, rounding a corner.

The stairway opened into a massive room—a cave—lit by flickering torchlight. A turquoise lagoon rippled in the center, winding into dark nooks and shadowed corners.

Salt stained the steps and crusted the rocks jutting out of the water.

"What is this?" I asked. "An elven spa?"

She grinned, and it loosened something in my chest. I thought I'd never see that smile again. "Geothermal pools. Said to have healing properties." Taking off her shoes, she strode to the edge and sat down, dangling her feet into the shimmering blue water. "No idea if that's true. I just find them relaxing."

Wasting no time, I pulled off my booties and joined her, the steam a welcome blast of heat. One toe in the water and I was melting. "This is incredible."

"Isn't it?" The water's reflection shimmered in her eyes. "You lost your necklace."

A statement so similar to ones I'd heard before, usually meant to disarm me—but when it came from her mouth it didn't make my skin crawl like it did with Flóki or trigger an inner alarm like with Leif.

"Yeah." I dipped my chin, my fingers curling around the empty space above my heart. "Chthonia's cronies came after me, too. They stole it." I forced myself to meet Olivia's midnight stare. "Along with so many other things."

"I'm sorry." Remorse pinched her face. "I know that was important to you."

"It was all I had left of her," I said.

"Not all…"

Source pulsed through me, like a lazy cat flicking its tail.

"You mean her magic?" I snapped my gaze to the pool, leaving my hand fisted at my clavicle. "I can't even use it without the necklace. That was my conduit."

"You released the Álfur River. That thing's been frozen for over a century." The outline of Olivia's face appeared next to mine, rippling in the water. "How do you explain that?"

I forced air out of my nose. "Honestly, I don't know."

"You tapped into your emotions. You allowed yourself to feel, and…?" The rest remained unspoken in the grin that softened the furrowed lines of her face.

"Listened to my heart," I finished. This is what she'd said, what she'd been trying to achieve in our therapy sessions before she was kidnapped.

Her shoulders rose with a steady inhale. "When people pass over to the next realm, they leave behind a unique imprint of energy—particles of creation that cannot be destroyed, so they redistribute back to the environment. Or in your case, transfer."

Butterflies whirled in my gut, the sensation ballooning into my chest, moving upwards until a lightness filled my head.

"Your mom's necklace was an heirloom you can never replace. But it's not the only thing channeling your powers. Sure, it helps do it faster, and with less mental strain." In the crystal waters, she tucked a stray curl behind her ear. "But her Source, your Source, lives in your heart. That's the biggest conduit of them all."

For a moment, I swore another pair of eyes stared back at me from the water. Ones so much like mine, curved and curious, but also like hers—my mom's. A piercing, flame-like blue, full of secrets. I swished my feet, the ripples shattering my reflection.

I focused on the stillness between the tiny wakes, but it was me once the water settled. Olivia shifted next to me, clearing her throat.

"I was saying, I wanted to be there for you, and I wish I could have told you all this earlier—" I bristled at the statement, but she held up a hand so I wouldn't interrupt this time. "But after I escaped Chthonia's clutches, I had to fake my death, or they never would've stopped hunting me. So, I came here."

"Why here?"

"Same reason as you, I assume? To find Gaia."

"Did you get detained at the lighthouse, too?" I bit back a smile.

"Surprisingly, no." She laughed. "I was able to contact the elves before I arrived and arrange my visit…" That spark of joy slowly tapered off. "Corbin hid so much from you. I get that was his form of protection, but… I think it did the opposite."

"Yeah." Leaning forward, I curled my fingers around the smooth edge of the lagoon. "So, um… Are you even a real therapist?"

"Yes!" Her jaw dropped playfully as she feigned offense, hand shooting to her heart. "Licensed and insured."

"Sorry." I cringed. "I had to ask. Well… What do we do now?"

"It's a good question." She sighed, relaxing her spine. "Not in a million years did I expect you to turn up here. It changes everything."

I peered into the pool's opaque surface again. "Any leads on the Angel of Earth?"

She shook her head. "Unfortunately, no. From what I gleaned when I was captured, I don't think Chthonia has any either, though."

"That's good." I wiggled my toes beneath the warm silky surface. "Are they looking for her, then?"

"Hard to tell exactly what their next move was going to be. Between the threats and the blindfold and whatever they slipped me, I was pretty disoriented." Olivia shuddered. I wanted to reach for her hand, to tell her I was sorry again. "They'll start soon if they haven't already. In order to bridge the realms, they need her—they need you. They need the Watchers' Source."

My fingers grazed my lips, and I chomped at the nails. "The queen promised to take me to Gaia's lair in the fjords after I completed her silly little task, but she kind of just bowed out."

"Jarðarbæli, right? The few other Nephilim I spoke to in Reykjavík made it sound like an abandoned tourist attraction. Said no one's been there in a decade." She frowned. "That the cave was cursed and the highlands make the journey impassable, anyway, and to not waste my time."

My ears perked. "The highlands, you said?" Flóki had mentioned he was stationed out there.

Olivia nodded.

Tendrils of unease curled in my gut. "Something here is off."

"Agreed. I can't put my finger on it, but the Galdur almost seems…" She gently kicked her feet, stirring the water. "Restricted?"

"Right? Like, why did Hildur need me to clear the moat? Why couldn't she do it?"

Dropping her voice so the swish of the lagoon masked her words, she whispered, "Something is definitely up."

"What do we do?"

"When do you see the queen next?"

"Tomorrow, I'm assuming?" I shrugged. "She didn't give me a clear answer."

"Okay." She rose to her feet. "Since there are no other Nephilim here, I'm going to the archives to see what I can find out about Jarðarbæli. It'll look too suspicious if we both go there now—she has Eyes everywhere."

The birds, the wind, even the hills have eyes for their queen, Hildur had told me.

I craned my neck so my gaze roved across the ceiling, the stalactites, all the nooks and crannies, for a flicker of movement, for a spy.

"What about Akosua?" I said suddenly, softly—a question I'd cycled through endlessly in my mind. "She left Empyrea too, not unlike my mom. Worse, actually. She betrayed them."

"I—" Olivia sucked in a breath. "I know. My captors mentioned her."

I picked and pulled at my cuticles until the skin was tender and bright. "I know she was disappointed about my mom's decision. Hurt. Angry. But what I don't understand is…" I tore at the jagged tip of a nail. "How she could do that. Side with the enemy. Go against everything she stood for. And for what? Revenge? A change of heart?"

"Grief changes people," she said, and if anyone understood that it was me. "Eternity is a long time to mourn. Imagine the stress of trying to protect a realm on top of that, and with only a fraction of the strength you once had."

Blood welled on my nail bed. I tucked it under my thumb, putting pressure on it.

A shadow passed over Olivia's face. "Who knows what Akosua's breaking point was? Maybe she was desperate. Maybe she felt betrayed. Maybe she thought she had no other choice."

"Desperation, betrayal…" *Grief,* I wanted to add, but couldn't find it in me to say. "It can eat you up inside."

My eyes fluttered, thoughts a flurry of Javi's stark white hospital room, and the smeared blood at Crescent Rock, and the cemetery that held Olivia's grave.

A gentle hand cupped my shoulder. "Let's touch base tomorrow. Are you going to hang out here?"

"Actually," I pushed myself off the ground, Source and adrenaline shooting through my veins, "do you know where the sparring ring is?"

CHAPTER 21

T HE TRAINING GROUNDS TOOK MY BREATH AWAY—OR maybe that was the lack of oxygen.

I'd taken the elevator to the highest floor, an experience in itself. A curling gazebo carved out of ice shielded me from the wind as I stepped out of the car and onto a plateau that overlooked a slate-gray hollow.

Hundreds of people gathered in this open space between the mountain's peaks. From here, they dashed around like little ants, running in circles over the barren terrain.

A crumbling set of stairs carved into the rock face snaked to the area below. Grasping the thick rope railing, I descended the nearly vertical path, my heart thrashing against my ribs at the dizzying altitude. At least it was free of snow—the steps had been swept clean of stray pebbles and ice, anything that might have someone tripping and breaking their neck. The height and the angle could do that on their own.

When I finally reached the bottom in one piece, I put my hand to my brow, shielding my vision from the icy glare of the surrounding snowcapped ridges.

My breath clouded in front of me, lungs working harder in the thin air. Elves darted across the flat land, grouping themselves into formations, clinking swords, lifting bar-bells, climbing the sides of the mountain. Some gathered around a raised platform—the sparring ring.

Craning and squinting for a good look, I could only make out a gloved hand, a flash of pinkish blonde over the audience clustered along the bright ropes. Cheers erupted.

After waiting for a line of soldiers to jog past, I walked over. Anxiety stabbed me in the gut, sharper than any sword or spear I saw hanging on the many weapons racks.

This wasn't just a standard outdoor training facility. This was where warriors were made.

The mat-covered area I'd initially assumed to be a normal gym sent a shiver down my spine: half the machinery didn't even remotely resemble workout equipment—it looked more like torture devices.

Beyond those, the base of the slopes were lined with pits: pits with metal spikes, pits with bubbling tar, pits with—oh God—*snakes.*

Nope. I swung my head in the direction of the sparring ring, picking up my pace. I would not be getting anywhere near those pits.

An elf darted into my path, flushed from their workout, a damp sweatband around their forehead. Three more raced after them, heading for those dreaded holes in the earth. Laughing, smiling, as if they were about to do the unthinkable: enjoy them.

Coming up here was definitely the wrong decision. I knew I should have just headed back to the comfort of my rooms. I had overexerted myself with the frozen waterfall. I should take a nap. There was plenty to talk to Eldi about, or

I could join Olivia. I was sure I could disappear back into the elevator, make myself invisible before…

"River!"

Or not.

I swiveled in the direction of my name to see a familiar figure jogging towards me.

"Gunnar," I said, already feeling as if I'd used up all of my oxygen.

He stopped a few feet away, his hair pulled into a low pony, biceps poking out of his tight black shirt. A trickle of sweat lined his brow. "What are you doing up here?"

"Great question," I panted, and it was totally due to the air, not the way the stretchy fabric sculpted his chest. "I'm… exploring?"

"I thought you'd be spent after that performance for the queen." Wiping his forehead on his sleeve, his skin glistening from his workout, he added, "That was pretty badass, by the way."

"Thanks." Heat flashed down the back of my neck, up my cheeks.

He nodded towards my clothes. "You changed."

I glanced down at my black leggings and my matching zip-up. "Yeah," I said, tucking the short layers of hair that'd come undone from my braid behind my ear. "I did."

"Hey, angel!" a girl called from the ring. Freyja. She curled her fingers. Beckoning—taunting. "You're up."

"O-oh, no." The blood drained from my face.

"Oh yes." She leaned on the elastic barrier. "G, bring her up here."

Gunnar hesitated, wide eyes darting between us.

She tilted her head. "That's a command."

"Sorry, River." Gritting his teeth, he stalked back to the enclosure, legs strong and slow. No threatening words, no touch, no force. They weren't needed, anyway. I was a rabbit in the den of wolves.

Heels skidding in the dirt, my feet grew heavier, more leaden with each tentative step.

"Shoes off," Gunnar said at the edge of the mat.

"Gloves off?" Freyja perked.

"*On,*" Gunnar and I said together.

At least two of us were on the same page.

Pushing off the ropes, Freyja gave me a vicious grin. She moved to the center of the ring—hopping, weaving, punching the air—practicing what she'd inevitably be doing to my face.

More elves drifted over, suspicious glances tracking my every flinch. I could've sworn I saw copper and silver coins change hands. Bets were definitely not on me.

"Pick your gloves." Gunnar gestured to the racks of gear with blue, red, gold, silver, and neon pads on display within the shelves. "I'll help you wrap your wrists."

Adrenaline burned through me. How had I ended up here? I just wanted to go for a walk, had wanted to burn off the confusing wave of optimism and power and rage that had bubbled up in me.

I unzipped my hoodie and shrugged it off, my stomach peeking between the high waist of my leggings and my sports bra. Alright, maybe I had wanted to do something, prove something—hit something. That was why I stumbled up here. That was why I changed after chatting with Olivia.

Goosebumps flooded my arms, but I hardly felt the cold.

I settled on a pair of all-black mitts to counter the princess's hot-pink gloves flashing in the corner of my vision.

Grabbing a roll of ivory cloth, Gunnar took my wrist. His touch was delicate, despite the fact that he could probably kill me with one punch. He unrolled the material, wrapping it around the base of my hand, then began slowly weaving it between my fingers. My red, raw fingers, utterly destroyed by my picking.

Heat crept up my neck again. Ugh. It was just a simple task, a mandatory one for a fight.

Still—this close, I could feel the warmth radiating off him, and when his skin grazed mine…

"Sorry," he murmured. But he didn't flinch.

I turned away, and a glint of silver caught my eye. The top of a dome peeked out behind a smaller ridge, the rest of it backed by nothing but sky, as if it dangled on the edge of a precipice.

"What's that?" I asked.

"The Terrordome," he said, not breaking from the rhythm of his work.

"What's it for?"

"Fighting."

"Isn't that what we're doing here?"

"Here, we're training." He dropped my right hand, picking up the left with a gentle touch. "There, you fight to the death."

"Don't tell me loser goes to the Terrordome, otherwise you might as well perform my last rites now."

A smile slipped along his lips, but his eyes remained on his task. "Nah, it serves more as a reminder of the past." He tucked the edge of the material into another layer on my palm. "You ready?"

No. "Yes," I blew out, swallowing thickly against the rush of my nerves.

Gunnar snagged a squishy helmet and placed it on my head. My nostrils flared at the lingering smell on the inner padding. Bending slightly to clip it beneath my chin, he brushed away the rogue strands of hair tangling in the buckle, fingers lightly skimming my neck in the process.

I laughed. "Sorry." My shoulders shot to my ears. "Tickles."

He bit the inside of his cheek, trying and failing to hold back a smile. "Done."

Folding my lips between my teeth, I then slipped on the gloves.

My opponent hadn't stopped dancing around—her feet quick, her gloves blurring into swipes of neon pink. Air hissed through her teeth with every jab, the extension powerful and swift. She didn't even sport a helmet—she was *that* confident.

I dragged my feet, apprehension making every step unsure and heavy. Gunnar held up the ropes. I slid beneath them and onto the mat.

Freyja waited in the middle, shoulders hunched, smirk gone, gloves grazing her chin in her fighting guard stance. And with the way her silver eyes pinned me… we might as well have been fighting to the death.

Why did she have it out for me? Sure, I'd mishandled my intro and made them drive in circles in the middle of nowhere, but out of anyone, *she* should understand why.

And it's not like she didn't do the same damn thing.

"Hey," Gunnar called. "Punches only. No Galdur."

A bell chimed.

Dukes up, she started a slow prowl around me. I mimicked the move, my thoughts stuck on why she hated me so much. She lunged forward, taunting. I scrambled back, almost tripping over my bare feet. Hushed laughter erupted behind me.

I blew it off, gritting my teeth.

Elbows pinned to her rib cage, fists beginning to circle, she scooted closer and closer, pushing me to the edge of the mat.

The world around me faded into a blur of lava rock and snow, as my angel senses took control and homed in on the threat—her.

She launched a fist at my face, fast as a pit viper's strike.

Somehow, I managed to duck and spin out of the way, keeping myself righted as the very edge of the pleather shielding her hand breezed my shirt.

I took the moment to catch my breath and dodged another punch, my arms aching, lungs out of breath. Sweat tickled my temple. I went to wipe it.

Her fist lunged the second my gloves dropped.

"Oof!" Pain swelled under my chin, radiating up to my jawbone, my teeth. The horizon shifted—oh wait, that was me, going down, down, down.

I slammed onto my back and the wind left my lungs completely.

A silhouette blocked my view of the sky, followed by a heavy weight dropping onto my core. Tears distorted my vision, but I saw through them enough to strike Freyja back, my biceps screaming. She swatted my hand away as if it were a flimsy, irritating paper airplane.

I pulled my elbows in to deflect her, but her fists rained down, her knees digging into my stomach.

"C'mon, River, this can't be all you have!" She laughed. "Give me a real fight!"

Blows landed on the side of my rib cage, on the sore muscles of my forearms, on the other side of my throbbing face. I tucked myself in tighter and tighter, closing my eyes, clenching my jaw. Somehow, I knew this was only a portion of her strength—this was her going *easy* on me—and it still hurt like hell.

"That's enough!" I screamed, but she couldn't hear me— too focused on the brawl, on the moment, the adrenaline taking over, turning her eyes into silver slits. Source pulsed in my veins, strength building in my bones. "GET OFF ME!"

I thrust my elbows up in defense—forgetting how strong I was now. Freyja was flung to the other side of the mat, slamming into one of the padded corners. My words echoed across the hollow, ringing through the white-capped mountains.

Hundreds of feet overhead, the snow shimmied. A dramatic rumble stirred the air.

"Shit," I whispered.

But it was too late.

The thick layer of powder rippled, dimpled, caved inwards, burrowing into the crag. In a few breaths, it tore off in a sheet of rock and ice and swiftly slid down the side, propelled towards the plateau. Towards us.

A cry rent the air. "Avalanche!"

Someone whistled.

An alarm blared.

Dropping their weapons, the elves training along the outskirts raced away from the base of the mountain's peaks at speeds not humanly possible.

I flung off my helmet and unfastened my gloves, rolling up to my knees.

The slide was already a quarter of the way across the terrain. I considered getting up and running, but then it slowly tapered out.

My shoulders fell, the far end of the training grounds now covered in piles of muddy snow. No one moved. No one so much as breathed. But their eyes were all fixed on the ring.

Face red, Freyja stomped towards me. "The rules were no magic, angel!"

"I—I didn't mean to!" I shot up, arms arcing over my face, my torso hunching, readying for a sucker punch.

A flash of dark brown hair and skin darted between us.

Gunnar stuck his arms out, separating us. "Frey, it was an accident."

Those words meant nothing to her. Snarling, she pushed against his strong body.

"Hey!" he said. It was direct, sharp, spoken like a command. "She didn't mean it."

Freyja stopped pushing against him, blinking as if she'd been in some sort of trance.

Gunnar nodded sharply. "Shake hands."

Crossing her arms, Freyja tilted onto a hip and looked away. My cheeks burned. I put my hands on my waist, my shoulders hardly able to bear their own weight.

"Shake. Hands," Gunnar repeated, his voice a low growl.

Tsking, Freyja dangled her manicured fingers, the wrappings worn and tinged crimson. At this point, I wasn't sure whose blood it was.

"It's just a hand, River." She rolled her eyes, so nonchalant, like she hadn't just been trying to beat the crap out of me. Like I should be *honored* she was offering it up.

I reached out, closing my fingers around hers—at least, as much as I could with the bulky padding bundled around our palms. "What would you call whatever that hand just did to my face for the past five minutes?"

A sly grin. Typical Freyja. "A favor."

My chest was going like I had just run all the way up the mountain.

"Good match." With a final shake, she released her grip, ducking out beneath the ropes. Elves flocked her, patting her on the back, handing her water.

"Nice work, angel." Gunnar slid into my view. "Don't worry about the snow; the plows will come later and clear it."

Pulse thrumming in my ears, raging in my chest, I flexed my fingers—the knuckles pink from the cold, the tips tingling with Source. The rush of it all hurtling back to me.

I stared down at myself: weak, breathless, exhausted, not in control of my powers. I was so underprepared—for this mat, for this journey, for whatever war was coming.

And Freyja's words… An obvious dig meant to annoy me, but they only ignited me.

Maybe she *did* do me a favor.

"You okay?" Gunnar's voice snapped me back to the moment.

"That was actually… kind of incredible," I breathed, grinning. "Let's do it again."

CHAPTER 22

Tʜᴇ ᴇʟᴇᴠᴀᴛᴏʀ sᴛᴏᴘᴘᴇᴅ, ᴅᴏᴏʀs ᴘᴀʀᴛɪɴɢ ᴏɴ ᴀ ᴘʀɪsᴍ of glass and light. I strode into the Sky Tower's foyer. The last strands of sunset filled the circular chamber, reflecting off the gilded accents and igniting the space.

Every square inch of me was sore. My feet, my nails… my arms didn't have it in them to redo my braid, and now my hair was a tangle of damp, matted layers.

But I didn't care. This feeling… it was magnetic. Ever since I'd landed that first punch, a jab to Gunnar's chest, after the match with Freyja, the adrenaline hadn't stopped coursing through my veins.

We'd stayed in the ring after all the other Eyes had left. Until our noses were numb and our knuckles were raw and our sides were sore from blocking.

I shot him a glance, the orange, red, and yellow streaks funneling through the windows illuminating him in the alpenglow. My steps grew heavier as we left the naturally lit foyer into the stone-walled hall. I froze in front of my door.

"How am I supposed to go back to this cage?" I huffed out a cold laugh.

Dimples indented his cheek. "Because that's what the queen has ordered."

My muscles quivered, weak from being knocked to the ground so many times.

I let myself slouch against the doorframe.

Gunnar followed the movement. "You should get some rest."

He was right: I should go inside, I should listen to him, I should avoid pissing Her Royal Highness off.

But the thrill from today, from this very moment, tore away reason, so instead, I blurted out, "Let's do something."

He raised a dark brow.

"I deserve a little fun," I added. "I got the shit kicked out of me today."

"And you were a total champ about it." He bit his lip to hold in a smile.

"I won't be in Iceland much longer—your queen is supposed to guide me to Jarðarbæli tomorrow. After that, I'm out." I should get points for persistence, right?

"Providing encouragement in direct conflict with the queen's orders is flirting with treason." Clasping his hands, he walked backwards towards the elevator, dark eyes gleaming with mischief. "But if one was interested in having dinner and drinks outside their gilded prison with off-duty Eyes, one might head to the lower tunnels."

The lower tunnels. Was Gunnar inviting me to… something? Butterflies whirled in my stomach. "Where might one find those?"

"Rumor has it they're two floors beneath the main level."

Putting his palms up, he added with a smirk, "But what do I know?"

Hand hovering over the doorknob, I asked, "And when should one expect to be there?"

He seemed to weigh the risk of replying. Just as the elevator doors slid shut, he answered, "Eight thirty."

Palms sweaty, I pushed open the door, warmth from the fire welcoming me immediately.

I hustled across the room, past the mirrored hutches and cabinets, in a blur of damp black nylon and messy brown hair.

My phone lay on the coffee table, where I'd left it. Finger tapping the screen, I huffed out a breath. Seven forty-five. No time at all to shower, change, and successfully find Gunnar's meeting point.

"You're back late." The voice had me almost jumping out of my skin, but of course it was Eldi.

"Sorry, I…" *Forgot you were there* felt a bit rude to say. "I had a draining day."

The flames billowed, almost playfully. "I can see that."

There was so much I wanted to ask her, so much I wanted to tell her, but I didn't have the time. Pulling off my shoes, I headed for the bedroom, the hardwood creaking beneath my hurried steps.

"Where are you off to now?"

"Dinner! With some of the Eyes." Ripping off my hoodie, I craned my neck just past the doorframe. "The queen won't care, right?"

Fiery shadows flickered off the floral wallpaper. "I can't say she'll be thrilled. All the more reason to go, in my opinion."

"I like the way you think."

I rushed into the bathroom and stopped on the threshold, the ivory stone cool beneath my toes. The tub was already filled. Steaming, with bubbles.

"Helga," Eldi called, picking up on the silence. "She filled and drained it twice. She didn't know when you'd be back. I would've just kept it heated for you, but I'm in here."

My palm covered my heart. Bless her.

There wasn't enough time to soak and actually enjoy the bath, but at least I could lather my hair with shampoo and conditioner, which I did as fast as humanly possible, even if it meant rinsing it out as soon as it went on.

Water dripping off my skin, I wrapped myself in a towel and tiptoed to the vanity.

I pulled out a drawer. The handle fell off the wood, screws clattering to the floor. Oops. I'd packed my own toiletries, but most of those were nearly empty, their caps having busted open on the airplane. But these… Picking up a glass bottle, I pulled off the lid, and sprayed—vetiver and jasmine. These looked new, and lavish, and smelled better than anything I'd brought.

First, I tackled the essentials: deodorant, moisturizer, brushing my teeth. The blow-dryer was convenient, if out of place. But that's how everything in this castle was. A hodge-podge of magic and electricity, ice and stone, everything so at odds.

After drying my hair, I tried another drawer. Stuck. I pulled harder, and it abruptly shot forward, stopping just before it crashed to the floor. Oops, again.

Makeup: an even more foreign concept. My body trembled with the swell of nerves as I fanned out the concealer, blush, liner, mascara. The first did an okay job covering up the faint bruising along my jawline.

I opened a compact next, the powder bright and shimmering. Bronzer? I feverishly applied it to my cheekbones and moved on to my eyes, swiping neutral color on my lids, then combing out my lashes.

There. Stepping back, I looked in the mirror. Ugh, those brows. They were utterly untamable without Mau. My entire face was. No amount of makeup could hide the bags under my eyes, or the swell of my lip where Freyja had decked me earlier.

Why did I care so much? It's not like this was a date; it's not like this was just the two of us. Gunnar was my friend. He had invited me to some kind of get-together. Other people would be there.

I backed away from the counter and headed straight to the armoire, throwing open the doors.

My shoulders curled in relief. I don't know why, but I was fulling expecting sparkly dresses and frilly blouses. It did have those, including a lacy pajama set I wouldn't be caught dead wearing, but other than that…

"It's spelled to have what you need," Eldi called, as if she knew where I was standing just by the pattern of my footsteps, by the squeal of the rusty metal hinges.

As I riffled through the layers of fabric, I realized I was missing a majorly important detail. "Shit. I forgot to ask him what to wear."

"Knowing the Eyes"—a log snapped in the hearth—"I'd recommend stylish but practical. They like their posh dinners, but they also have no problem wrestling an arctic yeti after dessert."

"Noted." Given that detail, I landed on a pair of ripped black jeans, ankle boots—good for my dagger—an olive silk camisole, and a cropped wool jacket. My hair I swept into a bun.

As I strode through the living area, the trinkets shaking in their glass hutches with the heavy thuds of my heels, a quiet voice floated in the air, stopping me in my tracks.

"Have fun tonight." The slight sadness to her words was like a stab to the chest.

"I will, Eldi." I turned towards the fireplace, where her flames were tinged blue. "Thank you."

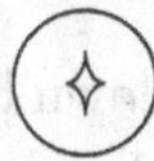

THE ELEVATOR DIPPED below the glacier, dropping me into what felt like the heart of it. A shudder ran up my spine, the air growing colder the lower I went.

Part of me figured the Eyes would've already left by the time the lift stopped—that it was all a joke to begin with, that when the doors parted and the soft light from the passage filled the car, Gunnar wouldn't be standing there in his dark pants, burgundy coat, matching beanie, back pressed against the wall.

But he was.

My breath clouded in front of me. "You're here."

Dropping the heel of his boot from the stone to the floor, he straightened. "You're early."

"Oh." My heart stuttered. Why was it doing that? "I thought I was late."

"Well, you're still earlier than I thought you would be."

"Hey." I smacked his bicep with a playful backhand, but a cool breeze pulled the smile from my face. "Where does this tunnel lead to?"

He put his hands in his pockets, curling his shoulders for warmth. "The royal driveway."

Royal. "Is Freyja coming?" The question knotted my stomach, especially as he easily strode forward, shooting me a backwards glance.

"She is."

I matched his quick steps. "Doesn't she have, like, official princess stuff to do?"

It was much less showy down here, no murals or pictures or decorative bowls, just mud and snow, the icy worn cobblestone, and the sporadic sconce.

"This is more pressing." The golden light from the flickering Galdur gleamed in his eyes. "It might be good to get you guys together in a less stressful environment. If—"

"She wasn't so stubborn we might get along?" I cut in.

"And what have you done to attempt to befriend her?"

"I've done everything! She just hates me."

"Freyja doesn't hate you. She has a hard time trusting people." His lips eased into the kind of grin that made me stumble over the flat ground. "Kind of like someone else I know…"

A cool draft funneled through the corridor. I pulled my jacket tighter, specks of snow catching on the wool, and focused on my feet.

"Honestly," he added, "I think she sees something in you."

"Like what?"

"Something she likes. And it spooks her." The shadows started to disperse, icy white moonlight pouring in from the end of the tunnel and pooling over the stone. "As a princess *and* a soldier, she has to work hard to find genuine friends. Even the ones that claim they're loyal are by her side one second, and the next they're talking shit about her."

"I'm not that kind of—" *Friend,* I almost said. But I choked on the word, images of Javi flooding my mind: Crying at the Boardwalk. Lying in the rubble. Screaming from a hospital bed. I had no shortage of memories of exactly what kind of friend I had been to him.

Maybe Freyja was right to steer clear of me.

Maybe they all should.

An iron gate creaked open, the sound pulling my focus ahead.

We spilled out into a large courtyard, the deep indigo night rising behind the snowy hills. Cars lined the left wall, stables the right.

Horse-drawn carriages would probably be more fitting for this castle, yet two SUVs idled in the center, plumes of steam piping out from their exhaust.

A few curious noses leaned over the gates at the stables, the animals whinnying, their hooves scuffing the dirt. One snorted, showing off its square teeth as if it were smiling, and I caught myself grinning back. It flared its light gray nostrils, rubbing its… *horn…* on a wooden pole.

My stomach flipped. "Is that a unicorn?" It was more breath than voice, but I swore the creature neighed in response.

Gunnar was paces away, opening the door to the idling black Jeep. "After you," he said, waving me into the car.

This four-by-four was so damn high, I had to stand on my tiptoes just to see the inside. I might as well have been asked to climb a mountain, and after today's training, every muscle screamed as I hiked myself up.

"Hello," I squeaked, as I crawled onto the leather to join the three elves already sitting in there, staring. No Freyja—she must be in the other car.

The driver nodded, his grown-out locks winging out from the sides of his hat. His hand was locked with the hand of the elf in the passenger seat, her fingers tight in his.

"Hi." Tossing her shiny black hair, the girl's russet eyes moved to Gunnar, who was getting in on the other side, pushing the dude in the middle seat closer to me.

The guy tugged on his chestnut curls ruefully. "I always get bitch."

"You like it, Fritz," the girl teased.

"Everyone, this is River—"

Gunnar had barely gotten the words out when the car skidded into motion, the steering wheel circling against the driver's palm. I flailed for the ceiling handle, my elbow slamming into Fritz.

"Sorry," I said.

He rubbed his arm, the fabric bunching over his warm ivory skin. "Trust me, I'm used to it."

We flew down an icy road away from the castle. Snow eddied out from under the tires, painting the windows. The music vibrated against the leather, almost too loud to think.

Buckle your seatbelt. Ryder's words echoed through my mind. *You know, that's a very bad habit of yours.* I almost resisted out of spite, but I scrabbled for it anyways.

"Don't worry," Fritz yelled above the bass. "You'll get used to Siebel's driving—" He cut himself short. We hit a bump. Unclear whether it was a rock or pothole or cat. Hopefully not a cat. Fritz gave me a wry smile. "Eventually."

"If I live long enough," I muttered back, clicking my belt into place.

As Siebel zoomed over a snowy mound, our palms slammed into the ceiling, the only thing stopping our heads from plowing into it.

Staying in my rooms would have been the more comfortable option, the safer option. Binds of anxiety tightened around my chest.

The girl in the passenger seat swung around, adjusting her navy cable-knit sweater, the stereo illuminating the layer of freckles on her nose and cheeks, her complexion pale and bright, like a fresh winter day. "You okay back there?"

With a clenched smile, I nodded, my grip tightening around the curve of the seat.

The mountain range raced by us in a blur of rock and darkness and ice. A streak of neon green flashed across the sky, the tail end of a northern light.

"I'm Eva, by the way." She turned the music down. "What brings you to Hamarinn?"

I could lie. I probably should lie, with a bounty on my head and support for my enemy rising every day, but I was tired of that. Tired of pretending to be who I wasn't.

So, I told her straight up. "I'm here to find Gaia, the Angel of Earth. The queen's taking me to Jarðarbæli tomorrow."

"Wow, I haven't heard that name in years. It's been forever since anyone's talked about it." Eva's eyes widened. "Do you all remember what happened to the last guy who tried to go up there?"

I blinked. The wind whipped past the glass.

Fritz tilted his head. "I do."

Gunnar cleared his throat, shifting in the corner of my eye. I wasn't sure if that was a message for the elves or if he was just... moving around.

"Never mind..." Pretending to zip his lips and throw away the key, Fritz turned his gaze to everyone and everything but me.

I wasn't going to just let that slide, not anymore. "Enlighten me. Please."

"Let's just say..." Eva tucked her fist beneath her chin. "He didn't make it back."

"But you will, of course," Gunnar quickly added.

"Of course," Eva echoed, that tight look on her face contradicting her cheery optimism.

"Okay." I crossed my arms. "What exactly aren't you guys telling me?"

"The only thing the Eyes recovered was a head!" Fritz blurted out, immediately slapping his palm over his mouth.

Narrowing my eyes, I asked, "What happened to the rest of him?"

"We don't know exactly." Eva gripped her elbows, a slight tremor rocking her shoulders, as if she were fighting off a chill. "There are... stories about Jarðarbæli. I remember the ones my dad told me when I was younger. Some are so gruesome they gave me nightmares for a week."

Right. That didn't sound ominous or anything.

Specks of light wavered in the distance, growing steadier as our tires sped nearer. Our floodlights swept over clusters of grass-thatched homes, steepled barns, glass greenhouses, until the concrete warehouses, cobblestone sidewalks, and vibrant streets of a city replaced the dirt roads.

"It's all urban legend." Gunnar waved his hand. "A friend of a cousin of a sister's ex type of situation, who knew someone that went up there. Nothing more than stories told to little elves so they won't go sneaking off into the highlands."

"It's true." Fritz nodded frantically, his curls bouncing as we veered around another sharp curve. "That's where the giants are, and giants eat elves, so maybe that's why no one ever goes—or comes back."

"Uh." Gunnar's face pinched. "I was thinking more because it's super remote?"

"No, Fritzy is right," Eva said. "Monsters find their homes there, and Jarðarbæli has some of the worst."

Gunnar palmed his face. "The goal was to make her feel *better*, guys."

Our next turn sent us rattling down a narrow alley at a pace that didn't fling me back into my seat—a speed I didn't think Siebel knew existed.

I chewed the inside of my lip, willing my heart to slow, too. "Do you actually know of anyone who lived to provide the details, or is this just based on rumors?"

"Kistuleitarinn."

The elves sucked in a collective breath.

"What?" Eva squinched her face at Fritz. "Why would anyone listen to him?"

Gunnar's brows dipped, lines indenting his forehead. "Kistuleitarinn is a known pathological liar—among other things."

Disturbing as this all was, I had to ask. "Who's Kistuleitarinn?"

Fritz's throat bobbed. "The Coffin Seeker."

My heart thudded in my chest. But before I could question Fritz further, before I even had time to digest what he'd said, Siebel eased us to a stop.

At first, I thought we'd pulled up to an empty lot, until I realized the building was under a mound of grass shaped like a hill. Faint wisps of light crept through the crack beneath the black doors.

After hitching the e-brake, Siebel got out, the cold turning his beige cheeks pink. Eva, Gunnar, and Fritz followed. From my perch, I watched a second car pull up behind us. Three elves leapt down. Freyja caught my eye and offered a sarcastic wave. Beside her, I recognized one of the others—Flóki.

Legs dangling over the seat, I prepared to lower myself onto the strip of lawn. "Where are we?"

"In the Valley of the Glaciers, on the outskirts of Álfaborg— our elven capital." Gunnar offered his hand, helping me land firmly on my feet. "We're in the Troll Quarters."

"Trolls?" My gut did a somersault. I knew nothing of trolls other than what I'd seen in comics and on TV, which didn't paint the best picture. "So, are… are they not like the giants Fritz was talking about?"

"Oh no." Gunnar whisked past me, the fire in the braziers at the foot of the path flickering over his features. Shooting me a sly grin, he said, "They're much, much worse."

CHAPTER 23

Hollowed-out horns slammed onto the table, amber liquid spilling over their tops and fizzing on the wood. Half a dozen hands shot to the center.

"*Skál!*" the elves cheered—the same thing everyone in this pub seemed to be chanting—clinking their mugs, er… *horns,* together.

The frothy liquid had barely touched my lips when a shoe whizzed past my nose. It knocked a decorative shield off the wall, the metal clanging on the floor.

"*Hæ!*" the barmaid waiting on the group next to us yelled, her thick red hair spilling out of her bun and over her hairy, rounded ears. "Do that again, you're goin' back to the bridge you crawled out from under!"

A rather beefy troll rose from his seat, his heavy fists slamming onto the table, the light from the candelabras flickering over his ruddy skin.

"I'll do what I please. Now get me another ale, *skessa.*" Pushing his thick neck forward, he let out a burp that was so loud, so foul, I was surprised everyone around him didn't pass out.

Squinching my nose, I slapped my palm over the lower half of my face.

"Disgusting," Freyja muttered.

"Get it yourself, ya stupid brute," the waitress spat, wiping her warty hands on her apron.

More growls, more shouts. More bickering back and forth, more things sailing through the air. I glanced up at the gabled ceiling. An iron chandelier hung from the beam above us, its loose chain swinging. Great.

An elbow nudged my arm—Gunnar. "Don't worry, this is completely normal for a Friday night at Wild Aven Tavern."

"Good to know." I took a sip, my gaze darting around the room at the trolls, on high alert for that second lethal shoe—or the chandelier—to drop.

Siebel rolled a silver coin between his fingers, sliding it to the middle of the table. "Bets that angry one won't make dawn."

Some of the others nodded, tossing their money into a pile.

My brows pinched together. "What do you mean?"

"Trolls can't be caught in daylight," Siebel downed the rest of his horn, "or they'll turn to stone."

"Most make it back to their caves by sunrise, but the unlucky few…" Gunnar trailed off.

"The *belligerent* few," Freyja chimed in.

"Check out the statues in the back when you have a chance." Eva gestured behind her, towards a door with a girthy troll standing beneath the rays of the sun carved into the wood. "All petrified trolls."

"That sounds horrifying," I said, reeling in my jaw, which had dropped to the floor, "and I will definitely be avoiding."

Freyja barked out a laugh, leaning into an elf I didn't know, twirling a finger around his long copper hair. I may not have bet on the troll, but I would've put all my money down on the laugh I just heard being a hallucination…if a tight smile wasn't still tugging at the corners of her mouth.

"It's not as bad as they make it out," a raspy voice quipped across from me.

I locked eyes with Flóki. Despite his obvious charm, even one word from him had a chill running down my back. "Sounds pretty bad—"

Vicious force slammed onto the tabletop, knocking over our drinks and sending sticky booze dripping through the cracks. Squishy palms pressed down, nails indenting the surface.

I flinched back from the troll just as he grinned at me, baring a smile with rows of square teeth that could crush a skull. He then slowly and deliberately met each one of our stares head on. "Which one of you is takin' bets on old Zulkis here?"

Siebel leaned back, crossing his muscular arms. "What's it to you?"

"Here's a bet, elf." The troll's voice rumbled through the long hall like an echo in a deep, dank, cavern. "Which one of you is goin' to end up as my midnight snack?"

Just like that, four pairs of hands slid to their waistbands. My sheath tickled against my ankle, hidden on the inside of my boot. One look at Gunnar told me this was normal.

Siebel rolled up his sleeve. "How about we wrestle for it?" His tone was casual, fearless. Reckless.

Zulkis let out a low chuckle, close enough that his hot breath blew my hair back. "Now you're talkin'."

Ramming his elbow onto the surface, he flexed his massive hand, leathered like a mitt and tinged a gray green.

Patrons bustled around, pushing to get closer, their empty horns clattering against the wood, their chants as powerful as their fists. Eva paled, her eyes widening at the growing crowd.

Gunnar gestured to her with a hand parallel to the ground, slowly lowering it. *Stay calm.*

Flóki swiveled around, pulling a joint out of his pocket. "As I was saying." He stood. "At least the trolls in the back don't pull this kind of shit."

Without a second glance, he wound past the crowd and slipped through the back door.

I looked at the rest of the group. Gunnar, Eva, Freyja, the elf next to her: everyone was preoccupied with Siebel and Zulkis as the match began. The two locked in, veins popping in their necks, their temples, their wrists.

Nobody batted an eye when I swung my legs over the bench, strode across the busy pub, and followed Flóki outside.

The lot was bigger than I'd assumed, rows of string lights holding back the darkness. Silhouettes dotted the night, still as statues, their contorted faces raging up at the stars. I stalled.

Trolls that didn't make it.

They *were* statues.

"Geez, it's like an open grave." I walked over to Flóki, shoes crunching in the compacted dirt. "Kind of morbid, right?"

"Kind of morbid, kind of beautiful." The end of his joint burned steadily with his long drag.

"What's beautiful about a sculpture garden made out of a bunch of dead people?"

"Serves as a reminder to us all." He blew out.

"A reminder of what?"

"That we can't escape death." In offering, he held out the tightly rolled hemp paper, the skunky scent billowing in the night. "At least they went out having fun."

Taking it from his hand, I tentatively pressed the unlit end to my lips. "Carpe diem," I said with an inhale, the smoke searing my lungs, my throat.

"Isn't that right." A trace of a smile lifted the corners of his mouth.

I fought to hold my muscles still to avoid coughing.

"So, tomorrow's the day," he said in a raspy drawl, playing with one of the many rings on his fingers.

I raised my brows, nearly gagging on the smoke as I passed the joint back to him.

"When you go to Jarðarbæli," he clarified, as if I had forgotten.

"It's supposed to be," I managed to get out without gasping too hard. I cleared my throat. "Got any advice? Nobody here seems to know anything, and the queen sure as hell hasn't told me what to expect. It's in the highlands." I remembered what he'd told me when I first met him. "That's where you're stationed, right?"

"I've poked around there," he said smoothly. "Never went in."

I stared at him expectantly. "And...?"

"Whatever's in that cave wants to be left alone." His eyes fixed on my heart, as if he were counting the beats. "But isn't that true of most good things? They're guarded."

"Great, so Fritz and Eva were right. There is a monster in there." The tickle in my throat finally subsiding, a tingling calm washed over me. "Apparently the only person who's been inside and lived to see another day is some dude lovingly named the Coffin Seeker."

"Ah, Kistuleitarinn." He took another hit. "That tracks."

"The others seemed…" Words floated outside my head, swirling with the bright auroras, painting the sky in scattered colors and thoughts and dreams. "Scared to even mention him?"

"Nothing to be scared of. He's in an oubliette in the ice dungeons."

"An oubliette?" Such a strange term. Such a strange sound. I giggled at the way my lips puckered when I said it. "How intense…"

"Yes, in the Dead Man's Zone. There's no escaping that place."

"What is he?" Innocence lined the question, almost awe. What could be so merciless, so evil, it had to be locked in a hole far beneath the ground?

"A demon."

"What?" My chin fell, gaze level with his. I hadn't even realized I'd been looking up at the stars. "The queen has a fucking demon under her castle?"

His mouth split into a grin, but it was all wrong. Menacing. He held out the joint.

Shaking my head no, I took a step back. I didn't think

I was *that* stoned, but surely I was hearing things. Because there's no way he just told me… "Are you for real?"

"Where else is she going to put him?"

"I—uh, I don't know. Why does she have him in the first place?" I squinched my lids closed, to shut out the world and give my thoughts a hope of being organized. But the shock and the buzz shuffled them into a meaningless mess.

"She keeps lots of specimens." Moving next to a petrified troll, Flóki ran the back of his hand over its cheek. "Before Kistuleitarinn was a demon, he was Einar the farmer. Born in a typical village. Lived a quiet life. Until… he didn't."

"He was human?"

"Part human, part angel. You probably know it as Nephilim." He paced around the statue, every so often stopping to run his fingers over the dips and grooves, like it were a work of art, and not a creature that once lived and breathed.

"What are you doing?" I gestured to the troll, its mouth contorted in an infinite scream, fear apparent even in its stone stare.

"Hm? Oh." Brushing his palms together, he took a step back. "Sometimes I wonder if this is just a shell, and their souls are still trapped inside."

"So," I laughed breathlessly, the horror and revulsion warring in me against the absurdity, "somewhere along the line, Einar became a demon?"

"All demons have some angel lineage, River. They're different sides of the same coin." He tilted his head, the silver hoops along his pointed ears reflecting the soft light. "It's funny. People are so afraid of Chthonia—but don't they know Earth has some of the biggest monsters."

My heart turned leaden, heavy in my chest. "Why do you say that?"

"Because here, that's what they choose to become."

After the teratorn attack, Ryder had told me that demons were the souls of corrupted angels, but I had been so wound up by everything else at the time, I hadn't fully digested the details. I also hadn't realized that applied to Nephilim—beings that were born of *this* world.

"What—" Despite the high, a chill ran down my spine. "What was it that turned him?"

"Bloodlust." His eyes, all pupil now, pierced me like daggers, roving over every inch of visible skin. "Elves. Female, specifically." Bile shot up my throat. I was going to be sick. "Don't look so scared. You aren't his type. He preferred them when they weren't breathing."

I glanced back at the building. Shadows flittered behind the small, circular, windows, but they were stained glass—no one could see us or hear us—and his words pressed in like the night, drawing goosebumps all over my skin.

"So, this demon," I said. "He's still alive."

Flóki nodded.

"Why?" A rush of anger slurred my words. "Why not give him the death he deserves?"

His cold fingers lightly touched my shoulder. "Because sometimes information is more important than justice."

Flinching, I shuffled out of his reach. "Hard disagree."

"Kistuleitarinn's older than Hildur—older than this kingdom. He's witnessed the rise and fall of many royal families, the bloody fights for the throne. He's lived through the Cross-Realm War, and the ones that came before that.

Some say he came from a completely different realm." A vein pulsed in his neck. "And some say he has the gift of Sight."

"So, what?" I said, crossing my arms. "The queen uses him as her own personal oracle?"

He folded his lips. "You didn't hear it from me."

My mind was racing. The coincidence… it was weird. What were the actual chances that the only person who'd successfully been to Jarðarbæli was a demon who happened to be trapped in a cell beneath the castle I was staying in?

For a moment, nothing but the wind blowing over the frozen dirt and grass filled the quiet space. And in that silence, a wild idea took hold…

"No," I said out loud. "It's not worth it."

"It could be," Flóki answered, as if he knew where my mind had strayed. "He's seen things, knows things, and like I said, he literally can't escape. He's a captive audience."

"Isn't his cell going to be, like, heavily guarded?" I couldn't believe I was asking that.

"They gave up on stationing Eyes there long ago. Too many things down there with a thirst for blood."

My pulse shot up.

"The entrance…" He dipped his chin, like he was weighing the words. "Different story."

"Well, that settles that." I scuffed my heel in the dirt. "There's no way I'm sneaking past an elven guard and not getting caught."

"Lucky for you, I'm part of the royal army," he crooned. "And I happen to know every hour a new soldier takes up position. I can distract them."

"That's an awfully short shift." Conveniently short.

"It's the darkness. It's all-consuming." A glimpse of that darkness flashed across his face, fluttering in my heart.

Suddenly I remembered the stairs in the courtyard, the ones leading down… The forlorn wails, the drafts of ice, the shadows seeping out: the ice dungeons.

"This is a horrible idea," I said, even though that same dangerous spike of interest that had flared through me back then tempted me now.

"I'll keep watch, distract whoever's working."

"And risk your job? Why?"

"You deserve to know what awaits you. Meet you beneath Töfratré at two forty-five?"

The back door flung open, crashing against the grassy wall.

"Riverrrrrr!" Freyja drew out my name in a way I found equally annoying and endearing. "We need you! Ragnar just bet against Zulkis you can turn water into wine."

"Who?"

"The guy who drove me and her here, her boyfriend—at least, the one for this week," Flóki hissed under his breath.

My head snapped towards him. That was uncalled for.

"What are you guys looking at, anyway?" Freyja said, stumbling over the gravel.

He shot me a look, like we were in on some secret.

"Nothing," I said quickly, backing away from the statues, from the elf, from the darkness. Music and laughter floated over the threshold in a steady stream.

Grabbing Freyja by the arm, I dragged her inside. Surprisingly, I was met with laughter, not a punch to the gut—could have gone either way.

We wove through the crowd, which had swelled to at least

quadruple in size; there were definitely some broken fire codes here, if they even had those sorts of things in troll country.

"Nice night to look at the stars," Freyja teased.

I rolled my eyes, releasing my grip. "What's Töfratré?"

"The tree in the courtyard?" She batted her lashes. "Why, you meeting him there later?"

"Frey!" Cheeks swollen and red, Ragnar waved us down. "Perfect timing."

Gunnar shot me a playfully crooked grin as he scooted over to make room.

Four glasses of water sat in a perfectly straight line down the center of the table.

"You weren't kidding, were you?" I groaned.

"This'll be fun—this'll be easy." Sliding her arm around my shoulder, she whispered, "And I *really need* to drink something other than beer."

Huffing out a breath, I slid onto the bench, my mouth set in a tight line. I took in the faces of those gathered around—their crinkled eyes, toothy grins and infectious laughter, reminders of why I'd begged Gunnar to come. To let loose. To have *fun*.

So… I leaned back and got to work on the impossible: making wine out of water with my mind.

But the biggest miracle? Managing to avoid Flóki for the rest of the night.

At least, until we got back to the castle.

I WAS WAITING at the tree when I heard the whispers.

Two tall forms entered the courtyard, shafts of moonlight showering their silver chainmail and strawberry-blonde hair.

Careful not to brush against the leaves, I slithered between the dangling branches to get a better glimpse. My stomach dropped—it was the queen and a guard.

What was she doing out here, wandering the halls close to three AM?

"Someone breached the kingdom's defenses." The man's voice was stifled by the curtain of ice, but clear enough for me to catch his stressed tone.

I took a tiny step closer, the fronds clinking at the movement. The elves paused, turning towards me. Hildur's lavender eyes flared. I froze.

"What do you mean?" she asked finally. They resumed their walk.

I dared a step after them, keeping to the shadows of the sweeping willow.

"We found him stumbling about on the tundra nearly frozen to death. He's convinced we have something of his. We tossed him in the dungeon," the guard said, and my heart thumped in my chest. "That shut him up."

The air seemed to grow colder, my breath a wisp in the air, with just the mention of that wretched place.

"You did the right thing coming to me. This stays between us." Her words were light, but vitriol sharpened her tone. "I'll pay him a visit tomorrow. For now, no one can know—it'll only cause panic that the Galdur wasn't enough to ward him off."

"Yes. About that…" He cleared his throat. "There's been another breach, on the western end of the castle."

"Creature?"

"Ice."

"How odd."

"The glacier," he pressed with no absence of concern, "it's melting. The Galdur can't seem to stop it."

A moment of silence. Thinking they might have turned down a corridor, I left the safety of the branches, ducking when I saw their silhouettes.

"Gods." She pinched the bridge of her nose.

"Shall we send in the Druids?" the guard suggested.

"No, no." She waved a hand, her thick mantle hissing across the ground. "I have a plan."

They disappeared down a hall, the rest of their conversation muffled by the thick stone walls. Worry burned my throat and curdled my gut. If the Galdur wasn't enough to keep someone from trespassing, who's to say it had the capacity to keep these people—these demons—in their cells?

Cold fingers grazed my spine.

Shoulders stiffening, I turned.

Flóki's translucent blue eyes shone in the dark. "You made it."

I barely heard the words over the rush of my blood. "Where did you come from?"

"You ready?" he asked, ignoring my question.

With a slight nod, I sucked in a breath.

"Let's go." He offered his hand.

I didn't take it.

Instead, I busied my hands tightening my bun and wove behind him back through the foliage, the icy world passing by me in a blur. At the threshold of the branches, on the opposite side of the massive tree, he put his hand up.

A silent instruction to hold.

Footsteps echoed in the hall. A tired curse was muttered beneath breaths.

It was happening now—the change of the guards.

Flóki reached into his pocket, then chucked a circular object into the courtyard. It arced across the room. I only counted two heartbeats, but it felt like a lifetime had passed by the time it reached the incoming soldier. It landed with a hard bounce, rolling to a stop at their feet.

They stooped to examine it, jumping back a second too late as the object exploded in a burst of powdery white.

"Snow bomb," Flóki whispered. "More annoying than anything. Popular prank with the youth. It'll keep him busy for a second, but most importantly, it's our cover."

Following his lead, I dashed across the open space, the guard cursing and angrily waving off the flurry, and we crept through the castle. We were at the ice dungeon's stairs before I could comprehend it, as silently and smoothly as if we were nothing but a swift-moving draft.

Ice coated the steep slabs of stone, and the temperature dropped with each step.

The gaping arch of a doorway was covered in shadows so thick, the moon couldn't even penetrate the darkness.

Our shoulders grazed when we reached the landing, and we stared into the abysmal black.

Words framed the entrance, etched into the pumiced stone: *Hér býr hið illa. Gefðu gaum að sál þinni.*

"What does it mean?" I asked, barely daring to whisper.

I felt him turn to me, that preternaturally blue gaze heating my cheeks. "Here lies evil. Heed your soul."

"How welcoming," I whispered sarcastically.

"Here." He shrugged off his black bomber jacket, placing it around my shoulders. "Take my jacket. It's cold in there."

I slid my arms into the silk-lined sleeves. Rolling the cuffs five or so times so the fabric didn't devour my wrists, I drew a deep breath and tried something earnest: "Appreciate it."

"The Coffin Seeker is in the basement." My nerves twitched at the way his name rolled off Flóki's tongue, as if he weren't a devil but something to be revered. "Seven floors down. Access to his oubliette is through a hole in the ground."

"Got it." I fought to keep my voice steady.

"Take this." Grabbing a torch out of its bracket, he handed it to me.

"Thanks."

"Think of it like a practice run for Jarðarbæli. Take your time. I'll be here when you're done."

"Yeah, it's not like I'm in a rush to get out or anything," I tossed over my shoulder before crossing the threshold.

Immediately, the sphere of black swallowed me whole. It was like disappearing behind a veil; in a step or two, Flóki was nothing but the murky outline of a person—noise, details, scents, *air* were all muffled by the abyss.

I breathed in must and something… rancid. The smell turned my stomach.

The path sloped down, veering to the left and getting darker, colder—if that was even possible. I faltered down the slick staircase, fighting to keep my footsteps quiet, my breathing silent. The torch barely burned back the darkness, and I had to guess at where the next stair would take me.

After nearly half a minute, I stumbled when the pattern broke. I had reached a landing, a break in the stairs. I had made it down one level.

Six more to go. That's all there was. I could do that.

Eyes stinging from the frigid cold, I held up the burning wood, the flames dancing off the ice-bound cells. Wet cobblestone made for a slippery walk, the tips of my shoes already soaking.

Thick frozen walls separated the prisoners, the floor padded in snow that helped throw the light.

Most remained silent, but I knew I was no longer alone by the itching feeling of eyes on me. Some crowded towards the torch's flame, shedding tears, prayers, vows. Some had written final messages with their nails, old blood streaking the walls.

Nothing in here resembled elf or human. They were only the shells of their former selves—and broken ones, at that. A low moan erupted from one of the lumps shivering on a bed of hay. I kept my eyes forward, my footsteps light. Nothing good would come from poking around.

Another sigh, and the shake of metal. My traitorous eyes drifted to one of the cells.

Tattooed fingers wrapped around the steel. A lean upper body curled over knees, black jeans digging into the powder. The crown of their head rocked against the barred door, dark hair a flat curtain over their features.

The realization wrenched the air from my lungs. All feeling left my limbs.

Even my pulse was lost to the shock.
It was him.
"Ryder," I whispered.

CHAPTER 24

HIS SHOULDERS STIFFENED AT THE SOUND OF MY voice, the steel bars shaking in his pale, frozen hands.

A thin shaft of light shone through a vent in the ceiling—the only source of illumination, besides the torch in my grasp. It curved around him, casting shadows that stretched the broadness of his shoulders over the walls.

I lowered into a crouch just outside the slatted door. The hem of Flóki's jacket soaked up the dampness from the floor as my hand hovered in the space between us.

I needed to touch him. To prove he was really there.

Desire surged under my collarbone in sharp, confusing waves. It was coated with bitterness and hatred, but it pulled me in just the same. At the last second, when we were a hair's breadth apart, I snatched my hand away, thinking better of it.

Clearing my throat, I repeated his name, a touch above a whisper now. "Ryder."

A ragged exhale clouded the air in front of his lips. He barely had enough strength to lift his chin. Icicles were crystalized along his eyes. Lashes frozen together, he strained to pull his eyelids open.

How long had he been down here? *Why* was he down here?

He brought his fists to his eyes, clearing the frost. Then he looked up at me.

Gasping, I flinched back, stumbling down to a knee.

The torch slipped out of my grasp, sputtering on the cobblestone.

His eyes were black.

There was no green, no life. Just two shadowed pits. The blood drained from my face. I shot to my feet.

This wasn't Ryder, this was a ghost—a stranger.

But then again, he'd lied to me our entire relationship, so maybe this was worse.

Maybe this was the real him.

His empty stare fell to the floor, before slowly dragging up my legs, sliding up my body, the way my arms tucked under my ribs. They caught on the dip of my silk camisole, which suddenly felt paper-thin, lingering over the flush of my chest. A weak smirk pulled at his lips.

"Nice jacket, baby." That wasn't his voice, either. It was barely a grating rasp, like his vocal cords had been shredded. "Black always looked good on you."

I pulled the bomber tighter around me, but I wasn't sure who needed it more. Because a rush of that same want flared through me, burning brighter than the torch.

"What are you doing here?" I demanded. "Who told you where I was?"

Moving first up my neck, his gaze flickered over my face. I was certain he was assessing me, cataloguing all the new scars and bruises I carried.

A flash of anger twisted his features, as if he bore them himself.

"Your hair is up." Crimson stained his teeth. "You never wear your hair up."

A chill far colder than the icy air in this elven prison, trilled along my bare neck. I stumbled back, suddenly all too aware of the tension dragging us closer. "Stop it."

"What, can't I give my girl a compliment?" he said through one side of his mouth.

"Do you have amnesia?" I spat. "I'm not your girl."

His smile told me he knew, but didn't care. And that was the kind of look that made me forget what we were now: mortal enemies. I couldn't let this conversation go on—not knowing that something molten and dangerous below my belly button was dragging me closer to him, inch by inch, steadily, inexorably.

Before I could lose my nerve, I thrust my hand into my boot—fully acknowledging and absolutely hating the way his eyes followed the motion, the way his lips tugged up when my cami scooped down—and whipped out the dagger Nemuik had gifted me from my ankle strap.

Ryder only grinned when I grabbed his hair, held his face to the bars, and brought the sharp tip to his neck.

"Now tell me, *hunter,* what you are doing here before I drive this blade into your throat."

I'd forgotten how still he could become, how he could school every inch of himself until he might have been carved from stone.

"Aw," he finally cooed, those black eyes glistening up at me "Are you trying to turn me on?"

I yanked on his brown locks, hard enough that the side of his head banged against the bars. "Don't fuck with me,

Ryder." Blood trickled down his throat as I pressed the blade in. My hands shook—whether it was from anger, or fear, or something else, I couldn't say. "Answer the question."

"Fine," he croaked, that subtle lilt I used to know and love hanging in the air. "I came here for you."

My grip tightened. "Why, doing Chthonia's dirty work? Proving your brother right? You going to try and siphon my powers right here?"

"Because I can't stay away from you." He rolled his neck slowly, the blade leaving a thin red line across his neck. "No matter what I do, where I go, I can't get you out of my head."

"You already hunted me down once and succeeded," I said, my tone cooler than the chiseled ice that made up the dungeon. "Don't you have someone else to obsess over now?"

"You got away," he rasped. A droplet of blood slipped down, coating the crystal knife. "I'd hardly call that a success."

Vindication, white-hot and so intense I almost couldn't see, sliced through me. I knew it. The tattoo, the contract. That's all this was. "Then why didn't you grab me in the woods outside Crescent Rock? I know that was you."

That same deep chuckle I'd heard that night in the forest rang through his cell. It drilled into my heart, under my skin. "Too easy."

Easy? "Oh, so this is a game to you." I pushed the knife in a touch harder. His leg kicked out on reflex. I had to admit, it was nice seeing him squirm for once. "Then I'm going to make it the most difficult one you've ever played."

"Careful." Even with the pressure on his vocal cords, the word was a silky threat. "Those are the kinds of things that only make me want you more."

Lowering the weapon, I tossed him out of my grasp before the swell of emotion muddied my thoughts. He caught himself before he tumbled into the snow.

It struck me then, the conversation I'd overheard between Hildur and one of her guards—it was Ryder they had found out on the glacier. He was clearly addicted to the hunt, to the rush it provided, and I was the prey that escaped.

"I know what it's like to feel that obsession…" Running the tip of my blade just under my sleeve, I lifted the fabric until orange wisps poked out—the wings of my butterfly tattoo. It was powerless now, but a soft pulse of that fixation flared at the touch, a reminder of how good it had felt to pursue. "I couldn't eat, breathe, sleep, think—I couldn't do anything without wanting my target. I would have burned the world down to get it in my hands."

His wild eyes roved over me, landing on the weapon in my hand, flicking to my exposed skin. Turning flinty, dangerous. "So you made it." It came out as a growl. "Good girl."

I narrowed my eyes, tilting my head. "Was that your plan all along, then? Herd me to the Night Stalkers so they could do the *actual* dirty work for you?"

"I did it to protect—"

"Your famous fucking words." I tossed the dagger upwards, the blade arcing, spinning. I caught it by the handle, and I knew full well what I was doing, curving my spine like that, bending low to place the weapon in its sheath. His hungry stare traced the shape of my body. "Well guess what? I don't need your protection, Ryder."

He wanted me. Even more so now. And I'd show him what he would never get, not ever again—even if my insides

287

flinched seeing him like that, beaten and down. But why? He'd lied to me, he'd hurt my friends, he'd joined Chthonia's cause.

I picked up the torch, the flame dampened by the water, but still lit. "Now, if you'll excuse me, I have a demon to get to."

"Wait," he cried. His voice twisted upward. Needy. Pathetic. "River, please, don't go."

My name echoed through the dank halls—an endless plea that drilled into my heart so deeply, so strongly, it could have carved itself into the mossy stone walls.

I shook it off. I *had* to, or I might end up crawling into that cell with him, giving into that same raw hunger. I'd hate myself for it tomorrow. And every day after. Because this relationship wasn't *real*.

Tightening my grip on the torch, I turned the corner and entered a windowless stairwell.

The spike in confidence from seeing my ex destroyed and begging pushed me on, but I wasn't sure how long that would last.

Already, the adrenaline was waning, turning jagged and sharp. By the time I reached the next landing, it had turned on me completely—a stabbing pain in my stomach.

The second floor was an exact replica of the first. A dozen glacial cells, wet cobblestone, evil in the air.

On my left, a bulky silhouette prowled the length of its chamber. In the bleak light I swore I caught a glimpse of a flowy lion's mane, but there were too many eyes and one set too many legs and an irregular shape jutting out of their back that resembled wings.

No good would come of investigating the cells and their prisoners. I'd learned that lesson.

I hurried to the next level, flinching at the sound of my own footsteps.

Every few breaths, Ryder screamed my name, his cries getting fainter, hoarser, the deeper I went.

By the time I reached the fifth floor, the stairs were so eroded they resembled slippery ramps. The fire sputtered.

Stone crumbled beneath my damp soles, and ice crept across the floors, the bars, covering every cell with a thin, frozen film.

But it was the silence—a heavy, haunting presence—that made my skin crawl. At every turn, there it was, tickling my ear, weighing on my shoulders, touching me, even though I knew nothing was there.

I cupped a hand over my mouth and huffed out air, trying to contain the warmth against my numb lips. My shoes were a sopping mess, the liquid from the stagnant puddles seeping into the soles, drenching my socks. Freezing cold.

I finally reached the sixth floor.

Down here, I was way too scared to shine the light anywhere but directly in front of me. I didn't need to see the cells, or the walls, or what lay beyond them—I just needed to find the hole, slip down, ask the Coffin Seeker some questions, then get the fuck out of there.

It was so pitch-black, even the fire seemed to be afraid, shrinking in on itself.

Towards the end of the corridor, where the floors above had sloped to a lower level, there was a break in the ground. A hole. One that required me to climb straight down, because as the last and final level, it wasn't accessible by the main stairs.

Just as Flóki had said it would be.

I crept closer. Smeared letters on the wall spelled out *Dauða manna svæði,* then beneath it, *Dead Man's Zone.* Other messages in Icelandic had been scribbled in the same ashy ink alongside another language I couldn't place.

With a big inhale that still left me feeling breathless, I set the torch next to the rim before lowering myself. I placed one foot on a rusty rung, grabbed the light, and descended into the darkness.

The metal ladder shook under me. If I had any intention of making a stealthy entrance, it was completely shot. Even Ryder probably heard me, all those levels above. I imagined him gnashing his teeth, struggling against the bars at the idea of me coming down here.

The heat of that, at least, was a welcome flash of warmth.

Because what came next was numbing fear.

My staccato exhales echoed off the stone chute, blackness above and below. If I reached out—if I moved my head—I would strike stone.

It didn't feel real, like I was suspended in time—like I was entering a different reality.

I finally broke out of the tight, narrow space into a circular room, where the ladder stopped a few feet shy of the ground.

Even though my hands trembled, I released their grip and landed with a splash in a small pool. More mystery liquid, and bone-chillingly cold.

I held up the fire, the flames shrunken to half their original size.

Cringing, I looked around.

There were no cells here, just empty halls and thick metal plates in the ground—if this had ever been anything remotely resembling a prison, it was nothing more than crushed walls and piles of mildewed wood in the corners now.

Enormous slabs of ice jutted out of the ceiling, the undersides dripping an endless stream of water onto the floor. Brick arches crumbled between them, bearing the weight of the six levels above. No wonder they referred to this place as the Dead Man's Zone—the entire dungeon had been carved into a glacier, and this was right below. If the ice so much as shifted, whoever was in the basement was done for.

The guard's warning to his queen circled in my head. If the glacier melted, what would happen to the prisoners? Would it kill them or… release them?

A clanging noise came from above, metal slamming shut. There was only one open door I had seen on my journey: the entrance to the dungeons. My entire body stilled. Had Flóki locked me in here?

Craning my neck, my gaze pierced upwards, as if I could see through the layers of stone and into the courtyard above. Instead, I noticed crimson blotches covering the ceiling— blood.

Get out get out get out. My heart beat with the command.

Sprinting towards the ladder, I stumbled over a mound of cobblestone jutting out of the putrid water, catching myself on my knees. The torch landed on top of it, on a round iron cover punctured with four small holes. My fingers froze as I reached for the stick.

Those were air holes.

I leaned in to get a closer look at the words embossed in the metal. *Kistuleitarinn.*

This was his oubliette.

I jumped back, the frigid muck swishing at the frantic movement.

Oh my God, could he see me? Hear me? Smell me? Did he know I was in here?

A menacing curl of laughter slipped through the holes, its deep rumble shaking the ice. Flakes of snow drifted to the ground.

"Come, child. Do not be scared." The voice slithered through the chamber like the low howl of the wind on a stormy night. I could taste the rottenness of it in the air, heavy on my tongue.

But I didn't dare move.

"Your heart is beating so fast. And your blood, the way it's rushing through your veins…" A sigh tickled my spine like a sharp claw running up it. "The living body is my favorite symphony."

I flinched as if his words had touched me.

That unearthly chuckle echoed throughout the room once more. "Let me at least get a good look at you, child. I haven't come across another one of my kind in far too long."

My kind. I huffed. Source pulsed from my fingertips, sloshing water into the holes.

I crouched down for him to see. "We are not the same." My glare drilled down into the pit of black.

Shadows moved in the depths. A smoky black plume shot out, caressing my cheek. "We're more alike than you'd care to admit."

"Yeah? How so?" I brushed the wispy cloud—his Source, *him*—off of my face with a little too much force, my hand slamming into my own jaw when my fingers met only air.

"We've committed the same sin." He casually blew out the last word, as if it were the smoke of a cigar giving him a high. Dread razed my insides. "Murder is a very unique bond—very unique indeed."

"That was an accident," I snarled, the scene from that fated day at the beach when I was eight swimming into my mind. I'd worked hard on freeing myself of that guilt. I wasn't going to let this demon make me carry it again. "I got caught in a rip current and my mom swam out after me. I didn't murder her for sport."

"So, when you killed the teratorn and Finis, you did not feel an ounce of satisfaction?"

"That's different." The grate rattled beneath me. I was shaking with cold, unforgiving rage. "They were demons."

"Perhaps then, but demons are not born. They were something else before."

I swore I saw a hint of color in the darkness: the whites of eyes.

"Alright," I said, my hands dangling between my knees, getting comfortable, even if the panic was like a parasite trying to burrow its way under my skin. "I didn't make this trek for the small talk. I need something. If you can't give it to me, I'm out."

"Forgive me, my Nephilim sister. It's been so long since I had a visitor."

"Don't call me that." My nostrils flared. "We are not kin." But even as I said it, the truth festered inside of me: all demons were once angels.

He sighed. "So go on. Tell me what you wish to know."

The help I needed was right there, but another question formed on my lips. "Is this what Hildur uses you for?"

"Is that really what you care to hear? I am not amenable; it's best to be forthright."

It was a valid reminder—as human as his tone sounded, I wasn't dealing with a person. I wasn't even dealing with a ghost. I was dealing with the closest thing to the devil.

In the silence, he grew impatient. "Shall I help you decide?"

A breath of a shadow swirled up from the holes drilled into the metal plate. Billowing into color, into movement, into a vision that I recognized immediately—the one from the Pearl of Truth.

"Stop that!" I shouted as the scene enveloped me, bursting into color and reality.

Surrounded by scorched hillsides and battered elves led astray by an evil with claws and fangs, I batted fruitlessly at the smoky vision, which would not dissipate.

"You know I have the gift of Sight, but did you know I'm also a Projector? It was always part of what I did. Perhaps that makes me less of a monster? Yes… I played their favorite memories while I made mine. That's got to mean something, right?"

The vision changed into the halls of this prison, to a screaming dark-haired guy behind bars. Golden-green irises rimmed the black depths of his eyes. Ryder, on his knees. Pleading. Craving. Heat burned through me, but it wasn't him. It wasn't *real.*

"I said STOP IT!" Dozens of hairline cracks shot across the brilliant sheets of turquoise ice above me.

"Careful," he tutted, and the drawl of it threw me off guard. It was him but it was Ryder, rasping behind his iron bars. "This glacier is melting fast enough as it is."

Swatting at the air, I felt myself tip.

The ground rushed up to meet me, and my hip slammed into the metal, the sharp edge of the oubliette slicing my thigh. Red blossomed like a rose through the fabric.

A moan crept up the shaft, one of disgusting, aching want. "It's not as sweet. Not the fruity notes of elven blood," Kistuleitarinn purred, "but delicious in its own way. You taste… like power."

Grimacing, I pushed myself up. Searing pain slit my skin.

"How?" I asked, ignoring his sickening comment. "How is it that an ancient glacier is all of a sudden melting at a rate that *magic* can't stop it?"

"Is that your final question?"

No, but I wanted it to be, if only so I could leave and get as far away as possible from this godforsaken place.

Curling my fingers, I gritted my teeth. "I need to know about Jarðarbæli. Hildur is taking me tomorrow—er, today."

"Is she?" That tone made my insides twitch with unease.

"Um, yeah." I gulped. "Anyways, apparently you're the only one who's been and lived to tell the tale."

"Not the only." The shadows swirled in his pit. "But as of your generation, yes."

"Why is everyone so scared of it?" Water dripped off the ice, plinking onto the sleeve of my jacket. My angel senses homed in on every drop, almost tearing me from the conversation.

"You can guess why."

"Because it's spelled to keep them out? Because there's

an abominable snowman stalking the fjords? Because Gaia threw some caution tape up?" I crossed my arms, bearing my weight on the hip without the gash in it. "Look demon, if I knew, I wouldn't be down here."

He chuckled, and I felt the ground rumble beneath my feet. "There's a monster in that lair most simply cannot face."

"Which is?" I tapped my foot, the stale water seeping into my shoes.

"Themselves."

"Themselves?" I repeated, scrunching my nose.

"The parts of you that you bury deep down and keep hidden are the biggest threat of all." Kistuleitarinn's gravelly voice was like an icy chill down my spine. "But it secretly calls to you. All of you."

"So it's like…" Realization burned a hole in my stomach, my insides gurgling. "Facing a mirror image of yourself, but the absolute worst version? A doppelgänger?"

"See? You don't need me."

"Maybe I don't." Tension grated the air. He didn't like that response. "But Gaia did," I quickly added. "Why?"

"She wanted to know more about the Angel of Water."

"She had direct access to her."

His voice drawled through the drill holes. "The new Angel of Water."

My heart rammed against my ribs, like a caged bird trying to escape.

"So, so fast it beats," he murmured. "Noisy. Distracting. So much sweeter when they're quiet."

Gunnar's words rang through my mind. *Kistuleitarinn is a known pathological liar—among other things.* No wonder he didn't elaborate on those "other things." A shiver made its way over my shoulders. I wasn't an elf, but after so much time in that wretched hole, I doubted the demon was picky about his next victim. "Wh-what did you tell her?"

"To be worried."

An invisible weight sank into my chest, my breaths stabbing and labored. "Why?"

"Because you have something the others don't."

"What's that?"

"Free will."

It felt like a skeletal hand gripped my windpipe.

"Angels cannot give in to their desires. If they do, there is only one fate."

The Fall.

A draft blew through the dungeon, angry and biting, just like it had when I stood atop that precipice and watched them all drop.

If I listened hard enough, I swore I'd hear their hopeless screams. I saw the flailing bodies, the battered wings, the endless gray sky in my nightmares regularly—but unlike the memory in Madame Myrian's crystal ball, my mom's tortured, wind-whipped face was at the center of it all.

Because that's where fate ultimately brought her—the Angel of Water—and the others had warned her of it. Earth, Air, and… Fire.

"I know of one angel who went against duty." The name pulsed through me in a fierce wave of apprehension. Akosua. "The Angel of Fire is still walking free, and she sided with the enemy. Where's the wrath of fate for that? Did it let her off easy?"

"Desire and desperation are different things."

I blinked. Such careful, careful words he chose.

"Yes, but Finis said she willingly—"

"You, though…" Darkness danced up through the grate, unspooling and threading around me. "You are born of the stars and flesh."

I crossed my arms. "Annnd that makes me special or something?"

His shadows pulled back before billowing outward. "That makes you dangerous."

"Says the person locked one hundred feet underground."

"The Angel of Earth couldn't grant me what I wished for." The torchlight flickered as he spoke. "But maybe the Angel of Water can."

My eyes narrowed. "Which is?"

"Forgiveness."

Grabbing the torch, which was at this point little more than embers, I glanced back at the ladder, every instinct screaming at me to get out. "Forgiveness for what, exactly?"

"What I did to Gaia's scribes in that earthly lair they called a shrine."

The way he described it… Jarðarbæli was sounding less like a creepy hole in the side of a mountain and similar to my mom's shrine at Natural Bridges. Sacred.

"They all paid tribute to the Angel of Earth in that cave in the highlands," Kistuleitarinn continued, eerily on par with my racing thoughts. "Nephilim, Huldufólk."

But they didn't anymore. Why? When I finally found my voice, it was barely a whisper over the blood violently rushing to my head. "What did you do to them?"

He answered with a close-lipped laugh. "Killed them all."

Bile stung my throat.

"Count the bodies when you get there."

I stumbled back.

"The ones in the inner caverns are the worst." Wraithlike tendrils quivered at my ankles, curling. I shook them off, but they slithered right back.

"Was this before or after you turned into a demon?"

"During." He paused. "But it really sealed the deal."

"You." Slowly, I walked backwards, towards the shaft I'd climbed in from. "You're the monster—or at least, you created it, when you converted Jarðarbæli from a sanctuary to a crypt. You're the reason everyone avoids that place now."

"Most people see their mirror image as evil: the monster inside. But the Angel of Earth, she showed me goodness: a saint." The inky coils spun upwards, swelling into a funnel of wind and shadow. "What would you see?"

Darkness stirred inside me—the kind that whispered in the late-night hours, the kind that called to me when I'd opened that depthless portal to hell and sent Finis back to her dimension.

I took another step towards the exit, farther away from him. Shadows twisted around me, tickling the baby hairs around my temples and the nape of my neck. He was in an oubliette. This was just a trick—a projection. He couldn't actually do anything to me.

"Source is like a muscle," he snarled, as if he could read my mind. "It can weaken over periods of unuse, but it's still there just the same. With the right circumstances, motives, it can spring into action. And I haven't eaten in years."

Drumbeats of fear pounded with my heart.

"The remnants of my last meal are still on the ceiling. I didn't get to play with that one after. Too starved…"

I didn't look up.

"So, I say to you what I said to the Angel of Earth: forgive me." Phantom tentacles rose from the Coffin Seeker's cell. They darted for my knees, wrapped around my wrists, constricted my waist.

Before, they had seemed insubstantial as shadow, but now I could feel the strength of them, choking me, lifting me off the floor just to slam me back down, into the filthy water and cobblestone and ice.

Pain seared my spine like a bolt of lightning.

Gasping, fighting to regain my feet, I waved the dying fire in front of me. The shadows sizzled, leaping back at the contact.

Despite the trembling in my limbs, I found my way to standing.

I channeled all that agonizing energy—the scream of my lower back, the tightness of my throat, the fear of being pulled into that dark, dank cell—into the chaotic Source around me and redirected it back at him.

Clenching my jaw, I raised my arms.

Wind blew through the dungeon, knocking the shadows back to the corners of the room. The water lapped at my feet—cool liquid churning, swirling, pouring into his oubliette as if it were a storm drain.

Fingers appeared at the holes, clawing for an escape, for air. Whatever was left of the demon wheezed and gagged, thrashing and banging the sides of the underground cell. It was beautiful. Poetic. *Powerful.*

A rumble tore through the room, drilling into my ears, my bones. The glacier was shaking. A massive crack splintered a wall. I didn't stop. I wanted to be the monster, be the darkness, and I never, ever wanted to be powerless again.

Chunks of ice broke off the ceiling. The glassy shards rained down, bouncing off my head and shoulders. The floor shuddered as if the glacier were shifting.

Something rustled in my heart. A warning. If I continued, this dungeon would collapse, and we'd *both* be done for.

I released the magic with a gasp, my elbows dropping bonelessly to my sides. I stumbled back until I hit the ladder, the floor slick but free of the smelly, stagnant pool.

"No wonder…" Kistuleitarinn hacked and coughed. "I see why she keeps you now."

With one hand gripping the torch, the other a rung of the ladder, I hoisted myself up the narrow chute, not daring to look back. When I reached the next floor, I ran.

Slipping, sliding, slamming into walls.

Hair unbound, skin prickling, coat waterlogged.

I finally reached the first floor. Sprinting over the snow-padded cobblestone, the faintest whisper of my name stopped me in my tracks.

Chest rising and falling in deep, ragged breaths, I moved my chin ever so slightly, until the corner of my gaze met his.

Ryder's eyes went wide. For a heartbeat, there in the depth of blackness, I found a trace of golden green. Mouth gaping open, he moved to speak.

Maybe I was lonely, maybe I was scared, but he still ignited a wanting part of me.

I started running again, his words lost to the wind. Up the staircase, up through the bleak darkness that didn't ease or give any hint of whether I was nearing the world once more. Only then did I remember that sound I'd heard in the Dead Man's Zone, the clanging of metal—of an iron door slamming shut.

I was truly hoping I'd just been imagining things, but as I tore through the archway, frost covered everything. Still, even slipping on each step as if they'd been cut into the ice themselves, I thrust myself right up to the locked door.

I banged on the metal, screaming, cursing, my knuckles turning bloody and numb.

No one answered.

Where was Flóki?

Source prickled my skin, or maybe that was the cold cutting off my circulation.

Pressing my palms against the flat face of the door, I pushed, using every bit of strength I had left. It flung open. I bounded up and out, like a bat out of hell.

There was no one there.

I sank to my knees. Finally, I was out of that horrific pit of blackness.

The first signs of a pink dawn streaked the sky, stirring an emotion in me that made my eyes sting. I caught the silhouette of someone down the hall, drawing nearer. It must be on the hour mark exactly: the changing of the guard. I had to get out of there before anyone found me.

Spine curling, I hacked out a phlegmy cough, the gash on my thigh and the bruise on my tailbone pounding with each flex of my lungs.

I welcomed the pain, because even if I was hurting, I was alive. I was free.

Light crept over my cheeks. I inhaled the fresh air as if I'd been starved of it.

How long had I been in there for?

Bed. I needed a bed, and a bath—I glanced at the wound on my leg, already festering—and probably an antibiotic.

Shivering, sopping, I rose to my feet and walked towards the elevator.

In this part of the castle, nobody else was in sight, but I knew a piece of that haunting darkness followed me back to my rooms—and I wasn't sure if I was ready to face it.

CHAPTER 25

Searing light forced my eyelids open, the bright streaks of another icy day pouring over my face. The curtains parted abruptly as someone—tall, regal, a diadem resting between her pointy ears—pulled them open.

It took a second for my brain to finally catch up with what I was seeing.

Eyes widening, I rolled onto my back, wiping the dried drool off my jaw.

"Hildur?" I rasped, pushing up onto my elbows. "I mean, uh, Your Highness?"

"Just what do you think you're doing?" With an abrupt flick of her wrist, she opened the next set of curtains. Sunlight rushed in. "Galivanting all night long, sleeping until noon. This isn't a hotel."

Noon? I shot up, the sheets crinkling around last night's clothes.

The day for Jarðarbæli had come. "Are you taking me to Gaia?"

"Soon." Facing me, she tapped her fingertips together. Her layered gown draped off her in waves, the sage fabric pooling on the floor. "I need a favor from you first."

My chest caved. More favors. More things. The Coffin Seeker's words rang through my mind—the tone especially. *Is she?* wasn't the response I'd anticipated when I'd told him where the queen was taking me today. He knew.

With a heavy sigh through my nose, I asked, "What is it this time?"

She rested her fist beneath her chin. "There's been an avalanche."

My breath lodged in my throat. I'd taken things too far last night—the glacier shifting, walls melting as I feverishly channeled my Source, throwing all my energy into destroying the demon even if that had meant destroying the castle.

Destroying myself.

I thought I'd stopped myself in time. "What happened?"

"Those mountains along the west side of Ískastali." She tsked, flicking her fingers in their direction. "Very unstable."

"So… it wasn't the glacier?" I gulped.

She shook her head no.

All the air whooshed out of me in one relieved exhale. The next heartbeat, I was out of the bed and running towards the armoire. "Is everyone okay?"

"We lost a few honored members of the kitchen staff." Squeezing her lips tight, Hildur dabbed the corners of her eyes with a handkerchief. Emotion crept into her voice. "The Eyes have been able to dig out most of the survivors and get them to the infirmary, but we need the debris cleared before we can begin repairs."

"On it." Grabbing a fresh pair of clothes and my dagger, I headed to the bathroom for a quick refresh, not missing the way she scowled at my bloody thigh.

Pain blasted through me as I slowly peeled off my pants, the fabric sticking to the yellow crust around the gash. It needed to be cleaned, but the best I could do was a quick dunk and rinse in an already pulled—and very *cold*—bath. Helga deserved a huge tip when I finally left.

I ran the soap over my skin, cringing at the bruising. In a weird way, it reminded me of the castle. On the outside, everything seemed mostly fine. But underneath?

The Galdur should have been impenetrable, regardless of what spurred the avalanche. How long had this kingdom been pretending to be strong when it was actually wasting away? And how far gone was it? How long before the magic totally failed, the elevators dropped, the entire glacier melted, the prisoners escaped?

Dangerous thoughts—and I knew better to state them. I'd tuck this away for later.

If innocent people were in trouble, it didn't matter what caused the avalanche; I'd do whatever I could to fix it.

I snagged my towel off its hook, dripping water as I went.

Careful not to rub the wound, I pulled on some leggings and a comfy sweatshirt, loosing a breath when the fabric brushed against my tailbone, and I had to pull up my tender arms to tie my hair into a braid.

Hildur waited in the living area, the fire hissing in the hearth, casting her shadow across the floral walls.

It was hard to imagine the Queen of the Huldufólk—sparkling crown, stacks of silver on her wrists, bejeweled gown trailing behind—descending the ladder to the deepest, darkest part of the castle to seek the help of a demon who murdered her own kind.

Yet why else was the Coffin Seeker there? I wondered if he was really serving out a punishment or if she collected demons as if they were rare coins.

Last night hung over me like a dark cloud, but I pushed through it, tugging on my boots. Bitter quiet followed us as we left the room and strode down the hall.

Only when we reached the elevator and began the drop down the transparent chute did she broach the silence. "I need you to create a barrier between the mountain and the castle."

"Don't you already have something like that?" I blinked, recalling the one I passed through when I first entered the grounds. The frozen moat, the ice giants, the drawbridge. "Fortress-style?"

"Yes, but it is old, and the avalanche happened to hit a weak spot." She stared ahead.

Another coincidence. Another twist of unease in my gut.

"So… what exactly are you asking me to do? Make an indestructible wall of ice that will protect your kingdom forever?"

The car slowed to a stop, the doors sliding open. "Temporary is fine."

"You know I can't do that." Wincing, I hustled to match her long-legged strides. It felt as if I'd fallen down all seven flights in that dungeon and hit every step along the way.

"You must." She turned down a narrow staircase, her feet swift and light.

"I…" *Can't,* I started to say, but I let it drop. It was no use. It'd mean nothing to her. She didn't even have the courtesy to try and convince me, like how she'd dangled the threat of war to force me to unfreeze the moat. The options were clear: do it or get out.

As long as I needed something from her, she could ask me for anything in return.

She disappeared around a corner, her long hair whipping behind her like rose gold ribbons.

Inhaling an icy breath, I followed, the passage growing tighter, windier, the tips of my fingers skimming the wall all the way down for extra support.

My knees buckled when I reached the final step, the stairwell opening into a wide hall.

Elves scurried past me, carrying whatever they could fit in their hands: vegetables, fruits, ale, each other. I hopped over a broken oak barrel, sliding on the mushy remains of what looked to be potatoes. Fallen crates of food littered the floor along with bits of blood and snow.

Stepping over the crumbled remnants of what clearly used to be a wall, I followed Hildur out onto the grounds, the thick layer of powder crunching beneath my soles.

A group of elves gathered at the foot of the avalanche, their colorful robes a stark contrast to the harsh, white, world.

"Your Highness." An elf ran over, clipboard angled against his gut: Kristjan, the same elf who'd been taking notes at the river the day before.

The queen pulled off her leather gloves. Without a moment's hesitation, he took them and guided her to the rest of her court. I struggled to catch up, warmth coating the side of my leg—my cut was open and bleeding. Damnit.

Mounds of rock idly tumbled down the mountainside, crashing into the ground.

"What's the plan?" I heard someone ask as I awkwardly hung on the outskirts of the assembled crowd.

I brought my hand to my brows, a shield against the intense glare.

"Gods, it's even worse than I'd imagined." The queen shook off her mantle, passing it to the air, knowing, expecting, someone to grab it. They did.

A flash of gray rushed by me. Tongue out, barking. Then another. Pink nose, furry ears, blue eyes. The royal huskies. They wove between the helpers, their curled tails shaking, paws digging into the compact snow.

"The dogs are searching for bodies. Whenever they alert, the Eyes are then pulling them out." Kristjan glanced at his notes. "The kitchen staff is gathering what's left of the stockpile, but understandably, they're a bit shaken up."

"No doubt," Hildur mused.

"We started at the base of the mountain, where the snowpack was deepest and deadliest, and are making our way out."

"That area is clear then." It was never a question with the queen—because if it wasn't done yet, it certainly would be after her statement. "Just in time for River to fix the barricade."

With a curl of her fingers, not even granting me the dignity of turning her head, she ushered me forward. Like I were a puppet—and I had no choice but to follow her summons.

"Very well." She ushered Kristjan aside. "Show us the worst of it."

Cutting across the ruined grounds, we carved a path along the perimeter of dirt and snow. The hollers of the volunteers grew softer the farther we ventured along the runout zone. But the whispers, those were as loud as ever.

The advisors slowed their pace, falling behind their queen.

"When are we going to address the matter of the Galdur?" one of them pressed. "That is the real issue here. Whenever we fix things, ten more issues pop up. Are we cursed?"

"A dark shadow has fallen over the realm," another said. "Just like what happened right before the Cross-Realm War. Something is coming, even if the queen doesn't want to admit it."

"It's the Nephilim," a third spat. "Things got worse when she arrived. I swear it."

My heart twisted.

Kristjan halted at the edge of the rampart, a huge chunk of it lost to the ice. "It's best to stay here in case there are any other disturbances on the mountain, and there are sharp things beneath the surface."

"Yes, great point, Kristjan." Hildur turned, addressing the rest of us. "If the angel needs to cross over, that is fine, but we will stay here, where it is safe."

Hot air blew out of my nostrils. Cheeks flaming, I tested part of the snowy mound with my foot. It shot right through it, at least six inches deep.

Shredded rubber—a wheel—poked out of the debris. And a glistening sheet of metal. I tilted my head. "Is that…"

"A truck," Kristjan confirmed. "The service road runs, erm…ran, parallel to here."

Whoa. He wasn't kidding.

Grasping the rough edges of the blown-out wall I assumed was supposed to provide a barricade for this sort of thing, I treaded the more compact snow, slipping around to the other side.

My breath caught in my chest. A swell of fog rose from the snowpack, billowing into a sparkling cloud. Tendrils of shadow curled through the haze—traces of dark magic.

There must've been dozens of elves, both Eyes and royals, helping clear the road—the number of footprints gave that away. Why hadn't anyone mentioned… this?

Same thing as yesterday: no one had made a single comment about the black veins trickling through the frozen moat. Clearly, we weren't dealing with a natural problem. It was supernatural. Evil.

The queen was far too cunning a woman not to know that. Far too powerful a being not to notice it. What was she hiding?

I crossed my arms. The shadows trembled, gathering together like an incoming storm.

Doubt pressed in on me like a cold front, curling my spine. Sure, there'd been a handful of times I'd called upon water—but that felt more like a miracle than a testament to my magical abilities—and it was purely redirection. I'd never *created* something out of water; that sounded about as possible as pulling something out of thin air.

Fuzzy dots speckled my vision. I'd been staring at the snow for too long.

Turning away and finding—surprise—*more ice,* something caught my eye: a pair of fresh footprints, but instead of the toes heading back to the castle, they pointed in the opposite direction—towards the mountain. Strange.

Even stranger, the fog hadn't dispersed at all despite the frigid gusts rolling off the ridge, seeming to be suspended over the debris.

Someone else was out here. Maybe the one who'd caused this mess.

I glanced back at the rampart. Between the thick layers of stone and the massive mound of ice and snow, the queen and her minions couldn't see me—and I doubted they could hear me, their own conversation muffled on this side of the wall.

Squaring my shoulders, I shut out the noisy fear and followed the mysterious tracks into the heart of the mountain.

PALMS PRESSED AGAINST my thighs, I hunched over, the air thin and stabbing.

Those damn footprints had disappeared, leaving me alone and confused on a narrow path between the peaks. But, of course, only *after* I'd climbed over piles of rubble and dodged the icy rock still dropping down from the avalanche and reached an elevation where I could hardly breathe.

A draft tunneled through the pass, whistling in my ears.

I looked over my shoulder, the immediate area surprisingly free and clear of debris—aside from the small towers of rocks stacked along the cliffside, which were arranged a bit too perfectly to be a natural phenomenon.

From here, I could make out the entire lay of the land. The castle, a glistening carving of ice. The elves, nothing but specks.

The sun beat down. Sweat gathered along my forehead. I wiped my brow on my sleeve. For an arctic world, it was so *hot*.

As much as my body screamed to turn around, I spotted a shadowy alcove ahead, and I needed some shade before making that hellish trip back.

Blisters rubbing against the heel of my boot, I hobbled along the trail.

The alcove was bigger than I'd thought, a glistening hideaway carved into the side of the mountain, sheets of translucent ice creeping over the stone.

A cauldron sat in the middle. I peeked inside, relieved to find it empty.

Sticks, leaves, bits of hay and flower petals scattered the floor—remnants of a bed. I kicked an apple core, the bittersweet stench of rot tickling my nose.

Who or what had been living here?

The hairs on the back of my neck stood on end. The quiet, the stillness—it was too staged, as if someone was watching. Assessing.

As I spun around, a pair of glacial eyes greeted me from the wall. I sucked in a breath.

In a few short strides I was standing in front of them, gaze tracing the curious drawing: the sweep of their lashes, the smudged outer corners, the lines drawn in ash and paint— the same turquoise as the ice that crept over the sides and the ceiling of the cave.

I reached for the surface.

The second my skin touched the rock, those blue eyes whipped through my mind. They sat deep within the folds of an aged, wrinkled face, one I did not know, crinkled in manic delight.

I jumped back, my heart ramming against my rib cage.

A sadistic cackle ripped through the space, a harsh echo in my skull. A gust nipped at my clothes like fingers; the eyes pierced me as if they saw into my soul.

Without a second thought, I sprinted down the trail, not stopping or slowing when I slipped on the frosted gravel, not once looking back.

That creepy laugh intertwined with the howl of the wind, seeming to follow me all the way down. I paused at a lower elevation, before the path dropped nearly vertical to the base of the mountain.

The elven kingdom sparkled in the distance. That mysterious cloud still hovered above the runout zone; in the short time I'd been away, more misty plumes had drifted up the cliffside. Tendrils of them slithered into the compact snow. Fissures broke through the white surface, the outer layer of powder trickling down the slope.

Horror hit me like a bone-chilling cold. The evil magic threaded in the strange fog was going to trigger another avalanche.

I glanced at the glacier. The elves were still nowhere near done clearing the first one, and if I peered closely… the sage satin robes, the fur-lined mantle, the silver armor flocking— the queen was right in its path.

There was a bustle of movement next to her, much too animated for a guard or one of her dreadfully old court members, paired with a flash of pink hair. Freyja. No doubt Gunnar stood next to her, and Eva and Siebel and Fritz. Another person hustled towards them, her raven curls bouncing. Olivia.

Loud booms, like thundercracks, rattled the air.

The escarpment shuddered. Fragments of rock broke off the crags, tumbling towards the messy pile below.

Projecting my voice, I cupped my hands around my mouth. "Get back!"

It was no use.

Those eerie, arctic eyes from the cave zapped across my mind. A mass of ice and snow and shadow separated from the mountain and sped towards the fortress.

Towards my friends.

That witchy cackle that'd been bouncing off the pass, echoing in my mind, roared in the debris. Between one blink and the next, the second avalanche was already halfway to the bottom.

Colorful specks skittered in the distance, aiming for the castle—people had finally caught notice and started running, but it was too late.

The snow was moving like it was ravenous, too fast, too deadly.

It shot by me, spraying me with a violent wave of rubble. The ground shook beneath me, splitting the path, knocking me to the ground.

My fingers grazed my temple, coming back wet, soaked with blood.

Head pounding, vision blurred, I tapped into the only thing left—the one thing that felt like home in this iced-out world: my Source.

Readily, it flared beneath my skin, spreading to my hands, my heart.

There was no time to sit and channel correctly, no energy to spare on second thoughts. Power wrapped around my limbs, squeezing and tingling until the air left my lungs and it had nowhere to go but out.

Turning to the base of the mountain, I thrust my hands forward, transforming every bit of myself, every ounce of rage and hope and fear, into a shimmering streak of Source that shot past the sweeping snowfall and slammed into the ground.

The earth quaked. The dark magic shuddered. The service road—what was left of it, at least—parted in two, the ice folding in on itself. Everything—the frame of the truck, the boulders marking the lanes, the piles and piles of snow—was swallowed by an emerging crevasse that stretched wider, plunged deeper, each passing second.

With a final push and a broken scream, my upper body slumped over, palms meeting the frigid ground.

The avalanche plowed onwards, falling into the deep, icy pit I'd just made, narrowly missing the castle's defensive wall, where my friends had been gathered only moments before.

A white cloud pulsed up and out, billowing into the sky. My breath wisped in front of me, the cold air stinging my lungs. Gathering my senses, I slowly rose to my feet. The silence was harsh, grating, so at odds with the roar of the avalanche, as if the entire world was in shock.

Elves scurried across the yard, sneaking out from behind boulders and dips in the terrain. Fingers pointed and shouts rang out—for reassurance, for help.

A line of people slithered through the hole in the rampart, halting at the newly forged rift. Voices drifted up the slope, but they were too far away, too muffled for me to make out anything they were saying.

I slid down the last steep incline, landing on the skirt of rocks at the base, nearing the new seam in the earth separating me from everything else.

"Angel?" I recognized that pitch, that sense of disbelief lacing Freyja's tone.

"River, oh my God!" Eva's hands shot over her mouth. "Are you okay?"

"She's bleeding!" Gunnar yelled. "Can we get a medic?"

My pulse stuttered. I brought my fingers back to my temple, confirming I was very much still bleeding.

"What are you doing out there?" Freyja called.

"It isn't safe," Eva added.

Olivia rushed up to their side. "River, we're going to get you out. Are you okay?"

"Grab a ladder and line!" someone ordered as I approached.

Toes flush with the edge, I peered into the crevasse. The sleek ice walls disappeared into a pit of shadows hundreds of feet down. With an acidic swallow, I stepped back, unease lodging behind my ribs.

"I'm fine." I gave a halfhearted smile. It hurt.

Everything hurt.

Spindrift floated in the air, catching on clothes, dusting hair. The queen's lavender eyes narrowed when my gaze crashed into hers. I couldn't decipher the look, but it was something along the lines of pissed… or impressed.

Leaning onto my good hip, I crossed my arms. I'd built her damn wall, it just happened to be going down, not up. Maybe she should specify next time.

A silver ladder arced across the sky, thudding to the ground mere inches from the drop-off, right beside my feet. Royal guards hooked the ends into the snow while another one of them clambered across, the metal rocking with every determined shift of his legs.

Safely at my side, he fastened the lines, tying one tight around my waist.

Clipped in with nothing but a carabiner and a fistful of the nylon rope, I approached the first rung. Powder slipped down the steep walls, drifting into the depths of the glacier, glittering as it illuminated just how far I'd have to fall.

I gulped. Pretty soon that'd be me.

"Best to crawl," the guard grunted. "And don't look down."

Too late. Sinking to my knees, I wrapped my fingers around the rail, the aluminum rough and biting. The ladder tilted.

The elves watching gasped. Not helpful. My heart beat wildly, nearly leaping out of my chest. Gritting my teeth, I leaned in the other direction, snapping the shoddy, makeshift bridge back into place.

"Careful!" Olivia shouted.

Breathing in on a ten count, I held my chin high, and started again, avoiding eye contact with the wedge of shadows beneath me.

Wind blew through the pass, numbing my nose, my cheeks, my ears.

This was the worst, but at this point I'd do anything to leave this cursed mountain—this cursed place—behind.

CHAPTER 26

"Thank the gods you're okay." Eva wrapped her arms around me, giving me a squeeze. The air left my lungs as we tilted backwards, nothing but empty breeze to catch us as we teetered on the edge of the crevasse. "What were you doing over there? The mountain is no place to be after a slide."

"Do you want to, um, maybe…" I gestured at the rift behind me, still way too close for comfort.

"Oh!" Eva inched us back towards solid ground. "My bad. You probably don't want to be anywhere near that certain-death hole."

"Preferably as far away from it as I can get," I said with a tight smile as she finally let go and Olivia stepped in.

Linking our arms, she pulled me away from the precipice, from the gawking court.

Guards scurried by. More ladders bowed across the crevasse. The clang of metal on metal filled the blaring silence.

Olivia dropped her voice to a whisper. "Did the queen have you on cleanup duty?"

"Something like that," I mumbled back. "I saw footprints in the snow. Fresh ones."

"Footprints?" Her nose squinched in confusion.

"They led towards the mountain." I looked over her shoulder, my gaze sweeping the fragile rock face. "I had to investigate."

"Reckless River," Freyja muttered, leaning against an unscathed part of the defensive wall.

Olivia shot her a glare. "Whoever was out there could have been the cause of all this."

"Okay." Freyja dropped her heel from the stone. "And did you find anyone on your little mission, angel?"

My brows furrowed together. "No."

"That's because it was just an avalanche." The princess curled her fingers, like suddenly her nails were the most interesting thing in the world. "We get those from time to time, living on a glacier and all. It sucks, but it's a part of our life."

I loaded my chest with air, only to huff it out in a long breath. The dark veins, the shadows, the neon-blue eyes—there was nothing natural about any of it.

"What about the fog?" I challenged. "Suspended over the debris like that? And didn't you see the shadows poking through?" Turning to Olivia, I asked, my tone pleading, "Did you?"

Guilt crinkled her forehead. "I got out here too late to get a glimpse of anything."

"I know you're only part mortal, but you've heard of clouds before, right?" Freyja threw back. "I'm sure it was a trick of the light."

Royal blue flashed in the corner of my vision. "She's over here!" a voice called.

Lips pulled in a thin line, Gunnar jogged over, decked in full uniform. An elf trailed after him, white coat flapping in the wind. The medic, I assumed. I was so frustrated with the situation that I had forgotten my head was bleeding.

"Perfect timing, G," Freyja drawled.

His palm gently grazed my arm. "Hey. You okay?"

Javi's words, the same question he'd ask every time I went into sensory overdrive and my brain went fuzzy and my world went black. Before my body had started adjusting to my angel senses, before he'd ended up in a coma, that phrase used to bring me back from just about anything. I thought I'd never hear them again. They hit me like a gut punch.

I didn't have it in me to respond, so I nodded, even if the movement angrily zapped my nerves and Olivia had to steady me.

"We were just having the most interesting conversation," Freyja said.

"Conversation or interrogation…" Olivia muttered so only I would hear.

"Oh yeah?" Gunnar shifted his shoulders, colorful patches on the fabric of his uniform rippling with the movement. "About what?"

Freyja jerked her head at me in a challenge. "Go on, River, tell him what you saw."

I narrowed my eyes. Was she baiting me?

"Footprints, shadows," she went on, her tone casual as if we were all out on a leisurely lunch date and a medic wasn't blotting my temples and wiping away the dried blood. "But I don't want to steal her thunder."

Eva gnawed on her lip a safe distance away. "If I didn't know any better, I'd blame this all on Grýla."

The doctor stilled, gauze pressing against my cheek.

Freyja's attention swiveled in her direction. "Oh please, that's a folktale."

"Yeah." Eva's boots scuffed the snow. "I'm just saying."

A breeze tickled my skin, tossing my hair. If I listened closely, I swore a hint of that eerie laugh echoed across the ravine.

"Who's Grýla?" Olivia asked, and I was glad I didn't have to.

Relieving me of the pressure to my cheekbone, the medic dropped their hand and reached into their bag, pulling out an amber bottle full of sticky, yellow liquid.

"An evil witch who has a long-standing feud with the elves. Rumor has it that she used to be a queen, but now she's an ogress." Eva cleared her throat. "We used to dare each other to find her when we were little. No one did, of course—"

"I wonder why," Freyja cut in.

"Because she doesn't want to be found," Eva shot back.

"Because she's not real," Gunnar said, crossing his arms. The curve of his bicep brushed mine. "The Huldufólk have very creative ways to keep their elven children out of the caves. This is one of them."

Olivia and I quickly glanced at each other, a spark of suspicion passing between us. They had all said something similar about Jarðarbæli. But every myth had a true source.

"Regardless," Gunnar continued, "if River saw footprints, we should be investigating. No one said it had to be Grýla."

"They were probably from the victims. Or the volunteers." Freyja craned her neck in the direction where the wreckage once stood. "You saw the chaos this morning. Everyone was scrambling." She barked out a hostile laugh. "Clearly I'm a nonbeliever."

Gunnar shook his head. "Regardless of what you believe, we should still be suspicious."

"Eyes. Nephilim." A graceful purr silenced us. All faces snapped in its direction. The medic stumbled to their feet, ghost white. The queen picked an invisible string off her sleeve, even though the stitching looked perfect, intricate and shimmering. "Don't we have things to do?"

"Yes, we do." Bowing, Eva placed a hand over her heart. Her russet eyes darted to the other soldiers. "Excuse us, Your Highness."

Freyja dropped into a dramatic curtsey, shooting us a lazy grin. She and Eva stalked towards the castle, the doctor scrambling to fill their leather satchel and follow, tripping over the slush.

Olivia dipped her chin in respect. Gathering her skirts, she slid past the queen. "Meet me in the archives," she mouthed, before disappearing.

Hildur turned to Gunnar, raising a dark, arched brow. "Stelpths?"

"Your Highness." Palm flat against his chest, he shifted on his feet. "With all due respect, I think this area needs to be investigated. River saw tracks in the snow."

A thin line dimpled the space between her brows, the faintest crease of concern. "Oh?"

Gunnar nodded at me in encouragement.

"Yes," I forced out, making myself meet the queen's steely gaze. "They went up the mountain, into the crags. I lost them on one of the passes." I laced my fingers together, to stop myself from picking. Did she ever blink? "But I did find a cave. The walls were painted with eyes and there were scraps on the ground as if… as if someone had been living there."

"Grýla's lair." Letting out a curt sigh, she pursed her lips. "The youth have been sneaking into that cave since the inception of this kingdom. Eyes are on the milder side of what has been painted on its walls. You should have seen what they drew on there when I was young…" With a face like stone, she turned to Gunnar. "I hardly think some tracks in the snow and childish vandalism are enough to bring about a search party—"

"There's more." I stepped forward.

Expectation charged her stare.

"There was this… fog."

"Yes, snow and dust particles. Very common after a slide."

"No." I shook my head. The queen opened her mouth to insert another chiding comment, but I quickly continued, and she snapped it shut. "This was suspended over the rubble. It didn't disperse or drift away. Parts were dark and smoky, like a storm cloud. And if I'm being honest, I saw something equally weird yesterday. There were these… black veins in the frozen moat."

She waved a hand. "Well, if that were true, *everyone* would've seen it." The curved pads of her shoulders lightly shook off a chill, but I knew she wasn't cold. As a citizen of the glacier, she'd witnessed the iciest parts of this world.

What I'd seen struck a chord. And if *she* was nervous… I tugged on my collar, anxious heat swarming the back of my neck.

Dropping my voice to a whisper, I added, "I don't think this was an avalanche. I think it was an attack."

With the way her nostrils flared, it was obvious a part of her thought that, too. The real question was whether she'd confront it or continue to ignore it, like all the other broken parts of her kingdom.

"Very well." A breeze wove through her long strawberry hair. "Stelpths, gather a troop. Be discreet. We don't need everyone knowing about this."

"Yes, Your Highness."

The queen rounded on me. "Is that it, Angel of Water?" She tilted her head. A command gleamed in her bright eyes.

"Yes," I lied. That menacing, ancient laugh still echoed in my mind.

Her gaze narrowed, as if she could hear it, too.

"So, that favor of mine." I pursed my lips. "Can we mark it complete?"

"You ruined my road," she muttered under her breath, passing me with a thick swish of her skirts.

I bit back a satisfied smile. "Would you prefer that or the castle?"

Shaking her head, she strode to the elves installing the ladders, her nosy court flocking to her side.

Gunnar gently nudged me with his elbow. "Dude."

I turned to the elven guard, the muscles in his jaw tight. "Dude what?"

"Now that you're safe and bandaged up, I have a bone to pick with you." He pointed at the snowcapped rocks, finger stabbing the air. "You went up into the highlands, alone?"

"Yeah? I was saving your kingdom." I crossed my arms, holding them as if that could hold all of me together.

He closed the short distance between us, powder wafting from each strong thud of his boots. "You could've easily gotten lost, killed by another slide, or entered the wrong cave and been a troll's lunch."

"You're being dramatic," I said. The scent of him, open tundra and roasted chestnuts, swirled around me as he stopped just shy of my chest. "You said yourself you used to go up there and explore. What's the difference?"

"I'm an elf. I was born in this land," he gritted out. I watched him try to rein in whatever temper had bubbled up. He drew in a deep breath, his eyes softening. "I know every nook and cranny, story and spirit of those mountains. Most importantly, I know when to stay back."

Our pupils locked. "The queen made it seem like it was no big deal."

"Of course she did. It's *the queen.*"

Fair point.

"When are you going to stop treating me like a kid?"

"When are you going to stop being so reckless?"

For ten rapid heartbeats, we glared at each other, tension coiling in my stomach, in our shoulders, in the air. There was something on the wind, something electric, as if lightning might strike at any moment.

"People care about you," he finally said, a ragged jumble of words. "You're what we call a *skært ljós.*"

"What does that mean?" My voice was no more even.

"Someone that makes things better. Literally, a… bright light."

My chest went tight. It was beautiful and thoughtful, and I was a storm cloud; I was rain and thunder, not sunshine or a cloudless day. But I quickly said, "You're right. I'm sorry."

Immediately, his forehead smoothed. "Next time at least call for backup. We're trained for this. We can help."

A rogue snowflake landed on his lip. Fists tight at my sides, I resisted the urge to wipe it away. Metal splitting wood pierced the silence—people rebuilding, although for a second, it had felt like just us in our own little snow globe.

"Right." Gulping, I took a shaky step back. The shrill buzz of an electric saw drilled into my ear. "Next time, I'll ask."

Cheeks heating, I spun around, my insides somersaulting. My foot skidded, and I tumbled to the frosted ground, ass hitting the ice first. Ow.

Gunnar moved with shocking speed, at my side before I could blink. One firm hand steadied my shoulder; the other pulled me up.

Another gentle touch. More undeserved kindness. And my pulse, racing again.

"You good? Should I call back the medic?"

"Yeah, yes." I nodded, lungs working to catch the wind that'd been knocked out of them. "I mean no. Train with you soon? Later? Tomorrow?"

When he didn't answer quickly enough, and his brow only quirked, eyes skimming my face like they were holding a different question, the heat caught up to me, and I stumbled out of his hold.

Grasping the rough wall for support, I scurried away.

Okay. Sure, I think he said, but his voice was muffled by the construction, the commotion and, loudest of all, my pounding heart.

CHAPTER 27

I KEPT MY HEAD LOW AS I STALKED DOWN THE HALL, evading the looks of curiosity, the fists pounding against hearts in honor, the sneers of mistrust—few of those, luckily, but that was due to the fact that everyone was in the northern part of the castle, helping with the avalanche.

A young elf sprinting by had been nice enough to direct me to the archives, where Olivia told me she'd be. I *thought* I was heading in the right direction—nothing looked familiar.

I traveled up a spiraled staircase, pale light shining through the window slits.

The paintings lining this corridor were darker, more sinister. Fallen soldiers, contorted creatures, deathly stares frozen in time with eerie accuracy.

A set of silver-edged doors waited at the far end. I swallowed, the air stale and scratchy. Sputtering torchlight cast shadows over the tales of battle and blood etched into the wood.

Gut twisting, I reached for the handle. The metal was cool against my palm as I pushed the doors open, holding in a cough at the powerful whiff of must.

Darkness spilled out, heavy on my skin.

"Olivia?" I squeaked.

I wavered on the threshold, the cold curling out from the depths, before stepping in.

A bob of light flickered on—Galdur. It hovered near the ceiling, washing the room in a yellow light. Long, wooden tables filled the immediate space, matching chairs tucked in.

I took another step, which triggered more elven magic, revealing rows of metal cabinets stuffed with boxes of files that traveled further back, into the pitch-blackness.

The archives.

It was so quiet, so still that even the soft pad of my steps echoed through the circular foyer. But none of that was what took my breath away.

All along the curved walls, the domed ceiling, the floor, everything was covered in a vibrant mural. The carvings on the doors were nothing but a window to the story painted here: the whole history of the elves almost coming alive through the stone. Such raw emotions were etched onto the faces of the beings: elves, angels, demons, wolves, dwarves.

They were so lifelike I felt like a voyeur, their eyes weirdly following me as I ventured further into the room. My feet itched to step over them, as if I were walking over a grave.

"Olivia?" I said again. No answer.

A fabric-bound book lay open on a table. I strode over— my eyes catching on a thick silver band glinting against the wood next to it: a ring. Someone must've accidentally left it, I thought as I looked down at the page, where a hungry open maw waited and a dozen eyes stared back at me.

With a mane of hair, long muscular body, large head, round ears, and wide muzzle, the creature reminded me of a lion, but at some point, during its creation or perhaps after, something had gone very wrong.

A leg, hoofed and limp, grew out of its chest. Two more hung off the sides of its gut. A feathered pair of wings jutted out of its back, the tips extending past the title.

Jelmadag, it said. I flinched, as if the grayscale animal—monster? demon?—drawn onto the paper could snap its jowls at me.

There were details, formulas scribbled along the edges of the pages, and blocks of text beneath the creature's giant paws. I wasn't sure what any of it meant. Everything was written in a different language.

Prickles swept over the scars on my shoulder blades, a faint inkling of déjà vu.

Where on earth would I have seen this thing before? I racked my brain for a memory—a drawing, a dream—and came back with nothing.

"River?"

I spun around, tailbone digging into the edge of the table, foolishly looking at all the hyperrealistic faces on the ground before settling on the familiar one of my old therapist. "You scared me."

"I'm sorry." Olivia's eyes flared with curiosity—or maybe it was concern. "I went to my rooms to freshen up. I thought you might…" Her gaze roved my bloody outfit. I tucked a strand of hair behind my ear, my skin getting hotter, itchier, every drawn-out second. "Do the same."

"Oh. That would've been smart." I brushed my fingers against my temple, the light touch sending searing pain to the bone. "Ow."

"Don't touch it." She held a stack of folders against her chest. "We'll make this quick so you can make a pit stop at the geothermal pools."

"Great idea," I mumbled.

"How are you holding up otherwise?" The gossamer layers of her burnt-orange dress spilled over the floor art like rays of the sun.

"I—" I started, the painted eyes, the cackle, the magic from the cave flashing through my head. "I'll survive. But... something doesn't feel right. I don't think that was a natural disaster—I mean, you heard what I told Freyja. There was this thick fog, and tendrils of shadow running up the mountain. I saw the same thing yesterday in the frozen moat. It looked like dark magic."

"Did you relay this to the queen?" Olivia emptied her arms onto the table, the thick files thudding on the wood.

I rested my elbows on the surface. "I tried, but you know how she is."

"Defensive."

"Dismissive." Despite being alone, I lowered my voice. "What if it was Grýla?"

"The ogress?" she said, flipping through her materials.

I nodded. "The queen called the cave I found on the mountain *Grýla's lair.* And I know everyone said she was a myth, but every story around here seems to hold quite a bit of truth."

"A long-standing feud with the elves is one thing, but if Grýla is real and caused that avalanche... she didn't aim to break a few things. She aimed to kill." Olivia pulled a crinkled sheet out of a folder and set it down in front of us. "Let's come back to that. I found something."

Peering over her shoulder, I skimmed the numbers, the illegible comments scribbled into neat rows. "What is it?"

"Incident reports for their Galdur." She ran a finger along the date column, thin coils of raven hair framing her face. "The earliest recorded event is a century ago, near the end of the Cross-Realm War."

Brows pinching together, I scanned the top of the paper. She was right.

"There are no details around what happened exactly, but the issues get worse over time." More paper, more records, slipped out of the folder. "This isn't normal. Magic can grow weaker with disuse, but that's not what's happening here."

The memory of the Coffin Seeker's cell came on so strong I could feel that whisper of cold running up my spine. *Source is like a muscle. It can weaken over periods of unuse, but it's still there just the same.*

Olivia tucked her knuckles beneath her chin. "This whole kingdom is run by magic. And it's breaking."

"What would cause it to do that?"

"I don't know."

I chewed on the inside of my lip. "How do we figure it out?"

"It's got to be somewhere in here." She gestured to the rows of shelves that led into the darkness, then said nothing more, the shuffle of papers and the quiet hum of silence falling over us.

He'd been right, the Coffin Seeker.

He'd known Hildur wouldn't take me to Jarðarbæli today. I cleared my throat, fighting down the creeping burn. What else had he been right about?

As I considered this, my attention fell on the portrait of the lion-monster, its twelve eyes staring back.

"What's that?" I asked, chin nodding in its direction.

Olivia glanced at the open page. "A jelmadag. A demon."

Unease pinged through me. I fought the urge to slam the book shut, as if the illustration needed to be contained.

"Did you stop by before you went to your rooms?" I asked.

"No." Hunched over the table, Olivia stilled. "I thought you'd been looking through that book…" Her spine slowly unfolded as she stood upright.

"Definitely not." I shook my head. "Who else would come here?"

"Well, there are scribes, but they're usually sorting, not reading, and certainly not during a crisis." Her eyes narrowed. "Let me take a look at that."

I grabbed the book's worn corner and slid it towards her, the frayed red cover swishing against the wood.

The air around us grew heavy, haunting, a cold draft sweeping through.

She flipped to the front, the paper thin, nearly translucent.

"This is a grimoire." She turned the page to a table of contents. "With instructions on how to summon and banish demons, spells to contain…"

"That's—I'm sure it's—" I stammered. "Someone was probably just curious. Or maybe it was for a class? Demonology for Beginners?"

A muscle in her jaw ticked. "People don't normally look

up how to summon demons out of pure curiosity. And any professor would be a fool to teach them how."

"Maybe they were looking to, um, put one back?" It was a useless suggestion to cover up what we were really feeling, and we both knew it. "One that slipped through the wards?"

Angling the book towards me, she asked, "Remind me, what page was this on when you got here?"

I flipped through the first half, the entry lying somewhere in the middle. My heart raced at the chapter headers flashing by: *How to Conjure, How to Bind, Realm Walking, The Nature of Demons, The Witch Trials, Relationships with Mortals, The Devil's Contract...*

I slowed when I reached *The Encyclopedia of Demons (Condensed)*, creatures with too many limbs and claws and fangs getting even scarier, toothier, the further I went. Finally, the lionlike silhouette of the jelmadag appeared.

I positioned the book towards Olivia. "What does it say?"

With a tight inhale, she began reading.

"Among the most formidable entities in Chthonia, the jel-madag stands as a paragon of predator and prey. Manifesting with the majestic build of a lion, subtle marks of its inverse—the lamb—are scattered over its body, usually in the form of an extra leg, hoofs, ears, or snout."

Palms clammy, I twisted my fingers together, the shadows seeming to listen and creep closer.

"This lesser demon comes from the same classification as a hellhound, riding into battle alongside the Scale of Six. Its mane burns with a hellfire that can never be extinguished, and its dozen eyes mimic the swirling depths of the Abyss. The jelmadag's claws can pierce stone and bone. And its head swivels like a

serpent, elongating as it hisses a cloud of steam so hot it can melt skin. It is the opposite of its Empyrean origin—a griffin—in every way, aside from its wings. The feathers slowly fall out over the course of eternity."

Olivia blew air out of her lips, scanning the text, speaking quicker. "Okay, let's see… *Mortal weapons cannot breach its barbed fur…*" Pointer skimming the page, she jumped to another section. "*There are four in existence…* Hold on, there's an addendum. Huh." She met my gaze. "One went missing during the Cross-Realm War."

My hand flew to my chest, as if it could stop my heart from dropping. That sweeping rush of familiarity shot through me once again.

"Where would one of those be after all this time?" she wondered out loud.

"Olivia, what do you know about the ice dungeons?" The question burned in my throat.

She studied my face. "Not enough, it seems."

I'd been holding back, but right there, I broke. The tavern, Flóki, the Coffin Seeker, *Ryder,* the fire nymph trapped in my hearth; every secret I'd been keeping close spilling out.

And as I spoke, Olivia listened—like we were back in her cozy office in Santa Cruz, me sprawled in that leather chair and her sitting across the room, cool and composed.

"First of all," she began after my words ran their course like a rainstorm, "I will ship you back to California and deliver you to Corbin myself if you ever step foot in that dungeon again."

Despite it all, a smile lifted the corners of my lips. Forget Kistuleitarinn, I knew the real reason behind her fiery order, and it had nothing to do with the demon—it was Ryder's knuckles wrapped around the cold bars, strands of his dark hair iced against his forehead. It was his voice, a weaker, more desperate version of the real thing…

I could see it. Hear it. So, so vividly. If I went down there again, the worst monster of all might be let out. Him. Me. *Us.*

"Speaking of…" The lines furrowing Olivia's forehead smoothed out. "How's your dad?"

"He…" The question snapped me out of the dungeon, bringing me back to the archives. "Shanley's been covering for me. He doesn't know I'm here."

"River." Her face fell. "How'd you get to Iceland, then?"

"Savings and a cheap last-minute flight."

"What about summer school?" Suspicion cast off her in waves. "The semester doesn't end for another few weeks."

"Failed." That one stung. "Again."

Tucking her lips inward, she shut her eyes, and I could almost see her arranging her thoughts. "When you get back to Santa Cruz," she said finally, opening her lids, her gaze a burning midnight, "things are going to change."

I nodded, picking at my cuticles, fixing my attention on the dried skin. Anywhere but her face, draped with disappointment.

"I'm serious, River." Very much a *look at me tone,* so I did. "You know, at first…" She tapped her fingers against the table. "I was going to say this is an elven problem—that our focus should be on getting you to Jarðarbæli and being on our way."

"And now?" My heart skipped.

"And now… If the Galdur fails completely—which, by the looks of these reports, it will—and this glacier melts and the things in that dungeon get loose…" She chewed on her bottom lip. "That spells trouble for all of us."

"So, what do we do?" I pressed down on my knuckles, focused on the slight pressure.

"I think we need to confront the queen. But we need more evidence. In the meantime"—she whirled on me—"go to the pools, wash off and heal up, and maybe think about calling your dad?"

Horror seized my face; I could only imagine the look. *Call him?* I blinked.

"Text?" she amended. "Fine, I won't push it." Her cheeks tightened with the trace of a smile. "I'll meet you for breakfast first thing tomorrow. Demons, ogresses, doppelgängers," she tsked. "I'm about to pull an all-nighter."

"I'll bring you a midnight snack." My stomach gurgled. "Milk and cookies?"

"Okay, sure, but in this case, self-care comes first." She shooed me, flapping her hands until I hustled past her.

After crossing the elaborate fresco—the faces stamped by my dirty soles—I paused at the door. "Are there any spells in there for summoning a massive swell for surfing?"

"I'll check." Setting a pair of glasses on the bridge of her nose, she peered at me over the cat eye frames. "That your final request?"

"Are you open to more?"

Her eyes crinkled, her whole face softening. "Go."

Biting back a smile, I crossed the threshold, the golden light from the archives pouring into the stone hall. As I briskly walked down the spiral staircase, with no one to talk to, my thoughts ran wild with questions, with theories, with *hunger.*

When was the last time I'd eaten?

Pushing that nagging ache aside, I let another force drive me before I ended up in the pantry: intuition. It guided me like the magnet of a compass, pointing towards the ground level—below it.

If I really wanted answers, I had to look for them. They wouldn't be stuffed between the pages of an old book. They'd be kept out of sight, in a place deemed untouchable, dangerous, an area no one dared to go. I reached the landing. All remained quiet, still. The gut-rumbling chime of a clock rang out, signaling the start of the hour.

I had to do it now—when the events from this morning still turned conversations, still demanded the support of every quick-moving hand—but mostly because not knowing was even more dangerous than taking the risk to find out. And I was convinced the queen was holding that missing jelmadag.

Slipping through the unusually empty courtyard, I kept close to the shadows cast by the afternoon sun dipping below the castle's skyline.

A tendril of heat crept up from a stairwell, the salt-infused air heady, beckoning. If I were smart, I'd follow it down to the healing pools, but I wasn't craving calm, warmth.

I was craving cold, darkness, and most of all, answers. So, I left the geothermal sanctuary behind, cutting across the atrium until the slick concrete steps rose from the ground.

Shutting out the fear, the doubt, the silhouettes moving in my peripheral, I descended into the dungeon before the change of the guard was complete. At the foot of the stairs, I snatched the torch from its bracket and disappeared behind the veil of blackness.

CHAPTER 28

THIS TIME, I KEPT MY FEET QUICK. I DIDN'T SPARE curious glances—not even as a weak gasp rose from a familiar corner, as my name left familiar lips. That undeniable pull wrapped around my heart, attempting to drag me into the shadows. To him.

"River," Ryder croaked. "You came."

My feet tried, unwittingly, to stop in front of his bars. Out of the corner of my eye, I caught a glimpse of him, nothing but a pathetic heap on the iced-out cobblestone.

Something in me stirred.

I knew I was playing with fire, and it took everything to stay away from him.

A deep roar rumbled through the dungeon, and a draft, like hot, acidic breath, tossed my hair. It was terrifying, but at least it drew me away from the most dangerous part of this prison—Ryder's cell.

"Wait," he pleaded, his silhouette shuffling towards me. "Don't go!"

My free hand squeezed into a fist.

Unlike when I'd trekked all the way down to the Dead Man's Zone, this time I only had one more floor to go. Puffs of frosty vapor rose off the stone, enveloping the tunnel in a haze. A strange sense of *knowing* beat beside my raging heart, a rush of déjà vu prickling my skin as I entered the second level.

I held the torch farther out in front of me, the flames illuminating rows of wet cages.

The vapor was thicker down here, a dense fog. Weirdest of all, it was scorching. Maybe that's why there was so much putrid water covering the floor, it wasn't fog at all—it was steam. Traces of it wafted through the thin slits of the cell on my left.

I dared a step closer. I barely dared a shaking breath.

The whites of glassy eyes reflected in the torchlight. So many—too many. They all surveyed me, tilting at angles not humanly possible.

My heart sputtered in my chest.

The jelmadag.

It huffed hot air out of its wide, flat nostrils, jolting me back with the stench of rotting meat. Sweat trickled down my hairline, gathered at my temples.

I'd been right.

"What are you doing here?" I whispered, rolling to my tiptoes, holding up my light to try and see farther into its chamber. The demon hissed, its back curling up like a threatened cat, lips baring fangs that were sharp and dripping.

"Stop." The command swept through the chamber, deep and grating, masculine.

I spun around. No one was there. It was just me, and the dozen-ish eyes of the jelmadag, watching. A manifestation of my own fears permeating the silence, then.

Holding up the torch once more, I paced the length of its cage. The frame of a muscular body, the delicate outline of wings, flickered in the dim light.

A flowing mane mimicked the lick of flames, streaks of blue glinting against the dark strands.

It lunged, ramming its shoulder against the door. Breath catching in my throat, I jumped back. Something swung from the demon's chest, clanging against the metal—a hoof.

My dagger was heavy on my waist.

"Don't you listen?" A growl rattled the ancient bars. "I do not wish to be put on display."

Stomach twisting, I mustered up a response. "You can talk."

The jelmadag grumbled, retreating deeper into his icebox.

"I don't know why I thought…" *You were a feral beast* might get me mauled, so I settled for, "Sorry, I just wasn't expecting a response."

He curled into a ball of shadow on the floor. Throaty exhales rumbled in the air. My cue to go—but I didn't.

"Are you sleeping?" I whispered.

"Are you leaving?"

Fingers curling around the thick iron, I leaned into the door. "Who put you here?"

"Fate." The demon whipped his barbed tail, a flash of midnight against sparkling glacial walls. I shivered at the red streaks staining what should have been a sheet of white, at the pieces of bone bouncing off the stone when his heavy, cat-like appendage thudded to the ground.

A formidable creature, indeed. What else had the grimoire said—besides that he was basically a killing machine?

Part lamb, mostly lion, four in existence, one missing from the underworld…

"The book… it said you were missing."

A satisfied chuckle lilted through the space like a cathedral's copper bells. "They're writing books about me now?"

"Did the queen put you here?" I asked. "After the Cross-Realm War?"

That random lamb leg kicked aimlessly, more of a twitch. "The Queen of the Huldufólk is merely a device for fate."

As his wings fluttered closed, a feather slipped loose, adding to the piles scattered over the stone. *It is the opposite of its Empyrean origin—a griffin—in every way aside from its wings. The feathers slowly fall out over the course of eternity.*

One drifted near my feet, the edges serrated and sharp like the tip of a blade.

"Get that light out of my face." Three bright, intelligent eyes cracked open, narrowing in on my chest. "And those fingers out of my cage."

"Sorry." I snatched my hand back, angling the torch away from the cell with the other. "I can't see you without it."

"I do not wish to be seen."

I squinted into the enclosure. His body blended into the darkness seamlessly. I wasn't sure what compelled me to stay. Curiosity, recklessness. Loneliness.

Keeping Kistuleitarinn locked up was questionable, but his gifts did give the kingdom an advantage, I guessed. But this beast? What reason to hold him captive if he was just going to stay locked in a basement, wasting away in the corner of his cell?

It's not like the jelmadag could be rehabilitated. Evil was

in his DNA. If he ever escaped… it'd be not only a threat to Hamarinn, but a danger to the realm, like Olivia had said.

Hildur had the means to banish this being back to his home dimension. Why not do it, then?

Shadows from the burning torch danced across my wrist. I stared into the flames. There were others in this castle with no means of escape. Other captives. Other cages.

I must've said that out loud because the jelmadag answered, "Power doesn't always come from virtuous means."

The stick trembled in my hand. "The queen is using you to strengthen her powers? Why, because her own is dwindling? Are you loyal to her?"

His jowls parted on a toothy yawn. The force of it blew my hair back. The fire sputtered. My nostrils burned. "I am loyal to no one here."

"Then what happens when the Galdur fails? Will you…" I gulped. "Eat everyone?"

"Unfortunately for me," the creature said, rolling onto his back, all four paws, and that awkward hoof, dangling in the air, "she's discovered a solution to keep it running at the bare minimum."

"How? Collecting beings like yourself?" Anticipation ran through me. "Then what does she do with you?"

A sleepy growl rumbled in response. "You ask a lot of questions. If it wasn't obvious, I would like to be left alone."

My head slumped. "Sorry."

"You needn't say it again."

"Sor…" I cut myself off, the distinct sound of claw scraping stone bringing my shoulders to my ears. I peered down the hall, into the gloom.

The chill I'd been fighting snaked up my spine. "You're still standing there."

Resisting the urge to apologize, I twisted the hem of my shirt. "Leaving now," I said, not interested in learning what else lurked beyond the veil of ice and shadow.

I backed away, the outline of the cell fading into the blackness as if it never existed, as if it were nothing but a forgotten corner in a moldy basement.

Only when the ground began to slope, taking me to the upper levels, did I turn forward.

The energy hit me immediately—a dozen vicious gazes striking me like harpoons. I glanced over my shoulder, the torch juddering in my shaky hand.

A voice lilted through the chamber. "We're all prisoners here, one way or another. A lack of chains doesn't equal freedom."

The jelmadag's parting words hung in the air, haunting me with those invisible stares all the way up the ramp. Even when the first floor appeared through the archway ahead, I could feel them, hear them, my gut a pit of wild nerves.

As the next cellblock popped out of the void, the faintest hint of illumination streaking through the overhead grates, I couldn't help but feel like one of them. My cell just wasn't four glacial walls. It was worse.

It was the illusion of freedom.

The queen's favors, her excuses, the room on the top floor... *We're all prisoners here, one way or another.*

Low wails drifted into the corridor, their familiar timbre tickling my ears. I kept my head straight, kept my feet moving, but the mere proximity of him seemed to wrap around my senses, grabbing me by the chin, saying, *Look at me, baby, look at me.*

I halted in the middle of the walkway.

A jolt of something beautiful, something dangerous, pulsed in my chest. All of a sudden, it was as if gravity shifted. All of a sudden, I was in front of his cell.

Ryder. He was right where I left him. On his knees, his head bowed, hair frosted. Stiller than a statue, reverent even, as if he were in deep, dutiful prayer.

I had to fight every impulse not to wrap my hands around the bars, not to push the icy locks out of his face.

"You're back." His voice was so weak. So quiet.

"Seems I am." I ran the back of my finger along the iron door, the metal clinking under my shaky hand.

Shadows cast out from his spine, stretching along the length of his cell, flittering in the hollow draft, wing-like. He raised his chin, gaze locking onto mine. Those electric-green eyes, the ones I dreamed about, were still devoured by emptiness, his black gaze chilling me.

Placing his palms on the frozen ground in front of him, he lurched forward, his shoulders rippling, in a slow, desperate crawl. "Did you come to help me, baby?"

I bristled. There was so much desire under that whine, so much need in those trembling muscles. Tendrils of those same, messy feelings twirled in my stomach. Clenching my fists at my sides, I tried to hold them in, but he made it impossible, even if I knew this was all a ploy.

"Please, baby."

Fucking. Impossible.

A heady rush of air and emotions rustled my lungs. This wasn't a good idea. Not at all.

Muffled laughter echoed off the icy walls, barreling under my skin. "What?" he said between laughs, "Are you scared of me now?"

"You killed people at Crescent Rock," I said, tone lined with steel. "Of course I am."

"Wasn't me. Although my hands make steady work of my enemies." He broke off to catch his breath, his teeth flashing a predatory smile. "Would you like to see what I can do with them?"

Upper lip curling, I tightened my grip around the iron separating us. The door rattled. "In your fucking dream—"

A whistle wove through the air. The pitch was weak, wary, but shrill enough to run a sheet of goosebumps over my arms. Unsheathing the dagger from my waist, I whirled around, the soles of my shoes scuffing the cobblestone.

No one was there.

The crown of Ryder's head bumped the door.

Twisting to glance back down at him, my eyes caught on the sleek curve of my crystal blade.

"That's right," I whispered. I turned the silver handle over, weighing the weapon in my palm. Mined by the dwarves, it held a unique sort of magic: sniffing out the wielder's enemies with a single drop of their blood.

Lowering to a crouch, I set the torch on the ground. I took in Ryder's ripped black shirt, the bluish tint to his skin—bordering on hypothermia—the swell of his pants. Batting my lashes, I matched his desperation.

This was a game two of us could play.

"Come here," I purred.

He moaned, lifting his chin to meet my stare, exposing the pale column of his throat.

Before my courage failed me, before he could stop me, I shot my fingers through the space between the bars and with a speed I didn't know I possessed in this freezing cold, wrapped them around his nape.

He didn't resist, falling forward limply as I jerked our faces together between the iron, a hair's breadth of icy air the only thing between us. His breath danced over my lips. For a heated moment, we held there, inhaling each other.

Then I brought the knife to his neck.

"Again?" He chuckled, and it held no ounce of warmth. "You going to kill me this time?"

"No." I dragged the sharp edge over his vein. "I want my blade to memorize the taste of your blood."

"Because you can't stay away from me either. Admit it." The words were ragged.

"Because you're my enemy." Red carved down his skin, pooling at his collar. "And I want neither one of us to forget it."

"Who is this girl?" Air hissed out through his teeth. "I like her."

"Yeah?" Pursing my lips, I slowly shook my head. "You can't have her."

Darkness flickered in his eyes. "Get in here," he growled.

I tilted my head, nose grazing his. I tried to hold in the way my body trembled at the feel of his skin against mine, pushing the poison back into my voice. "What for?"

"So I can destroy you or devour you." His hand fell below his belt, adjusting. "I'm not sure which one yet."

"Tempting." Dropping the weapon, I pressed my thumb against his blood, slick on my fingerprint. His moan danced against my throat, a warm blast of air. "But no."

Still, I couldn't deny the heat creeping into my lower belly. We were close. Too close. I quickly backed away seconds before he snatched the bars with hands that, moments before, he would have wrapped around my neck.

"River!" he snarled, cheekbones pressed against the iron, the veins around his eyes turning black. "Don't walk away from me."

I bent to pick up the torch.

"Please." A tired gasp left his lungs, his tone losing some of its sharpness. "Don't leave me. Please."

I debated it. For a few heavy beats, I stood in that dank, haunted, prison thinking about what it would be like: to truly touch him again, to hold him again, to bust him out of that cell.

The dagger whistled softly, reminding me of the grim reality: he'd left me. Betrayed me. Ruined me.

Shutting out his cries, I stormed to the exit. This time, I didn't look back.

CHAPTER 29

MY BLOODIED CLOTHES DROPPED TO THE FLOOR with a whisper.

I stuck my toes in one of the geothermal pools to test out the temperature, steam rising between the stalactites.

With my mind swimming elsewhere, it was hard to enjoy the serenity of this place: Ryder only a floor beneath me, the impending war, the queen's use of the demons in her efforts to gain back her power—her secrets.

If the entrance to this salt-licked cavern hadn't sprung up first, I would've continued on my path to the archives. But as those tendrils of heat wafted up the stairs, the calling to relax and freshen up outweighed the urge. Plus, Olivia needed her space to do her research without me constantly interrupting—which I planned to do later, after I rinsed off, napped. Healed.

Slowly, I eased into the pool until I was up to my neck, the white muddy bottom soft and squishy beneath my feet.

Taking a deep inhale, I dunked. The water swirled around me, wrapping me in its velvety warmth, washing away the blood.

I bobbed to the surface, my body feeling lighter, thoughts clearer. Arms floating at my sides, I dipped my head back, and drifted.

If I just stayed there, Ryder's touch might rinse off my skin. If I just stayed there, the silica-rich lagoon might swallow the crushing anxiety—another thing I was prisoner to.

Water splashing against my cheeks and rippling in my ears, I closed my eyes and let it all float away, until my nerves finally untangled from the ball they'd been wound in.

The call of sleep had my heart beating steadily…

"Enjoying your dip?"

Choking on a gasp, I thrashed to my feet, keeping everything from my upper chest well below the waterline. "Oh my God!"

Flóki's bloodred lips curved into a menacing grin. "Interesting thing to say."

"What?" I spat out, along with the gritty liquid that had flooded my mouth.

His gaze moved from my face to my exposed collarbone, dropping even further, fixated on something beneath the surface. I sunk lower. "Didn't they teach you not to say that name in vain?"

"You know what's *interesting?*" Despite being fully submerged, my arms shot across my chest. "Locking me in a dungeon full of demons."

"There are standard inmates in there, too." That smirk, that chuckle. It was all too sinister, all too *familiar.* "Anyway, I must have forgotten that door automatically locks."

Even surrounded by the heat, I shivered. "What do you want?"

"This is a public place." Fingers latching onto the hem of his shirt, he pulled it over his head, pale muscles flexing, marred with scars and tattoos.

I stilled.

He gripped his waistband. "Do you mind?"

Breath catching in my chest, I spun around. The *clink* of metal—his belt. The *brush* of fabric—his jeans. The *thud* of rubber—his boots. Counting down the seconds until he slithered into my space.

With a flap of my arms, I pushed myself deeper, farther away from him. "There are a dozen other pools. Can't you find your own?"

Water swished. My stomach flipped.

"I like this one."

My brows pinched in annoyance. Sucking in a lungful of air, I turned to face him.

He swam near the steps, treading closer, his piercing gaze heating my cheeks. "Your hair looks nice like that."

The hollow praise probably worked wonders on others. There *was* something about him—burning blue gaze, a jaw that was all angles, an air of mystery—I just happened to see right through it. To know better.

Narrowing my eyes, I flatly said, "Thanks."

He ran his fingers through his hair, biceps swelling; silver rings glinted against the black strands. "How's mine?"

"Fine." I looked away. "I should get going. I'm already a prune anyways."

Bouncing on my tiptoes, I waded closer to the stairs, careful to keep to the outskirts of the pool, to keep myself covered by the milky lagoon.

Didn't matter. I could still feel him, the intensity of his stare, the threatening shift in his muscles.

I was nearly out. Just a few more strokes to the shallows.

"Wait." Wet fingers reached across the water, brushing my shoulder. "Super impressive, what you did today."

My eyes could have burned holes in his hand. "You were there?"

He nodded, droplets dripping down the side of his face, plinking onto the surface.

"Oh." My voice sounded small in the tightness of the cavern. "I must have missed you."

"You seem to miss a lot." The comment struck me like the fangs of a water snake.

I glared at him over my shoulder. "Excuse me?"

"Got a lot on your mind, angel?" That touch slithered closer, his foot grazing my ankle. "I can help make it disappear."

Source tingled in my fingertips, heating with a rush of anger. "I'm good."

Shrugging, he tilted his head back until the nape of his neck dipped beneath the surface, thin lines of a tattoo poking out from behind his ear.

I splashed the water away from me, and a small wave curled with the force and my magic, breaking across Flóki's shoulders.

He shut his eyes, throwing his arms over his head. I took his distraction as a moment to escape, slipping out of the pool and snatching my towel off a stalagmite.

"Tomorrow the queen is taking me to Earth's lair," I said, wrapping myself in the soft fabric. "After that, I'm on the next flight to California. Then we'll never see each other again."

"Tomorrow, tomorrow." He laughed, and it was smoky and suffocating and wrong. "Why isn't it ever *now?*"

"Do you know something I don't?" I spat.

"I know Hildur finds you very useful." He waded closer, as if he was going to step out—follow. I held my ground. "And you've been so willing to help."

"Was I supposed to let those people die?" I bit back through gritted teeth.

"Why would she take you to Jarðarbæli?" he returned. "Keeping you around solves many of her problems."

"I can walk out that door at any moment. I can find a way there myself." Even as the words left my lips, I wasn't sure I believed them.

He lifted his dark brows. "You honestly think you could navigate that glacier? Did you see the corpses, or were you too bewitched by the Galdur?"

Bile stung my throat. There… there had been a peculiar crunch beneath my crampons, but I'd assumed it was the culmination of ice and snow.

"Gunnar wouldn't"—still stuck on the visual, I almost gagged—"Gunnar wouldn't let me wander that wasteland until I was nothing but a pile of bones."

"Gunnar has a duty." Flóki licked his lips, as if to draw my gaze, then bit down, canines dimpling the plump skin. "Crush or not."

My face heating once more, I gripped the towel tightly around me. "So I'm trapped here." The Coffin Seeker, the jelmadag, Eldi—even those stories of Grýla—they'd all hinted as much.

Unbidden, my eyes tracked the vaulted ceiling, cringing at the hanging rocks as if, at any minute, they might come crashing down. "What do you propose I do then?"

He shrugged, bare shoulders flecked with water glistening under the low light. "You could enact elven law." He phrased it like a suggestion, not a warning. Yet still… why did the words hit me like a gut punch?

I kept my voice flat, bored—the very last thing I was. "And what does that entail?"

"A fight to the death."

My heart thumped erratically, the only sound ringing through the quiet cavern.

Flóki's face cracked in a grin that was all too sharp. "Ha! You should have seen yourself."

Was it me, or had his pupils doubled in size? "Ok, so what is it really?"

"It's a way to get what you want." With a jerk of his chin, he gestured to a towel folded next to his mess of clothes.

Grabbing it, I tossed it over and spun around, trying not to give in to the itch to turn at the sound of his wet steps. "How does it work?"

"You say the magic words."

"And then what?" My muscles clenched at the trickling of water surely raining off his abs, at the swish of the lagoon—

At the patter of his footsteps, growing closer. "Hildur will grant you a pardon, a mercy, a wish."

"A simple phrase and the queen just… gives me whatever I want? I don't buy that one bit." I knew how she worked— always strategic, always one step ahead. "What's in it for her? What does she get out of it?"

"Alright, so she may not *want* to comply, but it's an incantation so potent, so ancient, no one can interfere." Energy prickled my back. He was standing behind me. "Not even the gods."

Figures. Gods were never on my side, anyways.

"What's the catch?"

"You simply have to prove your worth."

"How?"

"You'll be publicly pitted against an equal match."

That could be anyone. A worrisome thought ran through my mind like the hair-raising drag of a claw. "Like in some kind of duel? What if I lose?"

"Hildur is the speaker of your fate."

My stomach flipped.

"Besides." A heated breath tickled the back of my neck. Every hair stood on end. "You're stuck here, and you know it. So, what have you actually got to lose?"

Fingers tucked in tight, knuckles white and veiny, I asked, "And what are these so-called magic words?"

Lips grazed my earlobe. My insides coiled, every inch of me screaming to run. "We have to whisper. Eyes everywhere, you know."

It took everything in me to keep those fists at my sides, to latch my jaw tight, to fight the unsteady lurch of my pulse.

"*Aelphicas leges advoco. Ad veniam proelium. Ad misericordiam certamem. Ad gratiam mors,*" he said, before stepping away.

When I turned, the cavern was empty.

CHAPTER 30

Aelphicas leges advoco. Ad veniam proelium. *Ad misericordiam certamem. Ad gratiam mors.* I repeated those words over and over under my breath on my way back to my rooms: muttering them in the twilit atrium, where an elf was plucking the leaves off the icy tree; memorizing the inflections down the gilded halls; keeping them on the tip of my tongue in the frosted elevator.

Nervously twirling the ends of my hair, I threw open the door to my rooms. My heavy steps carried across the floor, the mirrored hutches shaking. "Aelphicas——"

"River!" Flames billowed in the fireplace, a flash of smoky orange and red. Eldi's words were pitched and quick. "I don't mean to pry but I overheard Her Highness briefing you on the avalanche. Are you okay? Did the castle get hit? What about the elves?"

My stomach sank as if wrapped in steel chains. The poor fire nymph had been an anxious crackle of embers waiting for me to return. I fed her another log, letting the fire grow bright.

"I'm okay. They're…" I flopped onto the couch and rested my neck on the velvet arm. "Mostly okay. There were a couple casualties."

"Megi hvíla á himnum." It was barely a whisper among the flames.

As the cushions enveloped me, the day caught up to me, and my entire body grew heavy. Mesmerized by the elemental dance, my lids slowly started to fall. The ogress's cave, the chaos, the dungeon, the pool, all stolen by the swift cloak of sleep.

"I just…" I yawned. "Need to take a quick nap. Then I'll tell you everything."

"Of course." She billowed gently. "Get some rest."

"Can you tell me a story?" I asked sleepily.

A pop. "I—I'm not sure I remember how."

"Sure you do." I nuzzled my cheek into a fringed pillow. "Start with the truth. That's where all stories come from."

I'm not sure if Eldi ever told me that story—the low whine of the whistling flames was the last thing I heard before the room fell to a cozy blackness, and I drifted off.

THE YOUNG WOMAN *stood at the edge of the black cliffs, overlooking the bubbling lake of fire.* Pop, *it went.* Blurp, *it bubbled. Agitated, restless.*

It wasn't like Mount Etna to erupt like this. Not so frequently, not so violently.

Ever since the elves had declared their alliance with the angels, the country had become a bloody warfront. And those things. They crawled out of her crater, dripping in her fire. Grotesque, hungry. Fiendish.

Steam rose from the crags. The woman's bare feet were used to the searing heat, her bronzed skin dappled with moisture. To most, it would be incinerating, but for her, it was invigorating.

She turned away from her beloved volcano, a tear so hot it sizzled streaking down her face. This would be the last time. She knew it deep in her core.

Their entire world had come undone, yet the containment spell hadn't passed the boundaries of Lokahryggur. Why? Why were her people the only ones worth saving?

The woman's bright red hair flapped in the mountain's wind. In this light, it rippled like a flame.

The fire folk didn't usually act out of desperation, but that was the only emotion burning through her as she tore through the highlands.

With nothing but sheer will, she'd kissed her children goodbye that morning. Another last. Another wrong to fuel her anger.

It was that same will that drew her to Ískastali, that forced her to her knees at the foot of the throne of the Ice Queen herself. It coaxed the words out of her mouth.

There was a law. An ancient one without a book or a scribe. One passed through the generations in the late, desperate hours, when the lesser, born into ash and heartbreak—not gold and privilege—screamed at the stars.

"Aelphicas leges advoco. Ad veniam proelium. Ad misericordiam certamem. Ad gratiam mors."

It wasn't in the common tongue, but she could feel the magic, and even if it didn't promise freedom, at least it gave her a chance.

"OH, THIS IS ridiculous. You try waking her."

Pressure dug into my shoulder. My body jiggled back and forth. Everything was shaking, the volcano was erupting, the monstrous beings were crawling out of it—

Lids flinging open, I shot up, the air like fire in my chest. The man hovering at my side gasped, sending his clipboard clattering. His circular spectacles fell down his nose as he bent to grab it—Kristjan. A tall, regal figure towered next to him, silhouette lit by flickering candles.

I blinked once, twice. The queen.

"What are you—" A textured throw pillow slipped off the velvet cushion and dropped to the rug. That was right— I'd fallen asleep on the couch. Shit, Olivia. I was supposed to meet her at the archives. "What time is it?"

I looked towards the windows. The curtains had been closed. Craning my neck, I glanced behind the queen to the grate. The fire had gone out.

Hildur stepped into my line of sight. "It's nearing midnight," she whispered, a trill lining her normally calm tone.

"Why are you in—" The question caught in my throat as the front door flung open and a line of elves shuffled in.

Their quick steps whispered across the room, gazes fixed on the floor.

Commandeering what was supposed to be my dining area, they draped dozens of black garment bags over the table, filling the remaining space with cosmetics, perfumes, and tubs of glittery paint.

Just beyond the set of double doors, furniture legs ground against the hardwood, making room for a plastic sheet. The kind used for butchering.

The muted *whoosh* of water came from deeper inside the room. They were drawing a bath.

Eyes wide and unsure, I met the queen's violet stare. It was bright, glowing, sparkling with magic. Things never, ever ended well for me when she looked like that.

"You're going someplace very special tonight."

Jarðarbæli. My heart skipped. It was time.

Twisting my legs off the couch, I scrambled to my feet. "I'm ready, just"—wiping at a thick strand of hair stuck to my cheek, I continued—"tell me what you need."

Corner of her lip quirking up, she gestured to the bedroom.

I spun around and immediately rammed my knee into the coffee table—that was going to leave a mark—and then followed her silent order.

"Tonight, you'll be entering the Heimer Töfra, a spirit realm between dimensions," she said, trailing behind me.

The Heimer Töfra. So that's where Gaia's lair was located. Passing the open armoire—the satin and silk, the sparkling and bejeweled dresses hanging in a tight row—I tucked that bit of information away for later.

"To be granted safe passage, we must provide an offering, even if only temporary."

Her voice was calm—too calm.

"What kind of offering?"

"Your soul."

I froze halfway across the marble tile of the bathroom. "Pardon?"

I must have heard wrong. The water was running, and I hadn't shaken off the grogginess of sleep, because there's no way she actually said—

"Your soul," she repeated calmly. The faucet was off now.

When I whirled on the queen, she remained still, statuesque. The room fell quiet, nothing but the steady bustle of hands breaking the silence.

My face twisted in confusion. "How does that work?"

Hildur clasped her lean fingers, resting them against her mustard-colored robes. "We will conduct an ancient ceremony, where your spirit guides will burn the blooms from our Töfratré."

Their ice tree in the atrium—it was no surprise to me that it held magical properties.

Was this what the Coffin Seeker was referring to then, when he said that most couldn't handle Jarðarbæli because it meant facing themselves?

Our souls… They were just another version of us. Kind of like a doppelgänger. My gut twisted. *Kind of.*

I so badly wanted to ask her about all this, but I really didn't need her knowing I went snooping around her dungeons. Not yet, at least. What if she took this opportunity away?

"Once you inhale the fumes, you will be transported to the Heimer Töfra: the World of Enchantment. There's a network of caves in the highlands."

A steady line of woodsy, leathery smoke wafted in the air, tickling my nostrils. "And that's where Gaia's is?"

Placing her palm on my shoulder, she ushered me on with a gentle spin. "The Andavörður will help you."

Maybe she took my comment as a statement instead of a question. I went to ask again.

"So, Gaia's—" An elf lowered a burning stick onto a set of lava rocks—so that's what that smell was. They bent into a bow before gesturing to the tub. "I just got back from the healing pools. I think I'm good."

They stared at me expectantly. Tendrils of steam rose from the water, white flowers floating amidst the bubbles.

"Oh. Uh. Okay, sure," I said. "I'll get in."

Clearly, there wasn't any other option anyway. Hands fidgeting at my sides, I swallowed the prickles of fear.

"So, these caves," I tossed behind me, but Hildur had already breezed out of the room. The door clicked shut.

The Andavörður, two of them, didn't say much—probably barred from small talk—but they seemed kind enough, looking away when I undressed, pouring floral-scented pitchers of water over my head, softly scrubbing my back. Pressing cool washcloths against my brow after an intense plucking, applying lotion after a scream-worthy waxing, gently correcting my posture when I couldn't sit still during the hour it took to paint my body in intricate silver swirls. Their silken headdresses fluttered as they helped me into the flowing skirts of my ombre-blue dress and set my hair into loose curls, pinning the upper half.

Now dragging a trail of shimmering fabric, I entered the sitting area.

Hildur rose from the settee in a slow sweep. Kristjan quickly followed, clipboard to chest, swiping the porcelain cup of tea from her hand.

The remaining few Andavörður scattered.

"How"—my throat bobbed, unsure—"how do I look?"

A lethal smile split the queen's cheeks. "Like a most perfect offering."

"Um. Thanks?"

She crossed over the rug, meeting me at the threshold in bold, graceful steps.

Leaning over the table, she plucked something circular and sparkly from the clutter and placed it on my head: a diadem.

She spun me so I faced a mirror.

A soft gasp spilled from my glossy, pink lips. My hand brushed through my hair, the classic-looking waves spilling over my shoulders and the sapphire-studded straps of my dress.

"It's beautiful, but…" I blinked, the thick extensions on my lashes causing it to come off as a dramatic bat of my eyes. "Is this the right attire for a cave?"

"For where you're heading, yes," she cooed, tucking a curl behind my ear. "We must go to Galdrahöllin, the Hall of Mystics, now to conduct the ceremony. Kristjan will walk us to the elevator, from which I will escort you. Alone."

My breath stopped in my chest as her reflection flitted out of frame. Alone. The queen was never alone. There was always a guard, or a courtier, or a handmaid.

"Come. We must make haste."

Mouth pursed, I blew the air out of my lungs, even the smallest movement causing the fabric of my dress to ripple like liquid silver.

The hallway was silent. No words, no Eyes, no turn of the lock. The shadows seemed to follow behind us like living wraiths, swallowing our footsteps.

Glass panes of the Sky Tower's windows arched overhead. Darkness covered the land. I glanced at a wall clock. Well past midnight. Suspicion knotted my stomach.

I was sure there were "reasons" we were creeping around the castle, and that this couldn't have waited until tomorrow, but the silent presence of the elf queen at my back, a weight I could almost feel, drove me onwards and kept the concerns locked behind my lips—at least until I got to the archives. Because when I returned from Jarðarbæli, I was going straight to Olivia, and we would confront Hildur on her secrets—her failing magic and her fallen kingdom—together.

Olivia. My heart cinched. I hoped she wasn't starving. I'd promised cookies.

The elevator doors opened without command. Kristjan fell behind, a hunched form in the foyer, and then it was just the queen and me.

Alone.

The second my slippers crossed the threshold, the window-panes shimmered to black. Enchanted to keep the location a secret. I don't know why I was surprised. It shouldn't have been a surprise. But still. My nerves mimicked my fists, curling tight.

I cleared my throat, making room for my voice. "Any last words for me?"

The corner of the queen's lips quirked.

The car plummeted, only picking up speed, the wind an icy shriek.

Thin rivulets of water cut across the glass. It'd never gone this fast, this erratically.

My heart beat as if to escape my chest.

Something snapped and we lurched, and I could've sworn we were traveling sideways.

Flinging myself into a corner for support, I shouted, "Is this thing broken?!"

Hildur only stared ahead, her violet irises electric beads in the dark.

She probably couldn't hear me. I could hardly hear myself, the harsh air sucking up my voice the second it left my mouth.

"Through misted veil and midnight gloom…" Her words were haunting, heavy. A promise. A presence.

"Lies an echo of an ancient tomb…"

Another bang, another jolt. Pushing my spine into a glass panel, I fought to stay standing.

She hadn't moved.

"Where whispers linger, spirits roam…"

Tears beaded the corners of my eyes, the cold stinging as we dropped farther, faster.

"And a curse of old shrouds the land's stronghold…"

Bile prickled the back of my throat.

I squinched my eyes shut.

"Centuries bound, now is time to unfold…"

We needed to stop. I needed to get out. Needed to…

"Blood and bone, the ancient toll."

"*Enough!*" I thought, I screamed, I—I didn't know.

Everything was spinning, everything was black, and then—everything stopped.

A low screech filled the air, followed by a swish of fabric. The ground shifted. Instantly, the space felt lighter, emptier. The doors opened.

Already the queen had paced ahead smoothly. Eyes burning, I scrambled after her, each breath thunderous in the silent hall. Other than the bronze door looming at the end—no handle, thick as a vault—this place was barren. And with no windows, it was impossible to tell where I was.

Hildur stopped halfway, turning abruptly.

"I smell the burning Töfratré. It lingers." She sniffed the air. "The ceremony has started. I cannot go any further."

When I raised my nose, it didn't smell any different than the incense I'd been inhaling for the past few hours getting ready. "Oh. Okay."

"Now go." She pushed me hard, like I was a fledgling that'd stayed too long in the nest.

The corridor stretched before me, candles flickering in sconces, shadows wavering like a mirage. I didn't hear the queen leave. My head grew light, fuzzy, the stench growing stronger, sweeter.

Finally, I reached the end of the hall.

My hand hovered above the door, the metal indented with whirling symbols and letters in a language I did not know.

Even before I touched it, it groaned open. A cloud of white smoke wafted out.

Pulse pounding wildly in my chest, my wrist, my throat, I said a prayer to whoever would listen. Maybe to my mom. But, most importantly, I cursed the Coffin Seeker, Flóki, the jelmadag, all who ever second-guessed me, because this was it.

I was going to Jarðarbæli.

And I wondered what version of myself I'd face.

PART III
ANGEL OF VENGEANCE

CHAPTER 31

HEAVY SMOKE STUNG MY NOSTRILS WITH A SWEET, woodsy scent. It was unclear what the source was. In here, it was nothing but stone arches and columns, vaulted ceilings and empty space. No fire, no kindling, nothing to light, yet a haziness fell over the room.

As I batted my hand in front of my face, a dais seemed to rise out of the clouds of smoke. My muscles growing soft and buttery, I stumbled towards it—a twist of silk, a flash of gold.

I kicked a beaded pillow out of the way. Why was that there?

Someone offered me a hand. My chin swerved in their direction, sluggish, slow.

I blinked once, twice, my reflection awed and warped in a pair of glassy black eyes. A bird?

No, not a bird. A mask. A leather mask in the shape of a raven's head. Their gloved palm hung in midair. Static, waiting, as if it weren't a limb but a puppet on a string, waiting for someone to give it life.

I took another lungful of air, meant to steady myself, but it only brought in more of those heady fumes. My knees buckled. The raven caught me before I could fall.

One hand around my shoulders to keep me steady, whoever was wearing the mask led me up the small set of stairs.

Another person—also head-to-toe in black, wearing the same medieval mask—split the haze, tendrils of it skittering around them, collecting above their head like a halo.

They set an onyx bowl atop a pedestal. Smoke billowed out of it, creeping over the sides, over the dais, up my nose. Eyes watering, I bit back a cough. My chest caved and jerked.

When I slipped out of the first bird's grasp, the second was quick to grab my arm. Both righted me and helped me to the top of the dais—a pathetic seven steps, but I might as well have been summiting a mountain. I couldn't breathe, couldn't see. Couldn't think.

Their dark robes masked their bodies, marking them as nothing but living shadows. The smoke swallowed them up, growing thicker, stronger, swirling into the cavernous hall. Cackles rent the air like lightning. A pair of ancient, arctic eyes flashed in my mind. Seeing. Taunting.

"Gaia?" I croaked. "Is that you?"

Heavy air coated my throat.

I dropped to my knees. This time, there was no one there to catch me.

My hand rushed to my mouth. The metallic lines painted onto my arms, my knuckles, every inch of my body, seemed to lift and float away. The shimmering shapes rose and twisted, spilling across the room, tamping down the thick clouds until I could take a proper inhalation.

Crisp oxygen hit my lungs. At the touch of fresh air, blades of grass sprung between my legs. The muted flicker of torchlight became folds of sunshine. And the stone arches crumbled to dust, unveiling a pure blue sky.

The spirit realm. I wasn't sure what I'd thought it'd look like, but I hadn't expected this. Quiet, natural. Fields of flowers and meadows. A river, a waterfall. Warm, colorful. Spring. My fear started to recede.

Pushing myself up to standing, I glanced at the ridgeline, the way the mountains cut and dipped into the horizon, the path winding up the side, then back to the valley. A lone tree—white trunk, white leaves, sweeping white branches—fluttered in the gentle gusts of wind flowing off the canyon walls behind it.

A strong sense of knowing struck my veins, tiny hairs quivering on the back of my neck.

This was the glacier, the kingdom of the elves, except… there was no ice, no castle, no *people*.

Ryder had explained dimensions to me once—how realms could overlap and share features and coordinates and almost… coexist.

My eyes turned upward. That damned mountain. I grunted. I was really hoping I'd never see it again.

Huffing a piece of hair out of my face, I spun in a circle, scanning the dips and hills, the lichen-tufted rocks, the streamlets trickling through the vale like fingers.

There had to be a sign, an altar, a grove of trees, *something* to indicate the entrance to Gaia's hideout, like the notched runes above my mom's.

Fingers digging into my hips, my nose tipped towards the ground, I walked in lazy, meandering circles.

Hildur had given me zero information—no surprise there. Any details about Jarðarbæli had come from my *enemies:* Flóki, the Coffin Seeker…

Kistuleitarinn had warned me about the bodies. The inner caves were supposed to be the worst. Caves—she was in a cave, in the highlands. My eyes darted to the falls, to the statuesque cliffs of basalt.

Thunder broke the silence. I whipped in its direction. A mass of rocks tumbled down the mountainside, stone scraping against stone, soil sliding and skittering until they fell into a pile at the bottom. A cloud of dust puffed up into the air.

Those all-seeing, crinkled eyes cracked like a whip across my mind. The same ones from that ogress Grýla's lair.

I bunched the silky fabric of my dress between my fingers. If the terrain shared the same footprint as the normal world, there would be a cave up there.

Gathering up my skirts, I made my way to the base of the mountain. A gravel path glittered under the sun, smooth and compact, polished, almost inviting. So different than the mess of icy debris I'd had to scale in the real world.

Wind tousled my hair, breezy and balmy.

Small rock towers lined the trail. I'd seen those in the elven kingdom, too.

As I climbed, the air turned thin, each breath stabbing and short. I glanced over my shoulder to the vale unfurling below. I was close, just a few more yards.

I rounded the corner, the hem of my gown hissing against the ground. The overhang and alcove were just where I suspected they'd be, a gaping maw cut into the crag.

On the outskirts of Hamarinn, Grýla's lair had been abandoned. Here, it was lived in.

Cages dangled from the ceiling, the metal clinking in the breeze. An earthy scent stained the air, smoke spitting from the cauldron like a chimney.

A form—a being—hunched over the pot. Hums drifted from the shadows of their hood, light and spirited.

"Gaia?" The name tasted like sandpaper in my throat.

The humming stopped. I halted, sucking in a breath. Their shoulders stiffened beneath the emerald wool of their cloak, but they gave no response.

My pulse raged in my chest, louder than the wind.

They resumed their quiet melody, undisturbed.

"Gaia?" I tried again. When I was only met with silence, I inched forward. Tipping my chin, I attempted to catch a glimpse of their face. They twisted in the opposite direction, strands of white hair spilling out.

"None by that name here." It was a woman's voice, somehow both ancient and young, jarring and smooth.

"Oh." My heart sank. "Do you know where she is?"

Dumping turquoise powder into a mortar, she spun around to the cauldron, ladling a spoonful of liquid into the vessel.

The flap of her hood dangled over the dark pits of her eyes. "They call it Jarðarbæli."

They. "Yes." I dared a step forward. A creature squeaked in its cage. "Can you point me in that direction?"

"You think an old witch knows the path to the angels?" Snatching a pestle off a cluttered table, she ground the tool against the bottom of the bowl.

Emotion pricked at my chest, cutting through the muscle. I breathed out, pushing the air, the pain, away from my heart. "You're a witch, then."

She dipped a chalky-white finger into the paste, smearing it against the wall. The… bare wall. No markings, no eyes.

"What's your name?" While her back was still to me, I peeked into the pot. Smoke curled over the sides. A bone floated to the top.

I shot backwards as she turned and ladled more liquid, more potion—whatever it was—before returning to the wall and working the bright turquoise splatter into two distinct circles.

"Please." I meant for it to come off strong, but desperation riddled my tone. "Hildur did me up, tossed me in here, and gave me no other instructions. I'd love some help—" I angled my head as she dunked the tip of a thumb into a different bowl and traced two swooping black lines above the blue. "If you have any, I'm all ears. Otherwise, I'd better be on my way."

"Rushing off already, eh?" The witch clicked her tongue. Another sweep of her stained fingers, another arching black line, this time below the blue. "Dinner's almost ready."

Smacking her palms together, she placed her hands on her hips, chin tipped up at her work. Eyes. The same eyes that flashed across my mind, the same eyes in Gr—

She whirled on me then, rotten, jagged teeth reflecting the subtle light. "Grýla hasn't had a guest in decades."

Grýla. A scream caught in my throat.

What was she doing here? Hiding?

Hunting?

I staggered towards the mouth of the cave, the soles of my slippers skidding over the stray pebbles.

Grýla was fast, faster than I expected. Her nails cut into my skin—she was yanking my hair so hard my scalp screamed at the pain, and my head snapped back. "It'd be rude not to stay. You came all this way. You must be hungry."

She threw me into a chair at the end of her wobbly table, the glasses clinking and tipping over, smelly liquid pooling and fizzing on the surface of the wood.

A bowl of soup appeared in front of me, wafting putrid-smelling steam into my face.

Nails, *claws,* digging into my neck, she snarled, "Eat."

The vapor tickled my nostrils, carrying the stench of charred flesh and rotten fruit.

There'd been a bone in the cauldron. It didn't look any different than an animal's, but…

Bile collected in the back of my throat. I pushed it down. Puking would make her angrier. Puking would make me look weak. I was not weak. Not anymore.

The elves had called Grýla a folktale. I would have said the same about mermaids, yet they were *real*—and Gunnar and Freyja had tricked them into letting us pass through their waters with nothing but old trinkets and empty compliments.

My pockets were empty, but I had my wits. Maybe I could outsmart the witch—trick her somehow. At least to buy some time to formulate a real plan.

"Mmm, smells delicious," I lied. "What is this, anyway?"

"Elf, I believe." Releasing the hold on my scruff, she moved to a shadowy corner and rummaged through a pile of junk. An eyeball rolled across the ground.

My gut twisted. *To be granted safe passage, we must provide an offering,* the queen had told me, *even if only temporary.* Safe to say, the last *offering* she sent became a permanent guest.

I would make it out.

I had to.

Swiping a spoon off the table, I tucked it under my thigh. "I seem to be missing utensils."

She grunted.

I crossed my arms. "I can't eat without a spoon."

A blistered palm slammed onto the tabletop, splintering the wood with its force. In it, a flash of bent silver twisted, twinkled. "Here you are."

Plastering on a fake smile that soured my cheeks, I chirped, "Thank you."

I gripped the handle of the spoon, even against the trembling of my muscles.

Pushing empty bottles and trinkets aside, she plopped into the seat across from me at the other end of the table and opened a wicker basket.

"Delicious." I pretended to slurp, the foul liquid brushing my lips. Hints of rot and ash tore into my taste buds. Disgusting. "So, are you a collector of sorts?"

"Hm?" The angle of her head drifted from the knitting needles in her hands, to me.

I gestured to the cages, eyes falling on a rusted one in the corner with a soiled rag for a blanket. Is that where she'd kept her last visitor? Is that where she'd keep me?

Gulping, I shook the gruesome thoughts away. "You just have a lot of nice things."

"That *queen* sends gifts. Trying to ease tensions." I didn't miss the way her lip curled at the mention of Hildur, how her gnarled fingers tightened on her tools.

At my staring, she held up the thick implement, then dug the tip into a flimsy square, too translucent to be fabric, too delicate to be flesh.

A soul.

A blanket of them, stitched together like a patchwork quilt. Trapped in this realm, in this cave. I eyed the human-sized cage more closely. Red stains dappled the bars. Thin scratches scored the bottom—nail marks.

Horror clenched my insides.

Another fake sip, another gag, another lie. "Yeah, she's awful. You know, she talks about you *incessantly*. Grýla, Grýla, Grýla. It's her favorite topic. She's obsessed."

The ogress's fingers stilled. Loose cloth still shielded her face, but at this angle, I swore I saw a thin lip quirk up.

Resting my chin in my palm, I batted my eyes, the extra lashes heavy on my lids. "What did you do? Tell her off? Curse her kingdom?"

"You have things confused, my dear." Her nails curled inwards, growing longer, sharper. "A curse is not a curse when it is one half of a bargain."

"What kind of bargain?" I leaned in, like we were in on some secret. "A soul for a soul?"

"A soul for a kingdom."

A lighthearted laugh bubbled out of me, but neither one of us was smiling anymore.

"Bit by bit, until it crumbles," she sang.

My words were spitting, harsh. "You don't mean you're the one destroying the Galdur? Sending Ískastali to its ruin..." I trailed off. Judgement would get me nowhere. Flattery would get me... somewhere. I hoped. I swallowed my pride and sweetened my tone. "And all the way from here. How crafty of you. How do you do it?"

"The elves can banish me all they want, but I was forged from that land. I was there, in the rocks, in the moss, as a whisper on the wind, as a horse hoof scuffing the dirt, before anyone else showed up." With a wave of her skeletal hand, the dark green cloak, the painful hunch to her back, all of it shimmered away.

A wisp of a woman grew upward from the empty robes on the floor. An entire silhouette formed in front of me, growing together with roots and ivy, leaves cascading from her head like strands of hair, flowers sprouting over her torso, grass carpeting her limbs.

I glanced up at her, my chin kicking back as if I were staring into a forest's canopy.

And then she transformed.

The foliage fell to the floor, crisp and dry. The bark shriveled, turning dead and bleached. The years of wanting and waiting and cursing flashed by in a second, stealing her beauty, turning her eyes glacial, until she was no longer a woman of nature but a woman of revenge. The ogress.

"The elves may *have* the spirit of that island," she tsked, hooded and hidden within the folds of her cloak again. "But I *am* the spirit."

Grýla was sent here against her will. And now she was ancient and crooked, starved and lonely, consumed with rage. I rested my chin in my palm, my brows dipping. "Why would they banish you?"

"Bargains. They're only as good as your word, and she found a way to twist mine."

Eldi's warning floated to mind. *The elves are cunning. Creative. They'll use their words against you, even the ones you do not say.* "What kind of bargain?"

"Many questions." She rose from her chair, the legs clicking against the ground. "Didn't you know that hungry mouths are often silent?"

"Well, I have a right to know." Time. I needed more time. "I mean, if this is going to be my last supper, I'd at least like to understand what put me here."

"It was never our choice to fight. It was not our battle, yet it was our blood that was spilled." She pressed her knuckles into the splintered wood, the color draining rapidly beneath the tight skin. "The elf queen agreed to pull out of that war, and I vowed to shield her kingdom until her enemies retreated."

The incident reports Olivia had found—they'd indicated that the earliest recorded failure of elven magic was during the Cross-Realm War.

My eyes narrowed. That was a century ago. What was Grýla doing here?

"I've no other option, dear girl," she said, as if the question had been written on my face. "I performed my job too well."

My heart lurched.

"I'm *trapped,*" she emphasized, spit flying out with the word. "Just like you."

"No." My eyes darted behind her, above her, to the wall and back. "There's got to be a way out."

She lunged, teeth bared and bloody, stopping only inches away from my own. I shot back, the wooden legs of my chair lifting off the ground. "The only way out of here is through the cauldron, I'm afraid."

I stared into her dark cowl, into the impenetrable shadows. A chill slithered across my shoulders. It struck me then: without visitors, there would be no food on her table, no souls to keep her company—and no magic to shield the elven realm.

As long as Hildur had Grýla, her kingdom was safe and hidden. And even though Grýla tampered with the Galdur, it'd never *fully* fail—so long as the queen fulfilled her end of the deal and kept bringing the ogress visitors. Because the bargain had been twisted to last for eternity, so clever Hildur never had to worry about threats of another war, just broken pipes and moldy walls and endless winters; retaliation—inconveniences, really—the monarch was willing to endure for the protection she got in return.

Chin slowly dropping to my chest, my gaze caught on the sapphire straps of my dress, the metallic paint shimmering over my collarbone, the bangles collecting at my wrists…

That queen *sends gifts, in hopes to ease tensions.*

How do I look?

Like a most perfect offering.

Hildur had wrapped me up in a pretty little bow.

Vapor rose from my bowl. Sickly, sweet. Two fingers pinching my nose, I swatted it away.

A gnarled chin, a flash of teeth. "What's wrong, angel? You don't like your soup?"

Shit. "No—I mean—I do."

"You've barely touched it. Tell me, how does it taste?"

She hunched lower, lower, until the tip of her warped nose skimmed the lip of the bowl.

"It's great," I ground out, fists bundled in my lap.

I flexed my hand. Source crept up my veins, gathering in the tendons, a small surge of adrenaline and salt and power ripping through the muscle and then just… falling, fading, like a fire with no spark, like a flame that'd been smothered by a blanket.

The gravity of it carved a hole in my stomach; the weight of it pulling me down.

They were right—Flóki, the demons.

I bit down on my lip, the bitter tang of iron coating my tongue.

This wasn't Jarðarbæli. This was something different. Another one of the queen's games.

Tears flecked my lash line. I was so fucking tired of being a pawn.

The metal hidden in the folds of my dress bit into my thigh. I needed to act fast—if the witch could cause an avalanche, freeze a river, turn a castle to ruins *across realms*, there's no telling what she was capable of here.

And I was armed with a spoon.

I gently removed the utensil, holding my shoulders straight, keeping the bowl tight against my palm. It was far from perfect, but it'd have to do.

At least to get me a head start.

"You know what I think." I met that empty void, that soul-sucking emptiness where her expression should be, head-on. "I think you're no better than the Queen of the Huldufólk."

A howl of laughter erupted from her hood, so shrill it nearly splintered my bones. "You have no idea how ruthless they can be. What kind of grudges they hold."

"You killed innocent people with that avalanche."

"I was due a visitor. I had a point to make. They kill people for sport."

"And what do you think you're doing here, collecting souls?"

"Getting a taste of home."

Before the words fully left her lips I flew out of my seat, shoving the tip of the spoon *up, up, up* into Grýla's draping of fabric, into the shadows where an eye might have been.

A guttural shriek echoed off the walls, the cages rattling, the sky cracking, the cauldron tipping. Her clawed hands swished past me, reaching, smothering, squeezing the air.

My heart racing, I grabbed the back of the chair and swung it around, ramming it into her side. It knocked her against the table, the fabric flinging back just far enough to reveal something ancient and rotting, her skin like decomposed leaves, her eye sockets hollow like the cavities in a tree.

Skirts whipping behind me, I sprinted around the fallen pot. The soup spilled out, bones crackling beneath my feet as I tore out of the cave.

Clouds gathered above me, thick and swollen. Black threads spun through them, lightning—*magic*—just like the ones I'd seen suspended over the debris in Hamarinn.

Wood splintered. Ice shattered.

The whole earth seemed to shift.

I sped down the path, a whir of blue and gold and silver, slippers skidding in the dirt, hem snagging on the rocks.

Behind me, laughter rumbled with the thunder.

I dared a glance back. In that split second, I saw only the rock face, the roiling of the sky.

Still, my heart beat harder.

Maybe the ogress was hiding, maybe she was a speck of dust, maybe she was a whisper on the wind.

The valley unfolded before me. I needed to get out. I needed to go. But where? Where was the exit, where was—

Red. A speck of it, peeking out from behind a mossy slope. I'd scoped this entire field, every dip, every knoll. Nothing. Nothing but vast, open wildness. And now…

I drew closer. The red speck bloomed into the curve of a cupola, the hillside giving way to four pale walls. A chapel on the riverbank, next to the willow's weeping tendrils.

A shadow flitted against the stained-glass windows. Someone, something was inside—*help*. Lungs tight, legs burning, I sprinted to the door. It hung open a crack.

I burst across the threshold. "Hello! Help!" Dust wafted in the shafts of light funneling through the arches, spilling over the silent pews. Candles flickered at the altar, wax pooling onto the aged carpet. "Hello?" I called again, chest caving in with hopelessness.

In a fluid movement, quiet and swift as a wraith, a person stood up from the second row, turning to face me. And that guttered flame below my collarbone ignited into a wildfire.

"Ryder!" His name was a ragged exhale on my lips. Slippers thudding against the aisle, I crashed into his chest, winding a tight ball of his black t-shirt into my fist. "Please, she's coming! Help me, please."

He slid one of my loose curls between his fingers, twisting the ends. "You wore your hair half up this time."

I gave him a shake, my hair falling out of his grasp. "Ryder, you don't understand. She's coming."

"Who?" His long, dark strands fell over his forehead, framing his temples.

A different sort of heat burned through me, but I swatted it away—along with his hand. "Grýla!"

"That old hag?" A coy smile. That dimple I adored. "I can fight her off. But by the sound of it, you already did."

"You don't know how strong she is. I'm sure that wasn't the last of her." Releasing the fistful of cotton, I stumbled back. "Wait. Why are you here? Is this one of her tricks?"

He filled the short gap between us in one smooth step. "Our souls are bound."

"What—" I shook my head, coherent thoughts vanishing amidst the shock. "What do you mean?"

"I broke the cardinal rule of a hunter," he said, gaze sweeping my hair, fingers reaching for another rogue curl. "I second-guessed myself."

I stilled, hardly able to form the next word. "And?"

He pulled up his sleeve, the blue-and-white river tattoo— the only one inked in color—flowing along the curve of his bicep. "The blood oath never fully sealed."

That night at the Boardwalk, so many weeks ago, hit me with the force of a flash flood.

I sank into myself, my knees quivering. After Ryder had delivered me to the enemy—after he'd stood there and watched as I struggled to fight the Greater Demon's evil magic—he'd handed me the very thing he'd stolen off my neck: my necklace. My conduit.

As my brain worked to block the heartache, the chaos, the memory, I'd actually forgotten that in the end, he'd helped me. And then I'd escaped.

We were still tethered.

"So, when I got sent to this realm"—I inhaled a lungful of icy air—"you did, too…"

He tucked the lock of hair he'd been playing with behind my ear. "The real mystery is what kind of trouble did you get into to put us…" He took in the arched room. "Here?"

"I—I'm looking for Gaia." A step backwards.

A step forwards. "Did you find her?"

"I found Grýla. And…" My back thudded against a wall. "You."

There was hunger in his eyes, pupils dilated so that only a hint of green flared around them. When he braced his forearm above me, his gaze dropped to my feet, my dress—each curve barely concealed by the thin layer of silk—the ritualistic paint smeared across my chest, my arms, my neck.

His free hand swept beneath my chin.

I shook my head. "No."

A smirk, a parting of his lips, a nod.

"I'm not doing this." Heartbreak echoed through me, as if I were reliving it all again. "This"—the word caught in my throat—"is off-limits."

"Oh, totally." His brows furrowed, mouth pursed, every visible part of his body disagreeing.

"Worse, forbidden."

"That makes it more fun."

"Sinful."

"All sins are tempting."

My pulse fluttered. His focus darted to the tick in my neck.

"So," he said, our breaths tangling together. "What are we not doing?"

"I don't…" The words were lost, but the tone held an invitation. "I don't know."

"Being brave?"

"Being reckless."

"Right," he said, biting into his bottom lip. "Let's not do that."

Wrapping my arms around his nape, I pulled him in closer, my mouth crashing into his.

Without a flinch, a thought, he sank into my lips, our tongues desperate, as if this could be ripped from us at any moment. Tucking his arms under my knees, he lifted me up, waist pressing into the space between my thighs.

I squeezed my legs around him, drawing us closer, tighter, chasing the friction.

"Saints," he growled, "I've waited too long for this."

I tilted my head back, staring at the grooves in the vaulted ceiling as he stamped kisses along the base of my neck. "You know I'll go back to hating you after this?"

"Mmm." The sound vibrated from the hollow of his throat into mine. "And you know I'll go back to hunting you."

I let out a breathy laugh, grabbing his jawline. "Then let's make it count."

He swallowed the words, his kiss soft and longing as his silken lips pressed against mine.

Slowly, he unhooked me, coming to kneel at my feet.

Eyes fixed on mine, his hands trailed under my dress, wandering up my legs. The tips of his fingers explored the curves, the dips, sneaking under the lace, featherlight, wanting.

I shifted my hips to stand wider, pressing my shoulders against the wall. "Are you second-guessing yourself now?"

"Baby, I've never been so sure about anything." He pulled the fabric beneath my skirt aside, fingertips brushing the delicate folds of skin.

A whimper escaped me—a yes, a plea. That was all it took to undo him, to turn that dark gaze feral. The first finger slipped in.

Core shaking, I tilted around it. Another finger. More rhythm. From him, from me.

An intense wave of pressure built where another finger circled.

Hips swaying, I pressed a hand against the wall, the other fisting my hair, as I drove him deeper. "Oh, my God."

In one swift tug, the flimsy fabric I'd called my underwear was at my ankles. I stepped out of them, kicking them over the tiles.

Sliding the hem of my dress upward, he handed me the roll of silk, face flushed with awe and desire, a color I hadn't seen him wear since…

Anguish flickered like a weak heartbeat.

But then he was saying my name, brushing the word over my skin.

And then I was tugging at his thick strands of hair, hooking my leg over his shoulder.

"River, River, River." He chanted it like a prayer.

"Ryder," I answered, his name a praise, a song.

My body arched in response, waiting for those soft lips, drifting dangerously close to that aching, wanting piece of me.

He started at the top, at the tingling nerves. One lick. Two. A moan drifted out of me.

I pitched my legs wider, writhing in rotation with his tongue, every touch bringing us, bringing me, closer and closer.

His mouth swept higher, then lower, in and around, before I eased my palm behind his head. I held it there, in one trembling spot, twisting my fingers in his hair.

"Ryder," I sighed, knocking my head back against the wall.

Waves of pressure built, spilling into my thighs, my core, my heart.

My hips picked up speed.

"Don't stop," I gasped. "Right there."

A current tore through me, peaking between my legs, splintering off to the rest of me. I was soaring, I was weightless, my blood rushing, my body boneless.

My knees shook, hardly able to keep me standing, but he didn't stop.

And I didn't want him to—I clenched against every little zing, every little aftershock that swept through me.

Ryder was just as greedy, swallowing every last drop of pleasure, every last moan and shiver, until I was nothing but a limp, starry-eyed pile of cells.

He sat back on his heels, drinking me in. My silver and gold body paint dotted his cheeks, streaking his nose.

The hunger was still there in his gaze. It followed the rise and fall of my chest, the droplets of sweat, while I caught my breath. One taste wasn't enough for either of us.

But it had to be.

His hazel irises swelled, eclipsing the darkness that seemed to be a permanent part of him now. I let my hem fall to the floor.

Taking his bottom lip between his teeth, he seemed to steel himself, leashing whatever had possessed him. After a slow breath, he rose to his feet, then held out a hand.

I stared at his open palm, unmoving, unblinking. For a second, we weren't in the Heimer Töfra, in a realm etched out of the hollowed-out walls of the elven castle. We were on the beach, just north of Santa Cruz, getting ready to leave a secret cove, after having just watched the seals splashing and spinning.

A jolt of sadness rocked my heart. Would we ever get there again? To that place where it felt like us against the world, where I was just a grieving girl, and he held all the broken bits and pieces of me.

I locked my hands at my sides, curling them into fists to resist the temptation to touch him further, to walk out of those doors like nothing had changed.

Outside, the sky had grown darker, stormy. He followed me out, and I had to fight every urge to lean into the warmth of his body behind me. Lighting crackled in the distance.

"What changed?" A clap of thunder shook with my words. "Why break your oath?"

When he didn't answer, I turned to face him, my chin kicking up. Beneath those long, dewy lashes, he stared. "Because you were more addicting than the magic."

My gaze dropped to his sleeve, to the ripples of water inked beneath it. "We both know that's the tattoo talking."

He shook his head, his stare ignited by desire that felt far too real to ignore.

But Ryder had tricked me into thinking he'd cared about me once before. "Why come all the way here if you weren't just going to turn me in again?"

"I needed you to see that there's still a piece of the old me, deep down inside. That part of me you saw before you knew who, what I was." Grabbing my hand, he placed it over his thundering heart. "See? It's still there, beating for *you*. You're the only reason it hasn't stopped completely."

My own pulse skittered, and God if I didn't want to kiss him all over again. But I slid my hand out from his grasp. "You still gave me up. You still betrayed me. You still lied. I will always hate you for that."

"You hate me? How's this: I hate myself." He fisted his hair, tugging so tightly it must have been painful. A muscle ticked in his jaw. "It keeps me up every fucking night, playing in my mind, over and over. Your face. The rubble. Having to stay away from you. It's driven me mad."

My eyes slipped back to his arm. "Pretty sure we know why."

"You took a contract. You know how it feels now—what I risked, what it meant to go back on the oath. And that cursed magic claimed a piece of my soul." He grabbed the sides of my head, and his lips hovered just above mine. "But it was worth it. It's worth every stab of pain, every hollow ache in my chest, because I didn't care about anything—"

Our heated breaths danced in the sliver between us.

"Until I met you."

Rain started to fall. Icy pellets drenched my silk dress, smearing the paint on my arms even more. Silver wisps streaked his chin, outlined his nose.

"Promise me something, baby?" A shadow of madness twisted his face as his mouth grazed mine. "Don't forget about me when I turn."

That final word was like a cold front, breaking the spell. I pushed him off. "Too late."

Before I could get anywhere, he latched onto my wrist. "I have eternity to make it up to you."

"What?" I spat.

"We're stuck here for good."

"No," I breathed. "There has to be a way out."

"Maybe it's better this way," he said, his thumb stroking the butterfly on my wrist.

If I listened closely, I swore a cackle wove its way down the mountain.

I met Ryder's darkened gaze. "You're not serious."

"Let the realms fight it out. We can stay here. Together," he said, as an arctic wind curled around us.

My free hand grabbed his chin, and I pinched it so hard, my fingertips hurt. "This isn't the ruthless hunter I know— because he would never willingly stand down and put his tail between his legs. Now, snap out of it, Ryder. We need to get out of here."

His face hardened, cheeks faintly blushing as if I'd struck him.

Latching my fingers around his tight grip, I took off across the fields. I dragged him behind me as sheets of rain spilled from the clouds, the ground muddy and sloshing, weighing us down.

My head swiveled, taking in the mossy cliffs, the shallow streams, the endless horizon.

"You can't run from me forever…" Grýla's voice echoed all around us, shaking the earth, my teeth, my bones.

Desperation thrummed in my veins.

Fingers squeezed mine. Ryder. I turned to face him, and the kernel of an idea, a saying, floated to the top of my mind.

"Aelphicas leges advoco," I whispered, clouds mottled with the linings of black magic gathering over us.

His eyes narrowed, a question burning behind them, but I didn't have time to explain.

"Aelphicas leges advoco," I repeated, this time louder. *"Ad veniam proelium. Ad misericordiam certamem. Ad gratiam mors!"*

Lightning struck. The world ripped in half. Ryder was flung out of my grasp.

And I enacted elven law.

CHAPTER 32

Brisk footsteps echoed around me, unbearable against the pounding in my head. And the ground, it was so *cold,* so *hard.* But of course it'd be: Grýla wasn't in the business of making her captives comfortable.

I rolled to the side, the space next to me empty. My eyes fluttered open and shut.

"Ryder?" I rasped.

Black spots dotted my vision, and for a moment, I swore I was back in that dimly lit royal hall beneath the tall archways, curled up on the ivory stone.

Wait a minute.

Sucking in a sharp breath, I propped myself up on my elbows. My skirt splayed beneath me in a pool of liquid silk. The footsteps crept closer. I *was* in the castle. I'd made it back.

My heart pinched. Oh my God, I'd made it back.

With those ancient words I'd enacted elven law, and it'd ripped me from the spirit realm, bringing me… here. My fuzzy gaze scanned the cavernous space. No bird masks. No Ryder.

Where was he?

My stomach tumbled. Was he still stuck in there?

The click-clacks slowed, and I knew who was behind me.

Spine stiffening, I glanced over my shoulder, and there she was: all violet eyes and sharp cheeks and cunning lips. Royal, regal. The person who had just tried to sacrifice me.

She lowered herself into a crouch, diamonds shimmering off her cream corset. I didn't so much as flinch when their bright and glittering reflection hit me in the eyes. "What did you do."

Not a question. It was an accusation, mixed with disappointment and barely leashed anger.

Something dark and twisted stirred inside me.

"You bitch," I said, hunched over my knees. "Where's Ryder?"

"Don't you dare talk to me like that." Her slim fingers pinched my chin, lavender gaze flaring bright. "I'm the queen, and you will give me your respect."

"You're no queen of mine," I snarled. "Where. Is. He."

"In his cell. Where he belongs." A vein bulged in her neck; her hold on her temper was slipping. "For now."

Relief swept through me—he'd made it back, too—but those last words cut it short.

Shoving me aside, she quickly straightened. "Do you know what you've done?"

"Me?" I pointed at my chest, flinching when I struck the bone a bit too hard. "What about you? Demons under the castle, unfair bargains, feeding souls to an immortal being you've locked away for over a century. You tried to sacrifice me! You gave me no other choice."

She steepled her hands, fingertips pressing against her red lipstick. "You have no idea what it takes to rule a kingdom, to keep my people safe."

"And part of that is choosing who lives and who dies?"

"Sacrificing the lives of a few to save the many from a bloody, pointless slaughter your kind will inevitably try to drag us into."

"You're not God."

"No." She barked out a laugh, cold and menacing. "But you've woken something much, much worse."

"I know how it works." Staggering to my feet, I grabbed the nearest column for support, fingers digging into the grooves. My body slumped against it, tender and shaky but ready to flee, as if I were still stuck in the Heimer Töfra. "You owe me a chance to fight for my freedom."

"Then you also know it's a public spectacle." Fingers laced behind her back, she did a slow circle around me, her emerald pants swishing with her long strides. "You also know it's a rite every being in the kingdom is called to attend. You know they'll cheer and pick sides, boo and eat popcorn, place bets on your life."

I... didn't know that part.

The queen must've seen it on my face, but hers remained impassive, carved from stone. "And because you're so well-versed in elven tradition, I'm sure you know your fate is now in the hands of the gods. The old gods. The fallen gods."

My blood ran dry. Flóki had made it sound like my fate would be in *Hildur's* hands. Not... I gulped. Not some ancient higher power. "Then I'll win. I'm the Angel of Water."

She tilted her head. "Dear girl, do you know who the old gods are?"

The clink of armor and the thrum of steady footsteps echoed through the hall.

A line of Eyes filed through the open door, helmets down, eyes slitted, jaws locked.

"What's this?" I squawked, flinching back.

The queen's eyes flicked to me. "Seize her." With the simple command, they formed a tight perimeter, circling me.

Were my friends behind some of those helms? Could they see my wide eyes and paled face, hear the plea on my lips? Would they do anything to stop this from happening?

Firm hands clenched my biceps, biting into the muscles. Power crackled through me, but I was too weak, too groggy, and their grip was too tight, too sure.

My gaze snapped to Hildur. "You were never going to take me to Gaia, were you?"

Pursing her lips, she forced air out of her nose, as if the question annoyed her.

"What about Gunnar and Freyja? What about the war?" I bucked against the guards, their metal chest plates digging into my back. "What about your Galdur?"

"Who needs that when I have people like you to keep my kingdom from crumbling?" the queen said with lethal calm.

My heart dropped. People like me. Like Olivia, Ryder. They were next. I had to tell them, save them. "You can't do this!" I yelled, fists slamming into the wall of armor around me.

Ignoring me, she nodded at the soldier on my right. *"Gestapennar."*

As the guards bore me away, I twisted, shouting back, "I will win your sick game, mark my words. And when I do…" Gritting my teeth, I fought against the hard grip pinning me down, managing to lift a hand, a finger. I pointed it at her heart. "You better hold on tight to your crown."

CHAPTER 33

THE CHANTING MADE PEBBLES DANCE ACROSS THE floor, made sand trickle out of the walls.

Hundreds, maybe thousands of elves yelled in delight, their voices distorted by the thick layers of earth between the stands they gathered in above and the cell I was in.

I rubbed my arms, the muscles still sore from the guards' firm grips when they dragged me from the Hall of Mystics and tossed me in here—some kind of holding area—a few days ago. My gut rumbled. The plates of food the servants had brought me were piled on top of a wobbly table in the corner, but I didn't dare touch them. Could be poison.

Dust fell from the ceiling into my hair. I plucked bits of dirt out of my braid, brushed off the grit collecting on my shoulders.

At least the elves had had the decency to lend me some clothes I could actually move in. The firelight flickered off my leather pants, my shiny boots, my thin black shirt.

The portcullis locking me in this makeshift prison rattled against the frame as the crowd grew larger, rowdier, ready for their sick death match.

My stomach lurched.

I grabbed an empty vase, ducked my head over it, and retched—even if I had nothing in me. Bile burned my throat, stung my nostrils.

The ceramic slipped from my grip, clunking to the floor. I stepped over it, pacing the length of the room—fourteen steps to the portcullis, then to the far wall. Again, and again, and again. I could not stop moving. I was like a lion trapped in a zoo.

Was Ryder still in the dungeon? And where was Olivia, I wondered. My heart twisted.

On what might have been my fiftieth circuit, someone called from the entrance, "Trippy, isn't it?"

I slowed to a halt, peering over my shoulder into the dim light. Despite the castle being fully equipped with an electrical grid, the elves had decided to go full medieval and use torches in this labyrinth of corridors and cells in…wherever the hell they'd thrown me.

But I'd know Gunnar's friendly voice anywhere.

"That's one word," I said. "Where am I?"

"Beneath the Terrordome."

The Terrordome. That sparkling silver building behind the ice-laden hills, the very place this same person once told me people fought to the death, while he was teaching me my jabs and crosses. Figured I'd end up here.

"It's a replica of the same coliseum they had in the realm the elves were originally from." The fire flickered, casting shadows over his face, the twists of his hair, his uniform— the tailored navy-blue coat and beret and slacks I sometimes saw him wear. "So they say."

"I thought no one was supposed to visit me." My eyebrows

dipped. "Or…" I trailed off. "Have you been assigned to make sure I don't escape?"

Gunnar huffed out a laugh, looking down beneath his long lashes. "Eva might have done a little switcheroo with the assignments during her last shift. Fritz is guarding the Hlið lífsins—the main gate you entered through—and he gave us special clearance to come in."

I didn't have the heart or the energy to explain that I'd been blindfolded on the chaotic trek in, presumably so I wouldn't be able to find my way out. Instead, I said, "Us?"

"A couple of people," he said, raising a brow. "You might know them as your friends?"

I fought hard to choke back the emotion creeping into my throat. But it was damn near impossible when his lips parted on a smile, and Olivia, then *Freyja* shuffled out from behind the wall.

"What are you guys doing here?" I wrapped my fingers around the metal and brought my face to the door.

Flipping off the hood of her maroon cape, Olivia grabbed on to the small parts of my hands I could fit through the lattice. "We're here to wish you good luck."

"Luck." I scuffed the dirt with my toe.

Olivia smiled, but the expression was thin on her face. "That's all we got."

Freyja put her weight on her hip, pewter gaze piercing me like the fine tips of icicles. "Is that not enough?"

"Of course it is," I said, but the words felt heavy.

"Good." Relaxing her face, she smoothed out her glittering green gown. "Because my bet's on you, angel."

Gunnar leaned against the grille. "Finalllyyy."

"Oh, shut up." Freyja gave a playful squinch of her nose.

Chewing the inside of my mouth, I bit back a smile. Her support—all their support….

I dug my face into my long, black sleeve, wiping away tears before they could fall.

"I can't believe the queen's doing this," Gunnar muttered.

"It's barbaric," Olivia spat, thrusting a hand through the air. "We've moved on from stunts like this. The old gods are nothing but trouble. They should stay sleeping."

"They should," I mumbled. "But I invoked them."

All three of their stares remained fixed on me as I walked them through the past forty-eight hellish hours. The tips of the elves' ears flinched when I told them how Grýla had caused the avalanche. Olivia's hand pressed against her heart when I explained how Hildur tricked me into entering the Heimer Töfra. Every mouth hung open by the time I got to the twisted deal the queen had made with the ogress.

"I'm telling you right now," Olivia said after I had gone quiet, "hell would have frozen over by the time I ended up in that old witch's stew."

I smiled somberly.

A horn bellowed above us. It was an instrument of war, loud enough to penetrate stone. A call to battle. Everyone's chins jerked up, grit falling upon us like snow.

"Look, as coldhearted as our queen can be, she did what any ruler would do: fought for her people." Freyja's stare lingered on the ceiling as if she could see through it. "Doesn't mean I agree with it. Honestly, I do think she'd prefer you out of the pit, but even she can't change this. Once law is enacted, it's in the hands of the gods."

The war horn blew again. Dirt wafted in the air. My shoulders sank even lower.

"Sounds like they're awake now," Gunnar said, swatting at the dust.

My heart fluttered in my chest. I willed it to stop. "What—what do they want?"

They spoke at once.

"Sacrifice."

"Blood."

"A show."

A roar echoed through the hall—deep, tortured. Inhuman. My attention flicked between my friends: Olivia, Gunnar, Freyja. They were here, so at least I wouldn't be fighting them.

"Who's my opponent?" I rasped.

"We…" Concern etched itself above Olivia's brows. "We don't know. We won't know until they step into the ring."

Another raucous roar of applause—fanatic, obsessive.

"The queen's arrived." Freyja glanced at Gunnar. "We need to go."

Unease twisted my stomach, burning my throat. "Is it really a fight to the death?"

"There's only one winner." Even though Gunnar kept a straight face, I could see the panic in his eyes. "Olivia's right. This is an old way of justice for an old way of life. Nobody does this anymore."

"What are the rules?"

"There are none," he said sadly.

"Every fight in this dome is a fight in those wretched gods' honor." Olivia shook her head, cursing under her breath. "Honor they don't deserve. There's a reason they were banished, why their shrines were torn down, why no one speaks their names anymore."

Before I could find out more, the metal slipped between my fingers as the portcullis rose with a groan. Screams and shafts of light funneled in from one far end of the corridor, where the ground sloped up from one prison to the next: the arena.

"That's our cue." Flipping her strawberry blonde tresses, Freyja gathered up her poofy skirts. "Mother will send someone for me if she hasn't already."

"Frey's right. If we get caught down here… One sec, though." Reaching into his jacket, Gunnar pulled out a curved piece of leather, etched runes glossy in the faint light.

A sheath, for a knife.

My knife.

"Where—" I gulped, swallowing a shaky breath. "Where did you get that?"

"Word gets out quickly in this castle. I snuck into your rooms before the Eyes raided it."

"Thank you." I took it into my hands, clutching it to my chest before hiding it in my boot. "Thank you."

"I'm rooting for you, Riv." He cupped my cheek softy before backing away. I didn't want him to go, didn't want to feel the cold, empty air where he once stood.

Olivia stepped forward, pulling me into a hug beneath the gate's pointed edges hanging above. "I'd tell you to run," she whispered, "but guards are stationed around every corner. The best I can promise is that when you're done with all this, we're heading straight to California."

"We?" I couldn't have heard that right. My pulse was pounding in my ears; the fear was warping her words. Olivia couldn't go back, not after what Chthonia had done to her—*would* do to her, given the chance.

She nodded. "You heard me. Running is what our enemy wants. We will not live in fear or hide in the shadows. Whatever happens next, we're in it together. Plus"—she squeezed tighter—"I think someone needs to talk some sense into your dad."

Another set of arms wrapped around us. "I love you guys," Gunnar sighed theatrically. "Frey, you want to join?"

Glancing past Gunnar's shoulder, I raised my brows. "Could be your last opportunity."

His chuckle reverberated to my core. "Morbid, Riv."

"What else is there to be right now?"

The ghost of a smile tugging at her lips, Freyja rolled her eyes. "Unless you want to include the dozen or so guards likely heading our way, I say we get the hell out of here."

We broke apart, all of us dabbing our eyes, stuck somewhere between a laugh and a cry.

Then my friends sprinted into one of a dozen narrow passageways, their swift footfalls echoing off the stone until they disappeared.

Again, I was alone.

I stepped into the corridor, the shadows moving and breathing as if they were watching, as if they were curious.

Flashes of movement and color wavered in the archway that led to the arena. The crowd was ready. Pulse thundering in my ears, I trudged towards them.

Something cracked beneath my boot. I lifted it to see the snapped ivory stick beneath—a bone.

Raising my chin, I kept my eyes forward, focused, ignoring the skeletal remains in the row of empty cells on my left, the stone pillars piercing the empty void of blackness on my right. My heart was an erratic thud in my chest. It was the only thing I could feel, hear—that, and the drumbeat of fear, a steady roar that grew louder with every step.

Source riled like a caged beast, a persistent, desperate pulse in my fingers, but there was no anchor in here. No life, no elements, just dust and darkness.

"River."

"Jesus!" I shouted, nearly jumping out of my own skin.

Flóki crept out from behind a wide, pointed arch. "Oh, were you expecting him?"

"Um, I—" Resisting the urge to place my hand over my pounding heart, I spat, "What are you doing here?"

"I came to wish you good luck." I hated that grin—it was so sleazy, so slimy, his icy blue eyes almost translucent in this light.

"Not needed." I crossed my arms, a shield. "Especially when all you do is speak lies."

He chuckled, eating up my fury as if it were something sweet. "I may have done a lot of things, but I never told a lie."

"You gave me half-truths. Same thing."

"Would you rather be in Grýla's cauldron?"

I bared my teeth.

"Fine." His tongue darted over his canine. "I may have left some parts out."

With a sharp inhale, I tightened my fists at my sides. "You pushed me to do this—you knew it'd be my last resort."

"Let me make it up to you." He took a vial out of his pocket, delicately rolling it between his fingers. "I come bearing gifts."

Gaze narrowing in on the jar of bright green liquid, I took a giant step back.

"Reindeer lichen." He closed the space between us, shoes crackling on the grit, the bones. "Grows on the sides of these mountains. In a highly concentrated form, it's extremely toxic. It can kill even the strongest man in ten seconds." Holding it up, he caught a shaft of light, presenting it as if it were ibuprofen and not something that could kill me in a few agonizing heartbeats.

My eyes narrowed. "What are you getting at, Flóki? You want me to kill myself?"

"That's a bit extreme, River, even for you." Grabbing my wrist, he placed the vial in my palm. "This is diluted. It won't kill you, but it can paralyze you long enough to fake it."

"I don't want your gifts," I gritted out, reluctant to show the tiniest hint of emotion, of the fear that threatened to undo me. "I want to know why."

"Someone had to wake those tired bastards up."

"Why not you? You seem like a great candidate."

He shot me a sheepish grin. "I'll take that as a compliment—"

"Don't."

Ignoring me, he curled my fingers around the glass. "Elves are forbidden from calling upon the old gods."

"Okay, so?" In my hand, the vial grew warmer, lighter. "It's not like you're in the camp of following the rules anyway."

"True." He chuckled, and it drove a chill up my spine. "But I'd be dead faster than you can say *Terrordome.*"

I narrowed my eyes. "How so?"

"For you, elven law is a courtesy. For me, it's a curse. Did you know," he said, his palm squeezing my knuckles tightly, "that in our home realm, these fights used to be routine?"

"No," I said, unable to hold back the shiver from his lingering touch. "And, honestly"—the war horn blared again, rattling my ear drums, pricking at my skin—"is now the best time?"

"We'd fight to honor the old gods and the mortals who ruled us, but mostly to break free of our chains." His eyes locked on the ground, as if he were tracing the footprints of his ancestors.

"For a pardon, a mercy, or a wish," I whispered, reciting what he'd told me at the healing pools.

He nodded, gaze snapping back to mine. "There was an uprising. When the elves escaped to this realm, they cursed the incantation. None of the Huldufólk can speak it; *really* speak it," he added with a wink, as if he knew what I was thinking, "without being struck down."

"How?" I rasped, the word drowned out by the cheers, by the haunting bellow of the instrument.

He shrugged. "Maybe they worked something out with the gods."

I tugged my hand back, out of his grasp. "And is that what you're aiming to do—make a deal with a bunch of ancient deities now that they're finally up?"

That wicked grin gave me all I needed.

"Why would they care about making a bargain with you?" I scoffed. "No offense, but they're *gods*. And you're… you."

"They were cast out of their realm—multiple times." His pupils flared, darkness taking over. "They have nowhere to rule. We can change that."

"Who's we?" As soon as it left my mouth, déjà vu rocked me, and I wasn't standing in an ancient tunnel beneath the Terrordome with Flóki, but on the Santa Cruz Beach Boardwalk with Ryder and Leif, cold and confused and demanding answers, before a demon whooshed out of the shadows.

Tilting his head, Flóki put his neck on display. A serpent coiled in grayscale behind his ear. The mark of the syndicate, of the hunter. "Look familiar?"

Seeing that tattoo… It ripped open the wound, the betrayal, heartache, pain flowing out of me like blood. But the design was missing a key component. "Where's the N and the S?"

Flóki's face twisted in disgust. "I'm not a Night Stalker."

Right. He was worse. He was poison, just like the one in my hand—just like that fringe group that attacked the werewolves and tried to siphon my powers and vowed to unleash hell on earth. Was that really why Ryder was here? Not out of love, but out of duty?

And had I fallen for it, again?

Flóki stepped forward, so close his breath tickled my face. "You take the lichen now, and we can guarantee safe passage to Chthonia. Otherwise… things may get a little messy."

Of course.

Of course he would be working with the enemy.

Air ballooned in my chest.

"Go to hell." I threw the vial to the ground, the glass shattering. "Without me!" I added as I stalked into the arena without a second glance over my shoulder.

CHAPTER 34

THE STADIUM CIRCLED AROUND ME, ROWS OF PACKED seats rising up into the curves of the dome, the cloudless blue sky twinkling behind the oculus.

Without the layers of earth and stone to pad out the noise, the elves' cheers were nearly unbearable. The acoustics made it worse, melding their shouts into one singular, ear-splitting roar.

Hands exchanged money. Lips whispered bets. Popcorn littered the floor. How were they excited for this? It was bloodshed, not entertainment.

Gritting my teeth, I fought the instinct to lower my gaze and cup my palms over my ears, to shut it all out.

But I needed to keep my chin up, to look them straight in the eyes, so they would think I wasn't scared—even if the fear was a steady rumble in my veins.

Right away, I found the royal box, positioned above another barred entrance directly across from mine. Symbols marked the ring of stone dividing the pit I was in from the seating.

I didn't have time to decipher what they meant—a whistle, steady and harsh, drifted to my ears. A silhouette walked across the sand, dark hair, stiff shoulders, arched shadows casting from their back.

As they drew closer, my dwarven blade sang a song so high-pitched it could shatter glass. I kicked the side of my boot where it remained hidden, mentally ordering it to shut up. It didn't, of course—it was just a weapon—and it'd been magically configured to warn me of his presence.

Ryder.

All the air left my lungs.

He halted several yards away. The whistling quieted. I could feel the hollowness of his gaze, the pity, roving all over me.

"What are you doing here?" I demanded.

Before he could answer, Hildur held up her hand. Cheers fell to hushed whispers, which quickly fell to silence, her ruthless, loyal followers bright-eyed and ready for blood. My angel senses pricked up as if they were a second pair of eyes, keeping watch on Ryder.

"My kingdom." The Queen of the Elves rose from her gilded seat, addressing the crowd with a soft sweep of her arm. "We have a very special event in store for today."

My gaze flicked to Ryder. He hadn't moved, but his face had gotten paler, and the dimple between his brows could almost pass for a sign of concern.

"This is quite unheard of," the queen said, tapping her fingertips together, "but it appears we have two participants."

Two? My pulse skittered.

In the break for applause, Hildur's indigo gaze met mine, eyes slitted. Assessing.

I bit the inside of my cheek, forcing an empty stare, not letting it drift away from hers.

"The Angel of Water has called upon the old gods for a pardon, a mercy, a wish. One that requires sacrifice, as was the way of our ancestors." She bowed her head. "Let's take a moment to remember their strength. To remember where we came from."

With the elves distracted, every head folded in silence, I seized the opportunity to shoot a quick glance at Ryder. He was already staring, lips pursed, cheeks flushed, panicked.

"What is going on?" I mouthed.

He held up his hands, shaking his head.

Unlike that night at the Boardwalk when he'd been all wry grins and harsh threats, right now he actually looked confused. He ran his hand through his hair, his sleeve crinkling up over his bicep, and I caught a tendril of inky blue.

His river tattoo—the one that tethered our souls and taken him to the Heimer Töfra, and the very thing that pulled him out and put him into this death game when I enacted elven law.

Yet, this time, only one of us would be making it out.

Jaw tight, I turned to the stadium, eyes raking over the crowd, searching for my friends in the audience. Freyja stood beside her mother, clasping her elbows, mouth tight. Gunnar patrolled one of the aisles, expressionless, steps featherlight. Olivia... *Where was she, where was she?*

As Hildur raised her head, I spotted Olivia in the second row.

"Today," the queen continued, "the old gods have been awakened. They have chosen a worthy opponent."

Sand shifted beneath me. The ground was shaking, moving. With a laborious groan, a third barred door to the arena rose up into the stone as the ones Ryder and I had come in through slammed shut.

Fanfare erupted.

Warning bells rang through my mind.

"It is with great honor I present to you the Ludi Mortales, our first in over one hundred and fifty years." The sage pieces of chiffon that made up her gown shimmered in the midday sun as she turned to meet the eyes of the eager elven spectators. Dropping her pitch, she spoke in an ancient tongue, *"Ab astris venimus, ad astra surgimus."*

"Numquam ignosces, numquam obliviscar," the entire room muttered back as one, with a reverence that was almost holy.

Shifting in the grit, I stared into the open maw of darkness on the other side of the arena, every hair follicle standing up. My knees bent, back arched, elbows out. Proper defensive form—I think.

Out of the corner of my eye, Ryder drew himself into a fighting position.

In one swift motion, I swooped the dagger out of my boot, the handle cool in my grasp.

I didn't need to acknowledge him—I could *feel* the shock radiating off him that I was armed. A smirk tugged at my lips; it was satisfying, really.

It didn't last long.

Growls came from the unlit chamber, rattling the single, circular windowpane high above, shaking silt loose from the walls. A line of steam blew out of the tunnel, scalding the ground.

Smoke rose from the scorch marks, dissipating in the tense air. With a quick nod at each other, Ryder and I crept towards the opening. The crystal fractals embedded in my hilt flared an electric blue, pulsing brighter as the space between us got shorter.

Three glowing white orbs appeared in the darkness, disappearing for a heartbeat before burning back to life. *Eyes*—curious, intelligent. Suspicious, but familiar—like this wasn't the first time they'd seen me.

I stilled. Ryder did the same.

Giant paws moved out of the shadows, blue-black flames lapping up the midnight fur, twisting towards the sky. Razor-sharp claws retracted, piercing the dirt.

The jelmadag stepped into the light.

"You," I whispered.

"Stay back," Ryder directed, arms wide, ready to strike. Although I wasn't sure how much damage they'd do to a cat made of fire…

Me. The word bellowed across the sand, my bones, an echo inside my skull.

The elves were so still, they were near lifeless. My head shot towards Ryder. He hadn't moved either, as if… no one else could hear the voice but me.

How? Tripping over my feet, I stumbled to create more distance. All dozen eyes homed in on the shift of my muscles, my pulse throbbing in my neck, cold and calculating. *Why?*

The dark flames threaded with the demon's mane shuddered in an absent draft. *I was summoned.*

No. I shook my head. *Why can I hear you?* I glanced at the elves, at Ryder. *And none of them can?*

"River," Ryder called, his accent smooth and enchanting. "Give me your dagger."

My face twisted. "Absolutely not."

"You don't know what this beast is capable of." He inched closer, as if *I* were the wild animal he needed to trap. "Hand me the weapon and let me deal with it."

"And then what happens?" I shot back. "You'll deal with me?"

I swore there was a wicked gleam to his eye—but even if I'd just imagined it, I couldn't take the chance: once the jelmadag was dead, he'd have no other choice but to turn the blade on me. There would only be one winner, and it wouldn't be the first time Ryder put his duty before me.

Seven sins, can we cut the small talk? Nostrils flared, the demon let out a chuff—coils of steam unfurled from his nose, snuck out the corners of his mouth. *I'm starved.*

My eyes went wide. *Y-you mean, you're going to eat us?*

Dear girl, what else am I to do with you two?

Maybe I should have given Ryder the dagger.

The jelmadag lunged—a flash of midnight shadow arcing through the air.

Cheers broke the heady silence. The noise swirled around me, catching my attention so I didn't hear or see Ryder coming. Almost a second too late, he grabbed my wrist and flung us out of the way.

"Focus, Riv. I'm not the enemy." Ryder snapped his fingers and pointed at the jelmadag. "That is."

Dark paws slammed into the ground, tiny licks of blue-tinted flames searing the dirt. The air around the beast was hot, warped, wavering like a mirage.

I've met plenty of other demons before, I said between breaths that stabbed like knives. A sharp tug dragged me away. *Ryder.* Dust kicked up from the thuds of our boots. *Why are you the first I can speak mind-to-mind with?*

Really? At least a third of the jelmadag's spider eyes rolled while the others stayed fixed on me. *The first ever?*

Well, there were others, but they were—

Angels. And angels and demons were… different sides of the same coin.

Was that so hard? Fanning his feathers, the creature let out a spine-curling roar. A thin silver chain glinted in the space between his shoulder blades, pinning his wings.

Thank goodness he couldn't fly.

That was rude.

Oops. Forgot he could hear me.

Now, if you'll excuse me, it's even ruder to talk with your mouth full.

My blood froze in my veins. *Wait!*

Pressing off his hind legs, he pounced.

Pinned wings or not, the jelmadag was fast—too fast. I narrowly dodged him again.

"We have to keep it moving, keep exhausting its energy," Ryder said over his shoulder as we aimlessly sprinted through the pit, "unless you're down to let me handle the weapon?" A knowing smirk darkened his stare, shadows eclipsing the golden green.

Arrgghhh. The demon's cry rang in my skull, a sound of pure exasperation. *Will you two just sit still?*

"No." I dropped Ryder's hand. I wasn't going to sit still or hand over my dagger—I was going to fight back.

I lashed out, hoping to catch my beastly opponent off guard.

Steel carving through the air, my blade met the creature's claws with a clang that vibrated down the metal to my hand, my wrist, my arm. My teeth clamped down.

This can't be how you face all your adversaries, I taunted. Sweat lined my upper lip. What do you do, bore them to death with your complaining?

The lone lamb leg growing out his chest kicked helplessly. Usually, I'm well-fed before a battle.

I twirled out of the way, slashing up in a quick, clean arc. My dagger met fur, resistance, and sudden heat burning up my forearm.

Lips curled back and steam spewed out of the demon's mouth, hot and hissing. I brought my knife in front of me, looking like a toothpick against his gigantic bone-crushing fangs.

Hot wind blew strands loose from my braid. When I looked up, all I saw were the blistered pads of paws, curled black flews, and the bottomless depths of an abyssal throat.

"River!" Ryder yelled.

I darted to the side. The jelmadag crash-landed, biting at the now-empty space I'd been standing in.

Ryder rushed over and tore the singed fabric off my calf. On the ground, it bubbled and scorched to a crisp. My skin screamed pink where the demon's fire had gotten me, but otherwise there were no blisters, no burns to my leg.

What's this now? Neck swaying like a serpent, the beast slowly pitched his head up.

I—I gulped. I don't know.

Do you know what hellfire does to those that come in

contact with it? His onyx mane rippled with the words. One lick of it should melt the skin off your bones.

Faint tendrils of smoke rose from the charred hole in my pants. My leg tingled, but it was true—there wasn't even a mark, as if it hadn't made contact with my flesh, but a body of... Water.

You should be a pile of ash right now. And yet you stand before me, whole.

Ryder wrapped his hand around mine, giving it a tug. "Let's move."

Planting my feet, I sank my heels into the ground.

"C'mon!" His head swiveled towards the jelmadag and back to me frantically. "We can't just stand here!"

I didn't go. Instead, I turned towards the demon, eyes burning hot, tears collecting on the lash line—probably from the steam seeping out of his pores.

"River." For the first time in my life, I heard Ryder gasp. "Your eyes…"

Is this a trick of the old gods? the demon demanded.

What? I thought. Bringing my blade parallel to my face, I peered at my reflection. Blue flames danced around my pupils, the irises transformed into heavenly fire, just like the angels etched into the stained-glass window in my dad's office.

My Source raged inside me, stronger than an ocean storm. It rushed over my skin, a cool and velvety current of power, like an invisible shield.

Like it was protecting me.

After all, water repelled fire.

"We'll be fine, Ryder." I brought the dagger to my side. Then with a confident smile, I said, "I'm the Angel of Water."

CHAPTER 35

Every single one of the jelmadag's eyes blinked, narrowing on me. He tilted his head, watching me closely, like I was no longer prey but a worthy opponent. An equal.

The crowd was still going strong, pumping their arms, hanging over the railings.

A steady stream of people filled the aisles, flocking to the lower levels. Rowdy elves, or maybe patrolling Eyes. Ryder's yells were muffled by the beast's steam, which was now enveloping me in a hazy cloud.

"River!" Louder, more frantic.

I turned towards Ryder's voice, waving my hand to see through the thick, hot vapor. A shadow floated into the bowl of the arena. Tricks of the light, of the flickering hellish flames.

A wisp of silver parted the steam, right past my nose. With a gasp I stumbled back, and an agonizing roar tore through the dome.

My spine stiffened. As the haze dispersed, I dared a step closer to the jelmadag—who lay in the dirt in a snarling heap of starless twilight. Pure, unbridled fury stared back at me. A sword pierced his neck.

"Who did this?" I asked out loud.

I whirled to find Ryder standing a few paces behind me. He wasn't alone.

Flóki left his side, stalking towards the injured beast—towards me. So that's who'd snuck their way into the ring.

Ryder grabbed the elf's arm, yanking him back. "C'mon, man."

The fracture in my heart that was just starting to heal shattered all over again.

I didn't want to cry—then I'd have to admit that I'd fallen for him, his tricks.

"What?" Flóki shoved off his grip. "Just trying to help."

I fisted a handful of hair, tugging my braid loose. "I told you in the tunnels, Flóki, I don't need your help, but let me make it even clearer to you: go away."

"Alright." Another metallic blur soared through the air—a throwing knife lodged in the jelmadag's shoulder. The demon screeched in pain. My nerves pulsed with anxiety. "But only if you come with me."

I scrunched my nose. "Not in your wildest dreams, dude."

On a clipped inhale, I dared to look at the stands. My knees buckled and the wind left my lungs at what I saw: pointed weapons, knives to throats, all black ensembles. People bleeding and running, mimicking the screams from the night at Crescent Rock. An undercurrent of terror pulsed through it all.

Not again, not again, not again.

My eyes darted around to find any sign of my friends, sweeping over the royal box. A flash of sparkling steel, a glint of purple silk. Gunnar impaled one intruder in the gut while Freyja kicked another in the chest. Their opponents stumbled over the edge of the balcony, landing face-first in the pit.

The queen and the rest of her royal, cowardly court held themselves flush against a wall. Kristjan held his clipboard over his head like a shield.

"River." An accent, a lilt of the R that still managed to reach some aching part of me.

Acid roiled in my stomach, burning up my throat, just looking at him.

Putting up his palms, Ryder inched forward. "Listen—"

I waved my dagger at him, the blade singing its high-pitched tune that promised violence. "Straight through your heart if you don't back the fuck up."

He stopped, a dark strand falling over his temple.

"Well played, my friend." Flóki wrapped an arm around Ryder's stiff shoulders, giving them a gentle shake. "You got her right where we want her. Your brother will be thrilled."

I forced my face to look bored even if the words were like a scythe to my gut. "Well," I said, hardly able to control the tremble in my voice, "I see you brought your crew. What's your next move, Flóki? Kill everyone here? They're innocent."

"It's an easy choice for them, really." Flóki twirled a knife along his knuckles, but it was his stupid, certain grin that made him the most dangerous. "Join us or die. It's not my fault these people are too proud."

"Good luck getting through the elven soldiers." Behind him, in the stands between the scared, civilian huddles, the brilliant blue uniforms of the queen's cavalry clashed against the shadows of Chthonia's. "They're much more experienced than your band of hooligans."

"Okay, I'll give credit where it's due." Flóki sucked his teeth. "But we only need to hold them off for so long."

"W-what do you mean?" I stammered, throat tight.

"The sword is blocking that monster's airway." He gestured to the jelmadag, lip curled as if the demon were a disgusting, mindless beast and not a living, sentient creature.

Tail cracking the air like a whip, the jelmadag shakily sank back on his haunches, deadly promise in his dozen eyes.

"The steam is trapped," Flóki continued. "It will start building in its gut. With no way out, it will explode."

My lips parted in horror.

He grinned coldly. "This creature is a ticking time bomb."

"Isn't he a demon?" My grip tightened on my dagger, the dwarven scrollwork indenting my palm. "He'd be on your side. And you're going to just… kill him with all the other victims?"

"Don't get soft on me." Bitter laughter coated his tongue. "There's plenty more monsters where that came from."

Despite the chaos, my world fell into silence.

Fight. A single word, an order. I gritted my teeth. *Fight, demon.*

I do not have access to my hellfire's steam. I cannot fly. His tone, so heavy with defeat.

You have claws, don't you? And fangs? Use them.

"How many minutes until this stadium gets leveled?" I asked.

Flóki's arctic eyes turned an abysmal black. "Seven."

No response from the jelmadag.

Look, I don't have my magic to play offense, either. I barely know how to throw a punch or even hold a weapon. I'm probably doing it all wrong—I glanced at the demon, his belly roiling and swollen. A shiver kissed my spine—*I know I'm doing it all wrong, but I refuse to go down without a fight.*

"Let's move." With a flick of his chin, Flóki gestured to Ryder. "The crew will open that gate. There's a tunnel we can take from the underground holding area. We'll follow that to the fjord. By the looks of it… not many will be joining us."

Desperation flooded my veins.

Is it because they fight in Chthonia's name that you disregard innocent life so easily? Did you even hear them? They treat you like a pest—they don't care about you. Muscles trembling, I repositioned my fingers on my dagger's hilt. *If I am to die today, I won't do it being the powerless pawn they assume I am. You might do the same.*

Alas. The demon released a bloody gurgle. *I will always be a monster.*

Prove them wrong.

Something unnerving glistened in the creature's gaze. Tears. Fear. *Will.*

A silhouette flittered in my peripheral. Ryder.

Spinning, I arced my dagger over my head, the steel screeching against his. "What a cute little bromance, you and Flóki. Did he lend you that blade?"

A guttural cry whistled through the arena, rattling hearts, weapons, bones. The jelmadag hissed, piping hot spit raining down around Flóki's feet.

The elf cursed, swearing torture and death upon the demon. It took effort not to smile at his frantic yells, the blubbering fool.

Ryder drew in close. Arms shaking, weapons crossed, blades straining against each other's, our heated breaths mixing in the small sliver of air. "Come with me."

"Never," I huffed, flinging my elbows out and pushing him off.

Those dark eyes narrowed, shadows eclipsing the ring of golden-green. A smirk curled his lips, cold and sadistic, and the veins along his throat pulsed black.

"What did they do to you?" I asked softly, so no one else heard.

Wincing, he took a stilted step closer, as if the effort physically pained him. "You promised me."

Fingertips grazed my chin, cupped my cheek. His skin was cold, so cold. I focused on remaining lethal and still, but a tremble worked its way through me. "What?"

That frigid hand slipped around my wrist. My pulse raged beneath his thumb.

He sucked in a breath. "That you wouldn't forget about me when…"

"When what?" I tugged on my arm. His grip remained firm.

I looked at him, really looked at him then. This… this person. They were just a shell for something I couldn't quite put my finger on—something that felt both vile and electric, tempting and taunting. An undercurrent. I'd experienced it before with Finis, with Kistuleitarinn, and even in the Heimer Töfra with Ryder.

It was evil.

Nervous heat turned my skin to fire.

What else had Ryder said in that twisted world of enchantment? No, not there. It was in the front seat of his car, speeding through the redwoods earlier that summer: *Demons aren't born, they're made.*

It was what the jelmadag just reminded me of ten minutes ago, what the Coffin Seeker had taunted me with below the castle: that we were more similar than I cared to admit. *That we were different sides of the same coin.*

Oh, no. My palm cupped my mouth. Ryder.

That cursed magic claimed a piece of my soul.

Oh, God. I was going to be sick. He—

I needed you to see there's still a piece of the old me, deep down inside.

He was turning into a demon.

"Are you scared?" he breathed, and it wasn't his voice, wasn't his smile, but when a soft sweep of his thumb traced over my skin, I still shuddered with longing that he mistook for fear. "Good—now follow my lead."

Dropping his hand, he stepped back, the steamy air, the screams, the death filling the space between us, leaching the want from my skin.

"Don't make this harder on yourself, River." With that phrase, with the way he drew out my name, as if it still belonged to him, I was catapulted back to that night at the Boardwalk. He'd said something similar, as if those damning words might comfort me. As if I'd actually listen. As if he wasn't actively trying to capture me again.

I barked out a cruel laugh. "Oh, I'll be fine. It's you I'm worried about."

He raised a brow.

Source thrummed in my heart. *Let me out,* it seemed to say with every beat. Welling in my fingertips, it spilled over the arena, hardly a shadow, a glimmer of movement in the corner of someone's eye. It dissipated quickly; the place was bare of elements, absolutely by design. *You got me this far*, I told it—told myself. *I can do the rest.*

Lowering into a crouch, I delivered a sweeping kick to the side of Ryder's leg. He fell to his knees, palms catching his weight. It wasn't even that hard, but I had the element of surprise. I knew he would underestimate me. Everyone always did.

Next, a boot to his face—that one probably did hurt, judging by the amount of blood.

I toed the knife that'd slipped out of his grasp until it spun just out of his reach. He was too busy clutching his nose to notice.

Whirling on him, I hooked my arm around his neck, bringing the tip of my whistling blade to his throat.

His hands shot up, scratching, pulling, begging me to release him. I only squeezed harder.

"Now it's my turn to ask." Lowering my mouth to his ear, his pulse raging wildly against my muscle, I whispered, "Are you scared?"

I inched the blade deeper, a drop of tarry crimson dribbling onto my sleeve.

"Yes," he finally croaked.

"Good, because now you're going to follow my lead."

"I'd follow you to the ends of the earth." His pale lips twitched, muttering far below the threshold of a whisper. "I'd follow you in death, in darkness, in light."

"Yeah, yeah, duty and all," I said, but still, my fingers slipped on the hilt. I straightened it immediately, but those words, the desperation—they did their job exactly, breaking me bit by bit.

His back flush against my chest, life hanging delicately in my grasp, I watched the horror unfold in front of me: the jelmadag's flames burning bright and blue, the tips so hot they turned colorless. Flóki loosely holding a knife at his side, waving it around like a dumbass, laughing and pointing at the poor creature. In the stands, Olivia holding her own against two merciless attackers, determined but weary. Eyes, clusters of them, swarming the royal box.

Two assailants in all black hopped over the railing, out of the luxury seating area, disappearing into the shadows of the stadium's corridors.

A guttural scream ripped through the arena. "MOM!"

My heart stopped.

A hand flopped against the stone, rings sparkling in the faint light shining down from the circular window above. Hems from the colorful gowns of hysterical elves shielded the rest of the queen's lifeless body from view.

Freyja tore apart the crowd, strawberry hair and violet chiffon flowing behind her, mowing down guards and hunters and courtiers alike—anything that stood in her way. Chest heaving, she stumbled to the edge of the balcony. Her bloodied fingers gripped the railing.

"You." The word, a threat. Her finger pointed down at the pit—at one of us—a mark for violence.

She hopped over the barrier, skirts sailing behind her, landing in a lethal crouch.

Flóki held out his arms. "Well, if it isn't the ice princess. Jealous to miss out on our fun?"

"I am not your princess," she seethed, every footfall a promise of blood.

"Fair point. If my men did their job"—he raised a blade towards the royal box—"which it looks like they did, that makes you 'queen'."

All the air rushed out of me. Sweat lined my palms. My knees buckled.

"Breathe, baby," Ryder said into my arm, the inflection vibrating against my skin.

"You shut up," I spat through gritted teeth. Tears burned my lids. "This is your fault; this is all your fucking fault."

"No weapon?" Flóki taunted the princess—the new queen. "You make this too easy."

Eyes darkening, Freyja raised her palms. "I have something better."

The arena began to shake. Silt spilled from the cracks in the stone. Then, in a roll of rock and dirt, the ground pitched down, then up. I jolted forward, bringing myself closer around Ryder's shoulders. Arm still tight around his neck, I rested my cheek on the crown of his head, using his chiseled body as my anchor.

Waiting out the tremors, I locked eyes with the jelmadag. Steam leaked out of every orifice, fur damp and blanched, gaze red and glassy.

We only had a few minutes. I only had one knife. And at least half the people down here wanted to kill me.

"Your useless Galdur can't do shit." Flóki's tone grew impatient, aggressive. "Have you forgotten I am of elven blood?"

"Betrayal will do that," Freyja snarled.

"What?"

"Make you forgetful. Turn you into a monster."

A scream leapt past Flóki's lips.

There was nothing human about it.

I am... sorry... The jelmadag's last words entered my mind.

No. Tears I'd worked so hard to hold in splashed my cheeks. *We'll stop this. I'll fix this.* What stupid, meaningless things to say. I knew the reality. I had no ounce of hope.

We were going to die here. We all were.

A violent sob racked my chest, my body shaking against Ryder's back.

Silver beads of light pierced my wet lash line—a reflection hitting me square in the eye. The chain. The one swinging between the jelmadag's shoulder blades, pinning his wings.

Pinning him *here*.

An idea took hold.

A foolish, reckless idea.

Nerves clawing at my stomach, I released the tight hold on my ex, my fingers skimming the collar of his shirt. He slumped forward, palm cupping the nape of his neck.

I took off running, heading straight for the jelmadag.

"River!" Ryder's scream was lost to the endless pounding of my heart, to the wind whistling past my ears.

The demon let out a wet snarl. Intelligence shone in his eyes. Suffering. Defeat.

As I drew closer, a blast of heat and humidity swarmed me—stray hairs stuck to my temples, sweat lined my upper lip, my eyeballs felt like they were on the verge of melting.

Stay away, the demon spat, writhing against the stone. *No amount of water can withstand these temperatures.*

With a prayer to whoever might be watching, I clamped my hands around the hilt of the sword lodged in his throat. Another call of my name—closer, more frantic.

Heat like I'd never felt, like the flare of a thousand suns, branded my palms.

Gritting my teeth, my tears vaporizing before they could even fall, I yanked as hard as I could.

Trapped steam rushed out of the beast's open maw as I slowly drew the blade out of his neck. An agonizing whistle roiled in his throat, like a teakettle left on too long. It dragged over my senses. The whole blade finally spilled out, thumping to the ground.

My arms were boneless, as if they'd melted off, but I swung the sword, bringing it down into the small space between his wings. The feathered limbs unfolded, quivering in the air.

Chest heaving, I dropped the scalding metal handle. I turned my hands over. Blisters bubbled along the joints. They stung, but they weren't in nearly as bad a shape as they should have been.

Arms wrapped around my waist, swinging me back.

"What are you doing?!" I twisted, kicking my legs, bucking my hips.

"Saving your ass!" Ryder said. "We need to get out of here. *Now.*"

Around us, glass shattered, stone cracked, and the *screaming*—it was feral, panicked.

Death coated the air.

I glanced over my shoulder. Through the mess of my hair, I saw a purple lump on the floor, strawberry strands of hair splayed around it. *No.*

Palm curled, arm rising as if he were uprooting invisible plants from the ground, Flóki stomped towards Freyja. A knife glistened in his other hand.

And yet she still cursed him, despite being sprawled on the floor, with a weapon headed straight for her neck.

"Let go of me!" My voice was desperate, ragged.

It was unclear if Ryder was ignoring me or just couldn't hear me, but I didn't have time to ask politely—my friend was about to be murdered in cold blood. My heel struck his shin.

He yelped in pain, loosening his grip just enough for me to wiggle out of it and run to the blood-streaked sword still lying in the open.

Skin sizzling, elbows screaming in pain, I lifted the weapon, buckling at its weight.

I'm not sure what propelled me forward—determination, supernatural ability, a blessing from the gods—but a heartbeat later, I was halfway across the pit.

Cyclones of dirt and sand and rock rained down upon Freyja's body with the steady flicks of Flóki's fingers. A dusty forearm blocked the crown of her head, but it wasn't enough. Her face was absolutely ruined. One eye black and blue, the other squinted open, blood pooling from her nose. A streak of silver flashed above Flóki's head. The knife.

I was close enough to see the horror in Freyja's eyes, but I wasn't close enough to stop it.

"NO!" I screamed.

Mustering every scrap of strength and magic I had, I threw the sword—I was too many feet away, too white-hot with rage. But still I hoped, and it was stupid, but once the hilt left my hands, hope was all I had.

Sunlight glistened off the metal, and as Flóki brought his blade down, mine slammed into his back. Immediately, he fell to his knees. I did the same.

Freyja pushed up onto her palms. Her lips moved, shaping words I couldn't hear.

A lump formed in my throat, my chest. My hands shook in my lap.

Wind rustled my clothes, batting the hair out of my face, but I couldn't see through the tears. Just a warmth, a shadow, a flicker of night.

Get on. A rasp of the jelmadag's voice thundered in my mind.

I didn't move. I couldn't. All I could do was stare. Red. Bubbling. Blood. Weapon. Red.

Growls rent the air. If they hadn't been deep enough to quake the earth, to rattle bones, I probably wouldn't have noticed. Don't make me ask again.

Body trembling, teeth chattering, I rose to my feet. Heat rippled off the demon.

"River, wait!" a voice called, a voice I'd recognize any-where, a voice I wasn't sure how to feel about anymore.

The jelmadag hissed, the ridge of fur along its spine standing on end. Permission to extinguish your boyfriend? I don't appreciate the way he's looking at me—or you, for that matter.

Lifting my head, I caught the outline of him. Tall, dishev-eled, black shirt, black boots, dark hair. Ryder. He's always like that.

Fine. Get on.

Are you snarling at me? I coughed. My lungs were burning. You're bleeding.

I've bled worse.

You're hungry.

I can find a horse.

When's the last time you flew? Do you even remember how?

Angel of Water, do not push me. I will take you where you need to go.

An arm's length away, Ryder halted. "Baby, we can get out of here right now, away from all this. Please."

Flashes of crisp blue uniforms descended into the pit. Eyes. Help. It was over.

"No pulse," I heard one of them say.

Gunnar sprinted to Freyja, dropping to his knees, and held her sobbing in his arms. Olivia leaned over a railing, head bowed, shirt torn, but alive and breathing.

The shadows had fled.

A tingle of relief and pure exhaustion washed over me.

"Ryder." I swallowed, and it was like gulping down sandpaper. "I need you to make *me* a promise now."

His throat bobbed.

"Show me you're that guy, the one you say is still there deep down inside. The one who gave me my necklace, the one who kissed me in the spirit realm, the one whose heart still beats." Make this worth it, I wanted to say. Don't give me this title for nothing. *Murderer.* "Surrender to the Eyes. Clean up this mess. Remember why you said you came here. For *me.*"

Gnashing his teeth together, he nodded.

I wanted him to hold me so badly. But I just turned and gripped the flowing tendrils of the jelmadag and hoisted myself onto his rippling back.

Are you ready?

A furnace of heat blazed around me, warping the air, warping *him*—emotion welled in Ryder's eyes, streaks of green cutting through the black.

Would mine suck up the darkness like that, too? After all, I'd done worse than kidnap.

I'd killed.

Yes.

On a steaming exhale, we launched into the air, a flash of matted fur and leathered wings.

I stole a long glance at the pit, and when the Eyes flocked around Ryder, their spears aimed at his heart, he slowly put his hands behind his head.

Hold on, the demon warned, and we shot through the dome's single skylight, glass falling like stars as we disappeared into the open sky.

CHAPTER 36

I KILLED A MAN.

Those were the only words I could hear, think, feel, as we scattered the clouds and soared above the vast Icelandic fjords.

Flóki's seized muscles, the bob of his head, the way his body sank to the floor. I shut my eyes, but under my lids, the images only grew stronger.

The jelmadag was silent—quiet thoughts, quiet wings, quiet breaths. Crisp air burned my lungs, cooling some of the hellfire, my Source roaring through me to shield its burn. As I sank into his mane, the blue-tipped flames tickled my face. I needed to get to Jarðarbæli.

Somehow, I was sure the demon knew that. But perhaps even more so, that I needed this: to let my tears fall, to fly even without my wings, to simply exist, no expectations.

I killed a man.

CHAPTER 37

We landed in a valley blanketed in moss, ancient layers of rock and lichen scattering at the beat of the jelmadag's wings. I slipped off the creature's side, landing on an onyx sandbank. My muscles flinched at the impact. Frigid wind ripped off the rugged slopes, some of the peaks so high they kissed the circling dark clouds. The air pulsed with power, feral and raw.

"Þórsmörk," the demon offered. "Land of the Gods."

Solid name. The mountains themselves were so breathtaking it was almost holy. Shallow grooves meandered through the vale, carrying the runoff from the ice caps.

Crouching on the damp bank, I peered into a glistening stream. My haggard reflection stared back. Mouth tight, lip split, brow bones bruised—murderous. I cupped my hands in the bone-chilling water, unable to stand the look of myself. I splashed my face, scrubbing at the dirt smattering my cheeks, picking out the dried blood beneath my fingernails.

Just like the blood of Flóki.

I shot backwards, tripping over my feet, my chest tightening, nearly cutting off my breath. I was exactly what the

Coffin Seeker had claimed I was. A murderer, a kindred spirit in death—

Do not be so hard on yourself. The jelmadag let out a steamy exhale. *We all do what we need to do.*

"I'm just like them." I bit back a sob. The grief had sunk its teeth into me, and now that it had latched on, it'd soon tear me to shreds, the sharp ache of it clawing at my heart, my stomach. "My instinct was to kill."

"Your instinct was to protect." A black tongue darted out, lapping up a shiny beetle. "You would be wise not to confuse the two."

"I suppose," I grumbled.

Turning to face the demon, I spotted a gaping hole in the mountainside. The mouth of a cave, etchings in the stone—indecipherable, at this distance, aside from the obvious circle with the four-pointed star in the center. The Empyrean symbol for earth.

I tossed my chin in its direction. "That it, then?"

"Þórsmörk, Land of the Gods *and* Throne of the Earth."

Jarðarbæli. Gaia's lair—more like tomb, after what Kistuleitarinn had done. Pretty sure I caught the pale glint of a femur from where I was standing.

Wiping my hands on my thighs, I walked around the jelmadag's midnight silhouette, the soil squishing beneath my tread.

"I dare not go any closer," he said.

Halting, I tossed over my shoulder, "What will you do?"

"Go home." Home. Even the wildest of beasts had a place where they belonged, a place they dreamed of. "But first, a farm. I'm hungry."

I chewed the inside of my cheek. "Will you fight for them?" I asked, Flóki's evil grin still at the forefront of my thoughts. "Despite what happened in the arena?"

"I will do what I am ordered to do, Angel of Water," he replied diplomatically.

"Got it." My shoulders fell. "Well… thank you for not eating me, and not taking me to them."

He nodded. "I only returned a favor."

Bearing his weight on his knees, he brought his belly to the ground, positioning himself to spring.

"Wait." My hand shot forward, as if I could stop him from leaving. "What's your name?"

"I am a jelmadag, lesser demon of Chthonia, bound and born to serve the Scale of Six."

"No, not what you are. *Who* you are. Your name. What people call you."

"I—that—" Words had never been a struggle for this beast. "That is not part of my identity."

I blinked. "You don't have a name?"

All dozen eyes blinked back. Snowcapped mountains twinkled in their reflections, and the threads of a conversation I'd had spun together in my mind: Gunnar in his blue uniform, something undeserving twinkling in his eyes… a jumble of words spoken on an icy cliffside. *People care about you. You're what we call a Skært Ljós.* God, I should have been nicer. *Someone that makes things better. A bright light.*

"Ljós." It rolled off the tongue. "That's your name. I'll record it in that book I found about you." I tilted my head. "I don't know if it's fate or coincidence that it was your page lying open on that table in the archives, but I'm glad it was."

Darkness streaked before his snout, a crack of its flaming tail. "Meeting you has been… the most pleasurable experience I've had in one hundred years."

Cheeks tightening on a smile, I sucked in a ragged breath and stepped back, giving Ljós some runway.

Wings shuddered and spread. Patches of feathers flittered off, dusting the ground. Warm gusts blew the loose moss and sand and the shorter layers of my hair out of my face as his paws left the earth.

And just like that, the demon left, becoming nothing more than a shadow floating through the sky.

Fingers wringing against my sweaty palms, I strode towards Jarðarbæli, ready to meet the ghostly double of myself.

It couldn't be worse than who I'd already become.

CHAPTER 38

THE CAVE WAS QUIET.

Too quiet.

When I crossed the threshold, even the low howl of the wind surrendered to silence. The murderous pound of my heart echoed off the dank walls, my soles thudding on the damp soil like a war drum.

My gaze bored into the shadows, sweeping the corners for silhouettes, for ghosts.

For that alternate version of myself.

Skeletal remains were scattered on the ground like ivory chips, practically glowing in the darkness—which was thicker here, mustier, the surrounding mountains blocking the light and casting the place in near pitch-blackness.

"Hello?" my voice chorused, calling a dozen times, echoing deep into the heart of the cavern. I expected one to talk back, but when they all faded, it was only silence that answered.

A draft cycled through, spreading the scent of mildew and decay. Between its whispers, I swore there was a laugh, a watchful eye—a sense of knowing.

Shivers raked my spine, but I trudged deeper, because the only way forward was inward.

If I turned back now, the desolate Icelandic wilderness would eat me alive. Miles, I was *miles* away—I'd counted at least three ridgelines and one vast lava field on the way here—from any form of civilization.

Remote wasn't even the right term for it; I might as well have been in a different world.

Since there was no alternative, I called into the depths of the cave again. "Hello?"

Soft light flickered in the blackness, dancing off the rock ahead. A low hum drifted to my ears. My heart leapt. There was someone else in here.

I broke into a jog, the path growing paler, messier, more densely littered with bones. A girl kneeled at an altar, her brown hair slicked behind her ears, her blue dress stained and torn.

It was me—other me.

Any semblance of confidence left my body, leaving my voice low and hoarse. "Hi there," I said to my doppelgänger, unsure how I was supposed to address *myself.*

She—*I*—held an old angel figurine, the color faded, the ceramic cracked, a wing missing. She was turning it over and over in her hands, her fingers raw and bloody.

I lowered myself into a crouch, my teeth clattering against the cold, my nerves, and met her at her level. The humming stopped. Her body stilled. Slowly her head turned as if it were separate from her body, on a swivel.

Candlelight flickered over hollow black eyes and sunken cheeks; thin black veins popped against ghostly white skin. All the air left my lungs, and I slipped backwards, catching myself on my palms. She grinned, a mutilated smile full of crimson-stained teeth.

I reached for my dagger.

She lunged.

I rolled out of the way, her clawlike hands drilling into the ground—where my chest would have been seconds before.

"What's wrong?" she said—I said—but it wasn't my voice, it was throaty and all wrong, and yet the words were leaving *both* our lips. "Don't like what you see?"

Her neck twisted, the tendons protruding, bones cracking at the harsh angle. I felt my own snapping, turning to meet her stare.

"What is happening?!" I said, and she echoed me in her creepy singsong of a voice.

I gasped, and she cackled.

I stumbled, and she charged.

In a streak of bluish black so fast it was like she flew, she tackled me, slamming me into a pile of skulls. I sank into the bones, the air thinning, fear crushing. Razor-sharp nails clawed at my clothes, at my face, at my hair.

The heel of my palm slammed into her shoulder, but she just brought her face closer, her rotten breath breezing my cheeks. Her pupils glinted with a savage hunger.

Fighting to inhale, to move, I snuck my hand into my boot, wrapping my fingers around the hilt of my blade.

She mimicked the movement, reaching into the skeletons. Cartilage snapped, and as I brought my weapon to my chest, she raised hers—a splintered bone—over my head.

Was this how it ended? Would I kill her—myself? My grip was slick on my dagger.

I shut my eyes and counted down from ten. On that last number, that last whisper, a calm flooded my veins.

This was it. It was over.

I pressed my elbow into the dirt, then pushed up.

"River, no!" An accented voice snapped my eyes open.

A shadow fell over us. The other me mirrored my look of surprise.

"You can't kill her!" Insistence draped the intruder's tone. Light and fluid. Female. "If she dies, so do you. She *is* you."

Seeming to waver between impulses—kill or listen— my doppelgänger and I released the hold on our weapons. They clattered against the dirt. She darted into a shadowy alcove and sank to the ground. Arms wrapped around her knees, she rocked back and forth, quietly humming.

She wouldn't look at me.

A hand, human, appeared in the empty space before me. After staring at it for longer than probably necessary— counting all five fingers, noting her fair skin popping against the dark cave—I took it.

Legs wobbling, I rose to my feet.

Divine presence swept over the room. Over me. An urge to bow. To sing. To worship. To pray. To kiss the ground.

Brilliant wings—so white they shone like beacons in the gloom, so tall the tips grazed the ceiling and the bottoms swept the floor—fluttered and folded, flush against her shoulder blades.

She was fresh-cut grass and fallen leaves and fields of flowers. She was rocky mountains and steep ravines and mossy canyons. She was sustenance, soil, nutrients, life. She was a voice, one of three, that had haunted my waking thoughts for so, so long.

She was Earth—Mother Earth.

Fiery green eyes flared, two beacons of chartreuse flame in this dark, musty, dirt world. "We finally meet, River Harlow."

CHAPTER 39

GAIA." WHISPERED LIKE A PRAYER, HER NAME TAN-gled on my tongue, as if I didn't hold the divine right to speak it.

She bit the inside of her lip, pale yellow brows rising, cheeks growing fuller as if she…

Was she holding in a laugh?

"Now that you've dropped to your knees, you owe me twenty pushups."

"I'm sorry." The words, my mind, were a confusing, bumbling mess. I scrambled to right myself, forcing my soft legs to hold me. "What?"

Leaning on the curve of her full hip, Gaia crossed her arms. The scabbard fixed to her belt shifted with the motion. "You get this a lot, I'm sure, but you remind me so much of your mother."

My throat bobbed. I could think of nothing to say. What *could* I say? I was a mere mortal beside her. I must have been staring. Fuck it, I *know* I was staring.

Airy laughter bubbled out of her, so light and carefree.

Oh my God, could she hear what I was thinking?

She waved towards the back of the cave. Come.

Her lips didn't move, yet her voice rang against the stones, the walls, the bones, the hard-packed mud, she and the elements fused as one.

She stepped into the gloom, wings softly glowing and illuminating the path, thick heels indenting the dirt.

I glanced at my doppelgänger, whimpering in the corner. A pang of hurt lanced through my heart. What about her? I thought.

You're not ready to face her, Gaia said, and I nearly jumped out of my skin. It'd been so long since she answered my thoughts, I almost forgot she could do it—almost forgot I'd spent a full decade giving up headspace to her and the other two archangels, Fei and Akosua. She'll be there when you are. Don't worry.

A chill raked my spine, as if the same emptiness that haunted that lonely girl in the corner had wrapped around me. I shook it off, jetting after Gaia.

Her silhouette burned back the shadows. When she turned down a tunnel, everything left behind pitched into darkness. Including me.

"Wait!" I said, hands flinging out in front of me as I fought my way through the lightless cavern, chasing after the faint glow of her wings.

She turned down a fork in the path. A faint roar rose from its depths.

My stomach twisted. Where are we going? I wondered.

I can't stand the sight of the bones, she sighed. Some of those belong to my friends.

Her scribes. I gulped. The Coffin Seeker. He'd gloated that the inner caves were supposed to be the worst.

My palm clapped over my mouth as we turned down yet another winding hall.

Water trickled over the path, my feet sloshing in the loose dirt. Or was it blood…

Gaia interrupted my thoughts. It's just water, River.

Just when my legs felt like they might give out, shafts of light streaked the dim corridor. I dared a glance at my feet. No bones, no bodies, only puddles and rocks. The roar I'd heard when we entered grew steadier, fiercer, louder.

The pathway opened up into a chamber, its ceiling as tall as a mountain peak. Ferns dripped from the walls and a waterfall thundered in the middle, its mist glittering in the air and dusting my cheeks.

A rainbow arced across the turquoise pool. I paused on the black lava bank, breathing in the ice and moss and magic.

Behind the falls, faint flickers of green and yellow and red poked through. Even with the obstructed view, I knew what they were—the Empyrean symbols for the Watchers—exactly like the ones in my mom's lair at Natural Bridges.

Gaia hopped onto a boulder, sitting still as the stone. The bottom tips of her wings grazed the ground.

The waterfall beat against the pool's surface, but it might as well have been my shoulders. "I killed a man."

Kicking a thigh-high boot over a knee, she tucked her fist under her chin. "I know."

"And you're okay with that?" Hot shame crept up my neck. "I'm a murderer."

Soft light radiated from her, painting her square face, her wide jaw, her slightly upturned nose, in an otherworldly glow.

"Isn't that against some heavenly law? It's against mortal law for sure." I glared at the waterfall, at the shining glyphs behind it, at the empty space where my mom's should've been burning bright. "Will I turn into a demon? Will I be sent to the Fall?"

We've all done things we're not proud of. The cavern pulsed with the words. I heard them in my heart, my soul, my mind just as much as my ears. *It doesn't make you evil.*

I scuffed the sole of my shoe on the ground. "You've killed people?"

She slid down the stone, coming to join me at my side. Her arm grazed mine.

"I convinced an entire elven kingdom to fight in a war I fear we will never win. Hundreds died—soldiers and innocents alike. So, guilty as charged." The tips of her wings shuddered. "And it's only going to happen again."

"It's inevitable, isn't it? This war," I said, pacing the waterline, my shoes sinking into the dark sand.

Gaia didn't answer, standing tall and straight like a chiseled, porcelain statue.

"I mean, there has to be an alternative to *more* violence," I pondered out loud as I walked back and forth, back and forth, following the crescent shape of the pool.

I twisted the sleeves of my shirt, the fabric drooping and soiled. Orange and black wisps of ink peeked out of the cuff.

Finally, the angel decided to speak. "I have one too."

Chin snapping up, I met her stare. *That* wasn't what I was expecting her to say. Her eyes flicked to my wrist. Green flames danced playfully behind her pupils, in place of irises.

"You have a tattoo?" My mouth hung open longer than I'd intended, but the shock was real.

Rolling up the gossamer sleeve of her forest-green tunic, she held out her arm to show a grayscale dragon, permanently in flight below her inner elbow.

"I have a few, actually. And this one—" She pulled up the platinum strands of loose hair that weren't braided along the crown of her head, and revealed a small anchor, blotchy ink and uneven lines on the back of her neck. "Lost a bet to a sailor one night."

Despite it all, a ghost of a smile danced over my lips. "No kidding…"

Letting down her hair, she bumped my shoulder with hers, broad and plush. "Your mother used to come here when she'd visit. When she wasn't off calming a tempest or rounding up mischievous river sprites or redirecting selkies back into the wild depths of the sea." Her gaze locked onto the shoreline, as if the memory was dancing before her eyes. "We'd sit on this beach, split a bottle of wine, dip our toes in the water, and gossip about the seraphim."

I filled my lungs with air, and for the first time in a long, long time it didn't feel stabbing, heavy. Haunting.

"I miss her." Emotion softened her rolling accent. "And while Mira's not here anymore"—she turned to me then—"you are."

Spoken as if that meant something, as if the fate of the realm wasn't truly doomed.

"I heard that." Her laugh was a shift of the earth, deep and rumbling.

My cheeks flushed. I really needed to tighten my mental

shield. If that was even possible; Gaia was looking at me like it wasn't, or at least, that'd it be really, really hard.

It was funny, I'd wished the Voices away for so long. But now that I had hers in my head again, I felt healed, whole—even if the whole telepathy thing was *extremely intrusive*.

She pursed her full lips, but it wasn't enough to stifle her smile. "With you, Mortal Earth stands a chance. We can fortify the realm. We can restore the wards."

"How? There are only two of you." I stopped when she raised an eyebrow, then corrected myself. "Okay, like two and a half."

"We have to summon the Angel of Air," Gaia mused.

"What about," I said, gulping nervously, "the Angel of Fire?" Akosua's voice of fervor and flame, her words—spitting and passionate—shot through my mind.

Our gazes drifted to the symbols behind the falls: earth, air, and fire. I narrowed my eyes, swearing a faint blue flickered alongside them—but it was probably just a trick of the light and the rushing water.

"We…" She trailed off, pulling at a silver thread dangling from her clothes. "We don't know."

"You don't think she joined hell like they claim she did?"

"I think that realm is founded on lies." Gaia curled her fingers, and a translucent wave of Source broke through her tight fists. Dirt shook loose from the walls. Ferns fluttered. The force of it rustled the air in my lungs. "Akosua wasn't thrilled with your mom's decision—none of us were—but she wasn't evil. She was steadfast in her loyalty to Empyrea. This switch to suddenly fight for the enemy, it just… doesn't make sense."

As if Gaia had turned on a faucet, all of a sudden the details from that night at the Boardwalk flooded me. And I let myself watch them, let myself *feel* the shock, the pain, the betrayal all over again. Facing Ryder and Leif. Surfing the concrete wave. Seeing Javi on top of the wreckage. Smoke and shadows and crooked limbs. Serpentine and avian, evil, gruesome. It was only when Finis had me alone that she revealed the reason why they hadn't just outright killed me.

They wanted my powers.

Desire and desperation are different things, the Coffin Seeker had told me deep in his haunted, wet dungeon.

I hated to think of him, hated even more that he might be right. Again.

"What if," I said carefully, "this is all just a ploy to try and get us to join them? You said yourself, Chthonia is built on nothing but lies."

It's true. Gaia's voice barreled into my mind. They thrive on deceit.

"When Chthonia's lackeys almost captured me earlier this summer, one of their Greater Demons told me they wanted my powers, that they *needed* them in order to bridge the realms, to rule Mortal Earth." As I spoke the words out loud, exhilaration grew in my chest. "What if that's what they have planned for *all* of us?"

A beat. To siphon our powers?

I nodded. "And they'll do it by whatever means necessary. Whether that's false promises, kidnapping, threats, violence, or straight up lies."

Which means Akosua didn't join Chthonia willingly. A white moth fluttered on the damp air. Gaia held out a finger.

"What if breaking our telepathic connection was a last resort?" I said, the idea unfolding like a winning hand. "Not to destroy us but—"

To save us, she finished, her answer coming through the foliage as a slight tremor in the earth. And now... The moth drifted in the cool air, closer, until it landed on her pointer. We need to save her.

"Alright." I rubbed my palms together. "What are the magic words?"

"Excuse me?" The warm light radiating from her wings bounced off the dainty insect's.

"You know, to summon the Angel of Air?" Was it hot in here, or was it just me? "That was our first task, right? I assumed there was a spell or incantation."

Squinching her nose, Gaia patted my shoulder. The moth took flight at the movement. "We call upon Fei the same way you called upon me. Walk into her lair with an open heart."

"Where's that?"

"On the outskirts of a village just outside one of my favorite cities on Mortal Earth: Ho Chi Minh."

My jaw fell. "Vietnam?" I hardly had enough money, enough *excuses,* to pull off coming here. How the hell was I going to go on another trip, let alone one on the literal opposite side of the world?! "Can't you just go back the way you came and grab her?"

"Empyrea's fortified. You know, threats of war and all that. Once you leave, you can't go back in. At least for now."

The pale lighthouse on that mossy Icelandic bluff whipped across my mind.

If Gaia was here, we could just go there right now. It was a portal.

"Those are also locked," she quipped.

My face turned wintry. "Hasn't anyone told you it's rude to read people's minds?"

She laughed, and flowers bloomed from the vines creeping over the walls. "There's the River I've missed."

I rolled my eyes. "Okay, so we go to Fei's lair, and then she just..." My brows furrowed. "Appears?"

"She'll receive the summoning. It's kind of like those chimes when you walk into a mini-mart that lets the clerk know you're there." She twirled a rogue strand of hair around her finger. "Ooooh, can we hit one of those on the way back to Ískastali? They have the *best* hot dogs."

"We?" I blinked.

She shot me a wry smile in return. "I'm coming with you. Obviously. But first we need to honor the monarchy. I know some of the queen's methods were questionable—"

"Unethical," I amended.

"Sure, but it was all for the sake of her kingdom. You might know someone who did the same?" She tilted her head, a knowing gleam in her eyes. "Who sacrificed everything to protect the ones they love?"

My heart twisted.

"Regardless," she went on, her wings ruffling behind her, "it's tradition."

I inhaled deeply.

I hadn't even thought about going back to Hamarinn, about who and what I'd have to face. Had they removed Hildur's body from the arena? Was the entire realm aware of what happened? Had Ryder kept his promise or had he massacred them all? Anxiety built in my chest, trapped and roiling like the steam in the jelmadag.

"But first," she said, "that hot dog."

My forehead crinkled. Here I was, shoulders heavy and caving, nearly crushed by the panic, and Gaia, the Angel of Earth—the literal epitome of strength and divinity and justice—was worried about… hot dogs.

"Lighten up, River." Wings shaking off the thin layer of moisture that'd accumulated from the spray of the falls, she patted me on the back, then strutted towards the tunnel, her holy light dwindling as she walked further into the shadows. "We've got plenty of dark times ahead."

"Don't they feed you in Empyrea?" I called after her.

"No!" she cackled. "Angels don't feel hunger. When I come here, my body shifts into a vessel that's much more mortal. Now, if you don't hurry up, I think I might faint of starvation, and then you'll have to *carry* me to Hamarinn!"

Tripping over vines and loose boulders, I sprinted after her, and we made our way back through the passage, but this time, she wasn't leading.

This time, we walked side by side.

We treaded through the labyrinth of darkness, over the bones, then finally past the altar, the candles now burning bright. It was empty, silent, not a sign of my doppelgänger.

As we neared the cave's gaping mouth, a silhouette stood beneath the overhang, painted in the coral tint of sunset. It was her—me—facing the vale, the mess of her hair blowing softly in the wind.

I slowed. "What is she doing?"

Waiting, the angel answered, crossing over to the mirror version of me. Gaia gave her a warm smile, her cheeks full and rosy.

"For what?" I breathed.

For you to let her go.

On a tight inhale, I approached the twisted image of myself, the soles of my feet sliding over the skeletal remains.

Only when I was standing beside her, my arm brushing hers, did she turn to greet me. My breath slipped at that haunting black stare. Muscles trembling, I reached for her hand. It was stiff and cold as a corpse.

Her eyes darted to my grip. Hollow, uncertain, but then her fingers wrapped around mine.

Our heartbeats synced, slowed, as we stood there, taking each other in, faces tinged by the deepening orange and pink hues of the world.

Between one breath and the next, one spontaneous blink, she was gone, and I was holding nothing but air. A ragged exhale left my lips.

Even though I could no longer see her, I knew she was still there. Part of my soul, part of my shadows, part of my Source. Part of me.

"Ready now?" Gaia asked, her curious emerald eyes ablaze.

I nodded, my gaze roving over her brilliant white feathers—those were going to draw *a lot* of attention.

As she crossed the threshold, her wings shimmered into nothing but a shadow, a play of the dwindling light. *There.* The word pulsed through my mind.

So, it wasn't just her stomach that shifted into something more human, it was all of her.

"You coming, Angel of Water?" she tossed over her shoulder, fiery irises deepening to a solid hunter green.

"Are we walking?" I asked, following her out into the open wilderness.

A star studded the sky, then another, and another as the sun dipped below the mountains, twilight taking its indigo hold. I shivered against the cold that Gaia seemed to embrace.

Her lips tilted into a mischievous grin.

Placing the tips of her thumb and pointer finger in her mouth, Gaia blew, letting out a shrill whistle that echoed off the canyon and rang through the natural hollow.

Hooves patted the soil. A moonlit horse galloped into view, silver-white mane flapping in the wind. Something glimmered on its forehead: a fractal of crystal, of pearl—a horn.

The unicorn came to a halt in front of us, the breeze kissing its silky hair.

My hand shot to my mouth. At the sudden movement, the creature took a cautious prance back, its nostrils flaring.

"She's a tad skittish," Gaia warned. "Let her take the lead."

Slowly, I extended my palm. "What's her name?"

"Rune. Pretty, huh?"

Whinnying, Rune pawed the earth.

Gaia's voice was soft and sweet. *"Sæll gamli vinur."*

"What did you say?"

"Hello, old friend."

Horn glistening, Rune kicked up her head, nosing my empty palm.

"Hi, girl." I gently pressed my free hand against her muzzle, running it over the velvet fur. "I wish I had a treat for you."

"The elves will have plenty at the stables," Gaia said, drifting to Rune's side. Dropping her face close, she whispered, *"Leyfi til að hjóla?"*

Tips of her ears twitching, the unicorn's front legs dipped low.

"Permission to mount has been granted." Gaia patted Rune's dappled white shoulder blades. "Come on. You first."

Grabbing a handful of Rune's lustrous mane, I hoisted myself up, scooching to the base of her neck. The Angel of Earth hopped on after me, sitting flush with my back. Taking two full strands of the unicorn's hair in her fists, Gaia lightly tapped her boots against Rune's sides.

With the speed of a falling star, we shot through the headlands, the caves and glaciers and meadows blending into one, as we rode alongside the icy wind.

CHAPTER 40

THE FIRE DANCED, HOT AND WILD, LEAPING TOWARDS the sky. Hildur, once a great ruler, was now nothing more than ashes, a whispered tale in the night.

I wiped my cheek, red from the wind, burning from the tears. Where did the elves go when they died?

Did they become the voices of the earth, or the echoes in the mountains, or the twisting strips of green and pink that streaked the sky?

Did they take the dried lupine, the muslin cloth, the branded weapons, all the offerings at their pyres with them into the next life?

Heat from the white-hot flames melted the layer of frost covering the ground. A slosh of mud and snow splashed the bottom of my dress. My hands twisted in the diamond-flecked sapphire fabric.

I'd have shown up in my crusty leathers and unbrushed hair, but Hildur was always one for tradition. So, when Gaia and I returned, I reluctantly took a bath then let Helga curl, cut, clothe, and scold me—*No weapons at a funeral, River!*— so I could honor the Queen of the Huldufólk one last time.

I righted the thin strap that'd slipped off my shoulder, the tiniest movement stabbing and aching.

My breaths felt like they'd never catch up, each exhale a punch to my rib cage.

The smoke probably didn't help.

But I wouldn't move. I couldn't, despite the service being done and over and the majority of guests now gathered inside the Great Hall, picking at a feast for a Harvest Festival that'd never come—one thing Flóki hadn't lied to me about.

He hadn't gotten a pyre, and I didn't dare ask what the alternative was.

Wind ran its hands through the soft waves of my hair.

A shadow flickered over a broken battlement, the fire casting the lean silhouette of a grieving straggler behind me—beside me.

Emerald-satin fabric brushed against my arm.

My gaze floated to the mountain that towered over the castle, the snow casting its rugged canvas in a shimmer of white. Two striking blue specks flickered along the ridgeline. My breath caught in my throat.

"Grýla," Freyja growled.

Those curious glacial eyes wavered.

Then they grew smaller, into pinpricks, until they disappeared completely, and I was left wondering if the ogress had really been there at all.

"What will happen to her?" I asked.

"The bargain's done. She's free. And if she knows what's good for her…" Freyja continued, pitching her voice up, "she'll mind her own damn business!"

The words echoed off the mountain face.

Spine straight, shoulders still, angel senses prickling, I waited for Grýla's answer—an avalanche, a snarl in the night. When those didn't come, I said, "Aren't you worried about your castle? Without her magic, it's no longer hidden from your enemies."

"We can't hide forever." Freyja curled her hands into fists. "With our Galdur restored, we are more than capable of protecting Ískastali without her help. I will make sure of it."

"Do you think she'll just…" Goosebumps dressed my arms like a second set of sleeves. "Let everything go?"

"My mom is dead," she said, but this time, she didn't fight the grief that'd been sneaking into her tone. "Grýla would be wise to let this feud die with the queen instead of taking it out on her subjects. Regardless… We'll be monitoring her movements."

"Freyja." Her name ripped out of my throat with a cry. "I'm so sorry."

The princess—the queen—nodded.

"Me too," she whispered.

Embers popped, stray tinder igniting in a fiery blaze. For a while, it was only the fire that spoke, spitting and whistling in a rhythmic crackle.

"My mother used to tell me when an elf dies, their spirit becomes part of the realm. That we'd be able to hear them on the breeze, feel them in the soil, see them in the stars."

Lungs aching, I held a sob tight in my chest.

"But," Freyja continued, her voice breaking, "I don't hear her, River. I don't feel her. The sky looks the same." She turned to me then, cheeks smattered with tears. "Where did she go?"

Biting down on my lip, I shook my head. "I wish I knew."

"This crown." Icy metal looped around her wrist, the silver reflecting the dance of the flames. "It's too heavy. It doesn't fit my head. I don't want it. I don't want this. I *can't* do this."

Part of me wished I had the energy to hype her up, but the truth was, I knew the feeling all too well. Thrust into someone else's shoes that would never quite fit—that would always feel too big, too bold. Unearned.

Words were failing me, so, instead, I tilted my head and rested it on her shoulder, taking her hand in mine. She squeezed back, her chest caving, shaking, and we watched the wood burn while the Northern Lights twirled above.

A falling star shot across the vast sea of midnight.

"The elves used to worship them—the stars. The brightest ones in the sky were said to be gods." She sniffled. "Have you decided what to ask of them?"

"What do you mean?"

"You enacted elven law. You survived the brutal games of the Terrordome. By right, you are granted a pardon, a mercy, or a wish."

My head shot up. "But I didn't defeat the jelmadag."

"I don't think the jelmadag was the real opponent," she said quietly.

Flóki. His stiff body, blood pooling out beneath him, the sword rigid and right.

"I thought that was just it," I said, cutting off my own thoughts. "A game. Are the old gods even real?"

"Guess we'll find out."

I stared at the fire. The smoke billowed, the flames seeming to snap hotter, wilder with the racing of my heart. Sweat tickled the hairline at the base of my neck. A presence weighed on the night. Powerful, ancient, watching with prying eyes, listening with meticulous ears.

Greed and power, vengeance and darkness pulsed in my veins.

There were no limits, something whispered, straight to my soul—I could do anything I wanted, be anything I wanted. A queen. A god. A legend. A ruler of the realm. Endless control.

"River," Freyja called. Not my name, but an order.

"Yeah?" A wall of flames filled my vision. "Oh, shit!" I was exactly one step away from being engulfed by the fire, as if I were a simple, mindless moth being drawn to the zapper.

How had I not realized I'd been walking towards it?

Wobbling on my chunky heels, I stumbled back to Freyja's side. The blood rushed to my head. A tightness seized my chest.

Taking a deep inhale, I glanced over my shoulder. The castle loomed a brilliant icy blue in the night. I'd lived through the fight, made it to Jarðarbæli, found Gaia, broken out of my cage.

I got what I wanted. There was nothing else to ask for. My attention snagged on the tower in the thin layer of clouds, glass turret sparkling in the moonlight.

But there were plenty of other souls far less fortunate, still trapped by these ruthless laws, waiting to taste the cool glacial air.

On a silent prayer, I wished for freedom, for life, a soul released from its grate. A nymph and her volcano, reunited with her fiery kin. The power to walk this land once more.

A fierce gust of wind batted the flames, tossing loose snow, the ash, my hair.

And then it was gone, it was done, and somehow, I knew, Eldi had finally left that godforsaken hearth.

"Your Highness," a guy sang from an outer corridor. Familiar, but too far away for me to fully catch or care. "Your court awaits you."

Freyja rolled her eyes, and suddenly she was herself again, the cool exterior slotting back into place over the frightened, mourning girl. "Best be getting back."

She didn't ask what I wished for. She didn't say anything about the gust of wind or the inexplicable trance she'd caught me in. She just gathered her green and lilac skirts and trudged towards the castle, the crown a bejeweled burden on her head.

"And what about you, angel?" that same person called, a tease of a smile in his voice. "You going to stay out here all night?"

Whirling around, I caught hints of the dark blue suit, the twists of his hair, the cut of his bright smile in the faint light. "Gunnar!"

Lifting the hem of my gown, I clambered over the slick courtyard, heels sinking into the ground, dress soaking up the slush. He met me halfway, scooping me up into his arms, twirling me beneath the constellations, burning brighter than ever.

Gently putting me down, he cupped my shoulders. "I am so happy you're not dead."

I thanked him with a playful smack to his chest, which probably hurt my fingers more than it affected him.

"Same," I said, and I meant it. "But I'm even happier I met you—all of you. Thank you for everything."

"It was my honor." Arm bent at the waist, he swept into an exaggerated bow. "Have you tired of our elven hospitality?"

"Can't get enough of it. In fact, I'm permanently taking up residence."

Brows furrowed, he looked at me beneath lowered lashes. "Really?"

"No," I laughed. "Olivia, Gaia, and I have a flight back to California tomorrow."

"Gaia? That's going to be rough. Last I saw her she was going shot-for-shot of Brennivín with some of the Eyes."

"Great, wonderful." I shook my head. "She is… both everything and nothing like what I was expecting. If that makes sense."

Gunnar bit the inside of his cheek. "I know someone else who's on that flight…"

Spine stiffening, I clipped out, "Oh, are you and Ryder buddies now?"

"Not quite. But after you left, he stayed and helped clean up the…" He cleared his throat, emotion seizing his words. A muscle ticked in his jaw. "Aftermath," he finished.

Ah, so Ryder decided to finally be a decent human? It didn't even make a dent in all the evil he had already done, but I had to admit, my chest felt a little lighter knowing he'd made the right decision, that he hadn't turned on them—on me—like a part of me worried he would.

"Well," I said, taking a deep breath, hoping to settle the slew of emotions swirling inside me, "it's about damn time he cleaned up his own mess."

Something burned in Gunnar's stare, something I wasn't

sure I was ready to address. "I saw the way you two looked at each other in that arena."

"Like we wanted to kill each other?" A shudder raked its way through me.

Folding his lips, he dipped his chin. "Like you were meant for each other."

Heat flooded my cheeks. "Gunnar, I—"

"River, you don't need to explain. I'm in Iceland, you're in Cali. It was fun getting to know you. When I say it was an honor, I truly mean it." Shifting to an arm length's away, he took me in, probably for the last time, like he was committing me to memory. So many unsaid things lay in that small shake of his head, in the twinkle in his eyes. "Maybe in another life."

Heart begging to say something but throat too raw to speak, I nodded.

Another step back. More distance, more space, and then he was two arms' length away.

I'd miss him. Miss his laugh, miss his warmth—miss what we could have been.

The electric spark that danced between us was sometimes the only thing that got me through some of my hardest days here. But he was right. He deserved someone with no strings attached.

This wasn't the right time for us.

"Now get in there." Gunnar nodded to the castle. "He's waiting for you."

CHAPTER 41

Shoulders back, I drifted into the great hall, heart raging in my chest. Each strut of my legs swished my dress, casting a mural of sparkles on the ivory stone.

Pausing just beyond the threshold, I scanned the arched room. The hem of my gown rippled at my feet, the slit parting at my ankle and running up to my thigh.

Whispers raced. Heads turned. Even the champagne seemed to bubble with excitement.

I kept my chin high, swiping a flute off a passing tray, trying and failing to emanate a vibe that was cool and unbothered.

But it was impossible to ignore the stares, the murmurs, the way the elven court looked at me as if they couldn't decide if they needed to be scared of me or worship me.

The sweet drink fizzed against my lips, bubbling all the way down. Only when the strings of the harp filled the room and the servers got back to their rounds did court politics and succession become the topics of conversation, prodding eyes getting bored and drifting away.

All except one pair.

I could feel his stare burning into my skin, gliding over the dips and curves of my body, pleading for me to turn his way—once I did, I knew it was over, knew I'd be crossing that floor in a storm of cerulean fabric and want and rage.

Then I saw him: an angel leaning against a marble column. Cutting jaw, slicked hair, a fresh scar on his throat, white collar open, tattooed clavicle exposed. Ryder's gaze, still rimmed with darkness but brighter than before, flared with a knowing heat.

It was so much worse than wanting. He was like gravity, like air. I *needed* him.

Placing my nearly full glass onto a table stocked with every cured meat known to man, I squeezed past the beads and jewels and flowing dresses, the bright suits and patterned ties.

The hunter didn't move, tracking me solely with his eyes. And then I was cutting across the empty dance floor, and then I was standing in front of him, my chin kicking back to take all of him in.

Face wild with that same yearning that set me ablaze, he towered over me.

The light softened, and the music seemed to fade.

Where did we go from here?

He held out a palm. "May I?"

It was probably just the shadows from the flickering candlelight, but I could have sworn he was trembling.

I took his hand. It was cold. Weirder, it was smooth, with none of his usual calluses. They must have faded from his skin during those lonely, weaponless nights spent in the dungeon.

Bringing us closer, he slid an arm around my waist. Timid, unsteady, so the opposite of him. "Is this okay?"

I nodded. "Yes." My free hand drifted to his back.

Who was this person?

Who was I?

We swayed to the gentle thrums of the harp, but my spine was stiff, my posture rigid and boxy.

There were too many questions left unanswered, too many things left unsaid.

"Thank you," I whispered.

"For what?" Strands of his dark brown locks fell over his temples. I wanted to run my fingers through them.

Instead, I said, "For not slaughtering my friends when I left the Terrordome."

He bowed his head.

"I have to admit"—blood flew through my veins in a dizzying rush—"I wasn't sure for a minute. You seemed awfully cozy with Flóki. Were you working together?"

His jaw worked to form the words. "He's a Chthonia supporter. Same rank as my brother. Handles the elven squadron."

My gut twisted. "And what about you?"

"What about me?"

"Who do you fight for?"

"You." A hoarseness lined his voice, the familiar lilt turned tired and raspy.

Butterflies whirled behind my ribs. "I'm sure Leif isn't too thrilled about that."

"I don't care." His minty breath danced over my cheeks. Heady, inviting.

I didn't want to lose him, lose us, not when I'd just gotten him back, but this was so much bigger than that—this was an act of war. "You'll be putting a target on your back."

His eyes flashed black. "I'll draw it myself."

Pushing off his chest, I tore out of his grasp, away from the darkness, the evil that seemed to be fully part of him now. "You'd turn on your family?"

He snatched my hand and placed it over his heart, his stare electric green again, burning. "River Harlow, I will go against everything I am, everything I know, to be with you."

His pulse thundered beneath my palm. Thump, thump, thump. *You're the only reason it hasn't stopped completely.* "Why?"

Slowly, Ryder dropped to his knees. Curious glances drifted in our direction. He ignored them, not daring to stray from my face. "There's a… hold on me… It's more powerful than the blood oath, more potent than my instincts. And definitely a hell of a lot more important than my duty."

"What's that?" My legs worked to hold me steady. His grip latched around my thighs.

"Love," he said, but it was unnecessary. It was written in the bat of his lashes, in the flush of his cheeks, in the glassiness of his eyes—all over his face.

I wrung my fingers in the empty space between us. God, there was nothing I wanted more than *him* right now.

But the shadows behind his stare, that demon clawing inside him—would it stay there forever, or would he one day fully transform?

I tugged on his hands, wrenching him off the floor. "How do I know this isn't another one of your ploys?"

"Maybe it is."

"To kill me?"

"To kiss you," he said at the same time.

My heart might have actually stopped. "What?"

Tucking a finger beneath my chin, he tilted it up. "I want to kiss you. Will you stop me?"

"No," I breathed, damning myself.

"Good."

Dropping his forehead against mine, he leaned in. Noses grazing, lips brushing, savoring this moment, breathing it in as if we'd been starved of oxygen.

Mouths coming together, his chest caved against mine, warm and surrendering.

The firm press of him, the way his tongue slipped past my teeth, the way he caressed me as if he never wanted to let go… I lost myself in him, in his touch, in the way our hearts seemed to sync.

His lips were soft but greedy, and I gave and gave. Falling deeper into the kiss, into each other, we grasped at fabric and collars as if no one was watching, as if we had all the time in the world.

"Never again." The pledge vibrated through me. He sealed it with another kiss, electric and longing.

I stared up at him, admiring all the secret features I loved: the two freckles on his cheeks, the ever-present furrow of his brow, the hidden dimples, the cutest little crooked bottom tooth.

He tucked a loose curl behind my ear, fingertips grazing my jaw, my neck, my collar. "Never again," he repeated. "Never again do I want to live in a world where this"—a ragged whine of a breath—"doesn't exist."

"Maybe don't try so hard to get rid of it this time?"

"Oh, she's a smartass, now." The drawl of his accent fluttered against my hair.

Slipping my palms between us, I pressed them against his pecs. "Seriously, Ry."

A growl rumbled in his throat. "It drives me crazy when you call me that."

I shot him a look. Eyes alight, he dished me one right back—attention flicking over every inch of my face, landing on my throat, where my skyrocketing pulse was flittering in that hollow part of my neck. Ugh. I was doomed.

Tucking my head under his chin, I rested my cheek in the open collar of his shirt.

He wrapped his arms around me tighter, cocooning me against his broad chest. "Never again."

I breathed him in, the faint traces of leather, sea salt, and pine. The scent of us. The scent of home.

"Never again," I repeated.

AKOSUA
ANGEL OF FIRE

S**HE WAS USED TO THE WARM, GOLDEN KISS OF THE** fire, but in this realm, it was all wrong. Here, it was blue, lifeless. Cold.

Akosua withdrew from her place before the hearth and resumed pacing the tower she'd been locked in. Her clever brown eyes swept over the courtyard beyond the row of slits they called windows. A horde of demons stalked the perimeter of the castle, horns and hooves and wings jutting out of their mismatched armor.

How this realm stayed fortified was beyond her.

When they weren't stabbing each other in the heart, its wretched inhabitants were playing dice, drinking themselves into oblivion, or daring each other to jump off the drawbridge. None ever survived the fall.

Fools. All of them, she thought.

Her gaze tracked the blood that smeared the ground below the windows. A clump of what looked to be skin and perhaps hair was wedged between the cobblestones.

Must have been what was left of the last guest.

A being made of hellfire and shadow swept through the purple sky. It landed in the field beyond the battlements, its deep roar shaking the windowpanes.

One of their sentries returning from patrol, she presumed.

The tops of dueling axes and swords glinted in the endless twilight: the closest things she ever saw to stars.

Here in Chthonia, she never witnessed a sunrise or sunset. It never got fully dark, it never got fully light. The realm was stuck. She was stuck. She was—

She slammed her palms onto the stone windowsill, stopping herself.

Spiraling would only blow her cover, and then she'd end up in a fiery pit or on one of the many spikes that lined the road.

Hand pressed against her diaphragm, she inhaled deeply, closed her eyes, and willed herself to breathe.

Akosua yearned to hear the calming words of her archangel sisters. Instead, she was met with the constant barrage of the demons' thoughts. It took all of her remaining will to block their twisted fantasies, their absurd questions, their croaky inflections out of her head.

It was enough to drive the sanest mind mad.

Even when she didn't hear them, she felt them—invisible claws raking through her brain as if it were a mine they could pillage and ransack.

Instead of Gaia's and Fei's familiar voices flowing through her mind like a soft wind, she heard a jewelry box chirp. Followed by a *creakkk* from the wooden four-poster bed and a rattle from the armoire's drawers.

At night, an unseen presence pulled the silk sheets off the mattress.

Everything in this room, in this godforsaken realm, was possessed. Cursed.

Even the air hung over her like a ghost, heavy and haunting.

A knock echoed through the bedroom. Her eyes shot open. The candles flickered. So did her heart.

Someone was at the door.

Akosua gulped, her throat dry, parched, aching with an endless thirst no matter how much water she drank.

The flames from the hearth cast a shiver down her spine. She wrapped her arms around her waist, holding in her body's warmth, the long sleeves of her red velvet dress dragging across the floor.

Flying imps scattered like moths as she opened the door. Pesky, nosy little critters—no doubt they'd had their ears to the wood, eavesdropping on her, reporting back to the demon king himself. Before her, one of his slithering regents stood, bug-eyed and hunched.

"Tharros," she said, mouth set in a firm line. "To what do I owe this pleasure?"

The lesser demon removed a ratty handkerchief from his pocket, dabbing his bone-white, scaly temples. Demons, they always ran hot. Meanwhile, another shiver raced down her spine.

"His Royal Highness has considered your request for an alliance." The words hissed out of his lipless mouth, the thin slits of his nose flaring.

"Oh?" She kept her face neutral, even if this news made her insides twist.

"There've been some advancements in the Mortal Lands,"

he stammered, a forked tongue darting out. Akosua found herself leaning farther back. "Xegdrelath accepts your offer."

Relief unfurled her spine.

"On one condition."

She stiffened.

"A betrothal."

Akosua gulped, suddenly needing to lean against the doorframe. "A—a what?"

Tharros gave her a smile that was all venom and fangs. "You will wed the demon king when Mortal Earth celebrates winter solstice."

The words spiraled around her; she could hardly hear them over her pounding heart. In earthly time, that was only a few short months away.

Coming here, presenting this…*alliance,* it was the only thing she could think to do to ward off the demons from torturing her sisters and using their magic to infiltrate Mortal Earth. Their Source certainly wasn't strong enough to protect them—not anymore, with the Angel of Water gone and her daughter stubborn as all hell, as human teenagers often are— and it would never be that powerful again, not until River took her rightful place among the Watchers.

But despite River's stubbornness, Akosua believed in her.

She'd seen the way the girl stared at the rain, how she maneuvered her surfboard, those days when she'd watch the ocean for hours—water called to her.

The lesser demon cleared his throat, tilting his head.

She had to be careful with these thoughts—that they weren't flashing across her face or leaking to another prying mind—but this was supposed to be *temporary.*

A betrothal would bind her here forever.

The little hope she'd been clinging onto guttered out. She couldn't bear to admit it, but… Perhaps she'd put too much faith in the Angel of Water's daughter.

"The tailor is waiting," Tharros continued, yellow eyes narrowing.

Her skin grew hot, and she hoped a flush wasn't rosying her ebony cheeks. "Now?" she managed to say, her head spinning.

"Something wrong?" he spat.

She snapped her gaze to his. "Nothing is wrong." Keeping her voice steady, she walked across the threshold, continuing the performance she'd been giving since the day she entered the realm. "I accept."

ACKNOWLEDGMENTS

AFTER SIXTEEN LONG months of pouring my heart and soul into this story, it's finally out in the world.

There were many moments throughout writing this book where, like River, I thoroughly doubted myself— where I leaned too far into the inner critic and convinced myself I wasn't good enough, strong enough, skilled enough, liked enough. But… I pushed past everything telling me I couldn't. And I did it.

Not alone, though. I'm so grateful to everyone who encouraged me, believed in me, and gave me some of their fairy dust along the way. Especially:

My sweet Kaia, the little girl behind every dedication. You're the reason my heart beats.

My husband, Tyler, for being so patient during my many deadlines and cheering me on during the hardest days.

My parents, and my parents-in-law, for your unconditional love and support.

My amazing editors, Sara Schonfeld and Lynsey G. I genuinely don't know where River would be without you two. You make me be a better writer, and I am endlessly thankful for your guidance.

Marina and Evan, for helping make the prologue and epilogue shine.

Jennifer, for helping me with that final editorial (and visual) pass—and always being in my corner.

My beta readers and sensitivity readers: your comments had me smiling and cackling and really helped shape the story into what it is today. Also, thank you for coming up with the term Horror Mermaids, haha!

Maddy, I can't thank my lucky stars enough to have you in my life. Since day 1 you've always been there for moral support, to offer a shoulder to cry on, to help me at a book fair, and to celebrate all the author (and non-author!) milestones in our lives.

Elizabeth Anne, for being my go-to gal for memes, writing woes, Charlie Hunnam gifs, and laughs. I am so grateful the universe brought us into each other's orbits.

Alissa, Olivia, and Nicole, my retreat roomies and planning besties. Your creative ideas, talent, wisdom, friendship, and our chaotic late-night retreat chats are something I will forever cherish.

Kate, thank you for always being there to answer my publishing questions, for giving me your ears for a good venting sesh, and for endlessly cheering me on. You are the best mentor I could ask for!

The Magical Mountain Mages: Emma, Heather, Reese, Mackenzie, Rebecca, Jessica P, Leila, Laura, Mia, Ginger, Jess C, Riley, Brianna, Kristy, and Nina. You are my sisters. My community.

Leila, for always being down to shoot a reel and hyping me up every chance you get.

ACKNOWLEDGMENTS

Kelly, from being a critique partner to someone I call a dear friend. I love bouncing ideas, swapping stories, and screeching about book boyfriends with you!

Margie, for being the best PA and helping me navigate the chaos of author life. I am happy to have you in my life and as my friend.

My Bookstagram friends, I am forever grateful for you. Your friendship, your support, the way you scream and kick your feet over River and Ryder… You help me get through some of the toughest days.

And the biggest thanks to you, dear reader, for letting these characters into your lives and loving them just as much as I do!

TORY GUYON grew up dreaming about dragons, pretending to craft potions, and eagerly awaiting to be summoned by the realm of the fae. She lives with her family in Santa Cruz, CA, and continues to actively seek out the magic of this world. Whether that's working with orangutans in the jungles of Borneo, summiting Mount Kilimanjaro's grueling 19,341 ft. peak, or looking for fairies in the redwoods with her daughter. Connect with her at www.saltandstarspress.com or on social media at @wri_tor.